DROLL STORIES

collected in the monasteries of Touraine
and given to the light by

HONORÉ DE BALZAC

Translated into modern English by
ALEC BROWN

With drawings by
MERVYN PEAKE

THE FOLIO SOCIETY
London 1961

The translator dedicates his work
to all who understand the spirit
of humane laughter

PRINTED IN GREAT BRITAIN

Printed and bound by Richard Clay and Company, Ltd, Bungay
Set in Garamond 11 point leaded 1 point
Illustrations lithographed by Novello & Co. Ltd, London

Contents

iii

Illustrations

iv

Translator's Note

THE *Contes Drolatiques* present a puzzle which calls for a key. Why did Balzac choose to couch this suite of historical romances in archaic French which, though a fascinating *tour de force*, was bound to be rather baffling to many readers? And why have I assumed the right to ignore the antiquarian cloak and make my translation in ordinary English? The first question is cardinal, and the second depends on it. What is the position? To the serious, and occasionally boisterous, yet delicate, treatment of a number of profound ethical-social themes, coupled with vivid sidelights and commentaries on the French Middle Ages, Balzac has added a purely linguistic theme, a very special *jeu d'esprit*. But if, as he wrote in August, 1833, to his great Ukrainian-Polish love, Countess Hanska, he considered these stories his 'principal title to fame in days to come', why did he disguise them?

Two answers are usually given. First, it is said that he wrote these stories as pot-boilers; secondly, he thought it expedient to avoid censorship by veiling their broad humour in obscure language.

The first suggestion can at once be dismissed. It is merely ridiculous. For an author of Balzac's inventive fertility, it would have been far, far easier to write stories which did not require such a very special setting, and were not conditioned by so much research. Nor was it a very pot-boiling desire to pack the stories with moral and ethical idealism, or—as with *The Succuba*—with formal experimentation. Apart from these considerations, the suggestion is based on a very crude misunderstanding of the psychology of any dedicated author. The annals of literature are full of titles of unquestionable seriousness—for which the author anxiously waited to be paid.

What of the second point, the suggestion that here we have stories deliberately made spicy to sell? This too I find nonsensical. One does not research into medieval history—many of the tales are founded on authentic records—merely to provide spice. True, Balzac is outspoken, and old French was no doubt a useful mask in a rather prudish period. But this was certainly not Balzac's reason for using such language. After all, one must presume that the authorities who might have censored him could also understand the texts.

I think we have the key in another letter to his future bride, written in October, 1834. Discussing his work as a whole, Balzac said that round the massive edifice of *The Human Comedy* he was, 'like a laughing child', weaving 'the arabesque' of the *Contes Drolatiques*.

v

In Balzac's mind the stories were clearly an integral part of his work. In *The Human Comedy* he wanted to depict what he regarded as the essential France. He described what we might call the end of the great age of princes. But he did not consider this by itself sufficient explanation of France. To reveal his country properly, he needed something more, namely to show its roots in medieval Christendom. Balzac was, after all, an ardent Catholic and a conservative at heart. He regretted what the French Revolution had swept away. The roots of vitality, he thought, were in the medieval, or pre-renaissance, age of soldier-princes, 'when there was much disorder', as he remarks in the *Prologue* to the *Second Decade* of the tales, and even in his language a man had 'elbow-room' and 'every poet . . . used to make his own language. . . .'

Here is the inner key to the riddle. Balzac was carried away by the gusto of his vision, intoxicated by his researches, and entranced by much reading not only of Rabelais and Margueritte of Navarre, but also of the earlier *fabliaux* and many an old chronicle. He had so soaked himself in that Gallic-Latin soil from which France had sprung that only by 'giving the freedom of the city to legitimate vocables, words in good usage, words we all know, but of which Milord Ronsard was ashamed', was he able to provide his imaginative powers with that scope and ebullient enjoyment which would ensure their being wielded to full success.

This being so, it may seem great temerity to strip away the 'antique' dress. Yet, such are the differences between our languages that if the English version is to give vital enough expression to the gusto of life which the stories express, the antiquarion dress positively must be shed.

Here are the reasons for this. Literary French, being an older language, began to achieve modern clarity of expression before English, so that early French prose is far easier to read than English prose of the same age. This is beautifully exemplified at the end of that early period—Montaigne, for instance, is so much more lucid and understandable in his original French than in Florio's contemporary English version. To translate Balzac's 'old French' into 'old English' would be to mistranslate, and add an obscurity which never existed in the original.

The *Droll Stories* were not buffoonery at all. Were that so, the costuming would be essential, for in it would reside the principal charm. But the inner humour of the old French, Balzac's picking and choosing of words and forms from all over the place, his playing with syntactical devices and even his inventing of words, all serve the ulterior purpose of expressing a viewpoint which English can better achieve in other ways. To Balzac the flamboyant play with language served as a catalyst, releasing a vital earthiness absent from his work. It was a deeply human, warm-hearted, and peculiarly innocent, naïve earthiness. Such humour is largely lost in the industrialized world, yet will be familiar to anyone who has lived in peasant communities. It is a vital quality which, it would seem, can today best be brought out by the more vigorous impact of the words we really understand and use.

In short, to re-tell these tales in the language of our own time, here and there perhaps enriched by an older word or a Balzacian coinage, is the way best calculated to make accessible in all its original honesty, this major work of Balzac.

ALEC BROWN

First Decade

Prologue

This is a highly carminative book, compact of exquisite love encounters, all well condimented for those very worthy wine-bibblers and most illustrious victims of gout for whom wrote our distinguished compatriot, the eternal glory of Touraine, namely, François Rabelais. Not that the author presumes to be more than a good Tourainian, keeping the generous mandibles of the illustrious gentry of that delightful, fertile land laughing. There is no country so prolific of cuckolds and cuckolders and high cockalorums generally, while it has also furnished France with many of her great men, including Courier, R.I.P., of spicy memory, Verville, author of *How to Get On*, and other well-known masters of the pen from whom we should perhaps weed out Descartes, since he was a depressive genius more prolific of vacant musings than of wine and good cheer, one of those of whom all the chophouse keepers and pastrycooks of Tours have a sober horror, rejecting and refusing even to discuss him, maintaining, if he is ever mentioned, that in their part of the country they never heard tell of him.

This work is actually the product of the merrier moments of the good old monks, of whom there were then still many scattered about our land, as at la Grenadière-les-St-Cyr, at the town of Sacché-les-Azay-le-Ridel, at Marmoustiers, at Verets, at la Roche-Corbon and in certain typothecary deposits of good yarns, namely, various canons of the church and worthy ladies who knew those good old times when folk made merry and if at every gust of their laughter their sides did split, and nag or sportive young foal burst forth, they did not worry as the young women do today, with all their straining to be happy solemnly, which fits our gay France about as well as an oilcan fits a Queen's head.

Therefore, seeing that laughter is a privilege limited to man, and that there is reason enough in the public affairs for tears without adding dismal books, I have considered it to be a patriotic act, devilishly so indeed, to publish a dose of cheerfulness in this age with its constant drizzle of misery, so thick and so wet that it soaks you through and through till it even begins to undermine and dissolve from under us those ancient ways of ours by which formerly as many as possible found pleasure in the public weal.

As things are, few of those old Pantagruelians remain who left God's business to God and the King's business to the King and, satisfied with doing the laughing, never meddled more than compelled. That breed is rapidly dying out. Therefore, I am most apprehensive

3

lest these distinguished fragments of old-time records should now lie for ever, scorned, effaced, fouled, fly-blown, spurned, condemned, all of which would leave me far from indifferent, seeing that I retain much lively respect for those scraps of our Gallic antiquity which have survived.

Further, you venomous critics, petty word-pilferers, harpies who ruin both a man's inventions and intentions, do remember that it is only in childhood that we laugh and that as we journey through life our laughter gradually gutters and dies out like a lamp without oil. This means that laughter requires innocence and purity of heart. Failing those qualities, men pinch their lips and contort their chaps and frown as if trying to conceal some vice or uncleanness. So do, I beg you, take this work as if it were a group portrait, a piece of statuary in which the artist cannot avoid depicting certain things and would be a twenty-two carat ninny to block it all out with fig leaves, such monumental works no more being made for convents than this book is.

At the same time, rather to my chagrin, I have been at pains to weed out from the chronicles some of the old words which were perhaps a little too youthful and might have jarred on some ears, dazzled some eyes, brought blushes to some cheeks, really giving maids-in-breeches and triple-lover, oh-so-virtuous ladies room to talk, for it is indeed also incumbent on us to do something to suit the vices of our own time, and circumlocutions are then politer than blunt words.

Yes, we are all old now, and we find tedious trifling more to our taste than the mercurial follies of our youth, for it tends to eke out our delight. So, softly with your attacks! Read these pages rather at night than by daylight, and do not on any account give them to innocent girls (if there still are any such things), lest the book catch alight.

With these injunctions I withdraw. I am, however, not apprehensive about this work. It has been drawn from a charming and elevated place, all the products of which have come off well, as well evidenced by the Royal Orders of the Golden Fleece, of the Holy Ghost, of the Garter, of the Bath and so many other striking things there taken and behind which I can shelter.

Therefore, loves, disport yourselves and enjoy yourselves, reading it all to the alleviation of yourselves and your loins, and may the Lubeck pox pock you if after reading me you deny me, as said our good Master Rabelais, to whom in token of respect and esteem as to the Prince of all Wisdom and all Fun, caps off!

I

Beautiful Imperia

To attend the Council of Constance, the Archbishop of Bordeaux included in his suite a very pretty little priest of Tours with most taking manners and a nice turn of speech, indeed, he passed for a son of La Soldée and the Governor. When Bordeaux called at Tours the Archbishop of that city had gladly presented this young clerk to his colleague, it being usual for archbishops to make each other presents, from awareness how inflamed the theological itch can be. So this young priest also went to Bâle and was quartered in the same mansion as his prelate, a man of the highest morals and great learning.

Philippe de Mala (as the priest was called) made up his mind he would behave well and serve his backer worthily. But though they were none the worse off for it, indeed, acquired more indulgences, more crowns sterling than all the others who were well behaved and steady, that mystigorical Council of Constance included many whose way of life was dissolute. Consequently, one night corrosive to his virtue, de Mala's ear and understanding received a hint from Satan that it was up to him to look after himself properly, for after all, the others were all busy dipping into our holy Mother Church's inexhaustible lap, in this miraculous wise proving the immanence of God, nor did the young Tourainian let Old Nick down, but swore to himself he would do himself very proud indeed, and, since it was feasible to do so without paying, for he was absolutely penniless, he would wallow, too, in the good cheer and other sauces of Germany. As, through modelling himself on his poor old Archbishop (who sinned no more because he could not do otherwise and hence was held to be a saint), de Mala had so far been extremely continent, he was forced many a time to endure unbearable flushes, followed by as many melancholizations, all because of the numerous lovely gay ladies, beautifully got up, though somewhat frigid to the poor, who had taken up temporary residence at Constance to bring clarity to the minds of the Fathers of the Council. It infuriated him not to know how to tackle these magpies. They had such panache that they would even snub Cardinals, Commendatory Abbots, Commissioners of the Rota, Legates, Bishops, Princes, Dukes and Margraves just as if they were ordinary penniless small fry of the Church. So, after evensong young Philippe would now try to talk to them and pick up the lovely language of love, and at least learned all the answers. But if the next day, before Compline, he came upon one of the same princesses, all togged out, reclining in her litter, with escort of well-armed pages, and all haughtiness, he just gaped like a dog thinking to snap at flies at the sight of that lively face which made him blush.

The Archbishop's secretary, a nobleman from Perigord, now made it quite clear to him that it was by dint of many presents, not relics or indulgences, but jewels and gold, that the fathers and justices and commissioners of the Church purchased the favour of being familiars of the topmost of those pampered pussies living under the protection of the Lords of the Council. So, in his naïvety and simplicity the poor Tourainian began to hoard in his mattress the rare angels which the good Archbishop gave him for special jobs of copying, and cultivated a hope that one day he might perhaps have enough for at least a peep of a cardinal's courtesan.

As to the rest of it, he just put his trust in God. He was a dedicated ecclesiastic from top to toe and as much like a real man as a nanny-goat in a night-cap is like a real girl. Nevertheless, spurred by his desires, he continued to roam the streets of Constance by night, careless of his life, ever risking having daylight let into him by the soldiery, and watched the cardinals calling on their women, when in those houses a multiplicity of real wax candles would flare up, and all the keyholes and embrasures glowed with light, and he could hear the saintly abbots and their company drinking away and merry-making, having an uproarious time, with ample love and singing of unheard-of alleluias and paying their mite too to the instruments which provided their music. The kitchens here worked wonders, with early morning services of crocks swimming rich, matins made of hams, vespers of tasty tidbits and lauds of all manner of sweet-tooth things. . . . And after the tippling came silence from these good ecclesiastics, while their pages played at dice on the stairs and the mules outside pawed at the cobblestones. All was well, for there was ample faith and piety, too. So that was how old Huss got burned, was it? How? Why, by putting his hand into the pot without being asked. But then, why did he have to be a Huguenot before anybody else?

To return to dear little Philippe, many was the time now that he got a good drubbing, but Old Nick proved his mainstay, prompting the conviction that sooner or later would come his turn to be cardinal to the wench of one of that ilk. His lust lent him the pluck of an autumn stag, so well indeed that one evening he slipped into the hall of the finest house in Constance, where he had often observed officers and senechals, varlets and pages waiting with torches for their masters, who were all Dukes and Kings, Cardinals and Archbishops.

'Phew!' cried Philippe to himself, 'she must be lovely, that one must and a gay piece, too . . .'

Thinking he belonged to the Elector of Bavaria, who was at that very moment leaving the building, and merely wanted to deliver some message from his lord, a heavily-armed soldier let him get inside the house. So up the stairs now went Philippe de Mala, as nimble as a March hare, to be guided by a delightful cloud of sweet perfumes straight to the bedroom, where he beheld the mistress of the house with her women, in the act of unfastening her girdle. He simply gaped with astonishment like a thief caught in the act. There the chambermaids and others were busily undressing the lovely lady from top to toe, baring her beautiful body with such dexterity and frankness that the sprightly priest gasped a gasp which was already redolent of love.

'And what might you be after, little-un?' the lady suddenly inquired.

'I've come—to deliver my soul to you,' murmured Philippe, feasting his eyes on her.

'You can come back tomorrow,' she replied, just to make a real fool of him, to which, scarlet now to the eartips, he replied politely:

'Without fail, Madame.'

The girl burst into a crazy fit of laughter.

Flabbergasted Philippe just gaped, but he did not desist from enveloping her with a glance whence shot little shafts of adoration of wonderful sharpness at her love delights: the lovely hair tumbling loose over shoulders and back of the most polished of ivory, all exquisite, gleaming curves of creamy flesh showing through countless wavy tresses of hair.

On her snow-white forehead gleamed a ruby-red spinel but it engendered far fewer waves of fire than those black eyes, now moist with tears, so heartily had she laughed. Indeed, she shook so with her laughter that she even sent one of her long-pointed shoes with gold-work fit for a shrine flashing through the air, and thus showed Philippe a bare foot daintier than the beak of a swan. She was in good humour this evening, or she would have had this little fellow with his tonsure tipped straight out of the window down into the street with no more concern than she now had for her first bishop.

'He has fine eyes, Madame,' remarked one of the women.

'But wherever did he spring from?' asked another.

'Poor child,' cried my lady, 'his mother must be looking for him!'

Without losing his wits for an instant, the Tourainian merely examined the gold brocade bed on which the lovely body of this hussy was about to rest, then made a gesture of great approval, and that

7

glance, so full of the spunk and knowingness of love, tickled the lady's imagination, so, half joking, but also rather impressed by the little fellow, she repeated:

'Tomorrow!' and dismissed him with a gesture which Pope John himself would have obeyed, the more so since now that the Council had depoped him he was indeed a snail without a shell.

'Oh, Madame!' cried one of the maids, 'another vow of chastity turned to the itch of love.'

There arose a cackle of laughter like a hail-storm, and, banging his head against the doorpost like a hooded crow, Philippe took his departure, so staggered was he, now that he had set eyes on this creature who was sweeter far to nibble than any siren of the waters. Outside, he took good note of the animals carved over the door-lintel and then made his way back to his good Archbishop, with a heart chockful of imps of Satan and bowels utterly sophisticated, back in his garret-room to spend the whole night counting his angels without ever making them more than four. And since this was all he had in his kitty he told himself he would be obliged to make the lady content with whatever else he had to give her.

'Whatever is the matter with you, Philippe?' asked the good Archbishop, when the clerk's spasms and groans finally alarmed him.

'Oh, My Lord,' replied the poor priest, 'I am merely astonished that so light and so lovely a lady should weigh so heavy on a man's heart!'

'But whomever do you mean?' insisted the Archbishop, and, good fellow, he put down the missal he was just reading for the good of others.

'Dear Jesus!' said Philippe, 'my kind Master and Protector, you will be very angry with me. What I have just seen was at least a Cardinal's lady. . . . And I wept when I realized that, even supposing you did let me undertake her conversion, I should need more than a miserable crown for her . . .'

The Archbishop knit together that circumflex accent with which his nose was surmounted, and was silent, while, most humble, the priest began to shake in his shoes for thus having spilled the beans to his superior, when without hesitation the holy man merely said:

'Really, is she all that expensive?'

'Oh, yes,' replied Philippe quickly, 'she has diminished many a mitre and crumpled many a cross.'

'Very well, then, Philippe, give her up and you shall have thirty angels out of the poor-box.'

'Oh no, My Lord!' replied the young fellow, fired as he was by the portion which he had promised himself, 'like that I should lose too much.'

'Ah, Philippe!' cried the good man of Bordeaux, 'so you are set on going to the devil, are you, and displeasing God like all our Cardinals?'

And the Bishop of Bordeaux was so grieved that he began at once to pray to St Gatien, protector of simpletons, imploring him to rescue his man. He made Philippe kneel down and also confide himself to that Saint, but in a whisper the wretched priest implored St Gatien to save him from failure, if, out of charity and mercy, his lady should let him in the next day, whereupon, perceiving what he thought to be his clerk's fervour, the kindly Archbishop cried:

'Keep your pluck up, my lad, and Heaven will exorcise you!'

The following day, while in the Council the Archbishop was holding forth against the shameful conduct of the apostles of Christianity, Philippe de Mala spent those angels of his, earned by so much toil, on perfumes, and washings and steepings and other frivolous preparations and so dandified himself up one really would have thought him one of those love-bird's little fancies. Off he went through the town to discover the house of his heart's darling (which he had only seen in the dark), but any whom he asked laughed in his face.

'Where's this scab-face been,' they said, 'not to have heard of fair Imperia?'

In the end he was very much afraid lest he had spent his angels very foolishly, for the name now told him what a fine mess he had deliberately got himself into. For the fair Imperia was the most costly and most exacting love lady there ever was, not to mention that she was held to be the most lucidifically lovely, no woman her equal to turn a cardinal into a hypocrite or an uncouth soldier and oppressor into a man of courtesy. She had her own brave captains, crossbowmen and lords attendant, all keen to serve her in any way. She needed but breathe a word to have any man who annoyed her cut down. It wanted but a slight twist of her lips for men to be laid low and it was no rarity, just to rag the clergy, for Baron de Baudricourt, one of the French King's own Captains, to inquire of her whether perchance she did not want anybody killed today.

Except for top-rank ecclesiastics, with whom she had a fine judgement in smiles, this fair Imperia ruled everybody with a rod of iron merely by reason of her lively tongue and her skill in love, by which the most insensitive and most virtuous men were entrammelled. This meant that she lived as cherished and respected a life as real ladies and princesses and was always addressed as *My Lady*, à propos of which, when a real lady of circumspect living complained about it, good Emperor Sigismund said:

'But, of course, the only difference is that whereas those good

9

dames stick to the decent norms of holy virtue, My Lady Imperia looks after the really sweet divagations of the Goddess Venus!'

Christian words which the ladies were very mistaken to find shocking.

Hence, when he recalled the glances he had received through his own speech, the day before, Philippe suspected that this might be all he would ever get. He was thus downcast and went quite off his food, trapesing about the town all the time, thinking the moment might come, so dandy and gallant was he, when there would appear some other beauty, a little less hard to accost than My Lady Imperia. Yet, when night fell, there was the little Tourainian again, all uppish with pride, caparizoned with desire, whipped on by his own choking sighs, suddenly slipping like an eel into the mansion of this lady who was the real queen of that Council, since all the authorities, learning and eminence of Christianity bowed down before her. The butler, however, failed to recognize him and was about to throw him out, when there was the chamber-maid crying from the top of the steps:

'Hallo there, Mr Imbert, that's My Lady's little 'un.'

Scarlet as a bridal night, stumbling with happiness and relief, poor Philippe now rushed up the stairs, where the chamber-maid took him by the hand and led him into the chamber where, lightly clad, *My Lady* was already enthroned, like a brave woman hoping for the best. Dazzling Imperia was, in fact, seated at a table draped with cloth of velvet, embroidered with gold, before her all the equipment of the best of bars: bottles of wine, ornate goblets, jugs of wine, punch, flasks of good Cypriot wine, sweet-boats loaded with dainties, roast peacocks, onion and parsley sauces and dainty hams, all of which would have delighted this gallant's sight had he not loved My Lady Imperia herself so much the more. She saw clearly that her little priest's eyes were all for her, and though accustomed to the heretical worship of ecclesiastics she was very pleased.

The fact is, the night before she had been quite taken by this poor little fellow, and Philippe de Mala had danced all day in her heart. The windows firmly closed, My Lady was well disposed, tuned up as she would have been to do honour to a Prince of the Empire. Hence, beatified by Imperia's sacrosanct loveliness, the little rogue at once grasped that tonight neither Emperor nor Burgrave, no, not even a Cardinal in the running for the Popedom was going to beat him, minor priest of minors though he might be, and in his purse nought but love and Old Nick.

Without hesitation he cast his lot and bowed with a grace which was far from silly, whereupon the lady rewarded him with a burning glance and said:

'Come close to me, so I may see if you have changed since yester-day.'

'Ah, I have changed, indeed,' said he.

'But in what?' she queried.

'Yesterday,' replied the trickster, 'I loved you. . . . But this evening we love each other. Thus have I turned from a miserable sufferer into one richer than the King.'

'Oh, little one, little one,' she cried, with delight, 'indeed you have changed, for I see a transformation from young priest to old devil.'

And they nestled together side by side before the good fire, which spread their intoxication throughout every limb. Thus they remained, ever on the point of taking food yet not eating, since their only thought was to bill each other with their eyes. But just as at last they were well established and utterly at their ease, there came a disagreeable noise at My Lady's door, like scuffling, and a cry from a maid, taken off her guard.

'My Lady, what do you think,' the girl cried, 'here's another!'

'What?' cried Imperia, haughtily, like any tyrant furious at being interrupted.

'The Bishop of Coire wishes to see you . . .'

'May the Devil take him!' she cried, while her eyes fondled Philippe.

'My Lady, he has seen the lights through the door cracks and he is making a great to-do . . .'

'Tell him I have the fever. And that's no lie, either, because I'm badly infected by this little priest, he has got my marrow all a-quiver!'

But just as, pressing Philippe's hand with devotion, she uttered these words, and he too was sizzling in his skin, the fat old Bishop of Coire appeared on the scene, panting and furious, to be followed by his men, bearing a trout, fresh from the Rhine, canonically salmoned, on a plate of gold, also sweetmeats in fancy boats and countless other dainties, such as liqueurs and compotes of fruit, all put down by the holy nuns of his various convents.

'Oh! Oh!' he cried in his rough voice, 'there's time yet for the Devil to get me without you having him flay me first, my pet!'

'One of these days,' cried Imperia, frowning, her laughing eyebrows suddenly turned most menacing, 'one of these days your guts will make a nice sheath for a rapier.'

'And this choir-boy, is he on the list of offerings already?' was his uncouth reply, and he turned his bloated glance on gentle Philippe.

'My Lord,' said Philippe, 'I am here to confess My Lady.'

'Indeed, and don't you know your canon law?' cried the Bishop. 'Confessing ladies at this hour of the night is a privilege reserved to

Bishops. . . . So Skedaddle! Go and get your feed with ordinary nuns, and don't let me see you here again, under pain of excommunication!'

'Don't you stir, my dear friend!' cried Imperia, raging, and lovelier in her anger than she was in love, since here it was a mixture of both. 'Please stay, you are at home here.'

Whereby Philippe at last knew that he was indeed the beloved.

'Is it not laid down in the prayer-book and the teaching of the church that in the Vale of Jehoshaphat you shall all be equal?' she asked the Bishop.

'Though it is certainly so written, that is an invention of Satan's, a doctoring of Holy Writ,' was the reply of this great hulk of a Bishop, who was anxious to fall to at table.

'Very well, then be equal in my company, since here on earth I am your Goddess,' said Imperia. 'Otherwise, Bishop, one of these days I shall have you gently constricted 'twixt head and shoulders, I swear it by the almighty authority of my own little tonsure, which is a more powerful one than the Pope's.'

And then, since she wanted that trout to be part of the dinner (not to speak of the gold dish, the sweetmeat boats and the dainties), she added neatly:

'Pray be seated. May I offer you a drink?'

At the same time the sly linnet, whose first piece of dupery this certainly was not, partly closed one eye, to signify to her darling that he need not worry about this German, whose liquor-bibbling would soon suit their book.

So the chamber-maid seated the Bishop at table and tucked his napkin well in for him, while, so furious that he was utterly speechless, seeing his good fortune go up in smoke, Philippe de Mala consigned the Bishop to more devils than he had ever known nuns. They had in due course got half-way through the repast, which the young priest did not touch at all, since he was only hungry for Imperia, close to whom he snuggled without a word more passing his lips, except that, of course, what he uttered with that fine tongue which the fair sex understands without any points or commas, diacritics or letters, ciphers or signs, notes or illustrations, while the pot-bellied Bishop, most sensitive and meticulous about the garment of ecclesiastical skin into which his late mother originally sewed him, had allowed My Lady's delicate hand to pour him out ample drenchings of the wine punch, so that he had already reached his first hiccough, when there was suddenly a tremendous clatter of horsemen down the street, the number of hooves, and the whoahing of many pages making it clear that some great lord all hot with love had arrived. And

12

indeed, but a moment later, the Cardinal of Ragusa burst into the chamber. Imperia's servants had been powerless to keep him out.

At this dismaying sight, the poor love-girl and her little-un were as abashed and ill at ease as freshly diagnosed lepers, for it was tempting Satan to think of getting rid of the Cardinal, the more so since it was still not clear yet who would be Pope, there being three claimants to the biretta for the good of Christendom.

The Cardinal, a wily Italian with a magnificent beard, and the great dialectician and prime mover of the Council, required but the feeblest thrust of his understanding to grasp the *alpha* and *omega* of the matter. He needed to put but a modicum of thought on to the scales to see what he must do to be sure of mortgaging his vital parts. For he had come here driven by a normal monastic appetite and if these were what stood in the way of satisfying his appetite he was a man ready to knife not one but two monks at once and even to sell his fragment of the true cross, which would have been very wrong.

'I say, my friend!' he said, to Philippe, calling him across to him.

More dead than alive, and now suspecting diabolical interference in his affairs, the poor Tourainian left the table.

'Yes, My Lord,' he muttered, waiting for orders.

The Cardinal took him by the arm, led him to the top of the stairs, then peered into the whites of his eyes and without any beating about the bush said:

'God's belly, you're a decent little cuss, I wouldn't like to have to show your topknot what your belly weighs. . . . That satisfaction might cost me several pious endowments in my old age. . . . So, choose quick! Marriage to an abbey for the rest of your time or marriage to My Lady tonight and death tomorrow!'

Desperate, the poor Tourainian stammered:

'And when you get over your fury, My Lord, may I come back again?'

It was hard for the Cardinal to be angry, but all the same, he cried grimly:

'Choose, I tell you! Gallows or mitre?'

'Why, if it's like that,' said the priest, slyly, 'a good big abbey!'

Hearing this, the Cardinal went back into the room, took a writing case and at the bottom of a deed parchment scribbled a note to the French Envoy.

While the Cardinal was making the abbey over, the Tourainian now whispered to him.

'My Lord,' he said, 'the Bishop of Coire isn't going to quit quite so easily as I do, you know. He's already got as many abbeys as the soldiers have pubs. Besides, he's in the Monarch's good books. Now, sir, I think that as thanks for so fine an abbey I owe you a tip of information. . . . You know how infectious that damned new disease, the whooping-cough, is and how badly it has caught Paris. Well, you tell the Bishop you have just been attending your good old friend the Archbishop of Bordeaux, and you'll be rid of him like chaff in a high wind.'

'Oho! you deserve more than an abbey!' chuckled the Cardinal. 'By God's Belly, here's a hundred crowns sterling for you, to cover your travelling expenses to Turpenay. I won the money gambling yesterday, and I'll give it ye!'

Hearing this speech and seeing Philippe de Mala at once vanish without shooting her the ticklesome glance full of amorous distillations that she hoped for from him, that lioness Imperia suddenly grasped what a coward the Tourainian was, and went as breathless as a dolphin. She was still not Catholic-minded enough to forgive any lover for letting her down like that and proving unprepared to die for his love-whim, and so Philippe's early demise was imprinted in the viperish glance which she shot at him to hurt him, a glance which put the Cardinal quite at his ease, for the rascally Italian never doubted that he would soon get his abbey back. Thus, apparently indifferent and unmoved by the storm, the Tourainian, with his ears down, like a drowned dog chased out of church during evensong, slipped away without a word.

My Lady heaved a heartfelt sigh. She could have torn the human species to shreds, so little she now valued it, for the ardour which had possessed her now went to her head, and there were flickers of flame leaping into the air all round her. And there was reason for it, too, for this was the first time a mere priest had ever let her down. Thus it was now the Cardinal who was smiling, thinking that by reason of all this he would have the greater pleasure and satisfaction. Was he not a smart companion, indeed? Besides, he had a red bonnet on his knob, hadn't he?

'Ah, dear confrère,' he said now, turning to the Bishop, 'how lucky I count myself to be here and how glad I am I was able to get rid of that little squirt who is unworthy of Lady Imperia, the more so since had you let him draw close to you, you stood a good chance of an unworthy end, and all through a common priest.'

'Oh, and why would that be?' asked the Bishop of Coire.

'Why, that little fellow is the Archbishop of Bordeaux's clerk . . . and that worthy was taken with that whooping-cough this morning!'

The Bishop gaped as if trying to swallow a cheese whole.

'I say, wherever do you get that from?' he asked, at last.

'Oh, it's true enough . . .' cried the Cardinal, taking the good German's hand in his, 'I have just been consoling the Archbishop with the extreme unction myself . . . As we speak the wind's set fair to take the reverend old gentleman straight to Paradise.'

The Bishop of Coire now demonstrated how light large men can be, since, by God's mercy, as recompense for their labours, well-paunched persons have internal tubing as expansible as a balloon. This Bishop now leapt nimbly backwards, all a-sweat with anxiety and already coughing like an ox swallowing goose-down in its feed, then, suddenly quite pale, he was off down those stairs without even a good-bye to Lady Imperia.

When the door was shut on the Bishop and that person was tearing away through the streets, the Cardinal of Ragusa burst out laughing and would have made a good joke of it.

'Why, my pet,' he cried, 'now don't I deserve to be Pope, eh? And, better than that, your gallant tonight!'

Only now did he realize that Imperia was worried about something, and approached her, intending to take her tenderly into his arms and caress her in cardinal fashion, for cardinals are better at embracing than other men, even soldiers, since they are idle and do not dissipate their essential humours.

'Oh! Oh!' cried Imperia, staggering back away from him, 'so you want to be my death, do you? You old metropolitan dunderhead! All you care about is enjoying yourself, you evil old ruffian. My pretty part's only an accessory to you, and if your pleasure's my death, I suppose you think you'll canonize me, eh? So you've got the plague and you want me, do you? Right-about turn, you brainless old monk, and look for it somewhere else, don't you touch me!' she added, as she saw him draw nearer. 'Or I'll stuff you with this dagger.'

With these words the fine wench slipped her hand into her bag and drew out a pretty little stiletto which she knew well how to use when needs must.

'But, my little paradise, my pettie,' said the Cardinal, with a snigger, 'surely you saw through my trick? Did I not have to get rid of that old ox from Coire?'

'Oh, indeed, my good sir. . . . Now, come on,' she added, 'if you love me, show it! I want you to leave my house this instant. If you've caught the disease, a lot you care about my death. I've had enough to do with you to know what price you would put on a moment of pleasure if you were on your deathbed. You would drown the earth, you would. Now, don't you forget, you boasted you would once, when you were tight. But all I love is my own self, my treasures and my health. . . . Outside! And if your innards are not frozen by the sweats, you may come to see me again tomorrow. . . . Today, my good Cardinal, I detest you,' she added, with a leer.

'Imperia,' cried the Cardinal, now on his knees, 'my sacred Imperia, don't play about with me.'

'I don't mean to,' she said, 'I never play with things which are holy or sacred.'

'Oh, you vile, foul-mouthed creature, I'll excommunicate you . . . tomorrow!'

'Gracious me, you're already out of your Cardinalian senses!'

'Imperia, you Satanic daughter of Old Nick! . . . I say, no my lovely one, my little . . .'

'You are losing your respect, Cardinal! . . . Not on your knees, sir, shame on you!'

'Is it an *articulo mortis* absolution you want? Is it my wealth? Or do you want a piece of the True Cross? Do you? . . .'

'Tonight, you would not purchase my heart with all the riches of heaven and earth!' she said, with a laugh. 'I would be the last of sinners, unworthy to receive the body of Our Lord Jesus Christ, if I did not have my whims.'

'I'll burn your house down . . . you sorceress! You have cast a spell on me! You shall perish at the stake! Hear me, my love, my darling hussy! I promise you the finest place in Heaven. . . . Well? No? To death then! . . . To death, you sorceress!'

'Now, now, I shall kill you, My Lord.'

The Cardinal fumed with frenzy.

'You are going out of your mind,' Imperia said, 'go away! . . . All this is tiring you.'

'I shall be Pope, and you shall pay for this wrong you do me.'

'Then you are no longer inclined to obey me?'

'What must I do this evening to please you?'

'Get out!'

Lightly as a wagtail she leapt into her inner room and locked the door, leaving the Cardinal to rage, till at last he had to leave the house.

When at last lovely Imperia was alone and sat down again at the table by the fire, but now without her little priest, she broke all her gold chains and cried furiously:

'By the triple horns of the devil, if that little one thinks he can cause me to treat the Cardinal like this and expose me to being poisoned tomorrow, without me taking . . . all my pleasure of him! I won't die till I have seen him flayed alive before me. . . . Oh,' she lamented, now weeping genuine tears, 'how unhappy is my life,

16

when the little happiness I do get now and then costs me a dog's trade, apart from my salvation. . . .'

Just as she was finishing her tirade, bellowing now like a calf at the slaughter, what should she see but the pink and white cheeks of that little priest! All this time, he had been skilfully concealed in her room, and was now peeping naughtily out at her from behind her Venetian mirror. . . .

'Oh,' she cried, 'you are the most perfect of monks, the loveliest little monk, you monkey, you, who ever monked a girl in this holy amorous city of Constance. . . . Oh, come, my darling knight, my beloved son, my own belly, my paradise of delight, I must drink your eyes, and eat you up and kill you with love! Oh, my verdant, blossoming, never-dying God! Why, I'll turn you from man of the church to king, emperor, pope, I'll make you happier than the whole lot together. . . . By God, you can put all here to fire and sword, I am Yours, and I'll show you well, too, for you'll be cardinal soon enough, if to make your biretta scarlet I have to spill all my heart's blood.'

Then with hands which shook, beside herself with happiness, she filled with Greek wine one of the goblets brought by the corpulent Bishop of Coire and offered it to her love, whom she insisted on serving kneeling, she whose slipper all the princes of Christendom thought sweeter of taste than that of the Pope ever was.

And all Philippe de Mala did was stare at her without a word, his eyes so greedy of love that she trembled all over with pleasure.

'Come, not a word, little one. . . . Let us sup!'

II

Venial Sin

How Worthy Baron Bruyn Took a Wife

Baron Bruyn, the one who completed la Roche-Corbon-les-Vouvray Castle, down the Loire, was a rough customer in his youth. He began playing havoc with maidenhoods when a mere boy. When he entered a household there was hell to pay, he could put Old Nick himself through the mill. Then suddenly he had to caulk his old man down for ever, after which he was in a position to see the clock round on the tiles every day of the week, and then he really did go at his pleasures as if he meant business.

However, by dint of sneezing away his cash, coughing away his codpiece, bleeding away his barrels, entertaining light birds and generally making mud pies, he found himself shunned by decent folk, his only friends the pillagers of the countryside and money-lenders. However, very soon even the money-lenders became as prickly as horse-chestnut husks, for time came when he had nothing left to mortgage but Roche-Corbon manor itself, and the *Rupes Carbonis* were a direct fief of His Majesty. And that put Bruyn in a nice mood, ready to lash out right and left and break other folk's shoulder-blades. He would quarrel with anybody about anything.

Seeing this, his neighbour, the Abbot of Marmoustiers, a man of great verbal generosity, told him that this was a clear indication of baronial perfection, that he was on the right road, though if *ad maioram gloriam Dei* he were but to go and slaughter some of those Moslems who were making a mess of the Holy Land, it would be better still, and he might also come home not only sinless, but also full of riches and indulgences, whether he ended up in Touraine or Paradise itself, whence originally all barons issued.

Bruyn marvelled at the good sense the Prelate talked and left the country forthwith. To the relief of his neighbours and his friends, the Monastery fitted him out and the Abbot blessed him. He then sacked many a city of Asia and Africa, striking at those miscreants without any warning, flaying Saracens, Greeks, Englishmen and sundry, caring little whether they were friends or whence they sprang, since one of his good points was his absolute lack of curiosity; he killed first, questioned after.

In this trade, so pleasing to the Almighty, to His Majesty and to himself, Bruyn earned fame as a good Christian and a leal knight and

18

had much fun besides overseas, since although he came across more decent poor men than perfect wenches, he would rather give a whore a crown than a poor man sixpence. But he was a good Tourainian, it was all grist to his mill. At last, however, fed up with Turks, relics and the other advantages of the Holy Land, Bruyn came home from the Crusade, to the great astonishment of Vouvray folk, loaded with crowns and precious stones, quite the opposite of some men who, rich when they set out, returned loaded with leprosy but light of cash.

When he thus returned from Tunis, our Sovereign King Philippe made Bruyn a Count and appointed him Seneschal of Touraine and Poitou. He was now greatly esteemed and indeed much liked, since apart from all his other merits he founded the church of Carmes-Deschaux in the parish of Egrignolles. This was to redeem the wildnesses of his youth. Thereby he was cardinally confirmed in the good graces of both Church and Almighty. From evil-liver and man of mischief he graduated to man of merit who as his hair grew thin was well behaved and a discreet rascal, rarely enraged, except when a man displeased God before him, which he would never suffer, having himself in his crazy youth displeased sufficient for others.

In short, he never quarrelled now, for, since he was Seneschal, other folk always gave way at once. For the truth is that he now always had his own way, which makes even a hell-cat tame and placid from skull to claws. Apart from this, he was the possessor of a castle planted up on a ridge over-towering the Loire, with jags at all the seams, as slashed as a Spanish doublet. The rooms were all Royal tapestry, fine furniture and show pieces, with Saracen decorations and fantasies which were the marvel of the folk of Tours, even the Archbishop and the clergy of St Martin's, to whom he gave—and without any strings, too—a banner with fringe of pure gold. All round the castle was a wealth of lovely lands, with mills and woodland and crops of all sorts to bring in revenues, and Bruyn could easily raise a thousand men to fight in the King's cause.

If, by ill chance, in the Baron's old days, his bailiff, a most assiduous man for hangings, brought in a poor peasant under suspicion of some misdeed, Bruyn would usually smile and say:

'Let this one go, Breddif, set him against all the guiltless ones I did in out abroad. . . .'

There were, however, many other occasions when he would have them swung up proud on an oak-tree or else hooked up on the Castle gibbet. But that was solely to have justice done and not to let the customs of his domains lapse.

Hence on Bruyn's lands the common folk were as well behaved

and as steady as nuns just out of their novitiate, and peace reigned, since he did protect folk from vagrants and malefactors, whom he never spared, knowing from experience what damage those accursed beasts of prey could accomplish. And, in any case, being a very devout man, who managed all his affairs with circumspection, whether prayers or good wine, he conducted his trials à la Turque, wasting no time and with many a quip for those who lost the toss. He would even dine with them to console them, and those he hanged he had buried in consecrated ground as belongings of the Almighty's, considering them punished enough by being prevented from living.

Finally, he never oppressed the Jews, except occasionally, and that when they were too swollen with money-lending and cash. He let them gather in their booty like honey bees, declaring them the best tax-collectors, and never despoiled them save for the profit and use of churchmen or of the King or of the province—or of himself.

This benevolence of his excited the affection and respect of every man, large or small. If he came back from a day on the bench and had a smile on his lips, the Abbot of Marmoustiers, of the same age as Bruyn was, would say: 'Oho! Count! I can see by your smile that somebody's due to swing. . . .' And when from la Roche-Corbon he rode to Tours the young hussies used to say: 'It's court day, there's dear old Bruyn.' Without any fear they would watch him ride by on the big white hack he had brought home from the Levant, and on Tours bridge the lads would pause in their marbles to cry: 'Good day, My Lord Seneschal!' And he would tease them and shout back: 'Beat it up, lads, till you get a tanning.' 'Yes, My Lord Seneschal,' they would reply.

Thus the countryside was so well purged of thieves and so happy that in the whole of that year when the Loire flooded badly there were only twenty-two rascals hanged in the whole winter, except for one Jew, though he was burnt at the stake at Château-Neuf for having stolen a communion wafer in that parish, or, some said, for having bought one, being a rich man.

One day, the following year, about St John the Harvester's Day (or as we say in Touraine, St Jean with the Scythe), some thieving bands appeared, of Egyptian, Bohemian or other such origin, stole some sacred objects at St Martin's, and in place of Our Lady the Virgin, as insult and mockery of our true faith, left, where she had stood, a shameless though lovely girl about the age of an old dog, stark naked, a show-girl and Moorish like themselves. This pagan forfeit led everybody, both King's men and Churchmen, to believe that this Moorish female should pay for it all, and be burned and roasted alive in St Martin's Close, near the fountain (where the herb market is).

But now with frankness and ingenuity this worthy Count Bruyn proved, in distinction from the rest, that it would be advantageous and most pleasing to the Almighty to win this soul of Afric for the true religion. In any case, he said, if the demon lodged in this female form were stubborn, it was not going to be burnt out with mere faggots, as the decision to burn the girl suggested.

This the Archbishop found to be soundly argued, most canonical, in full conformity with Christian charity and Gospel writ. The ladies of the city, however, and other persons in authority, were outspoken as to being cheated of a pretty little ceremony, since the Moorish girl was already sobbing her heart out in gaol and clamouring like a tethered goat, and of course she would if allowed be converted to God, so as to be able to live as long as any old crow.

To this the Seneschal's reply was that if this female alien should desire with due sanctity to commit herself to the Christian faith, there would be another sort of ceremony, also of great beauty, for he would guarantee to make the girl regally magnificent by being her godfather, and a virgin should be her godmother, to the greater delight of the Lord, since he himself was accounted to be innocent of sex, a *cocquebin*, as we say in Touraine of young men who are virginal, either being not married or counted as such, to distinguish them from husband and widowers, though the wenches all guess the truth well enough without any label because such men are more sprightly and cheerful than those grown dusty in connubial life.

The Moorish girl made no hesitation between faggots and baptismal water, preferring to be a live Christian girl rather than a dead Egyptian one. In this way, to avoid being summarily broiled she was to keep her heart a-glow all her life, since, for greater trust in her piety, she was entered in the Convent outside Chardonneret, where she took vows of holiness. The ceremony wound up at the Archbishop's Palace where for once there was dancing and festivity of the lords and ladies of Touraine, in honour of the Saviour of Mankind. Touraine is a land where there is more dancing and balling, more gustation and celebration, more lavish junketings and more jollity than in any other part of the whole world.

As his partner and godmother in this undertaking the good old Seneschal took the daughter of the Baron d'Azay-le-Ridel (later known as Azay-le-Brulé), this Baron, becoming crusader, having been abandoned on the field at Acre, a very distant city, in the hands of a Saracen who had now demanded a royal ransom, since this nobleman was of high standing, whereupon to get the necessary sum Lady d'Azay had mortgaged the estates to lombarders and extortioners and was left without a penny to her name, to await her lord in a wretched lodging in the town, without as much as a rug on which to be seated, though proud as the Queen of Sheba and plucky as a hound protecting his master's things, seeing which great distress, the Seneschal most tactfully called to request the unmarried daughter of this family to be godmother to the Egyptian girl, so he might have the right to assist Lady d'Azay.

Bruyn had indeed a memento of the capture of Cyprus, a heavy gold chain, which he intended to clasp about his gracious god-part-ner's throat, but however, the moment he beheld Blanche d'Azay dancing a *pavane* with the ladies of Tours, he added his lands and his white hairs, his cash and his stables, in short, all he had. For although, letting herself go on her last day, the Moorish girl was the admiration of the whole gathering for her pirouettes, her springs, her side-step-ping and toe-tapping and other acrobatic skills, Blanche by common consent beat her, so virginally and so daintily did she dance, and old Bruyn, too, marvelled at this sweet girl whose toes seemed to fear the floorboards and who with her seventeen years enjoyed herself as innocently as a cicada trying its first notes. He was now caught with an old man's desire, a desire apoplectic and vigorous with weakness, a desire which heated him from sole to neck, though no farther, his head being too deep in snow for love to nestle there. The old rascal then realized that he lacked a Lady of the Manor, and at once saw things more dismal than they really were. For what was a castle with-out its lady? No better than a clapper without its bell.

Indeed, a wife was the only thing left for him to crave, so of course he wanted one at once, for were Lady d'Azay to make him wait, he might in the meantime manage to quit this world altogether for another. However, during the christening festivities he gave little heed to his sore hurt, the less so since his eighty years had whitened his head. But all the same, he did find his sight clear enough for him to see his god-relation clearly and under her mother Lady d'Azay's instructions, she further plied him well with glance and gesture, tell-ing herself indeed that she was in no great danger beside so venerable a husband in the lord. So it was that, being naïve and uninstructed to a high degree, quite the contrary of all our Tourainian hussies, who are as alive to the facts of life as any Spring morning, Blanche first let the old fellow kiss her hand, then very soon, her neck, a bit low down, at least, so the Archbishop said who spliced them a week later, and it was a lovely wedding and she made a lovely bride.

This girl was indeed dainty and lively, without any peer. More than that, she was a virgin such as never virgin was, that is to say, she was a virgin with no knowledge whatsoever of love. She did not even know what it consists in or what it is for, she was a virgin capable of genuinely marvelling that some women so liked dallying in bed. She was, in fact, a virgin fully prepared to believe that babies are found in savoy cabbages.

Such was the innocence in which her mother had brought her up, without letting her even think of such trifles as how she had imbibed her soup through her teeth. She was thus a grown-up child with maidenhood completely intact, a child full of play and simplicity, an angel who only lacked wings to fly to Paradise. And when she left the lodging of her weeping mother to consummate her spiritual union with Bruyn in the Cathedral Church of St Gatien and Maurice, folk flocked in from all round to see the ceremony, rugs were laid out all down de la Sellerie Street, and everybody agreed that never had daintier foot stirred the soil of Touraine, never bluer eyes looked on heaven and never did finer festival bring out rugs and flowers into the streets.

The town hussies and those of St Martin and Château-Neuf together all envied those long, fair plaits with which it seemed that Blanche had hooked her county, but still more did they lust after her thread-of-gold frock and her exotic jewels, those white diamonds and those gold chains with which she played and which were to bind her forever to the Seneschal. That old soldier, moreover, was so stimulated when at her side that his happiness burst out through every wrinkle, in every glance, in every movement that he made. Though he was now about as straight as a bill-hook, he strutted so valiantly at Blanche's side that you might have thought him a German soldier on parade as his commander passed down the ranks. He could be seen to lay his hand on his diaphragm, like a man constrained to choking point by sheer delight.

When they heard the church bells ring out and saw the procession and all the pomp and ceremony of the wedding, of which there had been talk ever since the christening do at the Bishop's Palace, all the girls present craved there might be a whole vintage crop of Moorish maids, a cloud-burst of old Seneschals, and skepfuls of Egyptian baptisms. This, however, was the only one there ever was of the sort in Touraine, for that fair land is far removed both from Egypt and Bohemia.

After the ceremony, Lady d'Azay came in for a good sum of money, which she made use of at once to proceed to Acre to meet her husband. She travelled with a Lieutenant and some of Count de la Roche-Corbon's men-at-arms, and he fitted them out with everything they needed. She left on the very wedding-day, committing her daughter to the care of the Seneschal and enjoining him to care for her well. (Later she returned with Lord d'Azay, now leprous, and healed him herself at risk of being a leper herself, all of which was greatly marvelled at.)

The wedding accomplished and at last over (for to everybody's great satisfaction, it lasted three whole days), Count Bruyn took his young bride with great pomp to his Castle and there, by the custom of married folk, solemnly put her to bed in his own couch after this had been blessed by the Abbot of Marmoustiers. Thus, in this grand baronial chamber of la Roche-Corbon, which had been done out with green brocade with gold appliqué work, he came to lie beside her, but when, perfumed from head to foot, old Bruyn found himself flesh to flesh with this lovely bride of his, first he planted a kiss on her forehead, then another on one pretty little rounded breast, at the exact spot where she had allowed him to fasten her gold chain.

But that was all. The dear old boy had been a trifle too sure of himself, thinking he could shell his peas any farther. From that point on, despite the jolly wedding ditties, and the sounds of the epithalamia and lighter ditties rising from the floor below, where the dancing was still in full swing, love was idle. Instead of action, he comforted himself with a good swig of the bridal cup which, according to custom, had been blessed by the Church and placed at hand But though the spices of this certainly warmed his stomach, they did not affect the core of his defunct codpiece.

Blanche was not in the least taken aback by this felonious abstention of her husband's, for she was also utterly virginal in spirit as well as body, and all she could see in marriage was what all very young girls see, namely: gowns and festivities and horses and being Master and Mistress and having a county of one's own and enjoying oneself and issuing orders. So, child that she was, she merely toyed with the golden tassels of the bedstead and marvelled at the lavishness of the scarlet robes prepared for the funeral of her maidenhood.

Now, rather late, the Seneschal realized his guilt in the matter, but he trusted to the future. This, however, was merely to continue the steady decline of that with which he should have regaled his spouse. Therefore the Seneschal tried substituting words for deeds. He spoiled his wife in all possible ways: he promised her the keys of his cupboards, his barns, his chests, he promised complete control of his households and his lands, and with no supervision. In short, as we say in Touraine, he sliced the bread and strung it ready round her neck.

Like a young charger, with her manger thus brimming, Blanche thought her good man the most gallant of gentlemen. She propped herself up on the pillows, and broke into a smile. Now she saw the pretty green brocade hangings in lovelier light than before. From

now on she was at complete liberty every night to sleep in it all without any blemish whatsoever.

Seeing her ready thus to play ball, the wily old count, who had had little contact with real maids, but from much experience, since he had always had dealings with whores, was well aware that under their fine feathers all women are monkeys, became chary of any hand play or stolen kisses or those other little liberties of love which he had never failed to indulge in in time gone by, but which now would have found his responses as cold as a Pope's *obit*. So, fearing for his happiness he drew back to the edge of the bed, and to his all too enticing spouse he said:

'Well, my darling, so now, you see, you are a Seneschal's wife. Indeed, one might call you the Lady Seneschal.'

'Oh no,' said she.

'How so?' he cried, in great alarm. 'Are you not a grand lady?'

'Oh no,' she said, again. 'I shall only be a grand lady when I have a baby.'

'Did you notice the meadow-lands on the way here?' inquired her good husband.

'Yes,' she said. 'I did.'

'Well,' he said, 'they're all yours. . . .'

'Oh! Oh!' she cried, with a laugh. 'What fun I shall have catching butterflies in them!'

'Now isn't that a nice thought!' said her lord. 'And did you notice the woodlands?'

'Oh, I'd never dare go there alone! You must take me. Dear,' she added, 'will you give me a little drink of that cordial which the maid has taken so much trouble to make for us.'

'But why ever do you want that, my pet? It will put fire into your body.'

'Oh, but that's what I want,' she said, pouting with vexation, 'because I want to give you a baby as soon as possible, and I can easily see that that's what that cordial is for.'

'Pooh!' said the Seneschal, 'my dear child!'

From these words, indeed, Bruyn really did realize how virginal his Blanche was, virginal from head to foot. 'Pooh! Before all else you need God's good will for that office. Besides, a woman needs to be in a proper haysel condition.'

'And when shall I be in a haysel condition?' she inquired, with a smile.

'When it pleases Nature,' said Bruyn, intending the reply humorously.

'And what must be done for that to be?' she persisted.

'Pooh!' he said, 'you will need a cabbalistic, alchemistic operation, one fraught with much danger.'

'Oh!' said she, and was rather thoughtful. 'So that is why this metamorphosis of marriage made my mother cry so. But, dearest, Berthe de Preuilly, who's so set on being made a woman, too, she told me there was nothing in the world that was easier.'

'It's all according to age,' replied the Count. 'But, I say, have you seen that white hack in my stables that's the talk of Touraine?'

'Yes, it's a very gentle, nice horse, isn't it?'

'Yes, and I'll make you a present of it, if you like, and you can ride it whenever you want to and as often as you like.'

'Oh, how kind you are! So they weren't telling lies when they said . . .'

'Here, at La Roche-Corbon,' he resumed, 'here, my darling, everybody—the butler, the chaplain, the treasurer, the groom, the cook, the bailiff, even Lord de Montsoreau, I mean that young rascal Gautier who carries my banner, and all his men-at-arms and all his captains, man and beast together—they all are yours and are to do whatever you want to the letter, under pain of being incommoded by a hempen noose.'

'But,' she asked, 'that little alchemic operation—couldn't it be performed at once.'

'Oh no,' the Seneschal insisted. 'For that to take place, the first thing of all is that we both have to be in a perfect state of grace before our Maker, otherwise we should have a bad child, one all sins, and that is prohibited by church canon. That is why there are so many incorrigible scoundrels in the world—their parents were not sensible enough to wait till their souls were immaculate, so they gave their children bad souls. Handsome, virtuous sons come from perfect fathers. . . . That is why we have our beds blessed, as the Abbot of Marmoustiers did ours. Have you yourself not broken commandments of Holy Church?'

'Oh no,' cried Blanche quickly. 'Before mass I received absolution of all my sins and since then I have not committed the very littlest one.'

'You are indeed perfection,' agreed the crafty Count, 'I am overjoyed to have you for a wife. But I am of different stuff, I have sworn oaths like a heathen.'

'Oh, but why ever did you do that?'

'Because that dancing never ended and I could not soon enough have you all to myself to bring you here and kiss you.'

Thereupon, most gallantly, he took her hands in his and simply devoured them with caresses, babbling all manner of little nothings and charming trifles which made her quite happy. Then, as she was rather tired by all her dancing and the ceremonies, she lay down, as she did so, remarking to the Seneschal:

'Now, tomorrow I'm going to make sure you don't commit any sin at all.'

Thus she left her old boy, agog at her white loveliness, in love with her gentleness, but also as troubled to know however he was going to keep her in her state of innocence as he would have been to explain why cattle chew their cud. Though it all pointed to no good, he was so enflamed during her innocent, untroubled sleep at the sight of her exquisite perfections that he made up his mind he must at all costs protect this lovely jewel of love and fend off all dangers from it. . . . With tears in his eyes he kissed her lovely golden hair, her beautiful eyelids, her cool, scarlet lips, though very softly, from fear of waking her. . . .

This was all the old man's fruition, these silent delights which scorched his heart still more without Blanche even once stirring. Thus, poor dear fellow, he lamented the snows of his old age and it became clear to him that the Almighty had pleased to give him the walnuts he had always wanted now that he had lost his teeth.

The Seneschal's War with His Wife's Maidenhood

During the first days of his marriage Seneschal Bruyn thought out some remarkable cock-and-bull stories to foist on his wife, thus abusing her so pitiable innocence. First he discovered valid excuses for leaving her alone for longish periods of official duties, then he engaged her in country exercises, taking her out to the grape-harvest in his Vouvray vineyards and bamboozling her with countless fantastic notions, such as the yarn that the nobility did not do these things at all like lesser folk, or that the children of Counts were only to be planted at certain conjunctions of the heavens calculated by learned astrologers, or that one should always avoid making a baby on a Holy Day, because it was heavy work, which was prohibited. After that he observed all feast-days of the church like a man set on securing an unhindered entry to Paradise.

On other occasions he made out that if one or both of the parents happened not to be in a state of grace, babies started on St Clare's Day came blind, on St Genou's, gouty, on St Aignan's, ringwormy, on St Roch's, with the plague. Or it was a yarn about those laid in February being chilly mortals, those in March, too fidgetty, those in

April, worthless all round, whereas nice boys were started in May. He was, in fact, most anxious that his son should be perfect and take after them both, and this demanded the conjuncture of all the necessary conditions.

At other moments Bruyn told Blanche quite simply that it was a man's right to give his wife a baby when it happened to please him and him only, and that if she really wanted to be a virtuous wife she must fit in with her husband's moods. Finally, he said, they would have to wait till Lady d'Azay was back, so she could be present at the confinement.

All of this in the end led Blanche to the conclusion that the Seneschal was annoyed by her solicitations and was possibly right so to be, since he was old and full of experience. So she gave in, and thought no more of that longed-for child, except inwardly, which means that she was always thinking of it, just as whenever a woman gets any idea into her head, and she never suspected that by so doing she was behaving like any strumpet or beggar-girl, running after something she craved.

One evening, however, Bruyn himself happened to start talking about children, a subject he generally avoided as cats do water. The fact was, he groused about a lad he had condemned to death that morning for some serious crimes. He was quite sure, he said, that this was a boy born of folk with moral sin on their consciences.

'How simply awful!' said Blanche. 'But, dear, if you were to give me one when you were lacking absolution, I would repair the defects so well that you really would be pleased with him.'

Count Bruyn then realized that his wife was indeed very badly bitten by this burning notion of hers and it was time at last to tackle her maidenhood and make himself its master. He must somehow break it in, satisfy the thing, assuage it, indeed, he must extinguish it.

'Why, my pet,' he now said, 'do you want to be a mother? But look, you do not yet behave like a grand lady of the nobility, you are still not the complete Lady of the Manor.'

'Really?' she cried, 'to be a real Countess and lodge a little Count in my loins, must I really play the great lady? Then indeed I shall, and hard, too.'

Now, to obtain an heir, Blanche lent herself to the coursing of stags and deer. She leapt ditches, she galloped her hack up hill and down dale, through woods and through fields, she took great delight in watching her falcons fly, carrying them on her little wrist ever so daintily. She was always out a-hunting. Just, in fact, what the Seneschal had wanted. But all this riding to hounds merely gave her the appetite of a nun and a bishop put together. That is to say, she now

28

craved pregnancy desperately, she was all keyed up about it, and when she got home and her teeth got to work on her food there was no bridling her appetite. Besides, by dint of reading all manner of guidance writ large wherever she went and by unravelling in death the loves begun by birds and the creatures of the wild, she accomplished a certain occult natural alchemy which lent her cheeks colour and overstimulated her metabolisms, all of which was little likely to calm her combative nature. Indeed, it rather titillated her desire, which giggled and fidgetted and pleaded as never before.

By getting her to take to country sports, the Seneschal had thought to divert that treacherous maidenhood of his wife's into a safe channel, but his trickery had turned against him, for from those country sallies the unknown love circulating in Blanche's veins emerged more lusty than ever, crying out for jousting and tourneying as might any young page suddenly elevated to the knighthood.

The worthy Count then realized that he had taken the wrong road altogether. Once he was thus on the grill, there was no cool spot, he could no longer think what fodder to give her now she was so badly blown, and the longer he let be, the more restive she got. It was a duel fated to end in a dead man and a female assassin, a duel which now, God grant he wished far from him till he be gone for ever.

The poor Seneschal by now found it difficult to follow his hunting wife at all without coming off the saddle. He sweated like a bull under his harness and when his hot-stuff wife was just getting warmed up and enjoying it, he was at his last gasp. Often of an evening she would want to dance, when, weighed down by his cumbersome garments, the dear fellow found himself utterly worn out by the convolutions in which he was compelled to participate, either lending her a hand when she did the Saracen shakes or holding a lighted torch for her when it pleased her to do the candlestick dance, and all the time, despite all his sciaticas and his ossifications and his rheumatifications, he was obliged to grin and after all the twirlings and mummings and laughable pantomimings in which she indulged to take her mind off things, he was obliged to smile sweetly and murmur sweet gallantries and compliments, for he did still love her most dearly, and had she asked him to give her an oriphant he would at once have rushed off to look for one all over the place.

However, one fine day he admitted to himself that his loins were really too far gone to be the equal of his wife's lusty nature and so, humiliated as he thus was by this lusty knight Count May d'Enhood, he told himself he was now going to let everything go its course just as it would and from now on trust only in the modest piety and healthy sense of decency of sweet Blanche. All the same, he never slept more than a cat-wink, for, whatever he might try to persuade himself, he had a fundamental misgiving that after all the good Lord had made maidenhoods like partridges, to be taken on the spit and well basted.

One morning, in that sort of weather in which snails draw long trails, that dismal weather so fruitful of reflection, Blanche was at home. There she sat, musing in her tall chair, for there nothing is productive of more lively vaporation of the essential humours, nor is there any recipe, specific or elixir more searching, penetrating, piercing, enfevering than that insidious warmth which simmers twixt the down of an upholstered chair and that of a maid ensconsed therein. Thereby, against her will, the Countess was gradually inconvenienced by the said maidenhood, which had indeed begun to cause a metagrabolation of the brain accompanied by a process of attrition in all parts.

Her good husband was grieved to see her so melancholic, and he made a serious effort to drive away these cogitations, which in fact adumbrated the principle of extra-conjugal love.

'What makes you so sad, my darling?' he asked her.

'Shame,' she mumbled.

'Who then has insulted you?'

'Shame at not being a good wife,' she said, 'and I am not, because I have no child and you no heir. Am I a real lady, childless like this? Never! Look! All the ladies I know for miles around have children, and I too was married to have them, as you were to give them me. All the gentry of Touraine have their quivers full. Their wives have swarms of children, yours is the only one who has none. We shall be laughed at, I assure you! What will happen to your name? And your fiefs, your manors? A baby, too, is a woman's natural company, it is our delight to swaddle and beribbon it, tuck it up and dress it and undress it, pet it and dandle it, cradle it and take it up and put it to bed and suckle it, I feel that if I had only half a babe I could kiss it and wash it and swaddle it and unswaddle it and dance it up and down and make it laugh all day, as all other women do.'

'Were it not that in laying babies,' said Bruyn, 'women die, and because of that, you are still too small and too well knit together, or you would be a mother already . . .' replied the Seneschal, quite taken aback by this sudden burst of eloquence of his wife's. 'Perhaps you would like to buy one ready-made? That would cost you neither pain nor trouble.'

'But I want the pain and the trouble,' she said, 'without that, it would not be really ours. I know quite well that the baby has to come out of me, because that's what we are told in Church, Jesus was the fruit of the Virgin's belly, wasn't he?'

'Why then,' cried the Seneschal, 'let us pray to God it does happen! What's more, let us ask Our Lady of Egrignolles to help us. Many women have conceived after the *novena* in the *Calendar*.'

So, as soon as it was daylight, Blanche set out for the Church of Notre Dame d'Egrignolles. Mounted on her handsome steed, she was attired like a queen, her robe of green velvet laced with cord of fine gold but free at the bosom. The sleeves were of scarlet, on her feet were dainty shoes, on her head a towering headdress garnished with precious stones, about her middle a gilt belt which made the most of a waist slender as a flagstaff. All this fine array she intended to present to Our Lady the Virgin, a promise indeed for the day of her churching.

Before her rode young de Montsoreau, with eyes as keen as a buzzard's. He kept the folk in order, with his horsemen seeing to the security of the excursion. When they drew near Marmoustiers, the Seneschal, dozing off at last through the heat, for it was August, began to sway in his saddle like a diadem on a cow's head. Seeing so lively and charming a lady now riding with such an old crow, a peasant girl who had just squatted down to take a drink from her pitcher turned round to a toothless old hag gleaning and grousing nearby and said surely this princess must be on her way to the funeral of all funerals.

'Oh no,' said the old woman, 'that's our Lady of la Roche-Corbon, wife of the Seneschal of Touraine and Poitou, she's on her way to look for a babe.'

'Ha, ha, ha!' laughed the young wench, like a fly that's just been served, then, pointing to the dashing young knight who was leading the way, added: 'Let that 'un at the head gi' her one, that'd save her both wax and vow.'

'Pooh!' said the old one, 'you're not the only one, my lass, to be surprised she's going to Notre-Dame de l'Egrignolles, there isn't a good-looking priest in the place. She'd do far better to halt awhile in the shade of Marmoustiers bell-tower, she'd soon get in the family way there, the good fathers are quick on the draw.'

'A pox on your monks!' cried another harvest-girl, waking up at that moment. 'Use your eyes! Lord de Montsoreau's hot enough and handsome enough to find the way to this good lady's heart, especially since it's already gaping ready open for him.'

There was general laughter at this and de Montsoreau would have had at them and strung them up on a willow-tree by the road-side as punishment for their wicked talk, had Blanche not been quick to cry:

'Please, My Lord, don't hang them yet, that's not the last word of it, let's see on the way back.'

She then turned scarlet and Lord de Montsoreau shot her a glance right home as if there and then to thrust into her with the occult understandings of love, for of course the idle talk of these peasant wenches had by now somewhat clarified his wits and something was already ripening in his mind, for all maidenhoods are so much tinder, a mere word can catch light to them.

In this way, Blanche came to notice outstanding differences, including physical ones, between the qualities of her old husband and the perfections of this fellow, Gauttier de Montsoreau, a young nobleman who wore his twenty-three years most lightly, sitting his saddle straight as a ninepin, as wide-awake as early matins, while the Seneschal, on the contrary, was sound asleep beside him. What is more, Montsoreau was a person of tremendous driving force and some ability precisely where his master fell short. He was one of those fellows with real starch in him, whom at bed-time any fidgetty filly would prefer to any soft leather as hair-protector, with them they always soon stop worrying about the fleas, though there are of course some females who have not a good word for such men. But one needs tolerance both ways. Everyone to his or her own fashion of sleeping.

The Seneschal's spouse meditated at such length and so imperiously that by the time she reached Tours bridge she was covertly in love with Gauttier, head over heels in love, too, just as maids do fall in love when they have not a clue what it is, whereby she became a woman of fortune, that is, a woman desirous of the fortune of other folk, namely, the best part of a man. In other words, she was taken with love's sickness, plunging straightaway into the depths of her misfortunes, since between first initial longing and last desire all is fire, nor was aware, as however she now learned, that through the eyes there could be a flux of an insidious essence which caused great corrosion in all one's veins, in all convolutions of the heart, in all fibres of the limbs, in all roots of the hair, in all exudations of body's substance, in all regions of the brain, in all orifices of the epidermis, in all convolutions of the bowels, and in all canals hypochondrous or otherwise which now in Blanche were all suddenly titillated, irritated, heated, swollen, envenomed, disrupted and erected, as if there had been a thousand pin-cushions of needles in her. It was a very special lust, a virgin's lust, a lust which clouded the vision to such point that Blanche could not even see her aged husband, though young Gauttier, in whom nature is as broad as the glorious chin of any Abbot, was perfectly visible.

When the worthy Seneschal made his entry into Tours, he was

wakened at last by the cheering of the populace, whereupon with great pomp he proceeded with his train to the church of Notre-Dame de l'Egrignolles, formerly known as Notre-Dame *la Greigneur* as if to say: *the most meritorious*. Blanche then went to the chapel where one requested both God and the Virgin for a baby. She went in by herself, as was customary, while the Seneschal with some of his men and a handful of sightseers stayed outside the railings.

When the Countess saw the priest who was in charge of the special baby service come forward to receive her declaration of vows, she inquired of him if there were many barren women. To this the worthy priest replied that he had nothing to complain about, babies were a good source of revenue for his church.

'And do you often,' insisted Blanche, 'do you often see young wives with husbands as advanced in years as My own Lord is?'

'Rarely,' replied the priest.

'But have any such ever got heirs?'

'They invariably got them,' said the priest, with a smile.

'And the other barren women, whose consorts were less advanced?'

'They sometimes did. . . .'

'Oho!' she cried, 'so with a husband like the Seneschal, one is more sure of results?'

'Without doubt,' said the priest.

'And why is that?' she insisted.

'My Lady,' replied the priest, gravely, 'with a younger husband, it all depends on God alone, with the older ones, there is always human aid.'

At this time it is quite true that knowledge was altogether the preserve of ecclesiastics, so Blanche now made her vow, which was a very considerable one, seeing that on her back she had an easy two thousand crowns' worth.

'You are very happy,' said the Seneschal, seeing how on the way back to la Roche-Corbon she made her mare trip and skip and prance.

'Oh, of course I am happy,' she said. 'Now I am quite sure that I shall have a baby. The priest said other men have to do a little work, too. I shall take Gauttier to help.'

The Seneschal would then gladly have slaughtered that monk, but thought it would be too costly a crime, so he merely decided to plot a very cunning revenge with the aid of the Archbishop, and before he even sighted the roofs of la Roche-Corbon he intimated to Montsoreau that he had better seek a little shade in his own part of the country, which, knowing the liberties his master took, young Gauttier at once did. The Seneschal then engaged, in place of Gauttier, a scion of the house of de Jallanges, which was a sub-feudation of la Roche-Corbon Manor. This de Jallanges was a young lad, rising fourteen, René by name, whom he made his page and attendant till such time as he might be squired. The command of his forces Bruyn handed over to an old castrate with whom he had knocked about in Palestine and other parts.

In this way the good fellow fondly imagined he would be proof against ever donning the forked headdress of the cuckold, and able at his leisure to go on tightening girths and snaffles and reins on that fractious maidenhood of his wife's, now restive as any hobbled mule ever was.

When Sin is Merely Venial

The first Sunday after René's arrival at la Roche-Corbon Castle, Blanche went out hunting without her worthy spouse. Deep in the forest, near les Carneaux, she saw a monk pressing a girl a little harder than should be, so she put spurs on her horse, and cried to her men:

'Hi! Hi! Stop that monk, he'll kill her!'

But when she drew near, Blanche turned her horse about sharply. The sight she got of what that monk possessed stopped all her hunting. She returned home deep in thought. All at once, the dim lantern of her brain had flared up. There was suddenly brilliant light on many a scene in church pictures and other places too, also on old tales and lays of the troubadours, even on the domestic customs of birds. Thus all at once Blanche discovered the sweet mystery of love as writ in all tongues, even that of the carp. Was it not ridiculous that such knowledge should be sealed away from maids? That night she was quick abed and quick to say to her Seneschal:

'Bruyn, you have tricked me. Come now you've got to plough me as that monk of les Carneaux was ploughing that girl.'

Old Bruyn was reticent about the matter, but one thing he had no doubts about—his evil hour had come. There was too much fire in the glance he shot Blanche for there to be any fire at his other end.

Meekly, he replied:

'Alas, my love, when I took you for wife, I had more love than vigour, and counted on your benevolence and virtue, but it is now my life's great grief to feel all my strength concentrated in my heart alone. The anguish of it is shortening my life, so very soon you are sure to be free. Do wait now till I have departed from this world.

34

That is the only request that he who is your master and might command you makes of you, though he would rather be the first man to aid you in this and serve you. But do not betray the honour of my white hairs. . . . In such case there are men of our position who have put their wives to death.'

'Alas, so would you then kill me?' she asked.

'No,' the old man replied, 'I love you too much, my darling. Why, are you not the flower of my old age and the delight of my soul? You are my beloved daughter. The sight of you is the solace of my eyes and I could bear anything of you, even grief, as if it were happiness. . . . I give you complete licence in all things, so long as you do not too far displease your poor Bruyn, who at least made a great, rich, honoured and noble lady of you. Will you not thus make a lovely widow? Indeed, and your good fortune will at least sweeten my passing.'

With these words, in his dessicated eyes he found one tear more, which trickled all steaming down his pinecone countenance, to spatter on to Blanche's hand. She was very moved to behold this great affection of her aged husband, now even laying himself in the grave to please her, and with a smiling countenance she cried:

'Tut! Tut! Don't cry now, I will wait.'

The Seneschal then kissed her hands, and treated her to much billing and cooing. With agitated voice he murmured:

'Oh, Blanche, my love, if you but knew how when you sleep I eat you up with caresses, yes, here—and here. . . .' And with his two hands, just like two bundles of dry bones, the old baboon caressed her. He then continued by saying:

'Indeed, I never dared waken my little pussy, she would have throttled my honour, she would, in all this matter of love I embraced you only with my heart.'

'Oh,' she said, 'you can do all that when my eyes are open, if you like, it's all the same to me.'

When she said this, the poor Seneschal took the little stiletto which lay on the bedside table, placed it in her hand, and cried passionately:

'Come, my love, kill me outright—or let me think you love me just a little.'

'Why yes, of course I love you, darling,' she responded, quite frightened by this new suggestion, 'and I will see that I love you a lot, too.'

That is how this young piece of maidenhood finally got a grip on this old man and subjected him, for now, all by that malice proper to women, in the name of that lovely all so dewy paddock of Venus,

Blanche made her old Bruyn run at her beck and call like any miller's mule.

'Darling Bruyn, I want this, darling Bruyn, I want that. Come now, Bruyn, Bruyn!'

It was *darling Bruyn* the livelong day, so that the poor old fellow was worse done by when in his wife's good books than when she had been pestering him. She gave the man no peace, she wanted everything done out in scarlet, then at a mere wink from her he had to start all over again, and whenever she was downcast the Seneschal so lost his head that on the Bench the only sentence he could pronounce was: 'Hang him.'

Any other man would have died off like a fly in this virginal contest. Bruyn, however, was of so ferric a nature that it was no easy matter getting the better of him. One evening, when at la Roche-Corbon Castle Blanche had turned absolutely everything upside down, confounding beasts and men alike, and was still in such a black mood that she would have tried the patience of our eternal Father for all the vast stores of it which he has seeing that he puts up with us all, what did she say to the Seneschal, when they went to bed, but:

'My dear Bruyn, I've got such wild thoughts tonight deep down, they are biting me and pricking me and from down there they rise up to my heart and they overheat my mind and they incite me to evil things and at night I dreamt about that les Carneaux monk. . . .'

'My darling,' replied the Seneschal quickly, 'that is merely the work and temptation of Satan, which all monks and nuns well know how to subdue, so, if you want to save your soul, go to our worthy neighbour the Abbot of Marmoustiers and confess. He will give you good advice and holy guidance, how to get on to the right path.'

'I will go first thing tomorrow,' she said.

And, indeed, at daybreak off she cantered post-haste to that monastery of good monks who, astonished to see such a dainty lady calling, committed more than one sin that evening.

At once, in delight, they took her to their Reverend Abbot. Blanche found this worthy man in a green bower in a closed garden close in to the cliff, and for all that she was not used to giving white heads much consideration, she was overcome with respect by the holy man's countenance.

'God preserve you, Dear Lady,' he said. 'What have you so young come to ask me so nigh death?'

'Your valued counsel,' she replied, with a curtsey by way of greeting. 'And if you would please to guide so unruly a ewe lamb, I would be happy to have so wise a confessor.'

'My daughter,' was the Abbot's response, for old Bruyn had compounded this trickery with him and agreed the part to be played, 'had I not the chill of a hundred winters on this denuded pate of mine, I could not hear your sins, but speak out. If you enter paradise, it shall be my fault.'

The Seneschal's lady then delivered the trifles of her stock, and when she had unburdened herself of all her petty sins she came to the postscript of her confession.

'Oh, Father,' she said, 'I must also confess that I am daily fret with the longing to make a baby. Is that wrong?'

'No,' said the Abbot.

'But,' she went on, 'as the old women on the road said, nature forbids my husband ever opening up his stock to make the poor mite.'

'Then,' rejoined the man of God, 'you should live discreetly and refrain from any thought of this nature.'

'But I have heard Lady de Jallanges say that when one got neither profit nor pleasure from it, it was no sin.'

'There is always pleasure in it,' replied the Abbot. 'Besides, would you not count a baby profit? So get into your head once and for all that it would still be mortal sin before the Almighty and a crime before men to splice a babe to yourself by business with any man to whom Holy Church has not married you. Thus, those women who do infringe the holy laws of marriage suffer greatly from it in the next world, where they are at the mercy of horrible monsters with sharp tearing claws, who roast them in a multitude of furnaces as a reminder that down here on earth they warmed their cores a little more than is lawful.'

When she heard this Blanche scratched her ear and, after thinking it over a bit, said to the ecclesiastic:

'Then how did the Virgin Mary manage?'

'Ah,' replied the Abbot, 'that is a mystery.'

'But what is a mystery?'

'A mystery is something with no explanation, which one must accept, but never inquire into.'

'Indeed,' she said, 'then could I not make a little mystery?'

'That,' said the Abbot, 'only happened once, because it was the Son of God.'

'Woe is me, Father,' cried Blanche, 'is it then God's will that I die? Or, sound and healthy of understanding as I am now, am I to go out of my mind? There is great danger of that happening. When things begin to stir and heat together in me, I am no longer in my senses and heed nothing, to get at a man in such moments I would leap walls and cross open fields without shame and ruin everything merely to see what so irked the les Carneaux monk. And during those fits which rack me and prickle me, soul and body, neither God nor any devil nor even my husband exist, I prance and race about, I could smash any chains and all the crockery and the tools and the stables and the very household, in a way I cannot describe. Indeed, I dare not tell you all the things I could do because merely to mention them makes my mouth water and that part which may the dear God curse itches unbearably. . . . Suppose one day this madness so seized me that it penetrated me and destroyed my virtue. What then? Will God, who planted such great love in my body, then condemn me?'

At this pronouncement it was the Abbot who scratched his ear, for he was aghast that such lamentations, such deep wisdom, such sense and such arguments should be secreted by mere maidenhood.

'My daughter,' he said, 'God marked us off from the animals and made a Paradise for us to attain, and to that end he gave us reason, which is a rudder to steer us through the tempests of our overweening desires. There is still the possibility of overcoming that prime mover in your brain by fasts, by excessive labour and by other wise acts. So instead of fizzling and quivering like a monkey off its chain you must pray to the Virgin, sleep on hard boards, and reorganize your domestic life, so that you stop being idle.'

'Oh, Father, when, in church, I am in my pew, I see neither priest nor altar, only the child Jesus, who makes the thing attractive to me. And then, what if after all this my head does whirl, my understanding does go wild, and I find myself in the sticky lime of love?'

'If it came to that,' said the Abbot, with sudden imprudence, 'you would be in St Lidoire's position, for she went to sleep terribly soundly one very hot day with one leg here and the other there and very little on and a young man full of evil came up and very slyly filled her with child and as the saint was utterly ignorant that this wicked thing had been done to her she was very surprised indeed after some time to have to take to childbed. She had thought the swelling of her pouch must be some serious ailment. Now, St Lidoire did penance as for a mere venial sin, since she had had no pleasure from the wicked act, as the evil man himself bore out, for at the gallows when the noose was round his neck, he declared that the saint never even budged.'

'Oh, Father,' said Blanche, 'you may be sure I shall not budge any more than St Lidoire did.'

With this declaration she slipped away, all gaiety and charm and smiles, telling herself she could always commit a venial sin like that.

When she got back from the great monastery, in her castle court-yard hall she noticed little Jallanges cantering round and curvetting about on a fine horse under the instructions of an old groom. The lad was lending himself lissomely to all the animal's movements, as he dismounted and re-mounted, jumped and jousted, all very neatly indeed, thighs well up, so handsome, so able, so free of movement that it was a treat to watch. In short, a lad to inspire even Queen Lucrece, who killed herself for having been dishonoured against her will, with desire.

'Oh,' thought Blanche, 'if only this page had turned fifteen, I could have gone to sleep very soundly indeed beside him.'

So it was that despite the excessive youth of this charming servant, all through their afternoon refreshment and later during supper she quizzed those black curls, that white skin, that grace of René's, and especially his eyes, simply swimming with limpid warmth, simply ablaze with vital vigour which boylike he was diffident about aiming at anybody.

That evening, Blanche was seated pensive in the ingle-nook when old Bruyn asked what was worrying her.

'I was just thinking,' she said, 'you must have started love jousting very early to be so exhausted today.'

'Ah,' said Bruyn, with a grin, like any other old man asked for reminiscences of love affairs, 'I was only thirteen and a half when I first got one of my mother's maids in the family way.'

This was all that Blanche required. So she could indeed assume that young Page René might be equally satisfactorily equipped. This made her very pleased indeed and, revelling in her silent desires like a cook folding the flour into the cake mixture, she began to make up to her good spouse.

How and By Whom the Babe was Made

The Seneschal's wife did not waste any too much time devising how instanter to entice the page's love. She had soon found the natural ambush in which the crudest of men are caught. In this way.

In the midday heat good old Bruyn was used, Saracen fashion, to take a *siesta*, a custom he had never relinquished since his return from the Holy Land. While this was going on, Blanche would be out in the paddocks, alone, or else busy indoors with those little tasks of embroidery on which women spend their time, or, more often than not, she would keep an eye on the laundry, folding sheets, or at some such business. She now set apart this silent hour for the completion of the page's education by making him do some reading and recite his prayers to her.

The following day, therefore, when overcome by the sunshine, the most luminous rays of which heat the slopes of la Roche-Corbon to such an extent that unless inflated and sackbutted and freshly engingered by a devil of a maidenhood, one is inevitably drowsy, at midday the Seneschal went to sleep, Blanche draped herself most charmingly in her husband's great manorial throne of a chair, which, since she counted on the chance play of perspective, was not at all too high off the ground. Cunning wench, she snuggled into it as neatly as a swallow in its nest and leant her naughty head on her arm, like a child asleep, but, making ready thus, kept her greedy eyes open, smiling, marvelling in advance at the little secret promptings and sneezings, peepings and fits of ecstasy of the page who was to lie at her feet with no more than the hop of an old flea between them, and without a scruple she pulled the velvet hassock on which the poor boy was to kneel with whose soul and life she was going to play so close to her feet that had he been a stone saint his eyes would still have been compelled to follow the sinuosities of her gown and be led to wonder and marvel at the beauty and perfection of form of the shapely legs that filled My Lady Seneschal's white stockings. Like this there was no question but that a mere lad would be caught in a trap to which the stoutest-hearted of knights would have capitulated. When she had twisted and twisted again and shifted her body till it was in the position which might best engage the lad's attention, she called softly:

'Oh, René!'

René who, as she well knew, was at hand in the guard-room, did not fail to thrust his swarthy head through the curtains at the door and come running to her.

'What is your pleasure, My Lady?' he asked.

There he stood, with his cap of scarlet velour respectfully dangling in his hand, though it was not so scarlet by far as his fresh, bonny dimpled cheeks already were.

'Come here,' she murmured, very faintly, so powerfully did the boy now attract her that she was quite out of breath.

True, there was no precious stone that flashed brighter than René's eyes, no vellum whiter than his complexion, no woman, indeed, so gracefully formed as he. Besides, so near her desire was she that she found him still more finely fashioned. In addition, bear in mind that the lovely play of love was brilliantly reflected in all this youth, in the lovely sunlight, in the silence, in short, in the whole situation.

'Read me the litanies of Our Lady the Virgin,' she said to him, placing an opened book on her praying-stool. 'I want to see if your master has taught you well. Do you not think the Virgin lovely?' she asked, with a smile, when he took in his hands that book of hours, its illuminations gleaming azure and gold.

'It is only a painting,' he replied, timidly, with a swift glance at his so entrancing mistress.

'Come, read on. . . .'

Busily, René read out those litanies, so charming and so mystifying, and you may be sure that Blanche's responses of *ora pro nobis* became fainter and fainter, like the sound of horns ever farther across country, and when from the page's lips there came the ardent words: '*Oh, mystifying rose!*' the only response from the Lady of the Manor, who must have heard quite well, was a faint sigh, whereupon René suspected that the Lady Seneschal had fallen asleep, so lent himself to examining her at his ease, with no other desire now than to pronounce some litany of love of his own. His good fortune made his heart dance and leap as high as his throat, so that as if thus foreordained these two lovely virginities vied in gathering heat and, had you seen them, you could never have blamed either.

René feasted his eyes, contemplating a thousand culminatory acts by each and all of which this glorious love-fruit brought the water to his lips. Indeed, he entered into such ecstasy that he dropped the book, at which he was at once as confounded as a monk caught at young boys' play. However, the accident did at the same time serve to show that Blanche was indeed fast asleep, for at risk of greater peril—for she hoped for something more than the book to fall—she did not stir or even open her eyes.

Thus, you see, there is no more dangerous longing than the longing for pregnancy.

The page now examined his lady's feet, neatly shod in pale blue brocade slippers. She had, strikingly, placed one on a foot-stool, as the seat of the Seneschal's throne was too high up for her. It was a narrow-fashioned foot, lightly arched, two fingers broad and long as a gay sparrow (inclusive of tail). It was small at the tip, a true foot of delight, a virginal foot, a foot which deserved a kiss as a thief the noose, an impish foot, a sensuous foot, a foot which would ruin an archangel, a significant foot, a devilish stimulating foot, prompting the desire to make a couple more feet like it, and in this humble world of ours thus perpetuate the lovely creations of the Lord.

The page was now tempted to bare that persuasive foot, and to that end his eyes, glowing with the fire of his youthfulness, swept swift as a bell-clapper from the foot of delight to the slumbering countenance of his Lady and Mistress. He hearkened to her sleep, he drank in her respiration, then began to wonder hopelessly where it would be sweetest to plant his kiss, on My Lady Seneschal's fresh, red lips, or on this eloquent foot.

In the end, whether from respect or fear (unless it was from immensity of love), he chose the foot. He kissed it roughly, as any timid virgin would, then at once snatched up the book again, feeling his blushes doubling. Thus harrowed by his very pleasure, he cried out like one blinded: '*Janua coeli*, Oh, Heavenly Portal!'

But still Blanche did not wake, for she had trusted that her page would now proceed from foot to knee, and thence all the way to Paradise, and she was sorely disappointed when this new litany was brought to an end with no further harm done, and René, convinced he had had too much good fortune for one day, slipped out of the room, very subdued, though richer by that bold kiss than any thief could be by a poor-box.

When the Seneschal's wife was alone, she told herself that her page was clearly going to make rather heavy weather of it, if at his first service all he did was sing the *Magnificat* like that, so she resolved that tomorrow she would place her foot a little higher and so expose to the light the promontory of that lovely field which Touraine claims to be perfect for the reason that fresh air never spoils it and it is always dewy-fresh.

His desire well grilled and enflamed by the fantasies of the previous day, the page, you may well imagine, awaited with some impatience the hour for reading this breviary of gallantry. The summons came and the devices of the litany were resumed, nor did Blanche again fail to fall asleep, but this time René slid his hand along her lovely leg and made bold so far as to verify if it was the knee or something else that gleamed so creamily satin. At this vision, however, the poor boy, who had been bold against his will, so terrified was he, dared not venture more than the briefest of devotions and minor caresses, so though he did kiss that lovely material, he did so gently and lying low, whereupon, sensing by both spirit and the advice of the flesh what had taken place, the Seneschal's lady, making every effort not to stir, murmured:

'Go on, René. . . . I am asleep, you know.'

The horrified page, however, hearing what he took to be serious reproval, dropped the Book of Hours and the task in hand and fled, whereupon the Lady Seneschal immediately added this lamentation to the text: 'Oh, Holy Virgin, how hard it is to make babies!'

When he came in to serve his master and mistress at dinner, sweat poured down the page's back, but to his amazement all he got from Blanche was the naughtiest glance any woman ever gave a man, though very pleasing and powerful a glance it was too, for it transformed the child straightaway into a plucky man, so that the very same evening, as Bruyn stayed a little longer than usual at Court, René de Jallanges went seeking and, finding Blanche asleep, forthwith made her dreams very lovely ones. So thoroughly indeed did he ravish that which agonized her, and with such good husbandry did he sow his baby seed that there was really enough left over to have made a couple more, when suddenly the dear woman seized her page by the head, crushed him to her, and cried:

'Oh, René, you woke me up!'

True enough, no sleep could have survived that onslaught, and Blanche and René together concluded that the saints must sleep very soundly indeed.

Thus, without other miraculous intervention, merely by reason of a benign quality which is the principal servant of husbands, that charming, ornate plumage meet for cuckoos descended on the good Seneschal's pate without his feeling the slightest jolt.

After that lovely feast his wife most gladly took a regular siesta in the French style while Bruyn took his in the Saracen, and the experience of these siestas revealed to Blanche that the fine youth of the page tasted better than that of elderly seneschals. Consequently, at night between the sheets, she now huddled away far from her husband, whom she suddenly found devilish sour and malodorous. Then, by reason of waking so early that she simply had to take all these siestas, and by dint of saying those litanies, the Seneschal's wife felt the blossoming in her lovely loins of that offspring after which she had sighed so long, though now, it must be confessed, she liked the fashioning better than the residue.

Bear in mind, too, that René knew how to read, not merely what was writ in books, but also in his lovely lady's eyes. He would have cast himself on a blazing bonfire for her, had that ever been her whim. However, when they had laced themselves with tendrils numerous and wide-spreading (at least more than a hundred) the little lady began to get worried about the future of her love for the page and his soul, so one rainy morning when like a couple of children innocent from top to toe they were playing touch, Blanche, who was still in love, said to him:

'Come now, René! Do you realize that where I have only committed venial sins, because I was asleep, you have got mortal sins on your conscience?'

'Why, dear Lady,' said he, 'if that is sinning, wherever will God put all his damned ones?'

At this Blanche burst out laughing, and kissed his forehead.

'Sh!' she said, 'naughty! It is Paradise at stake, and, if you want to be with me for ever, we shall have to be together there.'

'Oh, my Paradise is here now.'

'Stop such talk,' she said. 'You are a miscreant, a bad boy, with no thought of what I love, and that is: you. You do not know—I am with child, and soon it will be as obvious as my nose. What will the Abbot say then? What will my Lord say? He is capable of killing you, in his rage. I think, little one, you had better go and see the Abbot of Marmoustiers. Confess your sins to him, and ask him to see what we had better do about the Seneschal.'

'Alas,' said the crafty page, 'if I tell the Abbot the secret of our delights, he will forbid our love-making.'

'I should certainly think he will, but your good fortune in the world to come is very dear to me.'

'Do you then insist, my darling?'

'I do,' said she, rather hesitantly.

'Very well, then, I will go, but now please hushabyes again, so I may bid you good-bye.'

This charming couple then recited farewell litanies in concert as if each was able to foresee that their love was fated to terminate in its springtide. Then, the following day, rather for the salvation of his dear lady than for himself, and also to obey her, René de Jallanges proceeded to the great monastery.

How Great Penance was Done
and Great Mourning Observed for this Sin of Love

'God in Heaven!' cried the Abbot, when the page had finished the long rigmarole about his sweet transgressions, 'are you then the accomplice in a crime of great enormity, and betrayer of your Lord? You page of Satan, do you realize that for this you will burn for ever, throughout eternity? Oh, wretched boy! I see you cast for ever into Hell's abyss, lest here in this world you pay God what you owe him for such grievance. . . .'

Hereupon, the good old Abbot, a man of that flesh of which the saints are made, and with great authority throughout Touraine, left the young fellow aghast by his piling on of reminders and Christian homilies, references to the commandments of Holy Church and as many other pieces of eloquence as would take Old Nick six weeks to seduce a maid with, and all to the final effect that René, still full of the submissiveness of innocence, said he would do as the good Abbot told him. Then, anxious to transform this child on the wrong road

44

into a man virtuous and holy for all time, the Abbot told René that he must first abase himself before his Lord and Master and confess his misbehaviour, then, supposing he came out of that confession alive, he must at once become a crusader and go straight to the Holy Land, to spend fifteen years on end there combatting the infidels.

'Alas, Reverend Father!' cried René, though staggered by this sentence, 'will fifteen years be sufficient to cleanse myself of such immense pleasure? Oh, if only you knew, it has been delightful enough for a good thousand years!'

'God will be kind,' said the old Abbot. 'Now off you go, and do not sin any more. As far as the past goes, *ego te absolvo. . . .*'

Thereupon poor René went back, most contrite, to Roche-Corbon Castle, and the very first man he met there was the Seneschal, polishing up his weapon and helmets and cuirasses and all that. He was seated out of doors on a big marble seat, enjoying the sight of his lovely armour gleaming in the sun, and recalling his merry times in the Holy Land, all his successes there, all the hussies he had had and so forth, and he was taken aback when René suddenly flopped down on his knees before him.

'What's the meaning of this?' he demanded.

'My Lord,' replied René, 'tell these men to withdraw, please.'

When the servants had done so, the page confessed his sin, relating how he had assaulted his Lady during her sleep and that he was sure he must have charged her with a child, just as the wicked man did St Lidoire, and he had now come, on his confessor's instructions, to place himself at the disposal of the injured party.

So saying, René de Jallanges lowered those handsome eyes, whence had issued all the trouble, and was silent, prostrate and without fear, his arms hanging by his sides, his head bare, awaiting the evil hour and submissive to the Lord God.

The Seneschal was not so white that he was unable to turn whiter, and he at once lost all colour, till he was like a newly dried sheet. He was speechless with rage. Then this old man, who lacked the vital juice in his veins wherewith to procreate a baby, suddenly discovered more strength than needed to slaughter a man. With his hairy right fist he seized his heavy mace, and raised it, brandishing it and handling it so lightly you might have thought it a skittles ball.

He meant to bring it down on the pallid forehead of this young René, who, knowing that he had indeed sinned against his Lord, remained calm, outstretching his neck, and thinking that he was about to pay for his love's sin in this world and the other too. But, for all his severity, such glorious youth and all the natural selection of this admirable crime found grace suddenly in the court of this old man's heart, and so Bruyn cast the mace far from him, to fall on a dog and make mince-meat of it on the spot.

'May a thousand million claws throughout eternity rend all the joints of the woman who made this wretch who sowed the oak which was made into the throne on which you put the horns on me!' cried Bruyn. 'And likewise those who engendered you, you accursed page of misfortune! Go to the devil whence you sprang! Out of my sight, out of this castle, out of this country, and bide not an instant more than needs be, or I'll see to it you roast to a slow death which will make you curse your foul strumpet twenty times in an hour!'

When he heard but the beginning of this pronouncement of the Seneschal, to whom a certain youthful sprightliness of oath had now returned, the page fled without waiting for the rest. This was wise of him, for, ablaze with foulest rage, Bruyn now rushed out into the gardens as fast as his loping legs would carry him, cursing all he came upon, lashing about him and swearing terribly, even over-tipping three crocks one of his men was taking the dogs their mash in, and so beside himself that he could not have told a hoer from a haberdasher. Then, suddenly, his eye lit on his demaidenhooded spouse. She was peering out of a window, up the monastery road, in expectation of her page, unaware she was never to see him again.

'Ah!' he cried, 'My Lady, by Old Nick's red trident, do you take me for a kid to feed on cock-and-bull stories. Am I to believe you've got so big a hole that that page could get in without waking you? 's blood! 's head! 's death!'

'But of course,' Blanche replied quickly, seeing that the mine had gone up. 'Of course I felt it, and nicely too, but, you see, as you never taught me what it was, I thought I was only dreaming.'

As suddenly as snow in summer sun, the Seneschal's great rage melted, for even God Almighty's greatest fury would have evaporated under a smile of Blanche's.

'May a thousand million devils take this alien child, I swear. . . .'

'Now then, don't you swear at all!' she said. 'If it isn't ours, it's mine. Besides, did you not say the other evening that you would love anything that came out of me?'

And Blanche raced down such an alley of arguments, with so many words of gold, plus plaints and grousings, tears and other feminine paternostrals—such as, first, that now the estates would not revert to the King, that never was any child more innocently cast in its mould and this and that reason, and endless other talk. She went on so long that at last the worthy old cuckoo calmed down. Then, snatching a convenient moment, Blanche cried:

'And where is the page?'

46

'He's gone to Hell!'

'What? Have you killed him?' she cried, and losing colour, nearly fell.

Bruyn just did not know what to do, seeing all the fortune of his old age crumbling away, and now for his own good he wished he could have shown her the lad. He even sent men to look for René, but, fearful of losing his life altogether, that young man was scurrying away at top speed, to travel oversea and accomplish the vow he had taken to Holy Church.

When Blanche learned from the Abbot concerning him what penance had been imposed on her beloved, she fell into a sore melancholy, crying again and again:

'Oh, where can he be, poor darling, surrounded by such dangers, all for love of me?'

Like a child who never gives his mother any peace till he gets what he wants, she never ceased crying for him, till her lamenting made the old Seneschal feel quite guilty himself and he strove to do countless things. Indeed, he achieved all, except one thing, to make Blanche a happy woman, for nothing could equal the choice feed that the young page had given her.

However, the day came at last when she gave birth to the child she had so desired, and you may be sure it was a happy day, too, for the worthy cuckold her husband, for, the features of the father being well carved on the pretty face of this fruit of passion, the child proved a great consolation to Blanche, and she somewhat recovered that kindly gaiety and flower of innocence which had formerly so rejoiced the Seneschal's old age, and by dint of seeing the child toddle about and by dint of watching the laughter exchanged between the infant and the Countess, in the end he too loved the boy, and would have been furious with anybody who did not think him the real father.

Now, as this business between Blanche and her page had never passed beyond the Castle Walls, it was assumed in all the land of Touraine that Count Bruyn de la Roche-Corbon had, after all, found enough stuff for a child. Thus Blanche's virtue remained intact and by means of that essential gumption which she had drawn from the natural reservoir of all women, she saw how essential it was to keep silence regarding that venial sin by which her child had been conceived. Thereby she became a very decent, well-conducted lady, quoted everywhere as the example of a virtuous woman.

Now, by exploiting it, she also experienced all her good husband's kindness of heart and, without ever allowing him to go anywhere below the chin, since she regarded herself as René's acquisition, in return for the flowers of old age which Bruyn offered her, Blanche petted the old man greatly, smiling on him and keeping him happy, cosseting him with all those devices and nice little tricks that good wives do employ on the husbands they deceive, all so satisfactorily that the Seneschal was quite loth to die. Huddled in his big throne chair, the longer he lived, the more used to life did he become.

However, at last, one day he did pass on, without clearly knowing where he was going, for as he died he said to Blanche:

'Why, my pet, I can't see you any more, is it night?'

That was indeed the death of a just man, and well merited, too, for all his labours in the Holy Land.

After his death, Blanche went into mourning deep and genuine, weeping for him as for a father, and she remained downcast, too, and would hear no talk of re-marrying, even if there were men of position who sought her hand, though of course quite unaware that she was already married at heart and lived in hopes.

Thus she was fated most of her life to live as a widow in fact as well as a widow at heart, for, having no news whatsoever of her dear one at the crusades, this poor Countess at last accounted him dead and for several nights on end woke up in tears, seeing him lying far off, wounded. In this way she lived for fourteen years in the memory of a single day of happiness till at last, in conversation after dinner, in the company of some ladies of Touraine, her little lad, who was then about thirteen and a half, and more like René than any child should be like his father, having nothing of Bruyn in him but his name, came running in, a merry, charming child, from the garden, perspiring, all hot and panting, knocking things over as he went, like any young boy, to run straight to his beloved mother's lap and, interrupting all the talk, cry:

'Mother dear, I must tell you something, there's a pilgrim out in the yard, he took me in his arms and he hugged me very tight.'

'Oh!' cried Lady la Roche-Corbon, turning to one of her men, whose duty it was to be companion to the young count and guard his precious life, 'did I not forbid you ever to let my son fall into the hands of any stranger, be it the most saintly man in all the world? You are dismissed!'

'Alas, My Lady,' replied the old groom, aghast at this dismissal, 'the man in question meant no harm at all, for he kissed the boy greatly, weeping all the time.'

'He wept?' she cried. 'Oh! then it was his father!'

So saying, her head sank back against the throne-chair in which she sat, which, just fancy, was the very one in which she had sinned.

Hearing this strange declaration, the ladies were so astonished that

48

they utterly failed to notice that the poor Lady la Roche-Corbon was dead, with nobody having any chance of knowing whether her sudden passing in this manner was caused by pain that her lover had gone again (for, faithful to his vow, René would not see her) or from great joy at his return and the hope she might have of rescindment of that interdiction which the Abbot of Marmoustiers had placed on their love.

There was then great mourning indeed, for de Jallanges lost heart at the sight of his lady being laid to earth, and took the tonsure as a monk of Marmoustier, which at that time some called Maimoustier, as if it was *maius monasterium*, 'the biggest monastery'. And, indeed, it was the loveliest one in France.

III

King's Darling

One of the smithies on the *Pont au Change* was at this time occupied by a goldsmith whose daughter was the talk of Paris on account of her very great beauty, though she was still more famous for her charm. Consequently, she was well pursued by men in the usual run of love interest, so much so indeed that some were even willing to pay the father a good sum to have that maid for wife, all of which pleased the goldsmith more than I can tell. There was a neighbour of his, a lawyer in the Supreme Court, who merely by selling his waffle to other folk had as many properties as a dog has fleas and he brought himself to offering the father a town house if he would but consent to this marriage, on which his mind was set. The goldsmith was certainly ready to meet the lawyer in the matter and without any regard either for the little detail that this fur-tipped old hood had the dial of a baboon, and scarcely a tooth in his jaws, and those he had shaky, not to speak of his smell, for he was filthy and stinking like the rest of the legal gentry who squatted all day on their legalistic middens and vellums and *olims* and all their mucky procedurals, and he issued the fiat to his daughter. But when that pretty lass saw the intended husband, she made her position clear at once:

'Heaven preserve me, I'm certainly not going to,' she said.

'I reckon different,' said the father, who by now had set his heart on that town house. 'I'm giving you him as husband, so pipe down, it's his affair now, he'll tame you.'

'That's how it is, is it?' said she. 'Well, before I obey you, I'm telling him just how it stands.'

The same evening, after supper, when the suitor began to put his ardent case, alleging how taken with her he was and promising her a good living for the rest of her life, she was blunt.

'My father has sold you my body,' she said, 'but if you take it, you'll only make a whore of me, because I would rather sleep with the whole street than you. I'm different from other girls, what I swear I'll give you is an unfaithfulness which will only end with death, yours or mine.'

Then she burst into tears, like any other unshod hussy, for after that operation they stop weeping with their eyes. The worthy lawyer, however, assumed her peculiar behaviour to be due to the usual little whims of maidens anxious to tempt a man and fan the flames and

turn their future's endearments into endowments. So the rascal took
no notice, just laughed at the lass's outburst and said:

'So when's the wedding?'

'Tomorrow as ever is,' said she, 'the sooner we get that over, the
sooner I can have lovers and lead the jolly life of girls who sleep with
whom they please.'

Whereupon, caught like a finch in a boy's lime, the silly lawyer
went straight off and got ready, put his case at the High Court, trotted
round to the Registrar, paid the special licence fees and pushed the
matter through quicker than any other case of his. All he could think
of was that beauty of his.

Meanwhile, the King, just back from an expedition, hearing much
talk at Court of this remarkable beauty who had refused the thousand
crowns of this one and snubbed that one, who, in short, would submit to none and had rejected all the most handsome lads who would
have let the Almighty off their share in Paradise in return for but
one day's dalliance with the serpent, the good King, that is, who had
a great tooth for such game, at once took a stroll out beyond the city
bounds, down past the smithies on the bridge, and dropped in at the
goldsmith's, his ostensible purpose being to buy some pieces of
jewellery for the lady of his heart, though it was really to bargain for
the most valuable item in the shop. He did not find anything he liked
among the gewgaws, or did not like anything he found among them,
so the old goldsmith began to fumble in a drawer under the counter,
intending to show the King a certain large diamond.

'My pet,' said the King thereupon to the lovely girl, while the old
man had his nose down under the counter, 'you are not made to sell
precious stones, but to receive them, and were you to give me the
choice of all the rings in this shop, I would say that I know one
about which folk in this town are crazy, one which pleases me,
too, and which I am always ready to be the subject or server of,
one the price of which the Kingdom of France itself could not
provide.'

'Ah!' replied the beauty. 'Your Majesty, I am marrying tomorrow.
But if you will give me that dagger which I see in your belt, I will
defend my maidenhood and reserve it for you, so I may do as the
Gospel says and give unto Caesar that which is Caesar's.'

The King wasted no time giving her that stiletto, and that admirable response did indeed so enamour him of the lass that he quite lost
his appetite. Off now he went, to make arrangements to lodge this
new mistress in a house he kept in Hirundelle Street.

Meanwhile, there was our lawyer, hasty to put the snaffle on himself, leading his bride to the altar, to the great mortification of his

rivals and amid the din of church bells. There were bands of musicians, and feasting enough to ruin any digestion till, in the evening, after the dancing, he retired to that room of his dwelling where the beauty should have already been abed, ready for him, instead to find, not a beauty, but a litigious demon, a rabid she-devil, who had refused to get into the lawyer's bed at all, and was now enthroned by the fire in one of his armchairs, toasting up alike her fury and her fancy.

Quite taken aback, the worthy husband actually knelt down before her, to invite her to the lovely small arms contest, but not a word from her, and when he made an attempt to raise her skirt, merely to take a glimpse of what had cost him so dear, she gave him such a clout that his bones chattered, though still she did not speak.

This little game, however, rather charmed our lawyer, for he thought it was all meant to lead up to, well, you know what. So in good faith he played back and put up with the sound blows the savage creature dealt him. By dint of much halloing and wheedling and forcible wooing, managing to tear now a sleeve, now a petticoat, he did at last contrive to slip his hand up to the dainty target of all this scrimmaging, but only at great cost, for the lass at once uttered a roar, rose to her feet, drew the Royal dagger and cried:

'What do you want of me?'

'Why, everything,' he said.

'Pooh!' she cried, 'a fine trollop I should be to give myself to you against my heart's dictates. If you thought you'd find my virginity unprotected, you were very mistaken. Here is the King's own dagger and I'll kill you with it if you try to come near me.'

With these words, keeping her eye on her lawyer, she took a coal from the hearth, drew a line across the floor, and added:

'This is the boundary of the Royal domain. Keep out. If you cross it, I shan't miss my blow.'

Having no intention of making love with that dagger, the lawyer was utterly flummoxed but just when he was listening to this harsh edict, the court dues of which he had already forked out, through the rents the worthy husband suddenly sighted such a fine specimen of firm white rotundity of buttock, in short, such a dazzling domestic lining, *et caetera*, sealing the holes in the gown, that death seemed sweet, could he but taste a bit of this, so he made a rush at the Royal estate, crying:

'Death's no object!'

He did indeed now make such a fierce descent on her that the beauty went flying headlong down on to the bed, but, not losing her sangfroid, she defended herself so furiously that the only advantage the lawyer got was to touch the creature's pelt, while at the same time he was the recipient of a dagger stroke up the chine which sliced off a good chunk of bacon, though without seriously wounding him, so that he might claim that his illegal entry of the Royal domain had not cost him too dearly.

This negligible gain, however, went to his head.

'I cannot live without having this lovely body and these wonders of love,' he cried, 'so kill me, then!'

And he lent himself more fiercely than before to the assault on the Royal preserve. But the beauty had her head full of King, and was utterly unmoved by this great passion, so she said gravely:

'If you threaten it with your pursuit, it is not you, it is myself I shall kill. . . .'

And her look was wild enough to daunt the poor man, who sat down, deploring the evil hour and spent this night, so happy a night to those who love mutually, in interjections, lamentations, supplications, and further promises about how well treated she would be, she could spend all she liked, she could simply guzzle gold, from simple maid he would turn her into a noble lady, by purchasing her a manor, and finally, that if she would but allow him to break a lance in honour of love he would free her from all else and end his life as she thought fit.

But when morning came she was still fresh, telling him that he could die if he liked, but that would be the only fortune she would accord him.

'You have not been tricked by me,' she said. 'Indeed, now I am giving myself to the King, I will let you off the street, I mean, all the porters and draymen I threatened you with.'

When it was fully day, she decked herself out in her wedding garments and fripperies, patiently waited till the good husband, whom she had refused everything, went out on business for a client, then was soon off to town, straightaway looking for the King. She did not have to go a crossbow-shot with her search, for the Sovereign had placed one of his men to watch and hang about round the house, and he at once addressed the bride, whose lock was still keyless:

'Are you not seeking His Majesty the King?'

'I am,' she replied.

'Right, then I am your best friend,' answered this fine gentleman and wily courtier, 'I would like your aid and protection just as I now give you mine,' and he told her exactly what sort of a man the King was, from what side to approach him, that one day he might be in a fury, while another day not a word came from him, in short, all the ins and outs of His Majesty. She would be well set up, he said, well looked after, but she must keep the King under her thumb. In short, he chattered so well on the way there that by the time she entered that house in Hirundelle Street where the Duchesse d'Estampes later lived, he had made the perfect tart of her.

When he found his fine wife gone, the poor husband wept like a cornered stag, and was most downcast. His colleagues mocked him and shamed him as badly as the mockers did poor St James at Compostella, but the cuckolded old fellow was so sore and fell into such a melancholy that in the end the other men wanted to cheer him up, and from sheer chicanery these fur-tipped hoods began to advance the argument that the poor wretched fellow was really not cuckolded at all, because his wife had rejected all jousting, and marriage was not consummated. Indeed, had the man who stuck the horns on his head been any other than His Majesty, they said, the lawyer could successfully have petitioned Holy Church for a bill of annulment.

The husband, however, was by now fatally mad on the hussy, and if he did happen to leave her to the King, that was only in the trust that one day he would be able to have her himself, in the conviction that a night with her would not be at all expensive, even at cost of lifelong disgrace. Now that really was love, and there are many loud-mouthed fellows who would scorn so great a passion, but the lawyer never ceased thinking of her. He neglected his briefs, his clients, his embezzlements and everything, and hung about the court, worried and careworn, like a miser looking for something he has lost, to such a point that one day, thinking himself up against the wall where by custom the lawyers discharged their waste, he urinated all over another barrister's gown.

Meanwhile the beauty was well loved by the King, both night and morning. His Majesty could not have enough of her, for she had ways of loving which were special and very nice, and was as good at kindling the fire as at dousing it. Today she would keep the King at arm's length, tomorrow it would be all petting. She was never twice the same, and she had some ideas, too, more than a thousand ideas. Otherwise, she was a very decent lass, using her beak as none other could, always laughing, always fertile in follies and little naughtinesses.

There was the Baron de Bridoré who committed suicide on her account, being unable to get her to grant him her love, even though he offered her the Bridoré estates in Touraine. (Those good old Tourainians who would give a manor for one jolly joust are, of course, no longer made.) This death saddened the beauty, and when her confessor laid the guilt at her door she swore an oath that, despite being the King's mistress, as far as it depended on her, she would be open to accept estates and save her soul.

This was how she began to accumulate that great wealth which excited city comment, though at the same time she certainly prevented the sudden demise of numerous noblemen. So well did she tune her lute and so inventive was she that the King simply had not a clue that she was thus helping him keep his subjects happy. The truth is that he had such a taste for her that she could have made him believe the boards of the room above were the floor of the one below, though of course this was easier for her than any other person, since in this house in Hirundelle Street the King was always a-bed, thereby losing all sense of orientation in the matter. He was indeed always plugging away, as if anxious to see if it were possible to wear out that fine material. But all he wore out, dear man, was himself, for he was eventually killed by much loving.

Though the goldsmith's daughter took care only to give herself to handsome men, and those best established at court, and her favours were as rare as miracles, the envious and outrivalled used to aver that for ten thousand crowns any plain knight could have a taste of the King's pleasure. That was falsity of falsity. When she finally quarrelled with her Sovereign, and he threw that slander in her face, her haughty reply was:

'I detest, I curse and I treadmill those who put such a falsehood into your mind! I never took on any man who did not produce at least thirty thousand as gate money.'

Angry though he was, the King could not help smiling at that and he kept her about for another month, just to put the stopper on the tittle-tattle.

At last, however, the future Countess d'Estampes saw she was never going to be either a lady or the King's mistress till her rival was ruined. But many would have liked such ruining, since the goldsmith's daughter was then married by a young lord who was even happy with her, so full of love and fire was she, enough and to spare for those whose cardinal sin is being too frigid.

I resume. One day, when the King's darling was out in her litter about town, buying laces, ribbons, slippers, bodices and other furnishings of love's business, and was so lovely and so beautifully dressed that any man seeing her (especially clerical gentry), would have thought the Heavens had opened, there was her worthy husband coming bang up against her near Trahoir Cross. Her dainty little foot was poking out of the litter, but at sight of the lawyer she plucked her head inside as sharply as if she had seen an asp. She was indeed a decent soul. I have known wenches who would have brazened it out just to injure their husbands, and out of sheer disrespect for those lords of the nuptial bed.

'But whatever is the matter?' cried de Lannoy, who from respect was escorting her.

'It's nothing,' she whispered, 'only—that man over there, that's my husband. How the poor wretch has changed! He was baboon enough before, but I reckon he's the picture of Job today.'

At this, like any other Court playboy, de Lannoy insisted on tackling the poor fellow and asking him if he thought that being her husband gave him the right to block her passage, and when she heard this, she roared with laughter, while, instead of being a man and killing her on the spot, the good husband just wept. The fact is, that laugh of hers lacerated him, head, heart, soul and all, so badly that he was on the point of attacking an elderly passer-by who stood titillating his own substance by gaping at the King's mistress.

Thus seeing that lovely flower, which he had once had when but a bud, but which was now fully opened, sweet-scented, white-fleshed too, and beautifully dressed, a fairy-like figure—all this together still more infected and maddened the lawyer, and beyond what tongue can tell. You would need to have gone through it yourself, and been intoxicated by a jilting girl, to have any adequate notion how frenzied the lawyer did now become. But it is indeed rare for anybody to to be so combusted with fury as he now was. He swore that he would risk life, fortune, happiness and anything else he had, but at least once he was going to be flesh to flesh with her and so regale himself with love that he might even abandon loins and guts on the battle-field afterwards. That whole night he spent crying:

'Oh! Aye! Ah! I—I shall have her, damn it, Heavens! I am her husband! Hell! . . .' banging his forehead, tossing about.

In this world accidents do happen so extraordinary that petty-minded folk simply will not credit them, because such coincidences seem beyond nature, though men of lofty imagination hold them to be true, since they are beyond invention. It was thus with this old lawyer, the very next day after that frightful night in which he so ate off his head.

One of his clients, a man with a big name who always had the entreé of the Royal presence, came to tell this good husband that he required a big sum of money without delay, something like twelve thousand crowns. To this the fur-tipped hood replied that one did not so often find sums like that at the street corner as the things one did find at street corners. Apart from security and guarantees of interest one needed a man who could easily cough up twelve thousand sterling and for all the size of that city and all the twaddle talked by masters of chicanery, there were few such men in Paris.

'My Lord,' he added, 'this must mean that you have a creditor who is exceptionally greedy and extortionate?'

'Indeed I have,' said the applicant, 'seeing the creditor I have in mind is the King's mistress. Don't breathe a word, but if I can only get twenty thousand crowns and throw in my Brie estate, I'm to take her measure tonight.'

At this the blood left the lawyer's cheeks and the courtier realized that somehow he had dropped a brick. The fact is, being a man fresh back from the wars, he was even ignorant that this beauty whom the King loved had a husband, let alone who that husband was.

'You've gone very pale,' he said to the lawyer.

'It's the ague,' was the lawyer's reply. 'But tell me, do you mean to give that woman all that money and the estate as well?'

'I certainly do.'

'And who has arranged this? She herself?'

'Oh no,' said this Lord. 'Far from it. These little arrangements and weighty trifles are contrived by one of her maids, and she is the nippiest chambermaid I ever saw, hotter than mustard, she certainly must have a nice little picking out of these nights she robs the king of.'

'Well, I have my own banker,' said the lawyer, 'he could certainly accommodate you. But nothing will be done and you won't get a single copper piece of those twelve thousand crowns unless that chambermaid comes to me to have the price of that most alchemical receptacle put straight into her purse. By heavens, that receptacle does transmute blood to gold, and no mistake!'

The nobleman laughed.

'And you'll bring off something too,' he said, 'if you can make that maid sign a receipt.'

The maid indeed did turn up at this crown appointment at the lawyer's office, as the worthy lawyer requested his client to bring her. Let me tell you too that when she arrived those gold coins were all finely set out in rows like nuns on their way to evensong, there they lay on a table, and so fine, so shining were those piles, so handsome, so noble, so young that they would have made a flogged donkey grin. But the worthy lawyer had not prepared the show for donkeys.

The dainty maid of course licked her lips. Most moist indeed were her chaps, as the monkey muttered her paternosters to those crowns. And when the King's mistress's husband saw this, he whispered in her ear words which just sweated gold.

'All for you,' he said.

'Oh!' gasped the girl. 'I never charge as much as that!'

'Ah, my pet, and you shall have them without me pegging you at all . . .' Then, turning aside a little, he continued: 'I can see that your client has not told you who I am, has he? No, he hasn't. Well, let me tell you that I am the rightful husband of that lady whom the King has used his position to debauch, the lady, that is, for whom you work. Now, if you will take her these crowns and come straight back here, you shall have as many again for yourself, on one condition, but one which won't displease you at all.'

The flabbergasted maid was much heartened by this, also very curious to learn how she was going to earn twelve thousand crowns without the lawyer touching her, and she did not fail to turn up very soon.

'Well, now,' said the husband, 'here are your twelve thousand crowns, ready for you. With such a sum one can buy estates, men, women and the conscience of at least three priests, so I trust that for the same sum I can have you, body, soul, whimsicals and all. Well, now I am going to trust you as lawyers do, for a *quid pro quo*, you know. What I want you to do is to run along now at once to the lord who thinks he's going to be loved by my wife tonight, and bamboozle him by giving him an urgent message that the King has suddenly announced that he is coming to sup with her, so for tonight he must turn his fancies elsewhere. Then I can come and take the place of either that fine fellow or the King.'

'But however will you manage that?' asked the maid.

'Look here,' said the lawyer, 'I've bought you, and your wits, and I don't think you'll need two looks at these crowns to find a scheme by which I can have my wife, why, that's a tie-up that involves you in absolutely no sin at all, for is it not pious work indeed to contrive the holy union of two spouses whose only conjunction so far has been that of their two hands at the altar?'

'By my fig,' said the girl, 'you just come along after supper. The lights shall all be out, and provided you don't speak a word, you can have your fill of my lady. Luckily in such moments of delight she gasps more than she speaks, indeed the only questions she asks she puts with her hands, for she's very shy, you know, she hates uttering those rude words that Court ladies use. . . .'

'Oho!' cried the lawyer. 'Well, here's your twelve thousand crowns, and I'll promise you twice more if by this trickery I get what's properly mine.'

They then agreed the hour, the door, the signal, everything, in short, and the maid went her way stooping under the welcome burden of that good cash piled up by the lawyer crown by crown from twisting widows and orphans and others too, all now to be poured into that little cleft that dissolves away everything save life itself, which indeed comes therefrom.

So there was master lawyer shaving and scenting himself and dressing in fine linen and doing without onions to sweeten his breath, prettifying himself and also fortifying himself and doing all that any High Court rascal might conceive to make himself seem a gallant man of high lineage. He assumed the airs of a young beau, pretended to be noble, even tried to disguise his loathsome physiognomy, though that was in vain, he still stank of lawyer, for he was not so spry as that pretty laundress of Portillon who, laundering her passage one day in her anxiety to be at her best for one of her lovers, slipped her penultimate finger a little way up you know what, sniffed at it and cried: 'Come, come, darling, still nifty, Heavens, I shall have to rinse you out in washing blue,' and without more ado she so steeped her rustic *cripsimen* that it would not stretch at all.

Our old lawyer, however, though of all trash the worst, now thought himself the handsomest fellow that ever was. Dressing lightly, though the cold nipped like a hempen collar, he set out, soon enough to reach the said Hirundelle Street. Here he had to kick his heels a longish time. But just as he was telling himself that he had been fooled, and it became pitch dark, there was the maid to open the door to him, and the worthy husband delightedly skipped into the King's lodging. The maid then locked him carefully into a clothes closet close to the bed where his wife slept and through the cracks he could see all her beauty, as in front of the fire she now undressed and donned a combat dress through which everything was visible. After which, thinking herself alone with her maid, she said some of the silly things women do say dressing.

'Am I not well worth twenty thousand crowns tonight? Look at these, aren't they worth a castle of Brie?'

As she said this, she gently raised two outposts, solid as keeps, capable of sustaining many an attack, especially seeing that they had already been savagely assaulted many a time without yielding.

'My bust alone is worth a kingdom!' she cried. 'I'll defy His Majesty to match it. All the same, God's truth, I'm beginning to tire of this trade. When you're at it all the time, all the enjoyment goes out of it.'

The little maid grinned and the lovely goldsmith's daughter then said:

'I'd rather like to see you in my place for once. . . .'

The maid laughed still more.

'Sh! My lady,' she whispered, 'he's here.'

'Who?'

'Your husband.'

'Which one?'

'The real one.'

'Sh!' said our beauty.

The maid then whispered to her all that had happened, for she wished to keep both the twelve thousand crowns and her mistress's favour too.

'Right then,' said the lawyer's wife, 'he shall have his money's worth. I'll see he's well cooled off. If he were to touch me, I would lose all my brilliance and become as ugly as a monk's monkey. Yes, you get into this bed tonight in my place, do a bit of work for your twelve thousand crowns. Only you're to tell him he's to clear out early, so he doesn't find out how you've tricked him. You see, just before daybreak I'll slip into bed beside him instead of you!'

Meanwhile the poor husband shivered and his teeth chattered, but at last, pretending to look for a sheet the maid came to him, and whispered:

'Keep your lust hot, My Lady's at her fussiest tonight, but you'll have a good helping, I can tell you, only work yourself up without any puffing and blowing, or I'm in for a bad time.'

At last, when the worthy husband was frozen through and through, all the lights were put out and the maid whispered loudly into the bed curtains to the King's mistress to tell her that her nobleman was there, then she herself got into the bed, while the lawyer's wife stumped out of the room as if she were the chambermaid. Patting himself on the back for his success, the lawyer then emerged from his chilly hiding-place.

The truth is that the maid did in fact give him more than a hundred thousand crowns worth, and the worthy fellow certainly learned the difference between the lavishness of Royal households and the miserly outlay of the women of the bourgeoisie. Grinning like a gaping slipper, the maid played her part to a T, regaling the old dry-as-dust with quite delightful gasps and wrigglings, leaps and convulsive double-bounds, flipping about like a carp in straw, crying 'Oh, oh, oh!' in a way which relieved her of the need for any other form of speech. Indeed, she made so many of those speechless requests and he answered all her questionnaires so amply that at last he fell asleep, as limp as an empty pocket, though just before the end of his labours this good lover, anxious to keep some little memento of his wonderful night of love, took advantage of one of the girl's somersaults to depilate her—his wife, as he thought—a little, where exactly I do not know, since I was not there, and in his hand he clutched that precious proof of the hot virtue of the lovely one.

Towards morning, when the cock crowed, the wife slipped in beside her good husband in the maid's stead and pretended to be asleep. Then the maid came into the room to tap the happy man's forehead lightly and whisper in his ear:

'Time! Time! Pull on your drawers and get away, it's nigh daylight.'

Gravely mortified at having to leave this treasure of his, the worthy fellow now felt a sudden urge to take one peep at the source of the delights now over.

'Why, good gracious!' he cried, matching up the evidence, 'my handful is fair and this is all jet black!'

'Oh! whatever have you done?' remonstrated the maid. 'My Lady's sure to see there's some missing.'

'That's not it, just look!' he insisted.

'Why,' said the maid, scornfully, 'did you really not know, you who know everything, that anything transplanted fades and dies?'

And without more ado she pitched him out, and she and the good trollop both roared with laughter.

The story came out and the poor lawyer, whose name was Féron, died of mortification, since he was the only man not to have his wife while she who was always called the 'well-shod *beauty*'—*la belle Ferronnière*—after she left the King, married a young Count de Buzançois, and in her old age used to tell the story herself, with much laughter, seeing that she never had been able to stand the stink of lawyers.

This teaches us never to be more attached than necessary to women who reject our yoke.

IV

Old Nick's Heir

There was in those days a worthy Canon of Notre-Dame in Paris who lived in a fine dwelling of his own in the Parvis, not far from St Pierre-aux-Boeufs. This Canon had come to Paris a simple priest, poor as a church mouse, but had since proved to be a fine fellow, well equipped in every way and so fruitfully constitutioned that if necessary he could do the job of several men without over-straining himself, for he rather specialized in confessing the ladies. He furnished the melancholic with gentle absolution, the ailing he gave a dram of his special balm and for each and all he had some sort of sweet thrown in. So famed was he for his discretion, his benevolence and his other ecclesiastical qualities that he also had clients at Court. Indeed, in order not to awaken the jealousy of the Court officiant (not to speak of husbands and others), in short, to give the stamp of sanctity to these worthy and profitable activities, Marshal Desquerdes gave him one of St Victor's bones, and all the Canon's miracles were then performed in virtue of that relic, so that if anybody got inquisitive, the answer used to be: 'Oh, he's got a bone that cures any woman,' which nobody could raise objection to, as it is not seemly to cast suspicion on relics.

Under the shadow of his cassock the worthy priest thus enjoyed the best possible name, that of a man who was a prodigious wielder of his weapon. Hence he lived like a king, raking the money in with his sprinkler and transmuting much holy water into good wine. Further, he became well embedded in the legal etceteras of wills or their caudicils, which some wrongly spell *codicils*, whereas the word comes from *cauda*, as if to speak of the tail of a legacy.

In short, this good frock-filler would have been promoted Archbishop had he but once jokingly said: 'I'd like a mitre for my topknot, just to keep it warm,' but out of all the benefices offered him, it was but a simple canonate that he chose, just in order to keep for himself the great advantages of his confessionades.

The day came, however, when the worthy Canon began to feel weak at the loins, for he was now a good seventy and had indeed made much use of the confessional box. So, recollecting all the good work he had done, he thought he might cease his apostolic labours, the more so since he had tucked away about one hundred thousand crowns, earned by the sweat of his body, and after that day he only confessed ladies of high lineage, though these he did thoroughly, so

62

that at Court it was said that however hard the finest young priests might strain, there was none left like the Canon of St Pierre-aux-Boeufs to bleach the soul of a lady of condition.

And so, at last, by force of nature, the Canon became a fine nonagenarian, with ample snows on his pate. His hands shook, but he was as upright as a bell-tower. So much phlegm had he spat without coughing that he now began to cough without spittle, and he who had stood so much from human kindness could now no longer rise from his chair. But he still drank his fill and ate heartily, and though he never spoke he was the very image of a live Canon of Notre-Dame de Paris.

Seeing the Canon's immobility and seeing the accounts of his evil living which for some time had circulated among lesser folk, ever ignorant, seeing moreover his silent seclusion, his flourishing health, his verdant old age and other things which take a lot of telling, there were folk who for the sake of sensation and to harm our holy religion spread the yarn that the real Canon was already long since defunct and for more than fifty years the good frock-filler's body had been occupied by Old Nick himself.

The fact is, his former clients at confession now conceived that only that person (Old Nick), by reason of his great heat, could possibly have furnished all those hermetic essences which they recalled having obtained, at their own wish indeed, from this worthy father-confessor, who certainly always had the devil in him.

However, as that devil was unquestionably well cooked and well done down by those ladies, and also since he would not have stirred for a queen of twenty years, there were worthy souls and folk not lacking in common sense, or middle-class folk who will reason about anything, the sort of folk indeed who will find lice on bald heads, did put the question why ever Old Nick should assume canonic form and go to Notre-Dame church at the hours when canons do go there and should even go so far as to sniff the scent of incense, taste holy water and do countless other unwonted things.

These heretical suggestions some answered by saying that no doubt Satan wanted to be converted, others that he assumed that form to mock the three nephews and heirs of this worthy confessor and make them wait till they themselves were ready to pass on before they should inherit the ample estate of this uncle of theirs, on whom indeed they called every day to see if his eyes were still open, though always to find them limpid, lively and sharp as those of a basilisk, which intrigued them greatly, seeing that they were very, very fond of their uncle—in words!

Apropos of all this one old woman told the story that the Canon must indeed be Old Nick, since two of these nephews of his, the lawyer one and the Captain, taking their uncle home one night without either lamp or lantern after a supper with the Inquisitor, made him stumble, inadvertently, of course, on a big heap of masonry prepared for the erection of a monument to St Christopher. First, as he fell, the old man struck sparks, then shouting for help and running to the old woman who told the story to fetch a light, his dear nephews found him in the flare of the torches on his feet, upright as a skittle and cheerful as a young falcon, saying that the Inquisitor's good wine had fortified him against shock and his bones were hard enough, he had endured worse strains than that.

The worthy nephews, who had thought he must be dead, were astounded. They now saw that since stones were no good, the time for their uncle to crack up was not going to come round so very soon. So it was not a mistake on their part to call him their good uncle. He was clearly made of fine quality stuff. There were indeed also tongues wicked enough to say that the Canon had found so many stones in his path on this occasion that after this accident he kept to his room, so as not to fall sick of the stone, and fear of the worst happening was the cause of his retiring life.

Of all these rumours and gossip it stands that, whether Old Nick or not, the old Canon did keep to his house, also that he would not die, and had three heirs with whom he lived as he did with his sciatica, his lumbago and other features of our human condition.

Of these three heirs, one was the most evil soldier ever issued from female womb, and badly he must have rent his mother's flesh too when he cracked his shell, since he was born already toothed and hirsute. In addition, this fellow ate in two tenses of the verb, present and future, having wenches of his own whose hair-dos he paid for, thus exhibiting his uncle's vigour and skill in the use of that which is often of use. In major engagements he endeavoured to deal out blows without getting any, which is always the only hard nut to crack in warfare, but in it all he never spared himself, and indeed, having no other good point but his courage, was Captain of a Company of Lancers and much liked by the Duke of Burgundy, who never made much inquiry into what his soldiers did in other parts.

This nephew of Old Nick was called Captain Cochegrue, though his creditors or any poor burghers whose pockets he emptied called him *Mau-singe* or Ill-ape, since he was as evil-featured as he was tough. But he also had a back ruined by the natural infirmity of a hump, and it did not behove anybody to pretend to get up on that to have a better view, for he would have cut them down on the spot without any inquiry.

The second nephew had studied the Common Law and with his uncle's backing too. He had made a good lawyer. He pleaded at the High Court bar, where he looked after the interests of those ladies whom earlier on the Canon had confessed most thoroughly. This one was known as *Pille-grue*, or pillager grue, a play on his real name, which, like the Captain his brother's, was of course Cochegrue.

Pille-grue had a miserable little body, fashioned as if he exuded very cold water. He was pale of countenance and had a physiognomy like a pole-cat's snout. In spite of this he was worth a penny or two more than the Captain and did feel a measure of love for his uncle, except that for the past two years he had had a crack at heart and drop by drop his gratitude had been oozing away, so that from time to time, in inclement weather, he had an urge to stick his feet into his uncle's shoes and squeeze out a little advance on that good inheritance.

Both he and his soldier brother found their portion very slender, since, to be correct, both legally and in fact, both by justice and natural law and reality, they would be obliged to give a third of it all to a poor young cousin, the son of another sister of the Canon's. This third heir, who did not seem to be much favoured by the worthy man, stuck to the country, where he was a shepherd, near Nanterre. This herdsman, however, though a common peasant, now came to town on the advice of his two cousins, and they installed him in their uncle's house, hoping that both by his stupidities and clodhopperish acts and the weakness of his wits, also by his general lack of gumption, he would prove so displeasing to the Canon that he would be struck right out of the will.

This poor fellow Chiquon, as the shepherd was called, had been living alone with his old uncle now for a month or so. Finding it either more advantageous or more entertaining to watch a priest than a flock of sheep, he had made himself the Canon's watchdog, his lackey, his staff in old age, ready with a '*God bless!*' every time the old man farted, a '*God be wi' you!*' every time he sneezed, or a '*God protect you!*' when he gurked, ever running out to see if it was raining or where the cat was, always ready to be silent, or to listen, or to talk, or to let the old fellow cough down his nose, seeing in his uncle the most wonderful Canon there ever was, and all quite heartily too. Quite frankly, quite unaware that he was licking up to the old man like a bitch with pups, while the uncle, who needed no telling on which side the bread was buttered, used to snub this poor fellow Chiquon and make him dance a fine tune, for ever sending for him while he grumbled to his other nephews that Chiquon was such a clodhopper that he was simply helping him into his grave. Whenever

Chiquon heard this he worked madly to suit his uncle, racking his brains how to do better, but as he had hind-quarters like a couple of pumpkins, very broad shoulders and thick limbs and was slow in the uptake, he was more like old Silenus than any fragile Zephyr. The fact is that a simple fellow like the poor shepherd could not re-fashion himself, so he just stayed the big fat hulk he was, leaving it to his inheritance some day to thin him down.

One evening, the Reverend Canon was holding forth about Satan and all the terrible sufferings, tortures, agonies and so forth that the Almighty kept on the fire ready for the damned, and there was good Chiquon, listening with eyes as big as oven doors to all this informa-tion, but without believing a bit of it.

'Come now,' said the Canon, 'are you not a Christian?'

'Why, of course I am,' replied Chiquon.

'Well, there's a Paradise for good folk, so don't you think a Hell is needed for the wicked?'

'Yes, indeed, Sir,' said Chiquon. 'But Satan too is not without his uses. . . . If in this house you had a scoundrel who turned everything upside down, would you not kick him out?'

'I would, Chiquon. . . .'

'Well then, Reverend Uncle, what a ninny God would be to let a wretched devil specially busy with spoiling things run loose in a world he has spent so much trouble making. . . . Nonsense, I don't admit there's any devil, if our good Lord exists. . . . I would just like to see fellow Satan, if he does exist. . . . Huh! A lot I fear his claws!'

'Well,' said the Canon, 'if I believed as little as you do, I shouldn't be worried at all, as in fact I am, about what I did in my youth, when I heard a dozen confessions every day. . . .'

'Confess some more, Canon!' said Chiquon. 'I assure you, up in Heaven it would mean so many good marks for you.'

'Get away with you, Chiquon! Do you really think so?'

'I certainly do, Canon.'

'Come, Chiquon, are you not afraid thus to deny Satan?'

'No more than I am afraid of a sheaf of corn.'

'That is a view which will cause you trouble some day, Chiquon!'

'Far from it, dear Uncle. God will keep Old Nick off me, because I think God is wiser and less brutish than the wise men make him out to be.'

At this point the other two nephews entered, and, realizing from the Canon's voice that he was really far from disliking Chiqon, and that all the complaints he had been making about this fellow were all so much humbug to disguise his liking for him, they exchanged sur-prised glances, then seeing their uncle laughing, put a question.

'If you were to make a will, Uncle, to whom would you leave the house?'

'To Chiquon.'

'And the rue St Denis rents?'

'To Chiquon.'

'And the Ville-Parisis holding?'

'To Chiquon.'

'Why,' cried the Captain in his great voice, 'then Chiquon would get everything?'

'No,' replied the Canon, with a smile, 'because, however well I drew up my will, it would be in vain, what I leave will go to the smartest of you three. I am so close to the future world that I can clearly see what's coming to you.'

And the wily Canon threw a malicious glance at Chiquon, rather like a light o' love giving some dainty fellow the glad-eye to entice him into her love parlour. The fire of that blazing eye now illuminated the shepherd, who from that moment possessed understanding and ears. All, in fact, was clear to him and his brain was as wide-open as a bride after the wedding night.

Taking these pronouncements as gospel prophecies, the lawyer and the captain were so done by the absurd prospects which the Canon saw that they bowed deeply and took their leave at once.

'Well, what do you say about Chiquon now, eh?' said Pille-grue to Mau-singe.

'I think, er, I think, er,' ground out the soldier, 'I, er, think that I think I'll lay an ambush in Jerusalem Street and bring his head down to the level of his feet and let him stick it on again if he chooses.'

'Ah no!' said the lawyer, 'you've got a special cut that's recognizable, folk'll say at once, "That's Cochegrue". What I suggest is to invite him to a party and after dinner we'll play putting each other in sacks, like they do at Royal fêtes, to see who can best walk thus clad, then we'll stitch him up and pitch him into the Seine and tell him to swim. . . .'

'That needs well ripening off,' objected the soldier.

'Oh, but it's dead ripe,' said the lawyer. 'Once our cousin's in Hell, the estate's ours to share between us.'

'I'm for it,' said the warrior, 'only we must work together like two legs of one body, for if you are as fine as a silk thread, I am as tough as steel, and daggers are as good as tapes, take note of that, my dear brother.'

'Taken,' said the lawyer, 'and all agreed, now is it to be thread or steel?'

'Oh, Hell's bells,' cried the soldier, 'is it then a King we're to undo? Is so much palaver needed for a mere clod of a shepherd? Look here, twenty thousand francs out of the estate to the one of us who first cuts him down! . . . I'll have good reason to tell him to pick up his brain-pan and put it on again.'

'And I to cry: "Swim, my lad . . . !"' declared the lawyer, laughing like the flaps of a doublet, after which they went off to sup, the captain to his tart and the lawyer to the wife of a goldsmith whose lover he was.

And who got the surprise? Chiquon! The poor shepherd overheard that plan to finish him off, although his two cousins had been pacing up and down the church close discussing it only as loudly as folk in church praying to the Almighty, so that Chiquon was hard put to it to know whether the words rose from the flags or his ears had dropped to ground level.

'Can you hear anything, Reverend Canon?' he asked.

'Yes,' said the Canon, 'the wood sizzling on the fire.'

'Ah!' replied Chiquon, 'I may not believe in the devil, but I do believe in my guardian angel, St Michael, and I'm off where he calls me. . . .'

'Very well, my lad,' said the Canon, 'only take care not to get wet or have your head lopped off, for I seem to hear running water and the rascals of the streets are not always the most dangerous.'

These words simply astounded Chiquon, but when he looked round at the Canon, it was to find him cheerful enough and his eyes bright, nor were his feet stretched out in death. But as he now had to make arrangements about that sudden demise which threatened him, Chiquon told himself he would always have time to admire the Canon and trim his finger-nails, and he scurried off at top speed through the city like any gay dame pattering off to her pleasure.

His two cousins, being utterly ignorant of the temporary outbreaks of divinatory skill to which shepherds are often subject, had in fact more than once discussed their secret devices in front of him, thinking him a nit-wit, and one evening, to amuse the Canon, Pille-grue had related how he had acquired the love of the wife of a certain goldsmith on whose head he had ever so neatly fitted horns carved, polished, sculped and historiated like any royal salt-cellar. According to his tale that fine wench was a very sprightly piece, so ever-ready that she was capable of dispatching an embrace while her hubby mounted the stairs. Nothing took her at a disadvantage. She could take her dose just like swallowing a strawberry; her only thought to twang her lute. She was a flibberty-gibbet indeed, always smiling, the most irreproachable of married dames, keeping her husband satisfied too, while he loved her as much as he did his own gullet. She

68

was as subtle as a perfume, to such point that for the past five years she had so well managed both household and love affairs that she was universally esteemed for her modesty and enjoyed her husband's full confidence, including the household keys, purse and all.

'So when do you play that sweet flute?' the Canon had asked.

'Every evening! Indeed, very often I spend the whole night with her,' the Captain had replied.

'But however do you manage that?' asked the astonished Canon.

'Like this. In the adjoining room there is a big linen chest. I get in there. When her good husband comes in from his pal the draper, where he goes to supper every evening, because as a matter of fact he often does a little job of work with that man's wife, my mistress says she's not very well and lets him go to bed by himself while she goes into the room where the chest is to have her wound dressed. The next day, I slip out when the goldsmith is down in his workshop, and as the house has one door leading to the street and another straight on to the bridge, I always go in or out by the door where he doesn't happen to be, my excuse being to discuss some pieces of litigation of his which I keep nice and healthy and never-ending. It's a cuckoldom that pays, for the petty costs and legal dues of the proceedings cost him as much as a stableful of horses, and he's very fond of me too, as any worthy cuckoo should be of the man who helps him fork and irrigate, plough and harrow Venus's natural garden. In fact he does nothing without me.'

All these little habits in the light which his danger shed, and instructed by those wise hints of self-preservation with which all creatures have enough to last them till their ball of life's all unrolled, now came back to the shepherd's memory. So off went Chiquon hotfoot to de la Calandre Street, where the goldsmith would be supping with his skirt. He knocked on the door, and when the little grill was opened and they asked who he was, said he was a messenger with State secrets, and so was admitted to the draper's house. He now went straight to the point, insisted on the merry draper's leaving his supper for a moment, got the man into a corner and said:

'If one of your neighbours planted antlers on your forehead and was then delivered to you bound hand and foot, would you not pitch him into deep water?'

'I certainly would,' said the goldsmith, 'but if you mean me, you'll feel my fist first.'

'Stuff and nonsense,' said Chiquon, 'I'm on your side, I am, I've just come round to tell you that as often as you've cracked up the draper's missus in here that lawyer fellow Pille-grue's been doing your wife for you, and if you care to drop in and look at your forge at this instant you'll find a nice little fire in it. But the moment you appear the fellow who keeps that you know what so nicely swept and clean will slip into your big linen chest. Now, what I'll do is come in and pretend to buy that chest from you, I'll have a wagon ready on the bridge, at your orders.'

Without a word the goldsmith takes cap and cloak and runs to his burrow like a poisoned rat. Getting there, he knocks. The door is opened and in he goes, pell-mell up the stairs, finds the table laid for two, hears the lid of the linen-chest clap down and meets his wife emerging from her love-chamber.

'Why, darling,' says he, 'only laid for two, I see.'

'Yes, sweetie, are we not two?'

'No,' says he, 'we're three.'

'Is your friend coming?' says she, looking towards the stairs with oh, what innocent eyes.

'No, I mean the friend who's in that chest.'

'Which chest do you mean?' she asks. 'Are you in your right mind? Where can you see a chest? Do we put friends in chests? Am I a woman to keep a lot of chestfuls of friends? Since when are friends kept in chests? Are you coming home cracked, to babble about these friends and chests of yours? The only friend of yours I know is Mr Corneille the draper, and the only chest is the one we keep our linen in.'

'Really,' said the goldsmith. 'Listen, wifey dear, a bad fellow came round just now to tell me you let our lawyer ride you, and that he's in the chest now. . . .'

'Me let him ride me?' she cried, 'when I can't bear the smell of any lawyer, they do everything upside-down. . . .'

'All right, darling,' said the goldsmith, 'all right, I know you are an honest woman. I don't want any bickering with you about any wretched linen-chests. The fellow who told me this happens to be a box-maker so what I'll do is sell him that damned chest, I shan't be able to bear the sight of it in this house any longer, he's going to let me have a couple of nice little ones for it, chests too small even for a boy to get in. Like that, these malicious tongue-waggings and all this talk of folk envious of your uprightness will be quenched for lack of food.'

'That delights me,' she said. 'I don't care a fig for the old chest, and it so happens it's empty anyway, all our linen is at the laundry, it can easily be fetched tomorrow first thing. Shall we have supper now?'

'Oh no,' he said, 'I shall have a better appetite if I see the last of that old chest at once.'

'I can see,' said she, 'it's going to be easier to get the chest out of this house than out of your head. . . .'

'Hi there! Hallo there!' shouted the goldsmith to his assistants and apprentices. 'I want you.'

In a jiffy the men were there and then, when the goldsmith had briefly instructed them how to handle the chest, this was lugged through the living-room, though on the way, since he was not used to being turned upside-down, the lawyer became rather fidgety.

'Look out,' said the wife, 'look out, the mainpost's shifted.'

'No, darling, it's only a little dowel.'

And without another word, the chest slithered very nicely down the stairs.

'Hallo there, wagoner!' cried the goldsmith.

And there was Chiquon, whistling to his mules, while the worthy apprentices heaved that litigious chest on to the lorry.

'Hi! Hi!' cried the lawyer.

'Master,' said an apprentice, 'that there chest's talking.'

'What language?' asked the goldsmith, giving the lad a sound booting between two pieces of ornament which fortunately were not glass, so that he went sprawling down the stairs and thus interrupted his analysis of chesty language, when, accompanied by the worthy goldsmith, the shepherd carted the load to the river's edge, without giving ear to the great eloquence of those talkative timbers. And then, tying some big stones to the construction, the goldsmith pitched it all into the Seine.

'*Swim, old pal!*' cried the shepherd, in tones which were quite sarcastic, as the chest broke the water nicely, like a duck, but none the less got rather wet, for it next dived deep.

Chiquon then continued along the embankment as far as the street of Port St Landry, near Notre Dame Priory, where, distinguishing the house and recognizing the door, he banged loudly on it.

'Open,' he cried, 'open up, in the name of the King!'

Hearing this, an old man who was none other than the notorious money-lender Versoris, hurried to the door.

'What is this?' he asked.

'The Provost has sent me,' said Chiquon, 'to warn you to keep a good watch tonight. He for his part is calling out his bowmen. That hunchback who robbed you is back. Keep yourself armed, the villain may well try to get the rest.'

Delivering himself of this, the worthy shepherd hurried at the run to des Marmousets street, to the house where Captain Cochegrue was junketing with Pâquerette, or Daisy, the loveliest of tarts and, so all the other whores said, also the one with the daintiest perversities.

Pâquerette was a wench with a lively eye, sharp as the blow of a stiletto, and she was so enticing to look at that she would have put all Paradise on heat. In a word, she was as brazen as a woman can be whose only virtue is her insolence.

Poor Chiquon had been much concerned on his way here, being most apprehensive lest he failed to discover where she lived, or to come upon the love-birds in bed, but a kind angel arranged everything just as he wanted. As he entered Marmousets street, what should he see but all the windows lit up and heads in night-caps thrust out, every trollop, every tart, every decent housewife and husbands and unmarried girls too, all out of bed, leaning out of their windows as if some thief were being led by torchlight to the gallows.

'I say, what's all this?' the worthy shepherd inquired of a burgher who had hastened down to his door with a halberd in his hands.

'Oh, it's all nothing after all,' said the good fellow, 'we thought at least it was the Armagnacs attacking, but it's only Mau-singe beating up Pâquerette.'

'But where?' insisted the shepherd.

'Over there, in that fine house with gargoyles of lovely flying toads on the pillars, a nice bit of carving, can't you hear the valets and chambermaids yelling?'

It was true, there was a continuous din of: 'Murder! Help. Hallo there, this way quick!' while inside one could hear blows descending, and Mau-singe's great voice bellowing: 'I'll slay the hussy! You dare dun me, you trollop? You want some crowns off me, do you, well take 'em!' And Pâquerette was groaning: 'Oah! Oah! He'll murder me! Help! Oah! Oah!'

There then suddenly came a great clank of iron and a heavy thump as the light body of that pretty lass fell, and after this a deathly silence. One by one the lights all went out, servants, merry-makers and others all withdrew indoors, and the shepherd, thus arrived in the nick of time, climbed the stairs with some of them. But when in the lofty chamber they saw broken bottles and slashed carpets and table-cloths, with crockery all over the floor, they were all subdued.

The shepherd, however, bold as any man with a one-track mind, flung open the door of the handsome room in which Pâquerette slept, to find her apparently stone dead, her hair loose, her throat slit. She lay bleeding on the carpet, and there too was Mau-singe, aghast, suddenly very tongue-tied, his voice hollow, puzzled to know on what note to intone the remainder of his litany:

'Come, my little Pâquerette, come, my Daisy, don't make tell me you're dead. Come, let me heal you. Oh, you sly girl, dead or alive, but you are so pretty in all that blood, I simply must embrace you!'

With these words, the crafty soldier took her and threw her on to the bed, but she fell all of a piece and as stiff as the corpse of a hanged man, seeing which her lover thought it was perhaps time to get his hump out of trouble. But before he left the scoundrel cried again:

'Oh, poor Pâquerette, my Daisy! However could I kill a fine lass whom I loved so much? All the same, I really have killed her. That's plain. When she was alive she never let her lovely titty slop out of her gown like that, Heavens, it's just like a crown at the bottom of a purse.'

But when he said this Pâquerette opened her eyes and peeped down a bit to look at her body, to find it white and firm, then, with a tremendous puff in the Captain's face, she came to entirely.

'That's what you get for slandering the dead,' she said, with a grin.

'But why ever did my cousin try to kill you?' asked the shepherd.

'Why? Because tomorrow the bums are coming to take the lot and he with no more cash than virtues threw it in my face for wanting to please a handsome knight who would have saved us both from distraint.'

'Pâquerette, I'll break your bones!'

'Come now,' said Chiquon, whom Mau-singe then recognized, 'is that really all? Don't worry, my dear fellow, I can find you a biggish sum.'

'And whence might that be?' demanded the astounded Captain.

'Come here and let me whisper in your ear. . . . If there were thirty thousand crowns loose by night in the shade of a pear tree, wouldn't you stoop down for the picking up, just so they didn't spoil?'

'Chiquon, I'll slaughter you like a dog if you're making fun of me, but I'll kiss you wherever you like, if you can show me thirty thousand crowns, even if to get them I had to kill three burghers in a corner on the embankment.'

'You won't even kill a bonnet. Here's how. I have a very faithful mistress and she's the servant of a money-lender in the Citadel, quite near where our good uncle lives. Now, I've just learned for sure that the old fellow left this morning for somewhere in the country, and before he went he buried a good bushel of gold coin under a pear tree, thinking only the angels saw him, but this lass of mine, who happened to have a frightful toothache and was taking a breath of air at her attic window, involuntarily saw the old extortioner digging and out of sheer love she's told me. If you'll promise to give me a good share, I'll lend you my shoulders to get up on the wall, and from there

73

you can jump to the pear tree, as it's next to the wall. Eh? Now will you call me a fool or a brute?'

'Indeed I will not call you either, you're a very decent fellow and you're my very loyal cousin, and if ever you have an enemy you want putting down, I'm there, ready to kill even one of my own friends for you, I am no longer merely your cousin, I am your brother! Come on, Pâquerette,' he cried to the girl, 'put the tables back, wipe away the bloodstains, it's all my property, I'm paying for it and I'll give you mine a hundred times over for what I've taken of yours. Draw some of the best, tuck those wild pigeons back inside and pull down your petticoats, girl, laugh, I insist, give an eye to the pots on the stove and we'll resume our prayers where we broke off earlier this evening. Tomorrow, I'll dress you better than the Queen. This is my cousin and I want to treat him, even if it means turning the house upside-down. We'll get it all back tomorrow in the cellars. Come on. Juice! Juice for our hams!'

Thereupon—and in less time than it takes a priest to say *Dominus vobiscum*, the whole dovecote passed from tears to laughter, just as it had earlier changed from laughter to tears. It is only in tart-ridden homes that women are wooed with knives and four walls see such hurricanes of delight, for those are things beyond the wits of high-stiff-necked dames.

Captain Cochegrue was now as merry as a hundred schoolboys when lessons are over and he treated his cousin to some good liquor. Chiquon tipped it all down with clodhopper equanimity, though he pretended to be tight and blathered a great deal of nonsense about how tomorrow he was going to buy all Paris, he would lend the King a hundred thousand, he would have gold to ease himself on, in short, talked such a lot of twaddle that the Captain began to fear lest he made some compromising declaration and, thinking his brain already befuddled enough, took him outside, with the firm intention, when it came to sharing out, of slitting Chiquon open to see if he had not some sort of sponge inside him, since he had imbibed a brimming quart of good Surène wine.

So they strode on, babbling endless theologicalities which got most complicated, till they slipped on tiptoe under the wall of that garden where the money-lender's crowns were buried. Now Cochegrue utilized Chiquon's broad shoulders and heaved himself up into the pear tree like any man expert in attacking towns, but Versoris, who was on the look-out, made a sudden nick in the Captain's neck and repeated the dose so hard that with the third blow that topknot rolled right off, though not before he heard the clear voice of the shepherd shouting:

'Now pick up your top-knot, old pal!'

This accomplished, generous-hearted Chiquon, in whom virtue thus received its reward, thought it better to go back to the good Canon's house, where that legacy was by God's mercy now most methodically simplified. So by strenuous use of his legs he reached St Pierre aux-Boeufs street and was soon sleeping like a newborn babe, no longer aware of what the term cousin-german meant. And when, the following morning, he rose, according to the custom of shepherds, with the sun, and went to his uncle's room, to inquire if the old man had spat white, or coughed, and if he had slept well, the ancient housekeeper surprised him with the news that when the Canon had heard St Maurice ring for morning service (that church was the first patron of Notre Dame), he had out of great piety gone to the Cathedral, where the whole Chapter was to take dinner with the Bishop of Paris. To which Chiquon cried:

'Is the Reverend Canon out of his mind to go out and get cold feet and catch a chill? Does he want to die? I'll go and light a big fire to comfort him when he gets back.'

The good shepherd then burst into the hall where the Canon generally sat, to see his uncle, to his great alarm, seated in his throne.

'Oh, what nonsense that old thing Burette does talk!' he cried, 'I knew you were too sensible to go to your choir stall at this hour of the day.'

The Canon did not speak. The shepherd, who, like all contemplative folk, was a man of occult sense, was not unaware that sometimes old folk have wise whims. They hold talk with the spirit of hidden things and deep within them contrive to mumble other-worldly things, so out of respect and esteem for the abstruse musings of the Canon he withdrew some distance from him and waited till the meditation should end, at the same time, without a word, checking the length of the worthy man's toe-nails, for they seemed about to poke through his slippers, when, thus examining his dear uncle's feet more closely, he was astonished to see that the flesh of his legs was glowing so red that it turned his stockings scarlet and seemed to show fire through the stitches.

'So he's dead,' said Chiquon to himself. But at that very instant the door opened, and he saw the Canon yet again, back from service, with his nose frozen!

'Ah, come now!' cried Chiquon, 'are you crazy, Uncle dear, do remember you ought not to be in that doorway at all, you are already snug in your chair by the fireside, for there cannot be two Canons like you in this world!'

'Oh, Chiquon, let me tell you that there was a time when I would

75

gladly have been in two places at once, but that is not vouchsafed to man, he would be too happy. Come, are you seeing visions? There's only me here!'

Turning now to the chair, Chiquon saw that it was indeed empty, and was most astonished, as you may well imagine. But he went across to the chair, and what did he see on the seat but a little pile of cinders, still reeking of sulphur.

'Oh, just look at that!' he cried. 'I see Old Nick has treated me decently. I must offer up a prayer for him.'

Thereupon he told the Canon quite simply how Old Nick had enjoyed himself playing at Providence and had helped him so faithfully to get rid of his evil cousins. This the Canon admired greatly, thinking it a good piece of work, since he had still a lot of sense left, and had often noticed things which were to the good account of Satan. So this veteran and worthy priest said that there always was as much good in evil as there was evil in good and hence one should never bother too much about the world to come—which was a grave heresy condemned by many a Council.

That is how the Chiquons got their money and in our day, through their ancestor's wealth, have been in a position to help build St Michael's Bridge, where Old Nick looks very well placed under the angel in commemoration of this story, which is recorded in reliable chronicles.

V

The Diversions of King Louis XI

King Louis XI was a boon companion, with a great love of joking and, apart from the functions incumbent on his position as King and feasts of the Church, a great man for junketings, also as well as hunting coneys and big game in the Royal forests he was much given to chasing skirts. Thus the ignoramuses who make him out to be a dour type merely show that they never knew him, for he was a good friend and a practical joker without equal.

It was he who when once in a good mood said that there were four things in life highly estimable and advantageous; warm privies, cold drinks, hard stands and tender meats. He has sometimes been charged with much mucking about with trollops. That is an unworthy invention, for his mistresses, one of whom he married, all came from big houses and founded distinguished families. He was no man for wild schemes or waste. He was very practical, and if because they found no crumbs for their picking some robbers of the public purse have rounded on him, genuine seekers of the facts of the case know that in private life this King was a very decent little fellow, quite forthcoming, indeed, and before he ever had any of his friends heads' removed, or otherwise punished them, they had to have deceived him badly, his vengeance was always just. It is only in friend Verville that I see this worthy sovereign recorded as making a mistake, but even so, a single error does not make custom. Besides it was more friend Tristan's fault than his own.

Here is that story, as Verville tells it, though I have a suspicion he was being funny, and only cite it because there are people ignorant of this work of my irreproachable compatriot. (I shorten and give only the substance, the details being abundant, as of course scholars know.)

Verville says that Louis XI had granted Turpenay Abbey (referred to in *Imperia*) to a lord who by drawing his revenues therefrom became known as the Lord of Turpenay Abbey. The King being at Plessis-les-Tours one day, the real Abbot, a monk, called on him and submitted his plea, arguing that both canonically and monastically the monastery was really his and the incumbent in question a usurper who did him most unreasonable wrong, wherefore he enjoined His Majesty to show him justice.

The King waggled his wig and said he would indeed satisfy that request, but the monk, being as persistent as all the Carthusian breed,

77

was always putting in an appearance just as the King left his dining-room, till Louis was so sick of that monasterial holy water that he summoned his trusty Tristan and cried:

'Friend, that Turpenay Abbey fellow gets on my nerves. He wants justice done. Do me the favour of fulfilling my promise.'

To Tristan, apparently, it was not only the cowl that made the monk, and he went straightway to the fellow who called himself Lord of Turpenay Abbey and did the necessary to turn his head about a bit, binding him and trying to get into that part of his anatomy the notion that the King wanted him to leave this world. That fellow did not comply at all lightly or perhaps one should rather say that once on the rope he did comply very lightly, but he was certainly not listened to, and without a trace of brusquerie was constrained 'twixt that head and his shoulders, so that he departed this world, and three hours later the King's great friend reported that the sublimation was complete. By chance, five days after this, the exact term at which souls return, the monk entered the Royal presence, to Louis XI's utter consternation. Tristan was present, so the King called him over and hissed into his ear:

'You did not do what I said.'

'Save your pleasure, Sire,' said Tristan, 'but I did. Turpenay's dead enough.'

'By *that Turpenay fellow* I understood this monk,' said the King.

'But I,' said Tristan, 'I understood 'tother one.'

'And you actually did the job?'

'Aye, Sire.'

'Right, then,' said Louis, turned to the monk and called the man to him.

The poor monk was terrified, but all the King said was:

'You may thank the Almighty he did not want you killed as I instructed. The fellow who took your name got it in your place. God has decided the case! Now go to your monastery and pray for my soul now, but don't you budge out of the place again!'

This story proves how kind Louis XI was. He might easily have had that monk hanged for being the cause of the error, but, on the other hand, the nobleman in question did die 'in the King's service'.

During the first part of his stay at Plessis-les-Tours, not wanting, out of respect for Her Majesty (a delicacy the successors of this King did not show), to hold his drinking parties and merry routs in his castle, Louis, having taken a fancy to a lady named Nicole Beaupertuis, who as a matter of fact was a burgess of the town, he dispatched the husband to the Ponent and established this Nicole in a house near the Cardonneret, where Quincangrogne street runs, that then being a deserted district, well outside the town.

Thus he had both husband and wife devoted to him, and by this Beaupertuis woman eventually had a daughter, who died a nun. This Nicole Beaupertuis was as sharp-beaked as a parrot, but well upholstered, complete with two lovely, abundant natural cushions, firm to the touch, white as angel's wings and further known for their fecundity of peripatetic modalities whereby with her the love act never became repetitive, so scholarly was she in the finer equations of that discipline, indeed, in all the ways of cooking those Poissy olives, not to speak of her methods for bracing of the nerves and the more abstruse doctrinal points of the prayer book, which suited the King to a T. Nicole was as cheerful as a finch, always had a song on her lips, was always laughing and never spiteful to anyone, which is the way of women whose nature is so free and open that so they are always occupied. . . .

You are a punster, sir! . . .

To continue, the King and his boon companions frequently resorted to this house and to keep it all dark he went by night, without any suite, but, being mistrustful and fearing ambushes, he had given Nicole all the fiercest dogs in his kennels and those Royal dogs recognized only Nicole and His Majesty. Whenever the King came, Nicole would let them loose in the garden, so that when the house door was well bolted and locked, and the King had the keys, he and his company were able to indulge in a thousand pleasures without fearing any betrayal. They would be up to all sorts of japes and wickedness, in a word, they had an uproarious time.

Those nights, it was good friend Tristan who kept guard over the surroundings and anybody who took a stroll down Chardonneret Mall stood a good chance of being put in a position for the laying not of his hands, but his feet on any other passer, that is, unless he had a pass from the King, for Louis often sent a man out to find other hussies for his friends or to bring in other folk to provide entertainment whenever Nicole or one of the guests had a bright idea.

The people of Tours, in other words, were there to satisfy His Majesty's minor pleasures, and well advised too to keep a still tongue in a wise cheek after. Hence it was not till the King was no more of this world that those little pastimes became known. It was then alleged that the party game of *Buss-my-cue* was an invention of the King's own, so, though it is not the real subject of this tale I am going to relate it, for it does serve to reveal the comical, facetious bent of that good fellow.

There were three men of Tours who were celebrated for their avarice. The first was Master Cornelius, a well enough known figure. The second was called Peccard. He sold ecclesiastical trimmings and trickeries and knick-knacks. The third's name was Marchandeau. He was a very rich vineron. In spite of their meanness, these latter two founded worthy families. Well, one evening King Louis was out at Madame Beaupertuis's place and in high spirits. He had already drunk a bibful, he had wisecracked to his fill too, and also said his own prayers before vespers in my lady's oratory, when, turning to his friends Le Daim, Cardinal La Balue and old Dunois, who were still busily soaking, he remarked:

'What we want is a good laugh, my friends. . . . If you ask me, there'd be good fun watching a miser faced with a bag of gold he cannot have. . . . Hallo there! Go and find my treasurer,' he told the man who ran up to his call, 'have him bring me six thousand gold crowns here without delay, then go and seize first my friend Cornelius, then that haberdasher of Cygne Street, then old Marchandeau and bring all three here, on Royal Orders.'

The company returned to their pots and to hair-splitting examination as to whether the fair sex were to be preferred nice and high or after lavish use of soap. They also discussed whether skinny or plump women were preferable, and as the flower of authorities on that subject was present, one and all agreed that the best was a lady whom like a dish of hot mussels one had all to oneself at the precise moment when the Almighty inspired one with the right notion to communicate to her. The Cardinal then asked what was most precious to one of the fair sex, the first kiss or the last, to which Nicole Beaupertuis replied the last, since then a woman knew what she was losing, whereas with the first she was ignorant as to what precious thing she was about to get.

While this talk and much else unfortunately lost to us was being bandied about, the six thousand crowns arrived, an easy three-hundred-thousand worth of today's money, so enfeebled do we become in every way.*

The gold crowns the King had spread out on a table under a good light, so that they glistened like the eyes of all the guests, which all lit up uncontrollably, causing much rueful laughter. And now very soon there were the three misers, led in very pale and anxious (except Cornelius, that is, for he knew Louis's little whimsicalities).

'Now come on, my friends,' said Louis to them, 'just look at those crowns on that table!'

* This comparison was made 125 years ago, since which we have all been still more prolific of noughts. *Translator.*

The three burghers did rub their eyes, you may believe me, even Nicole Beaupertuis's diamonds glinted less than their greedy little orbs.

'It's all for you—if you can win it,' added the King, when they had ceased marvelling at the money, and began to measure each other up. The guests now discovered that these old baboons were more expert than anybody else in grimacing, so wondrous did their physiognomies become, their eyes staring like cats at their milk or girls at potential husbands.

'Ya!' cried the King, 'that's all for the one who can say "*Buss-my-cue!*" three times to the other two, with his hand in the gold. But if he fails to keep as straight a face as a fly that's just raped its neighbour, that is, if he grins at all when he utters that password, he doesn't get a penny, but instead pays My Lady ten crowns. But each man can have three tries at it.'

'That's easy,' said Cornelius, whose mouth, since he was a Dutchman, was as often tight and grim as Nicole's lips were open and grinning.

So now, boldly enough, Master Cornelius clapped his hand on the crowns to make sure they were good mint, then solemnly grasped a handful, but when he looked up at the other two and politely said *Buss-my-cue*, and, mistrustful of his Dutch gravity, the other two misers replied with a *Bless you*, as if he had sneezed, and so made all the guests laugh, Cornelius laughed with them.

When the wine-grower tried to get the crowns, he felt such a tickling in his chaps that his battered colander of a face could not stop his laughter trickling through all its gaps just as smoke puffs out of a chimney's cracks, and he was unable to utter a word. It was then the haberdasher's turn. He was a little grim squirt of a man with lips as pinched as a felon's neck. Grabbing a handful of the coins, he looked round at everybody except the King and mockingly cried: '*Buss-my-cue!*'

'Is it turdy?' asked the vineron.

'That's for you to see,' replied the haberdasher, gravely, when the King felt sudden alarm for his crowns, especially as this fellow Peccard repeated the catchword the first time without laughing, and was in fact about to pronounce the sacramental phrase for the third time when suddenly Nicole nodded consent, and that made him lose control, his mouth crisped up at once, like a broken foreskin.

'However did you manage to keep solemn so long with six thousand crowns in front of you?' inquired Dunois.

'Well, My Lord Cardinal,' he said, 'the first time, I thought of a case of mine that's coming up before the court tomorrow, the second time I thought of my wife, and she'd wipe the smile off any man.'

The desire to win that fine sum of money made them try again and for nearly an hour the King enjoyed the contortions of these three physiognomies, the made-ready and the grimaces and the other babooneries of expression they assumed, but it was all in vain, and to such gentry, who so much preferred receiving to giving, it was a very scarlet pain each to have to fork up a hundred crowns to Lady Nicole.

When at last they were gone, Nicole turned boldly to King Louis:

'Sire,' she said, 'now would you like me to have a try?'

'God's Easter!' was the Royal riposte, 'no! I'll jolly well kiss yours for less than that.'

Words of a thrifty man, as indeed King Louis always was.

One evening, fat old Cardinal la Balue tried paying court to Nicole Beaupertuis by word and gesture a little more than canon law allows. But she, fortunately for her, was a keen-witted wench, better not ask her how many stitches her mother's shift had in it.

'Upon my word, Cardinal,' she said, 'that little bit which His Majesty likes doesn't need supreme unction yet.'

Then there came the Royal Barber, Olivier Le Daim, and she would not listen to him either, in answer to his idle chatter she said she would leave it to His Majesty to say whether he wished her to have a shave.

However, as Le Daim made no point of asking her to keep his advances secret, she suspected that these manoeuvres of his were all devices suggested by the King, whose suspicions must have been prompted by his friends, and so, being unable to avenge herself on Louis, she did at least want to ridicule the gentlemen in question, both pull their legs and amuse the King by the tricks she proposed to play on them. So one evening when they came to supper she had present a lady of Tours who in any case wished to speak to the King. This was a person of some standing who wanted to implore pardon for her husband, and, what is more after what happened, she got it!

Taking the King aside into a closet for a moment, Nicole told him to ply all their guests well with liquor and encourage them to do themselves well at table. He was moreover to be very cheerful, full of jokes, but when the table was cleared he was to be pernickety about something they had said, in fact, generally rather formal with them. If he did all this, she promised some good fun for him and would show all they were made of. Finally, Nicole said, and most important, he must do his best to be nice to this other woman and seem to be in earnest, as if she was in his favour, for she had very nobly agreed to play a key part in the whole diversion.

'Well, Gentlemen,' said the King, rejoicing to the company, 'and now to table! The hunting was long and good.'

So, polishing their mandibles in readiness, the Court Barber, the Cardinal, a fat Bishop, the Captain of the Scots Guards, an Envoy of the High Court, and a Justiciary who was a favourite of the King's all followed the two ladies into the banqueting hall. And how they did block out their doublets! Meaning? Meaning that they lined their bellies well, meaning their natural chemistry, meaning that they checked every dish, meaning that they stuffed their own tripe and dug their own graves with their own jaws, meaning play with Cain's sword, death to all good things in sauces, and long live all cuckolds, and meaning, more philosophically put, making turds with their teeth.

Now do you get me? How many words do you need to penetrate your thick skulls?

King Louis certainly did not fall short in his dispensation of a fine feast for his company. He stuffed them with green peas, he was repetitive with the hotpot, he sang hosannas to the prunes, he waxed poetic over the fish, to one guest he cried: 'But you're eating nothing!' to another: 'Come, let's drink to our dear Hostess!' and to them all it was: 'Come, gentlemen, do let's taste these prawns! Do let's kill this bottle! Never tried these faggots? And this lamprey, eh? Indescribable! Upon my word, if there was ever a mullet in the Loire like this one! Come on now, do justice to this pie! Why, but that's game of my shooting, it's a personal insult if you don't have a bite!' And it was: 'Drink up, the King's turning a blind eye! Do say a word to these pasties, they're our Hostess's own baking! Grapple with these grapes, man, they're off my own vines. Come on now, you can't say *no* to my medlars!'

And all the time he thus helped them fill out their basic *aposteumata*, the good King laughed with them and it was endless quips and quirks and gurks and smirks and wipings of jibs, as freely as if no monarch had been present. Moreover, the greater the inroads they made into the victuals and the more the fields of tasty food they laid waste, the more the flasks of wine they flushed it all down with, till their trunks were indeed well cardinalized and their doublets threatened to become schismatic at the seams, so stuffed they were, veritable Troyes sausages from funnel to main hoop of the paunch. When they got back to the parlour, in fact, they were in quite a muck sweat and puffing hard, even beginning to wish they had not tucked in quite so lavishly.

Now the King suddenly became taciturn. Everybody else followed suit. Indeed, they were the more glad to do so since all their energy was now so indrawn for the accomplishing of intestinal demaceration of all the platterfuls consigned to their bellies, which matter was now beginning to pipe its own tune, with immense gurgling.

One muttered to himself:

'How silly of me it was to have that dollop of sauce!'

Another grumbled because of that dish of chitterlings cooked with capers which he had stockpiled. Yet another's thoughts were that those delicious pork faggots were most litigious.

The Cardinal, the most paunched of them all, was whistling through his nostrils like a broken-winded mare. He it was, indeed, who was first compelled to give vent to a remarkable belch, when he would rather he had been in Germany, where folk say *many happy returns* one to another on such events, for, hearing that gastrophobic sound, His Majesty frowned and shot the Cardinal a dark glance.

'What does this signify?' he demanded. 'Do you take me for a common priest?'

This remark struck terror, for ordinarily His Majesty welcomed a well expelled belch. The other guests decided they must find some other way of getting rid of the vapours already paddling about in all their pancreatic convolutions. For some time, they did succeed in keeping them down, deep in their mesenterial pleats. At this stage, seeing them as well greased-up as tax collectors, Nicole Beaupertuis took the good monarch aside and whispered:

'Now let me tell you. I've had that image-maker Peccard fashion two large dummies just like this lady and myself. Now when the company begin to feel the urge of certain drugs with which I lined their glasses, and proceed to seek that throne to which we two womenfolk are now going to pretend to go, it will be to find the place permanently engaged. Then their contortions will give you some fun.'

With these words, Nicole and the burgess of Tours retired, ostensibly to ply the bow-drill, feminine fashion, the origin of which expression I may tell you elsewhere. After a decent lapse of liquid, Nicole reappeared, giving the impression that she had left the other girl in the den of natural alchemy. At once the King addressed the Cardinal, compelling him to stand up. Holding the Cardinal by the tassel of his amice, he began a serious discussion of public affairs. Whatever the King said, all la Balue could get out was 'Yes, Sire,' so anxious was he to be delivered now of the Royal favour and lower his breeks down, for his cellars were already water-logged and the bolt of his back-door had nearly given way.

All the guests, indeed, now became preoccupied with how to halt the forward progression of their waste matter, especially difficult since nature has imbued this even more than water with the quality of tending to find a certain level. The said substances meanwhile continued to soften up and to flow, labouring like insects in a frenzied anxiety to emerge from their cocoons, becoming wild and tormenting and indifferent to the Royal dignity, for there is nothing either so ignorant or so insolent as that particular form of matter, which at the same time is as freedom-loving as any prisoner.

So it was that at the least excuse they slipped out of that company like eels out of a net, not one but with the greatest difficulty and need for ingenuity not to make his mess there and then, in the Royal presence. Louis XI now took great delight in accosting each of his guests in turn, finding great enjoyment in the vicissitudes of their countenances, though these were but a reflection of the grubby grimacing of their bowels.

To Olivier Le Daim the Court Councillor said: 'I'd give my job now for a pint of minutes in old Turd's Vineyard.'

'True,' agreed Le Daim, 'there's nothing like a good rear, is there? I can tell you, I'm no longer surprised at the way flies do it all over the place.'

Thinking that by now, however, the lady from Tours must surely have cleared her books, the Cardinal suddenly abandoned the hairs of his tassel to His Majesty, and, making a backwards hop as if he'd forgotten to say his prayers, he made for the door.

'What ails you, my dear Cardinal?' cried the King.

'God of Easter, what ails me? Why—er—er—it's like this, Sire, you measure everything so lavishly, Sire,' gasped the Cardinal, and slipped away, leaving the others astonished at his quick wit.

Proudly La Balue proceeded to the nether apartment, loosening the knots of his pouch little by little as he went, only, when he snatched the blessed portal open, to find that lady from Tours still functioning on the throne like a Pope at inauguration, so, re-sheathing his ripe fruit, he hurried downstairs to go to the garden, but when he reached the lower steps, the barking of those hounds put him in peril of being bitten in one hemisphere or the other, so at last, utterly at a loss where to discharge his chemical products, he crept back to the sitting-room, shivering now like one who has caught a chill.

Seeing the Cardinal back, the others concluded that he had vacated his natural containers and demulcted his ecclesiastical sewerage and was to be reckoned a happy man, so Le Daim jumped up quickly, as if he rather wanted to examine the hangings and count the rafters, but contriving to reach the door before anybody else. Then, loosening his sphincter in advance, and humming a cheerful lay, he hastily made for the retreat, but once there, just like La Balue, was obliged to mutter his apologies to that never-ending female nature-easer, and closed the door as quickly as he had opened it, to go back with the same accumulating back-ballast of molecular aggregations encumbering his intimate conduits.

Thus, one after the other, the guests ventured forth, without one being able to get rid of his sauces, and soon there they were all, in the presence of Louis XI, as frustrated as ever and now eyeing one another, making more comprehensible conversation with their rears than ever with their lips, for the transactions of the natural organs are never circumlocutory, all in them is rational and easy to understand, seeing that it is a science which we learn with birth.

'If you ask me,' said the Cardinal to Le Daim, 'that woman's going to have the squits till daybreak. Whatever was Nicole Beaupertuis thinking of to invite such a diarrhoic here tonight?'

'Yes, may the ague take her, she's been a good hour now at what I could do in a jiffy!' cried Olivier Le Daim.

By now, mortified by colic, all these courtiers were beginning to stamp their feet, to make that importunate stuff bide a while, when the lady in question reappeared. How lovely, how charming they thought her, you may well imagine, they would gladly have kissed that which in themselves itched so badly and never was daybreak welcomed with greater delight than the appearance of that lady liberator of their poor suffering bellies.

La Balue rose. The others, out of respect, esteem and reverence for Holy Church, gave way to him as ecclesiastic, then, containing themselves, continued to grimace while the King and Nicole laughed to themselves, she aiding him now in hampering these lost creatures' respiration. The Captain of Scots Guards, who had exceeded all the others in his consumption of a dish to which the cook had added a laxative powder, now messed his breeches through trying merely to release an importunate little fart. At once he retired shamefaced to a corner, hoping that in the Royal presence the stuff would be well-behaved enough not to smell. At that moment, back came the Cardinal, horrifically metaspattericalized, for on the episcopal throne he had now found My Lady Nicole Beaupertuis herself. When in his agony he re-entered the sitting-room and saw her at her Lord and Master's side, all he could do was emit a Satanical:

'Ahh!'

'What does that mean?' inquired the King, shooting the great cleric a look which might have given him fever.

'Sire,' said La Balue, bluntly, 'all purgatorial matters are my province, and I feel obliged to warn you that there is witches' business going on in this house.'

'Come, my dear Cardinal, you must be joking!' said the King.

At these words, all present lost all sense of distinction between their doublets and their linings, they just dribbled from sheer fright, and the atmosphere became choking.

'What does this lack of respect mean?' cried the King, driving the last spot of colour from their cheeks. 'Hullo there, Tristan, my friend!' shouted Louis XI, rising suddenly and sticking his head out of the window, 'come up here, quickly, will ye?'

The Grand Provost of the Mansion did not dilly-dally, and as all present were mere nobodies whom the King had elevated, His Majesty, if out of humour, might, if such was his whim, just as easily dispossess them, so that when he arrived on the scene Tristan found all of them, except the cardinal, who trusted in his cassock to protect his neck, very strained and worried.

'Friend,' said the King, 'take these gentlemen at once to judgement on the Mall, every jack man has shat himself through over-eating.'

'Wasn't I a clever little joker?' Nicole asked him.

''Twas a good joke indeed,' said the King. 'But a damned stinky one.'

The final words of the Royal summing up had at least intimated to the courtiers that the King did not really mean to play with their heads this time. For so much mercy they blessed Heaven.

This Monarch was greatly given to such privy jokes, but he was not a bad man, as the guests all agreed, easing nature in a row along the Mall with Tristan who, like a good Frenchman, kept them company and escorted them home.

That, by the way, is the reason why ever since the townsfolk of Tours have insisted on turning that out-of-town walk into a public latrine. They have merely followed Court example. Nor will I leave the cloacal arrangements of this great King without setting down the great jape he played on an old maid, Mademoiselle Godegrand, who was most vexed at having utterly failed in forty years' existence to find a lid for her pot, whereby she was rabid as a he-mule in her tanned hide at still being a virgin.

She lived on the opposite side of the road from that house of Nicole Beaupertuis's, in what is now Jerusalem street. Hence, by leaning from the balcony it was quite easy to see what was being done, and hear too, in the ground floor room in which she spent her time, and many a time did Louis have some fine fun with the old girl, who had no notion she was so well in range of His Majesty's mortar.

Well, one open market day the King happened to have hanged a young burgher of Tours for raping a lady of the nobility rather advanced in years under the illusion he was accosting a young girl. In this there was nothing wrong and it would indeed have been to the lady's merit to be taken for a virgin, had the young man, when he found out his mistake, not heaped a thousand insults on her head and, suspecting her of deliberate trickery, taken it into his head to rob her of a lovely silver gilt goblet, to pay, so he said, for the present he had just made her.

The young fellow in question had a fine head of hair and was so handsome that the whole town wanted to witness the hanging, as a sort of sorrow, also from curiosity, and you may be sure there were more female head-dresses than male hats present. The young man swung very well and, dying gallantly enough, after the usage and custom of men on the gibbet in these days, with lance erect, which was the talk of the town, many of the ladies saying apropos that it was murder not to preserve such a darling of a codpiece.

'What do you say to putting that fine young lancer in old Gode-grand's bed?' Nicole Beaupertuis asked the King.

''Twould terrify her,' replied Louis XI.

'Not on your life, Sire, you may be sure she would be pleased to take in a dead man, since she so craves a live one. Yesterday I saw her going quite soppy about a young man's cap which she had stuck on to the back of a chair. You would have laughed at the things she said and did.'

So while this forty-year-old virgin was at evensong, the King sent men to take down the young burgher who had just wound up the final scene of his own tragic comedy, and then, dressing him in a white shirt, two valets got him over the walls into Mademoiselle Godegrand's garden and thence into her bed, pushing him across to the wall side. This accomplished, they made themselves scarce and the King mounted watch on the balcony of Nicole's sitting-room, toying with her while they waited for the old maid to go to bed.

It was not long before the old maid turned up, all sprightly-go-lightly, fresh from service at St Martin's, which was close at hand, for Jerusalem Street abuts on the monastery. In she came, put down her satchel and her chaplet and her rosary and all the other contraptions that old maids do carry, then uncovered the fire, blew it up, and warmed herself, then sat snug in her chair, stroking her pussy, failing anything better, then to the larder, to sup with sighs and sigh with sups, all lonesome, staring at her tapestries, then had a good drink, then farted a good fart, which the King heard.

'Oho!' cried Nicole, 'if only the corpse would pipe up with a *God bless you!*' and they both laughed a silent laugh.

Keenly attentive, our most Christian monarch then watched the old maid's undressing. As she took off her garments, she admired herself. Here she plucked a hair, there she scratched a pimple—one had naughtily popped up on her nose—then she picked her teeth and did all the other little things which, alas, all ladies, virginal or otherwise do, much to their annoyance, though without these slight faults of nature they would perhaps be too cocky and one would never be able to enjoy them. And when at last she had completed her discourse musical and aquatic the old dear slipped in between the sheets and then there came, oh, a lovely, an enormous, a vast and withal a curious cry, when she found there, age, and felt there the coolth of the hanged man and his fine odour of youth. After that, from coquetry, of course, Mademoiselle Godegrand leapt well back, but since she did not know that this really was a dead man, she came back to him, supposing him to be making fun of her and pretending.

'Get away with you, you naughty joker!' she said.

Nevertheless, take it from me, even these words she pronounced most submissively and in a very charming fashion, then, seeing the body still did not stir, she made a closer inspection, to be most amazed by the young man's outstanding human qualities. She now realized who it was, so she proceeded to conduct certain experiments, purely scientific, of course, in the interest of those to be hanged.

'But whatever is she doing?' whispered Nicole to the King.

'She is trying to bring him back to life,' said the King. 'A work of Christian humanity. . . .'

Indeed, the old maid did proceed to give the young man frictions and other reinvigorating treatment, imploring St Maria of Egypt the while to aid her in her labour of revitalization of this husband thus fallen amorous from the skies, when suddenly, her eyes on this corpse which she was so charitably warming up, she thought she detected a faint movement of the eyes, then, placing her hand on the young man's heart, felt a feeble beat. Finally, by reason of the warmth of the bed and of her affection and of course also by reason of the temperature of old maids, which is much higher than any hot wind of the African Deserts, she had the great pleasure of restoring life to this fine lusty fellow who accidentally had been very badly hanged.

'That's how my executioners serve me!' cried Louis XI, but laughing.

'Ah,' cried Nicole Beaupertuis, 'but you're never going to have him re-hanged, are you, he is too handsome.'

'The sentence says nothing about being twice hanged,' replied Louis. 'But he's going to marry that old maid. . . .'

Meanwhile, the good spinster had hurried away to find a surgeon, a fine barber who lived in the Abbey, and soon brought him back, and he at once took his lance, to bleed the young fellow. But as no blood issued, he said:

'Hm! Too late! The transference of the pulmonary blood has commenced.'

However, even as he spoke the good young blood did suddenly ooze out a drop, then all at once flowed freely, thus the hempen apoplexy, which had only just begun, was halted. The young man moved, becoming more alive, then, by the volition of nature, sank into great enfeeblement and profound diminution, with prostration and universal flaccidity of the tissues, whereupon the old maid, who let nothing escape her, and was following all these great and remarkable transformations in the person of the young victim, plucked the surgeon by the sleeve and, indicating the pitiable part by a strange glance, said:

'Is he always going to be like that?'

'By Heavens,' said the barber, truthfully, 'he is, and very often too!'

'Oh, he was so much nicer when hanged!'

When he heard this, the King burst into a loud guffaw, at which, looking out of the window and seeing him, both the old maid and the surgeon were terribly scared, for that laugh seemed to them to spell a second death sentence for their poor victim. But the King kept his word, and instead, he married the couple. Then, to complete this act of justice, he invested the husband with the title of Baron de Mortsauf, or Deathsafe, in place of the name he had taken to the gallows.

As Mademoiselle Godegrand had a nice little nestful of crowns, she and her young man made a good Tourainian household, which is still an honoured family, for the Baron de Mortsauf served His Majesty very loyally on many occasions. His only weakness was a shyness of gibbets and of old women, and he would never accept any rendezvous after dark.

This teaches us to check on our women well and be sure what they are, and not to make any mistakes about local distinctions between the old and the young, seeing that even if we may not be hanged for our errors of passion, there are still other considerable risks to be run.

VI

The Constable of France's Wife

Ambitious of great fortune, the Constable d'Armagnac took as wife the Countess Bonne, who was already deeply enamoured of young Savoisy, a son of Our Sovereign Lord Charles VI's Chamberlain.

D'Armagnac was an uncouth military type, of miserable appearance. A tough-hided, hairy man, foul-tongued too, always condemning men to the gallows, always sweaty too, from fighting or the engineering of any other stratagem than the stratagems of love. Hence this worthy military man was utterly indifferent about any seasoning of the conjugal stew, and treated his dainty wife like a man with his mind on loftier things, which is a manner that the ladies hold in grave mistrust, for they do not like their bedsteads to be the only objects to appreciate their minor caresses, let alone their major efforts. Hence, as soon as she had been to the altar the lovely Countess found her love for this young Savoisy more appetizing than ever, which was obvious also to this partner of hers.

Since this obviously meant that they both wanted to study the same music, it was not long before they had their lutes tuned to each other's. In other words, they solved their conundrum. It then became patent to Queen Isabella that Savoisy's horses were more often stabled at d'Armagnac's than at St Paul's House, where the Chamberlain had lived since (on orders of the University, as everybody knows), his original house was destroyed. This made that sober, circumspect Queen most apprehensive of serious trouble for Lady Bonne, especially as the Chancellor was a man as ready to whip out his blade as a priest to give a blessing. The Queen was just about as good at glossing over something as a lead dagger is at cutting, and a day or two later, on the way out of church after evensong she remarked to her cousin, whom she found taking holy water together with Savoisy:

'Darling, I think I can see blood in this water, don't you?'

'Nonsense, Madame!' says Savoisy, to the Queen, 'love likes blood.'

This rejoinder the Queen found quite neat. Indeed, she jotted it down, and later even implemented the assertion, when her own lord and King wounded one of her own lovers, the origin of whose favour you shall see in this tale.

From your own great experience you will of course know that in the springtide of love either of the lovers is always most loth to reveal the innermost workings of his (or her) heart and, both from fine prudence and also from the amusement which derives from the gentle deceits of courtship, will vie with one another at concealing it all—till one day of forgetfulness suffices to turn all past prudence to naught. The poor woman gets caught in the noose of her own happiness, her lover then marks his presence or rather his departure by leaving behind some trifle of his breeches, or by fatal accident there is a cloak or a spur left behind, and at once there's somebody's sharp blade cleaving down through all that canvas they have so sweetly gold-embroidered with their delights. But when one's days are full one should never scowl at death, and if ever there was one, the marital sword is a fine mode of exit for gallantry. Thus the exquisite affair of the Constable's wife was bound to end.

One morning early, when through the flight of the Duke of Burgundy, who had abandoned Lagny, d'Armagnac had time on his hands, it occurred to him to say how-de-do to his spouse. Moreover, so as not to make her cross, he decided he would waken her in rather a nice way. But alas, she was so deeply bogged down in a slumber as heavy as her night had been light, that she did not even flicker her eyelids in response to his accosting gesture, but merely muttered:

'Come on, now, Charles darling, that's enough.'

'Oh,' cried the Constable of France, hearing his spouse thus address a saint who was not one of the family calendar, 'so I've got Charles on my top-knot, have I?'

Without hesitation he leapt out of bed, and livid with rage and sword bared, rushed to the closet where the Countess's maid slept, suspecting that this was partly her doing.

'Ah! Ah! You strumpet of Satan!' he cried, by way of introduction to the subject of his wrath, 'say your prayers and don't waste time, I'm going to finish you off at once on account of this dirty business with the Mister Charles who comes here.'

'Oh, My Lord,' gasped the woman, 'whoever told you that?'

'Don't deceive yourself,' cried d'Armagnac, 'I'll slit your weazand without delay, unless you tell me every detail about these rendezvous, how it's all arranged, and if your tongue wriggles or stumbles, I'll nail you to the wall right away with this blade! Come on, speak up!'

'Then you can nail me up,' retorted the girl. 'You shall know nothing!'

This glorious rebuff did not at all please the Lord Constable, and so enraged was he that he did there and then nail the girl to the wall. After this he went back to his wife, on the way telling his groom, whom he met on the stairs, awakened by the girl's screams, that he could go up and look, he had 'corrected Billette rather severely'.

Then, before going on to discuss things with Bonne, he took his son, sound asleep as a child will be, and dragged him too very roughly to the bedroom. The mother now opened her eyes and wide too, as you may imagine, when she heard the child's cries, and was beside herself with anguish to see the boy in her husband's grasp, and the Constable's right hand dripping blood while his glance flashed to and fro between the boy and her.

'Whatever is the matter?' she demanded.

'Madam,' thundered this short-shrifter, 'is this the child of my loins, or those of Savoisy, your lover?'

At these words, Bonne went as white as a sheet and leapt to her child like a frightened frog leaping into a pond.

'Why, of course the boy is ours,' she said.

'Unless you want to see his head roll at your feet, confess everything to me, and answer straight! You have found me an assistant, have you?'

'I should think I have!' she said challengingly.

'And who is it?'

'Certainly not Savoisy,' she said, 'nor shall I ever tell you who it is —when I don't know myself!'

Hereupon the Constable rose to his feet and took his wife by the arm, preparing to truncate her avowal by the blow of his sword, but she shot him an imperious glance.

'Very well, kill me if you like,' she cried. 'In any case, this will be the end between us!'

'You shall live,' replied the husband. 'I shall keep a punishment for you worse than any death.'

With this harsh, bitter threat he left her, for he mistrusted all the traps, arguments and devices which, severally and collectively, the fair sex study night and day in all possible forms, and went straight to cross-examine all his men, showing them such a terrible countenance that every one answered him as if he were the Almighty himself on judgement day, when we must each give an account of ourselves. But not one of them knew anything of the grave misdeed at the bottom of this sudden wily cross-examination and from all they said the Chancellor concluded that not one of the men of the household had a finger in the pie, except perhaps one of his hounds which proved taciturn, and that moreover the one which he had selected to guard the gardens, so in his fury he took the animal in his bare hands and strangled it. This result of his inquiries led him to the peripatetic conclusion that his assistant had been entering the house by way of the gardens, out of which the only exit was the postern-gate on the river embankment.

93

Here a word for those who do not know the lay-out of the Armagnac mansion. This stood in a prominent place near the royal establishments of St Paul (where subsequently was erected Longueville
House). At this time, however, the Armagnac mansion had a fine
white-stone parade entrance in St Antoine Street. It was fortified all
round, the high walls on the river side, opposite Vaches Island
(where the Port de Grève is now situated), being furnished with
watchtowers. (The plans of this were on view for a long time in the
house of Cardinal Duprat, Royal Chancellor.) The Constable therefore thought hard and deep and at the bottom of his brain, of all his
devices, selected the best of all and so well adapted it to the immediate necessity that the gallant could not help falling into the trap
like a hare into a snare.

'God's Death!' he cried, 'now I've got the man who put the horns
on me, and I have time to think out well how I'll cook him when I
get him.'

Here then is the order of battle which at last this hirsute and
worthy soldier, who had waged war so well against Duke John the
Fearless, instituted to catch his secret enemy unawares. He took a
good number of his most devoted and skilled bowmen and stationed
them in the towers on the embankment side, telling them that under
pain of severest punishment they were to shoot down anybody, without distinction of person, except of course himself, who seemed to be
trying to get out of the gardens, but they were, whether by night or
by day, to let the lover, whoever it was, enter. The same arrangement was made on the entrance side, in St Antoine Street. The whole
household, even including the chaplain, was now ordered on no
account to leave the house, under pain of death, while keeping watch
on the two wings of the mansion was entrusted to men of the Constable's regular forces, with special orders to keep good watch on the
wide streets.

Like this, it was inevitable that the unknown lover to whom the
Constable owed his antlers would be caught red-handed when,
ignorant of all these preparations, he came round at the usual love
hour impudently to plant his standard again in the heart of the legitimate appurtenances of the Lord Constable. It was a trap which, unless of course as unfailingly protected by Lord God as good St Peter
was by our Saviour when he stopped him going to the sea-bottom
that day when it came into their heads to see if the sea was as solid as
terra firma, the wiliest man ought to fall.

The Constable that day had business out at Poissy, and was to ride
off immediately after the midday meal, so that, knowing this arrangement, poor Countess Bonne had the day before every reason to invite

94

her young admirer to that delightful tourney in which she was ever the victor, but while the Constable was thus encircling his house with eyes and death and, to be sure of getting his man, setting his archers in that special ambush near the postern-gate, to catch the gallant on the way out, his good lady was for her part not engaged merely in telling her fortune by tossing peas on a board or by deciphering black cows on the hearth.

First, you should know that the nailed-up maid-servant actually unnailed herself and dragged herself to her mistress, to tell her that her cuckolded husband had got no information and also, before expiring, to be able to comfort her dear mistress with the information that she could count absolutely on the maid's sister, who did the household laundry and was ready to let herself be hacked to sausage-meat to please my Lady, and was moreover the wiliest and spryest wench in the district, famous from the Law Courts to Trahoir Cross among the common folk as one most fertile-witted in love's extremities.

So, lamenting the death of her good maid, the Countess sent for the laundress and told her to leave her washing and rummage in her rag-bag of devices, for she was prepared to sacrifice all her own future happiness to save Savoisy. The two females' first thought of course was to let Savoisy know the Count's suspicions and persuade him to be wary. So the good laundress loaded herself with enough linen to defeat a mule and went to the outer door. There, however, she found an armed man who turned a deaf ear to all verbal argument. Therefore, in her great devotion, she decided to try taking the soldier by his weak spot and so thoroughly did she kindle him with her caresses that at last, in spite of being in full war kit, he had a grand bout with her, but even after that jousting he would not let her out into the street, and even though after that she tried to get her passport stamped by a number of the handsomest of the guards, thinking that perhaps someone else would be a better cavalier, not one of the bowmen, men-at-arms or others dared open even the narrowest cranny leading out of that mansion.

'You're very nasty, ungrateful wretches,' she told them, 'not to do me the service I've done you!'

Fortunately, however, all this business did enable the laundress to find out everything about the preparations, and she scurried back to her mistress to tell her all the Count's military dispositions, whereupon the two women resumed their conferencing, and had not even had time to get through a couple of *alleluias* about all those warlike marshallings, look-outs, defences and ambiguous dispositions, all so sly, crafty and diabolical, before, by that sixth sense with which females are furnished, they recognized that the poor lover was menaced by mortal danger.

Learning soon enough that she was the only one who had free exit from the house, the Constable's wife quickly risked all to take advantage of her right. But she did not get more than a crossbowshot from the door alone, for the Constable had ordered four of his pages to follow her if she did go out, while two ensigns of his company were also to keep her in sight. The poor lady then returned to her room, weeping as copiously as all the Magdalenes whom you see on church paints put together.

'Alas!' she cried. 'Like this, my lover really will lose his life, and I shall never see him again! And he so sweet-spoken and lovely to touch. . . . So that lovely head which has so often rested on my knees will be destroyed! Why can I not toss my husband some empty valueless head instead of that one so full of charm and valour . . .? A foul head for a perfumed one, a hated head for a loved one!'

'Well, my Lady,' suddenly suggested the laundress, 'what if we dressed that kitchen boy who is so crazy about me, and worries the life out of me, in noble clothing and thus gayed up put him out through the postern gate?' And at this proposal the two women exchanged most murderous glances.

'Once they polished off that sauce-spoiler, all this soldiery would disperse like so many starlings.'

'Yes, but would the Count not recognize the fellow?' cried the Countess, clutching her heart, and shaking her head. 'No, no, we simply must spill some noble blood, and not spare it either.'

But, after thinking it over a short while, she suddenly danced with delight and flung her arms round the laundress's neck. 'For saving my love by your advice,' she cried, 'I will reward you to your last breath!' and with these words, the Countess wiped away her tears, dolled her face up as if she were going to the altar again, took her vanity bag and her book of the Hours, and went straight to St Paul's Church, where the bells were just ringing for the last mass of the day. Now, as it happened, this was a service which ordinarily—like any other frisky lady of the nobility—they are all alike—the Countess never missed. It was commonly known as 'the dress mass', for at this service one saw nothing but all the fops and the fancy men, the young scions of the nobility and the ladies of Court, all highly prinked and perfumed. In short, it was a mass limited to those whose gowns carried coats of arms or ankles gilded spurs.

So off went Lady Bonne, leaving her laundress at home in great state of fluster to keep her eye on the granary, and so reached her parish church accompanied of course by her pages and those two ensigns with their men-at-arms. It is commonly alleged that among that band of handsome knights who fidgeted round the ladies at church, there was more than one whose delight she was and whose heart was sold to her after the fashion of our adolescence, in which we sleep with as many women as possible in thought, so as to be able to make sure of at least one of so many in reality. But among those fine birds of prey, whose beaks were always open and whose eyes flitted more up and down the pews and prayer-stools than towards altar or priests, there was one to whom the Countess had been wont to give the glad eye out of sheer charity, since he was less fidgety and seemed more profoundly involved than any other.

For this particular knight was not at all forthcoming. He always clung to the same pillar and did not stir from it. Indeed, it left him in the Seventh Heaven merely to gaze upon this lady of his heart's choice. His pale features reflected a sweet sadness, and his countenance was expressive of a heart of very fine metal, one of those that feed on fierce attachments and seem to revel in the very hopelessness of a love without prospects. There are few such. As a rule men prefer the ladies' you know what to any of those unknowns of love's enjoyment that flourish merely in the soul's profundities.

To the Constable's wife it seemed clear that, for all that his clothes were well cut, clean, trim, indeed, and revelative of some taste in their matchings, this must be a very poor knight, come from some distant place to seek a fortune with no more than his cap and his sword to back him. So, partly because she suspected his secret poverty, partly because he adored her so, but also a little because he really was so handsome, with his fine black hair, which he wore very long, and his stalwart figure, and because he was so meek and utterly resigned, she had already inwardly wished him both female favour and fortune. So now, in order not to suffer subsequently from a shortage of real gallants, and prompted too by her businesslike housewife's mind, she began to egg this young man on, as her wits instructed her, by various favours, such as a little swift glance or two sent wriggling towards him like well-fanged asps.

Thus like any Queen, accustomed to play as she pleased with things far more valuable than a mere knight, Bonne made light of the real well-being of that young life. For, after all, did her husband, as Constable of France, not often enough risk the Kingdom and all as you or I might a shilling at piquet? Finally, let us observe that it was only three days before this that as the congregation came out of church after evensong the worthy Constable's lady had with a sly glance pointed out that very same young worshipper to the Queen and chosen with a little laugh to say:

'A young man of parts, eh?'

This turn of speech, subsequently established in elegant discourse, was much used to describe courtiers, and it was the wife of Constable d'Armagnac and none other to whom the French language owes the pretty euphemism.

It so happened that the Countess had hit on the truth concerning the young nobleman. He was a bannerless knight, Julien de Bois-Bourredon by name, who, having failed to inherit enough timber on his fief-lands to make himself a toothpick, and realizing he had no other wealth than the abundant virility with which his late mother had so suitably equipped him, thought to draw both a living and a thriving from this at Court, since he was well aware how greedy high-placed ladies are for such fine revenues and what a fine high price they put on them whenever they can be collected without mishap between sun-down and sun-up. There are indeed many like him who have chosen to make their road up that narrow path in distaff country, but this young fellow, far from neat measures of his love in several cups, had put all his capital into one single dream the very first time that he set eyes on the triumphant loveliness of Countess Bonne at the parade mass. He had, in other words, fallen genuinely in love at once, which was a good thing for his crowns, since it put him right off his appetite and quenched all his thirst. Such love is the most dangerous, since while it keeps you on a very strict love diet, it also prompts a love of that régime, a double sickness capable of spelling a man's doom altogether.

So much for the young lord of whom the worthy Constable's lady thought, and whom she now rapidly approached, to invite him to his death. The moment she entered the church, she had espied the poor knight, faithful to his delight, awaiting her there, his back to the same pillar, like an ailing man dreaming of sunshine, of the spring, of daybreak. However, the moment she came near him, she turned aside from him again, and went to the Queen to request her aid in her desperate situation. The fact is, she took sudden pity of this young admirer. Then, however, one of the ensigns approached her and with firmness mingled with respect said:

'My Lady, my orders are not to allow you to speak to anybody, man or woman, not even the Queen or your own Confessor. I must assure you that our lives are at stake in this.'

'Is dying then not your recognized occupational duty?' she demanded.

'So is obeying,' was the soldier's reply.

So the Countess applied herself again to her devotions at her usual place, and there, examining her worshipper again, found he looked thinner and more cadaverous than ever.

'Hm!' she said to herself, 'perhaps I need not be so worried about his dying, after all he's already got one foot in the grave.'

Thus paraphrasing her intention, she threw the young man one of those flaming glances permissible only to the nobility and the professional ladies of love, and that false love evidenced by her lovely eyes at once dealt the young man by the pillar a sharp thrust. Who indeed does not love the hot assault of life when it thus floods about his heart and puffs up every part of his being? With a like pleasure which is ever fresh in the female soul, the Constable's lady was conscious too of the omnipotence of her magnificent glance. The knight's speechless response soon told her this, and that fluxion of the blood which turned his cheeks bright scarlet was more eloquent than the finest words of Greek or Latin oratory and quite as well comprehended too by her. And at that sweet revelation, in order to be quite sure that it was no accident of nature, the Countess took further pleasure in seeing exactly how far the vital essence of her eyes could go. And having thus heated her worshipper thirty times over, she was at last completely confirmed in the belief that he was ready to die magnificently in her service.

This notion indeed so touched Lady Bonne on the quick that thrice over between prayers she was tickled with a sudden urge to pile all the man's delights into one tremendous delight and to dissolve this for him in one single thrust of love, so she should not some day be reproached with having not merely thrown away the young fellow's life, but also his happiness. And when the officiant turned round to the nave to intone his *Be-off-with-you* to his fine gilded flock, the Constable's wife made her way out past that pillar against which her suitor stood and passed very close to him, endeavouring by one tremendous glad-eye to suggest that he should follow her. Then, to confirm him in his cognizance and purposive interpretation of that fleet invitation, the sly woman when past him turned her head back just sufficient to repeat the solicitation. She saw then that he had already taken a step or two forward but was hesitant to go on, so shy was he. But at this final indication the young knight was convinced at last that he was not being overweening, so, treading softly and with small steps, like any young sop timid to find himself in one of those good places which are said to be bad, he mingled in the company leaving the church. But now, whether he was ahead of her or behind her, to right or to left, the Constable's wife still contrived to shoot him numerous glances, the more to bait him and better to attract her to him, just like any fisher plucking at the line the better to hook a gudgeon.

To cut a long story short, so well did the Countess ply the business of a tart in her task of directing holy water to drive her water-mill (which is as good as saying that there is nothing so much like a trollop as a woman of noble birth), that when she reached the portal of her mansion this Constable's lady made no hesitation about going straight in, then pausing an instant to turn her head back towards the young knight and invite him to follow with a glad-eye so infernal that he at once ran to the Queen of his Heart as if she had said 'Come!' out loud. As he entered, she gave him her hand, and thus, both a-simmer and a-shiver, though from opposite reasons, the couple found themselves inside.

In that evil moment Lady d'Armagnac was, it must be confessed, ashamed of having behaved with such looseness, merely to help death, and also with being so faithless to Savoisy the better to save him, but that little twinge of remorse proved as lame as the big ones, and in any case, it was now too late, and, seeing that the dice were all thrown, Bonne leant heavily on the arm of her worshipper and murmured:

'Quick, come to my room, I have something to tell you.'

Unaware yet that his life was at stake, young de Bois-Bourredon was so choked by hope of a bliss so near that he was utterly unable to make any response at all. And when the laundress saw this fine young nobleman which the Countess had so swiftly taken, 'Damn it,' said she, 'it would take a Court lady to bring off a pick-up like that,' then vouchsafed the courtier a profound curtsey which was pregnant with that sarcastic respect due to a man brave enough to play so great a part for such a little part.

'Picarde,' said the Constable's wife, drawing her woman to her by the skirts, 'I am utterly unable to admit to him what awful price I am going to pay him for his speechless adoration of his and such lovely faith in the loyalty of woman.'

'Pooh, My Lady,' said the laundress. 'And why tell him at all? Dispatch him happy through the postern. There's many a man dies in the wars for nought. Is it out of the question for this one to die for something? Why, if that would be any consolation, I'd make another from him myself.'

'Get away with you!' cried the Countess. 'I shall tell him the whole truth. That will be my punishment for my sin.'

Thinking his lady was arranging some details and making secret arrangements with her maid so she should not be disturbed in the discussion that she was promising him, the unknown lover kept discreetly at a distance and watched the flies flitting round. He did admittedly think the Countess very daring, but at the same time, as

indeed even a cripple might, he found a thousand reasons to justify
her, and also thought himself fully worthy of inspiring such madness.
He was thus musing prettily when the Constable's wife opened the
door of her chamber and invited him to follow her. But, once there,
this lady of authority abandoned all her high-riding appearances and
fell to her knees at the knight's feet.

'Alas, noble knight,' she said, 'I have done you a terrible wrong.
Hear me! When you leave this house, it will be to meet your death!
My crazy passion for another man blinded me. And so, without being
able to take his place here, you will yet have to assume it before those
who lie in wait to assassinate him. There, that is the delight I enticed
you here for!'

'Oh,' replied Bois-Bourredon, burying dark despair in the depths
of his heart, 'but I am your grateful servant for so using me as a
chattel. . . . Indeed, I love you so much that I have become like
any lady, I dream every day of offering you something which can be
given but once. Then take my life, if you will!'

And, having delivered himself of this, the poor young knight compounded into one glance all those he would have given her for days
without end. But when she heard these valiant, loving words Bonne
suddenly rose to her feet.

'Oh,' she cried, 'were it not for Savoisy, how I would love you!'

'Alas, that certainly seals my fate,' replied Bois-Bourredon. 'I
knew from my horoscope that I was fated to die by the love of a great
lady. Heavens, though!' he cried, seizing his fine sword by the hilt, 'I
shall still sell my life dearly, and though I shall die, I shall be happy in
the thought that my demise assures the happiness of the woman
whom I love. I shall live a finer life in her memory than in reality!'

When she beheld the pose which this brave man assumed and his
gleaming countenance, the Constable's wife utterly took him to her
heart, only a moment later to be cut to the quick that he should seem
so willing to leave her without even asking a trifling favour of her.

'Come here, let me arm you,' she cried, and held up her lips to kiss
him.

'Ah, dear lady, would you then render my death impossible,' he
cried, damping the fire of his eyes with a hesitant tear, 'by making
my life too valuable?'

'Come with me!' she then cried, utterly defeated by such burning
love, 'I do not know in what this will all end, but come. After, we
can but die both together at the postern.'

One single fire consuming their two hearts, one harmony to pluck
the chords for both, they now mingled finely in a fast embrace, lost
in the lovely frenzy of that fever beyond reason which I hope you all

know, and thus utterly forgot the danger in which Savoisy or they themselves stood, forgot the Constable of France, forgot death, forgot life, forgot all.

Meanwhile, the sentinels at the main door had gone to inform the Constable that the lover had arrived. He was, they said, a young nobleman who was so enamoured that he had not even heeded the many warning glances which all through mass and on the way from church the Countess had thrown him to prevent his being done to death. But when these soldiers met their master he was already hurrying to assume his post at the postern, for meanwhile his archers on the embankment had also been whistling to him from a distance to tell him that Savoisy had entered by that door.

The truth was that Savoisy had indeed come at the appointed hour, and, like any lover, having no thought but for his lady, had simply not noticed the Count's spies, but had slipped straight in by the postern gate. This collision of lovers resulted in the Constable cutting short whatever his front door men wanted to say. With a gesture of authority, he warned them not to contradict him.

'I know we've got the beast caught,' he cried.

So, all together, with a great cry of 'Kill him, kill him!' they rushed to the postern and men-at-arms, bowmen, Constable, captains and all the rest of the mob came down at once on Charles Savoisy, nephew of His Majesty, and fell on him at the Countess's very window, so that by a remarkable accident the poor young fellow's groans as he perished dismally, mingling with the howling of the soldiery, clashed in a part song with the passionate sighs and the rather different cries uttered by the two lovers, who now sprang from the bed in great fear.

'Oh!' cried the Countess, white as a sheet, 'it's Savoisy, killed through me.'

'But I shall live for you,' replied Bois-Bourredon, 'and you will find me the happier to pay for my fortune at the price he has now paid for his.'

'Quick, hide in this chest!' cried the Countess. 'I hear the Constable coming.'

She was right, the Count d'Armagnac entered the room only a few instants later, bearing in his hand a man's head, which he placed all bleeding up on the mantel-shelf.

'There, My Lady,' he said. 'There is a picture for you which may teach you the duty a wife owes her husband.'

'You have slaughtered an innocent man,' replied the Countess, without changing colour a bit. 'Savoisy was not my lover.'

So saying, she looked the Constable proudly in the face, her countenance so masked with feminine deceit and audacity that the Constable felt as silly as a young girl who in a drawing-room full of people had slipped a note in her nether region and was struck with doubt whether she had not indeed committed a frightful wrong.

'Of whom then were your thoughts when I touched you this morning?' he demanded.

'I was dreaming of the King,' she said.

'Then, my dear, why on earth did you not tell me so?'

'Would you have believed me,' she asked him, 'in the animal fury you were in?'

The Constable plucked at his ear, then persisted:

'But how was it Savoisy had a key to our back gate?'

'Oh,' she cried, 'I just wonder, have you not enough respect for me to believe what I have just told you?'

With these words, the Constable's lady turned as lightly on her heel as a weather-vane in the wind, and pretended as if to busy herself with household affairs, when you may well imagine that the Count found poor Savoisy's head most embarrassing, while Bois-Bourredon, for his part, was at great pains not to cough as he listened to the Count muttering this and that all to himself. Finally, with two crashing blows of his fist on the table, the Constable cried:

'Those Poissy folk! I'll launch an attack and give them hell!'

With this, he made off, and when night fell Bois-Bourredon escaped in disguise.

Poor Savoisy was greatly lamented by his lady, who had done all any woman could to save her lover. Later he was more than lamented, he was regretted, for when the Constable's wife told Queen Isabel what had happened, that person soon detached Bois-Bourredon from the Countess's service to serve herself, so struck was she by the qualities of that young lord and his steadfast pluck.

Bois-Bourredon was indeed one whom Death had well recommended to the ladies. Indeed, he so valiantly put his shoulder to the wheel in the fortunate part which the Queen thus opened for him that when one day King Charles was in his right mind and Bois-Bourredon treated him badly, certain jealous courtiers told the king of his cuckoldom. Bois-Bourredon was then stitched in a sack in a jiffy and tossed into the Seine, as we all know, near Charenton Ferry.

I need not add that from that day when the Constable took it into his head to be careless with cutting instruments his worthy wife made such good use of the two deaths which he had caused that she threw them in his face many a time, till she had him as smooth as a cat's fur, and thus put him on to the proper road of conjugal life, when he declared her then to be a very proper, well-behaved Constable's wife, as indeed she was.

Since, following the model of the great authors of antiquity, in addition to the good laughs with which it will provide you this book should also add some lofty principles, I may point out to you that the essence of this Tale is as follows: In serious situations, a woman should never need lose her head, for the God of Love never abandons the ladies, particularly when they are pretty and young and of good standing; further, that when they go to love assignations, lovers should never do so like ninnies, but likewise keep their heads, and take note of everything about their love-nests, so as never to fall into traps, and thereby not lose their lives, for next to a good woman the most precious thing is undoubtedly a handsome gentleman.

VII

The Maid of Thilhouse

The Lord of the Manor of Valênes, a pleasant place, the castle of which is not far from the town of Thilhouse, had taken to wife a miserable woman who, whether from taste or distaste, pleasure or displeasure, sickness or health, allowed her husband to go hungry for those sweets and confectioneries which are stipulated in all good marriage contracts.

To be fair, one must add that the gentleman in question was a very foul, filthy fellow, always out a-huntin' wild animals and no more delectable indoors than a smoky chimney. Besides, for arithmetical reasons the said sportsman had at his back fully three-score years regarding which he was as silent as the widow of the executioner's puppet is of things hempen.

Nature, however, who sends us skepfuls of the crooked and the bandy, the blind and the ugly, bothers no more about such folk than about the handsome ones, for, like those who make the stitches of tapestry, she knows not what she does, and instils in them all the same appetite and the same liking for the hotpot. Hence it is that every creature in due course finds its match, whence the proverb, *no pot's too ugly for a lid*.

Now, Lord de Valênes was always on the look out for pots (pretty ones) that needed lidding, and often hunted such tame beasties as well as the wild ones, but married petticoat game at this time was becoming rather scarce in those parts and defrocking maidenhoods was expensive. Nevertheless, by dint of inquiry and much nosing, he one day obtained information that at Thilhouse there was a weaver's widow who had a real treasure in the form of a young wench of sixteen who had never been allowed to leave her mother's skirts, for out of maternal protectiveness the widow even took her daughter out to ease nature, and invariably had her sleeping in her own bed with her. She was constantly on the guard, getting her up in the morning and only letting her work at jobs which they could do together, by which they earned some eightpence per diem. On Holy Days, in church, she kept the girl on the lead, and it was only with difficulty she would even give her a chance to exchange a mere bantering word with the lads. It was moreover always *hands off* regarding that maid.

However, about this time conditions became so hard that the widow and her daughter had only just enough food to keep body and soul together, and though they lived with one of their poor relations they often lacked wood in winter and clothes in summer. They also owed enough around to frighten a bailiff, though such folk are never easily scared by other people's debts. In a word, if the girl grew in good looks, the widow certainly did likewise in poverty, and in order to keep her daughter's maidenhood she got badly into debt, like any alchemist concentrating on the crucible in which he melts his all.

Completing his inquiries, Lord de Valênes one rainy day came to the hovel where the two spinning-women lived, as if by chance, and to light a fire to dry himself sent for some faggots to a copse nearby. While he waited for these to be brought, he seated himself on a stool between the two poor women. By grace of the grey shadowy half-light of the hut he saw the charming appearance of this Maid of Thilhouse, bonny, firm arms, outposts solid as castle-keeps to keep the cold winds off her heart, waist as full of sap as a young oak tree, and all this also as fresh and trim and tender as a bud in April. In short, she was the loveliest thing in the world. She had eyes which were steady and of a modest blue and a glance which was more modest than that of the Virgin, since, never having had a baby, in this respect she had the advantage of that lady.

If anybody had proposed to her taking a little turn of pleasure, she looked so naïve and so little open to any inkling what that meant that she might well have replied:

'Of course, where do you go in?'

Hence good old Valênes fidgeted on his stool, sniffing meanwhile at the lass and stretching out his neck like a monkey after walnuts. This was quite obvious to the mother, but she said nothing, being rather afraid of the lord to whom all the land there belonged.

When a faggot was put on the fire and this blazed up, the worthy huntsman suddenly remarked:

'Ah, now that warms a man almost as much as your daughter's eyes do.'

'Alas,' said the widow, 'they are a fire that cooks nothing. . . .'

'Oh, but surely,' he replied.

'And how do you make that out?'

'Like this,' he said. 'You lend your lass to my wife, she has need of a chambermaid, and we'll pay you two faggots a day.'

'Ah, My Lord,' said the widow, 'but whatever should I bake on such a blazing hearth?'

'Why,' said the old rascal, 'good crisp loaves, I reckon. I'll give you twenty gallons of corn every harvest.'

'But then,' the old woman went on, 'wherever should I store it?'

'In your bin.'

'But I haven't got any bin, or chest or anything.'

'Right, then I'll give you some bins and some chests and some stoves and some washtubs and a good bed complete with hangings, in short, everything.'

'Upon my word,' said the good widow, 'the rain'll ruin it all, I have no house.'

'From here,' went on the Lord of the Manor, 'can you not see Tourbillière House, where my poor groom Pillegrain, the one that got gored by the boar, used to live?'

'I can,' said the old woman.

'Well, put yourself there,' he said, 'for the rest of your life.'

'Upon my word,' cried the mother, letting her distaff fall, 'do you really mean it?'

'I do.'

'But what would my girl get?'

'Whatever she earns serving me,' said the Lord of the Manor.

'Why, My Lord, you mock me.'

'No, I don't,' he said.

'You do,' said she.

'By Saint Gatien and Saint Eleuther and the thousand million saints swarming up above, I swear . . .'

'Right,' said the widow, 'if you're really not joking, I'd just like a lawyer to give these faggots of yours the once-over.'

'By Christ's blood and the daintiest part of your daughter, am I then not a man of chivalry? My word is worth risking!'

'Well, I don't exactly say it isn't,' replied the widow, 'but it's also true that I am a poor spinster and too fond of my daughter to abandon her just like that, and she is too young and too frail yet, service would break her, yesterday in his sermon, you know, the curé said we all have to answer to God for our children.'

'Damnation to you,' cried the Lord of the Manor, 'go and find your lawyer.'

An old woodcutter promptly ran round to the notary and he came and drew up a fine, proper contract, to which, being illiterate, Lord de Valênes put his mark, then when all was signed and sealed, he said:

'Now, good mother, are you now at last relieved of responsibility to God for your girl's maidenhood?'

'Oh, Sir, the curé said, "*till the age of reason*", and my daughter is very reasonable.' Then, turning to the girl, she went on: 'Listen here, Marie Ficquet, your most precious possession is your honour and where you are going every man, not to mention My Lord, will be

after destroying it, but now perhaps you can see what it is worth. . . .
So don't you get rid of it except with your eyes well open and all
your papers in order. And that means, not to contaminate your virtue
before God and man (except for legitimate cause) you should take
good care to have your little part well sprinkled at the altar before-
hand, or you'll go to the bad.'

'Yes, Mamma,' said the maid, and there and then left her parent's
miserable dwelling and went to Valênes Castle to serve My Lady
there, who did indeed find the girl quite to her taste.

When the folk of Valênes, Sacché, Villaines and other places
learned of the high price given for the Maid of Thilhouse, other good
housewives recognized that there was no more profitable a thing than
virtue and strove to bring up all their daughters well-instructed virgins. But it was as chancy a business as training silkworms, those
maidenhoods were so apt to collapse, for like medlars, they soon
ripen when well kept in straw. Nevertheless, there were a number of
girls, noted therefore in Touraine, in all the convents, who were
accredited virgins, though that is something I will not answer for,
never having checked the matter in that contest which Verville lay
down as the only valid one for a maid's perfect maidenhood.

Nevertheless, Marie Ficquet did follow her mother's wise counsel
and refused to give ear to a single one of those gentle pleas, gilded
words or apish devices of her master, unless he had her previously
sprinkled at the altar, and whenever the old gentleman seemed about
to jump his fences, the girl would flare up like a cat with kittens
when a dog comes near, and cry:

'I'll tell My Lady.'

Indeed, six months had gone by and Lord Valênes had not recovered even the price of a single faggot. However much he sup-
plicated, Marie Ficquet was only the more rigid and firm, though,
one day at last he asked rather nicely, she did go so far as to say:

'All right—but, when you've had it, will you give it back to me?'
which was a teaser.

On other occasions, however, she informed him much more tartly
that if she had as many holes as a colander, there still wouldn't be one
for him.

'You are so ugly,' she said.

The dear old fellow took this rustic language as the flower of
virtue, and did not stint his little gestures, his endless speeches and
his hundred thousand oaths, for by dint of much sight of this lass's
heart-protectors and those magnificent buttocks which at certain
movements stood out in wondrous relief through her skirts and by
study of other things which were enough to put a saint into a fine

state, the old boy became really enamoured of her with a genuine old man's passion, which is one that, in distinction from the passion of young fellows, increases exponentially, for the elderly love with their weakness, which augments, whereas the young love with their vigour, which diminishes.

Finally, to close the last loophole of this damned wench's refusal Lord de Valênes took one of his stewards into his confidence. This was a fellow of over seventy, whom he persuaded that to warm his hide the old fellow should take a wife and that Marie Ficquet was the girl for the job. The old steward, having earned three hundred Tourainian crowns sterling by his various services to the household, had in mind to live in peace now without opening any more front doors, but his master begged him to marry just a little, to please him, and assured the old fellow that he need not worry about his wife at all, so to be obliging the old man did at last make the mistake of engaging in the marriage.

On the wedding day, Marie Ficquet, now deprived of any argument and unable to raise any further cause against her suitor, finally stipulated a good dowry and marriage settlement as the price of her maidenhood, after which she did at last tell the old bounder that he might come and do his best in her bed, promising him moreover as many tosses as he had given her mother grains of wheat, though at his age a bushel ought to be enough.

The wedding over, Lord de Valênes did not fail, and, as soon as his wife was between the sheets, off he slipped to the well decorated, well carpeted, well be-rugged room in which he had put his pullet, his money, his faggots, his house, his wheat and his steward's wife.

To cut a long story short, be assured that he found the Maid of Thilhouse the loveliest girl in the world, incomparably beautiful in the gentle light of the fire flickering in the hearth. She was however rather captious between the sheets, most difficult, in fact, most odoriferous indeed of maidenhood, and there was no doubt about it, the old man found the price of this jewel well spent. But, being unable to prevent himself hurrying over the first mouthfuls of this tasty Royal morsel, de Valênes next proceeded, like any past master, to attempt to embroider his young formulary, and then it was that by excess of greed this over-fortunate fellow began over-finessing, and slipping, in short, proved not quite up to the pretty trade of love. Seeing which, after a while, this good lass quite innocently remarked to her old cavalier:

'My Lord, if you mean to do anything about it, as I suppose you do, do swing your bells a bit harder!'

For this remark, which got about, I know not how, Marie Ficquet became famous, and in our parts people still say: *"She's a regular Maid of Thilhouse,"* when, to mock a bride, they wish to suggest she is rather a *friquenelle*. And what is a *friquenelle*? That is what we call any girl whom I would not wish you to have between the sheets on your marriage night, unless you have been brought up a stoic and are not surprised by any naughtiness. There are, however, many men who are forced to be stoics in this droll situation, which is still not at all infrequent, for though Nature may turn, she changes not, and there are always good Thilhouse maids in Touraine and elsewhere.

Now, were you to ask me in what the moral of this Tale consists, or should I say bursts, I should be in the right if I told the ladies that these *droll tales* are rather designed to teach the morals of pleasure than to provide the pleasure of making morals. On the other hand, were it some fine old worn-out rascal who accosted me on the subject, I should tell him, with polite regard of course for his wig, whether yellow or grey, that God wished to punish Lord de Valênes for trying to purchase goods which are made solely to be granted gratis.

VIII

Brother-in-Arms

Early in the reign of the second Henry of that name, who so loved fair Diane, there was still in existence a ceremonial observance which has since then entirely faded out, like many other things of the olden days. This lovely, noble custom was the choice of a brother-in-arms made by every knight by which, having got to know each other as two trusty, lusty fellows, such a pair would be married for life to each other. They became brothers, each defending the other in the field against any assailant putting his life in danger, or at Court against slanderous friends. In the absence of his companion, a brother-in-arms was expected to address any man accusing his brother of any act of betrayal, mischief or felonious scurrility with the formula: 'By your throat, but you lie!' and go into the field without delay. So sure were brothers-in-arms of each other's honour. Nor need one even add that whatever the business, bad or good, one brother-in-arms always seconded the other, or that they shared everything, fortune and misfortune alike. They were indeed more than ordinary brothers, merely linked by the chances of nature, for they had made themselves brothers by the bonds of a special emotion which was involuntary and mutual.

Thus brotherhood in arms was productive of fine deeds, as glorious as those of the ancient Greeks or Romans or others. That however is not my subject here, all such matters have been written by our country's historians, and every man knows them. My story is that at this time there were two young noblemen of Touraine, one of whom was the younger de Maillé, the other a de Lavallière, who concluded brotherhood in arms on the day they earned their spurs. They had come from the household of the Duke de Montmorency, in which, under that military leader's excellent guidance, they had been brought up, which shows how infectious valour is in such fine company, for at the battle of Ravenna they earned the praises of the oldest knights present.

It was in fact in the course of that arduous day that de Maillé, being rescued by de Lavallière, with whom he had been through a number of skirmishes, saw that this was a noble heart of a gentleman, and as they had both had their doublets freshly slashed, they christened their fraternity with their blood and were tended together in the same bed in the tent of their master, the Duke.

Here it should be noted that, exceptional to the usual run of that family, who were all comely, the younger de Maillé was far from handsome. Indeed, almost the only good points he had were Satanic ones, though otherwise he was as lissom as a greyhound, broad-shouldered and of athletic build, just like King Pepin, who was a terrible man at joustings. In distinction from him, young Lord de Chateau-Lavallière was one of those dainty young fellows for whom fine lace and fine hose and slashed shoes seem to have been invented. His long flaxen locks were as lovely as any lady's coiffure and he was, in a word, one of those pets with whom the ladies would gladly play. Hence it was that the consort of the Crown Prince of France, who was a niece of the Pope's, remarked one day laughingly to the Queen of Navarre, knowing that she rather fancied such drolleries, 'that page would make a fine cure-all plaster, wouldn't he?' which made the pretty little Tourainian flush scarlet, since, being under sixteen at the time, he took those coy words all wrong, as a reproach.

When he got back from Italy, the young de Maillé found a marriage slipper all ready for him to slip into. It was an arrangement of his mother's, in the person of Lady Marie d'Annebault, a charming girl, good looking and well furnished with all the necessary, also a fine town house in Barbette Street furnished with Italian furniture and pictures, and besides that, ample estates bringing in a good revenue. Now, some days after the demise of King François, a disaster which implanted much trepidation deep down in the ladies of his Court, seeing that the poor sovereign had died of the Neapolitan Pox, so that from now on there was going to be no security even with the most elevated dames of the peerage, de Maillé was obliged to leave Court and go to Piedmont to settle certain matters of profound importance. You may be sure that he much disliked having to leave behind this nice wife whom he had just acquired, who was so tender of years, so enticing, so frisky too, but whom now he would have to leave beset by all the dangers and solicitations, the ambushes and the surprises of the band of Court gallants, which did include many fine young fellows, all bold as eagles, proud of glance and as amorous for the ladies as any man for a slice of ham on Easter morning.

Because of such a high level of rivalry to leave behind him, the world turned black to de Maillé, and after thinking it over he at the last moment came to the conclusion that he had better padlock his wife as I shall now relate. The day before he was due to set out, he sent for his brother-in-arms, and on that grim morning, as soon as at last he heard de Lavallière's horse in his courtyard, he leapt out of bed, leaving his sweet, white-skinned better half deep in that luxurious half sleep which all those who greedy of idle delights so much enjoy. In came de Lavallière, and, withdrawing into a window embrasure, the two friends shook each other heartily by the hand. De Lavallière at once said:

'I know I ought to have come last night when I got your message, but it so happened I had a love suit to investigate with my lady-love, she had at last given me a rendezvous and I simply could not miss that, but I left her before it was light. . . . What is it, brother, do you want me to go with you? I told her about your mission, and she made me a promise to be faithful while I am gone. . . . Besides, if she does deceive me, a friend, after all, is worth more than a mistress.'

'Ah, my dear brother,' replied de Maillé, much moved by these words, 'what I mean to ask of you really is a supreme test of your great heart. . . . Will you stay and look after my wife and defend her against everybody, be her guide, keep a tight rein on her and be responsible with your head for her integrity? You shall stay here while I am away. You can have the green room, and be my wife's faithful knight.'

With a frown, de Lavallière said:

'It is not you or your wife or myself that worries me, but only the scoundrels who may take advantage of such a situation to entangle you and me like two skeins of silk. . . .'

'You need have no worries on my account,' said de Maillé, at once, pressing de Lavallière to him. 'If it were God's will to cuckold me, 'twould hurt me less, were you the one to profit thereby. . . . Though, I do swear, I should die of grief, even of that, for I am crazy about my dear, gay, precious wife.'

So saying, he turned his head away, to conceal from de Lavallière the moisture which came to his eyes. But the handsome courtier did not fail to notice that seed of tears, and he squeezed de Maillé's hand in his.

'Brother,' he said, 'on my faith as a man I swear that before any man touches your wife he shall feel my poniard in his belly. . . . And, save my death, when you return you shall find her intact of body, if not of heart, for thought, you know, is beyond the power even of a knight. . . .'

'Then is it decreed in Heaven,' cried de Maillé, 'for me ever to be your devoted servant!'

Thereupon this good fellow took his departure at once, lest he should be too softened by those laments and tears and other solvent sauces which the ladies produce when they bid farewell.

After accompanying de Maillé as far as the city gates, de Lavallière returned to the house, where he waited till Marie d'Annebault rose, to tell her that her husband had gone and place himself at her orders, a duty which he accomplished with such charm of manner that the most virtuous of women would have been tickled by the desire to keep that fine knight at her side. Not that there was however any need for such fine palaver to instruct the lady, since as a matter of fact she had overheard the two friends and been greatly outraged by her husband's mistrust.

Alas, there is no gainsaying it, only God is perfect. In all that any man's mind performs there is always a bad side, and for all its being the great art of life to get hold of the right end of everything, even a stick, it is an impossible art, and the reason for the particularly great difficulty there is in pleasing the ladies is that there is one part of them which is more feminine even than they themselves are. Indeed, were it not for the respect due them, I should use another word for it.

However that may be, we should never awaken the imagination of that naughty part of their nature. In any case, perfect management of womankind is always a task to drive a man crazy. We do far better to stay subject to them, for that, I think, is the best way of solving the most exacting enigma of married life. Therefore, though Marie d'Annebault was delighted with the fine manners and offers of the gallant, there was in her smile a spirit of malice, indeed, to put it bluntly, a real determination to see her protector torn between honour and pleasure, and so solicit his affection, so reward him with kind attentions, so pursue him with glances so warm that to the profit of gallantry he should betray friendship.

Everything indeed conspired towards these cunning services, because of the contiguity into which Lord de Lavallière was brought with Marie by mere reason of living in the same house. And as there is nothing in the world that can thwart the whims of a woman, whatever the situation, that female monkey strove to ensnare him in her love-net. She would keep him at the fireside with her till midnight, singing him songs, and of all manner of subjects, too, and displaying the lovely shoulders and the snowy temptations of which her bodice was full, indeed casting countless scorching glances at him, though of course all without her expression ever revealing her inner thoughts. At other times, she would have him go strolling with her all the morning in the gardens, leaning heavily on his arm, pressing close to him, sighing, having him re-lace for her those boots of hers, which were always coming undone at a particular spot. Or there were all those delightful little speeches and other things which the ladies know so much about, little attentions to the guest, going to see if he was quite comfortable, if his bed was as it should be, if the room was clean, if it was aired enough, making sure at night there were no draughts, or by day that there was not too much sun, begging him not to fail to indicate his slightest desire. She would ask if he were not used to taking a little light refreshment in bed in the morning, or something to drink, perhaps, a glass of mead or of milk—or some dried fruits. And did he find the routine of meals in the household suitably timed?

'I will fit in with whatever you might care for,' she said, 'you only need to tell me. . . . I think you are afraid to ask me. . . . Please don't be hesitant!'

All these fine cossetings she accompanied by endless other sweet little ways, such as when she came into the room where he was, saying: 'If I worry you, please send me away. . . . But of course, you want to be alone. . . . I will withdraw . . .' which always inevitably produced a polite invitation to stay.

Further, the cunning piece was always lightly dressed. Indeed, she revealed sufficient specimens of her beauty to raise a whinny from even a patriarch as dilapidated by the years as Lord Methuselah must have been at one hundred and sixty.

But, being as wily himself as a silken thread, de Maillé's faithful brother-in-arms gave full rein to all the lady's trickeries. He was even somewhat pleased to find her so preoccupied with himself. That seemed so much gained in the matter of keeping others off, though of course, as loyal brother, he constantly endeavoured to keep the absent husband in his hostess's thoughts. One evening, however, after a very sultry day, de Lavallière got quite alarmed at the lady's pranks and felt obliged to tell her how greatly he loved de Maillé. As husband, he said, she had a man of honour, a very noble man, who was passionately fond of her and also very sensitive about excrescences on his crown.

'But if that is so,' she objected, 'why ever did he instal you here?'

'Was that not a lofty prudence?' was de Lavallière's reply. 'Was there not a need to entrust you to somebody who would protect your virtue? Not that a protector is needed, I mean, except to protect you from malicious persons. . . .'

'In other words, you are supposed to be my guardian?' she cried.

'And proud indeed to be it!' cried de Lavallière.

'Upon my word!' she declared, 'it was a very bad choice.'

She accompanied this assertion by a glance of such frank naughtiness that to reprove her the worthy friend assumed a very frigid expression and there and then left her to her own devices. This tacit refusal even to begin the contest of love vexed the lady, and she was most thoughtful for a time, wondering what obstacle it could be that she had come up against, for no lady likes for a moment to think that a handsome knight would scorn the offer of that trifle which is so much prized and worth so much. These reflections of hers now so well knit together and matched up, hooking one into the other, that when she had laid them all out and offered the result up, she found herself genuinely head over heels in love, which should be a lesson to the ladies never to play with a man's weapons, on the principle that he who plays with birdlime gets sticky fingers.

Thus Marie d'Annebault ended up where she should have begun: with the realization that in order thus to escape from her snares the good knight must be caught in those of some other lady, whereupon, making a good search about her to discover where her young guest had found a sheath that suited him, she picked on 'Fair Limeuil' (as she was called), who was one of Queen Catherine's three ladies-in-waiting, for since Ladies de Nevers, d'Estrées and de Giac were all known to be great friends of Lavallière's, it must be one of them that he loved so madly.

This discovery added the reason of jealousy to all those others which had thus prompted Marie d'Annebault to the seduction of her Argus, though of course she had no intention of cutting off his head, all she wanted to do was kiss it and perfume it, without hurting any other appendage. But she was unquestionably younger, prettier, more appetizing and daintier than her rivals. At least, that was the pleasing conclusion to which her mind came. So, ripe in all the chords, heart springs and other physical causes which are femininity's prime movers, she returned to the charge, to assail the knight's heart once again. The ladies particularly like taking a bastion that is well buttressed.

So now she played the demure pussy, snuggling up against him, tickling him so softly, taming him ever so gently, petting him so daintily that one evening when she was in a very black mood indeed (though deep at heart quite cheerful), she actually brought her guardian brother to inquire what ailed her. Dreamily she replied (while he listened as if it were the sweetest of music) that the truth was, she had married de Maillé against her heart's promptings and it really made her very unhappy. She was forced to live in utter ignorance of the sweet things of love, her husband did not understand her, her life was a vale of tears.

In short, Marie now made herself out to be a veritable virgin at heart, indeed, in every sense, since she also declared that the act of love had only brought her unpleasantness, whereas, she went on to say, she was quite sure it ought to be most fecund in sweets and all manner of dainties, seeing that all women ran after it, craved for it, and were jealous about those who did supply it, for some women had to pay a very high price for it. She said she was so curious herself about it that she would give her life and be for ever her lover's servant without a murmur, were it not that the one man with whom it would most please her to engage in the commerce of love refused to understand her, although, so much did her husband trust her, if she and this man did go to bed together, the secret need never come out. She ended up by saying that if he went on refusing her, it would be her death.

Thus were sung all the possible variations of that little canticle which all the ladies are born on their lips with, all interrupted by many silences pregnant with heartfelt sighs, and accompanied by much posturing and crying to heaven, eyes in the air, together with sudden little blushings and hair all awry. . . . In fact, the stew was seasoned with all possible incantations of St John's Day herbs, and as behind all this advocacy there was a penetrating desire such as can make even the ugly handsome, the worthy knight fell at the lady's feet, clutched them, watered them with his tears and covered them with kisses. This dear woman, you may be sure, was delighted to have her feet kissed. Indeed, she did not pay too close a regard at all to what he was at, let him have his way with her gown, for, after all, to raise skirts one does need to take hold of the hem.

Nevertheless, this evening it was written that she should remain good. Full of despair, handsome de Lavallière suddenly cried:

'Ah! dear Lady, what a miserable, unworthy sinner I am!'

'No . . . no . . . go on,' she said.

'Alas, 'tis denied me, the happiness of being yours.'

'How so?' she asked.

'I dare not confess the truth about myself. . . .'

'Is it then so bad . . .?'

'Alas, 'twould bring blushes to your cheeks.'

'But speak up,' she said. 'Look, I will hide my face in my hands!'

And the cunning wench covered her eyes, and so well that she was able to see her dear one quite well between her fingers.

'Alas!' he replied. 'The other evening, when you spoke such kind words to me, I was so traitorously inflamed thereby that, never dreaming my happiness so close, nor daring to confess my fire, I went to one of those houses of pleasure to which noblemen do resort, but there, through my love for you and also to save my brother's honour, whose crown I would be ashamed to sully, I was so nicely caught, that I now stand well to die—of the Italian Pox. . . .'

Marie d'Annebault was most upset. Indeed, she was terrified. She began an outcry like a woman in her labour pains, and though very gently, thrust de Lavallière from her. Poor de Lavallière. Now indeed was he in a lamentable condition. He turned to leave the room.

But he had not yet even reached the tapestries of the door when his lady again took an interest in him, murmuring all the time to herself:

'Oh, the pity of it!'

De Maillé's wife now fell into a great melancholy, muttering to herself her laments on the young nobleman's behalf, but feeling only the more in love with him now that he was thus trebly forbidden fruit.

'Were it not for Maillé,' she even said one evening when she found him more handsome than ever, 'I would gladly catch your complaint so that we might suffer the same trials together.'

'I love you too much,' the brother-in-arms assured her, 'not to behave myself.'

Leaving her now, he went straight to see his fair Limeuil. You may however be sure that, since now he was unable to refuse to receive the burning glances of Marie d'Annebault, there was a fire piled up at meal times and in the evenings which warmed them very greatly, though she was prevented from otherwise touching the knight. Nevertheless, now that she was thus engaged, Marie d'Annebault was better fortified than ever against all the Court gallants, for there are no walls more impassable and no better watch-dogs than love itself. It is like the devil, enveloping its victims with flames.

One evening, however, when de Lavallière had escorted his friend's wife to a dance given by Queen Catherine, he ventured to partner the fair Limeuil, of whom he was indeed most fond, for in those days knights boldly conducted their loves in twos, even in companies. This made all the ladies very jealous of Limeuil, while she was just contemplating favouring handsome de Lavallière with all a man could desire, and before she took part in the quadrille she had given him the sweetest of rendezvous for the following day, during a hunting expedition. Then our great Queen Catherine, who used to foment such love affairs from reasons of high politics, stirring them much as pastry-cooks poke the fires in their ovens, shooting a glance at all the charming couples caught in the toils of her special quadrille of wenches, turned to her husband and said:

'Now, I ask you, while they joust here like this, are they capable of forming leagues against you?'

'Ah, but what about those Protestants?'

'Pooh!' she cried. 'In the end we shall get them too. Why, look, there's de Lavallière. Is he not suspected of being a Hugenot? Yet, as you see, he's quite converted to my darling Limeuil now. She's not doing badly for a maid of sixteen, is she? He'll soon have her on his list.'

'Oh no, Madame, he won't,' interrupted Marie d'Annebault.

'Don't you believe a word of it, de Lavallière has caught the same disease that made you Queen.'

At that fine piece of naïvety, Catherine, pretty Diane and the King, who were all in the group, choked with laughter, and the story swiftly went the rounds, exposing de Lavallière to shame and endless jibes. The poor fellow now had so many fingers of scorn pointed at him that he would have given anything to be in somebody else's shoes, for Limeuil, whom de Lavallière's rivals had lost no time acquainting—laughing, of course—with the danger in which she stood, at once started back from her lover, so great was the effusion and so grave the fears of that nasty complaint.

Thus, de Lavallière found himself abandoned all round like any leper. The King said something extremely unpleasant to him, and the good knight left the party, followed by poor Marie, who was most disturbed at all that had been said, for she saw that she had now utterly ruined the man she loved. She had demolished his honour and damaged his career, for all physicians and surgeons declared it unquestionable that men Italianized by that love complaint were sure to be robbed of their best properties by reason of it and lose their generative virtues. Their bones they said, were blackened by it. Hence from this time on there was no woman who would allow the finest lord in the whole land to marry her, were he merely suspected of being one of those whom François Master Rabelais called his 'priceless scabby-wags'.

As the good knight was now very silent and melancholic, when they got back from Hercules House, where the party was being held, his companion said:

'My dear Lord, I have done you grave harm!'

'Oh, My Lady,' replied de Lavallière, 'my harm is indeed reparable. But what about your plight too? You had no reason to know anything about the dangers of loving me!'

'Ah,' she replied, 'then at least I am very sure of always having you as mine, since in reward for this great shame and dishonour I have done you, I should for ever be yours, more than mere hostess and lady, indeed, your servant. So it is my will now to devote myself to you, in order to efface the traces of that shame and cure you by endless care and nursing, and if the gentry of the faculty do still insist that the disease has taken too deep a root and you are doomed to die of it like the late King, I shall demand your company, so I may perish gloriously, by dying of what killed you. In all truth,' she declared, bursting into tears, 'there is no torture that can atone for the harm I have done you.'

These words were accompanied by bitter sobs. Her very virtuous heart failed her and she fell in a true faint. Horrified, de Lavallière took her to him and lay his hand on that heart which beat beneath a breast of incomparable beauty. At the warmth of that beloved hand, the lady recovered her senses for a moment, only to feel such burning delight that she again lost consciousness.

'Alas,' she cried, when she came to again, 'this horrid, superficial caress is from now on to be the only delight for us in our love, yet still it is a thousand points above any of the pleasure poor Maillé thought he rendered me. . . . Let your hand rest there,' she murmured. 'It is indeed on the very core of me and my soul feels it there.'

At this speech, still most piteous in countenance, the knight assured the lady that he for his part felt such delight at that contact that the pangs of his ailment were thereby greatly augmented, and death was preferable to the torture he felt.

'Then let us die!' she said.

But the litter was in the courtyard and as there was no other way of dying, they each went to bed apart, both of them heavy with love, for if de Lavallière had lost his fair Limeuil, Marie d'Annebault had gained delight without parallel. By this unforeseen mishap, however, de Lavallière found himself banned from love and marriage alike. He no longer dared show his face anywhere. He had learned that protecting a lady's part was a costly business. On the other hand, the more honour and virtue he lost, the more pleasure he discovered in his lofty sacrifices to his brotherhood-in-arms. Nevertheless, towards the end of his watch he began to find his duty most arduous, most prickly and insufferable to execute.

Her avowal of love, which she now believed to be shared, together with the wrong she had done her knight, coupled with this discovery of pleasures hitherto unknown, all now lent fair Marie great boldness. Fallen as she was into this platonic manner of loving, slightly alleviated by sundry small licences of conduct which involved no real danger, she passed on to those devilish delights of *goosey-goosey* invented by the court ladies who after the death of King François were afraid of infection, yet wanted to belong to their lovers, and to play his part of guardian to the end de Lavallière was unable to refuse himself those cruel contactual delights.

In this way, one evening after another, this sorrowing Marie held her guest close to her skirts, her hands in his, his eyes feasting her with kisses, his cheek laid softly close to hers. In this virtuous style of love's union, in which the knight was as captive as Satan in a holy-water stoop, she endlessly told de Lavallière about her great love, a love without any limits, seeing that it could fill all the infinity of space with desires unexorcized. All that fire with which the women-folk instil their corporeal love when night has no other illumination but their eyes, she now transferred to the mystical movements of her head, the exultation of her soul and the ecstasies of her heart. And then, quite naturally indeed, with the exquisite delight of two angels, the lovers coupled in spirit alone, jointly intoning those lovely litanies which the lovers of those days used to repeat in honour of love, anthems which the Abbot of Thelema paragraphically rescued from oblivion by having them carved into the walls of his abbey, which, as Master Alcofibras decreed, was situated in our Chinon country, where I myself saw them in the Latin tongue, here to translate them for the profit of Christians.

'Alas!' said Marie d'Annebault, 'you are my strength and my life, my fortune and my treasure.'

'And you,' he replied, 'you, my angel, are a pearl!'

'You, darling, are my seraphim.'

'You—my soul.'

'You, sweet, are my God!'

'You—my evening and my morning star, my honour, beauty and universe!'

'Darling—my great, my divine master!'

'You—my glory, fame, religion!'

'Pet, my charmer, my handsome, brave, noble, dear knight, my defender, my King and my love!'

'You, my fairy, flower of my days, dream of my nights!'

'Sweet dear, my every moment's thought!'

'You, my eyes' delight!'

'Dear heart, you are the voice of my soul!'

'You, light of the day.'

'My own one, you are the strength by which the very night does glow!'

'You are the best-beloved of all women!'

'Most precious, never was man so adored as you!'

'You are my blood, a self better than my own being!'

'Dear sweet, you are my heart and all my light!'

'You—my saint, my only delight!'

'To you, sweetheart, I grant the palms of love, and great though mine may be, your love, I know, is greater still, for you are my only Lord.'

'No, you it is who are the queen of love, my goddess, my Virgin Mary!'

'No, dearest, I am but your servant, your maid, a mere nothing, for you to dispose of as you please!'

E 121

'No, no, 'tis I who am your slave, your faithful page, I whom you may use as a mere breath of air, on whom you may trample as on a mat, my heart to be your throne.'

'But dear love, no, for your heart transfixes me!'

'Your glance consumes me!'

'But dearest, 'tis but by you I see at all!'

'And but by you I feel!'

'If so, then lay your dear hand on my heart, your hand alone, and when my blood assumes the warmth of yours, you will see me grow utterly pale.'

In these struggles their eyes, already so ardent, would flare up anew, and the good knight was not a little guilty for the delight which Marie d'Annebault felt in the hand which he pressed to her heart. And then, as all his strength and all his thought of the matter in question were concentrated in that airy contact it happened that he did indeed grow faint and completely lost consciousness. Their eyes then wept most scalding tears, and they seized each other in hot embrace, as fire seizes hold of buildings. But further than that they did not go, for had not de Lavallière promised to render whole and unblemished to his friend, her body, if not her heart?

When de Maillé announced his return, it was high time, for no virtue could long have withstood that grilling labour and as the licence left to the two lovers diminished, so did the delight they found in their imaginations grow. Now, however, this friend-at-arms at last left Marie d'Annebault and went forth to meet his friend as far as the Bondy country, so de Maillé should pass through the forest there without misfortune, after which, as ancient custom was, the two friends slept together in Bondy town. Here, lying in the same bed, they related, the one the events of his long journey, the other, all the Court gossip, and all the tales of gallantry there had been. De Maillé's first inquiry, of course, was concerning Marie d'Annebault. Solemnly, de Lavallière swore she was intact in that precious part wherein the honour of husbands is lodged, and doting de Maillé was greatly pleased to have that news.

The following day, all three friends were reunited, to the great mortification, however, of Marie, though, with that supreme sense of justice which women do possess, she greeted her husband well, while with one finger and charming sidelong glances she pointed out her heart to de Lavallière, as if to say:

'This belongs to you.'

At dinner, de Lavallière announced that he was now going to the wars. De Maillé was very distressed by this grave decision, and would have accompanied his brother-in-arms, had not de Lavallière categorically refused to permit it.

'Madame,' he said secretly, to Marie d'Annebault, 'I love you indeed more than life, but oh, not more than honour.'

He turned very pale as he said this, and Lady de Maillé too turned white as a sheet when she heard the words, for never in all their games of goosey-goosey had there ever been so much true love as in these words.

De Maillé insisted on accompanying his friend as far as Meaulx. When he got back, he discussed with his wife the unknown reasons and mysterious causes of de Lavallière's hasty departure, when, shrewdly guessing at poor de Lavallière's mortification, tactless Marie cried:

'I know, it is because he has been so greatly put to shame here, for everybody knows that he has the Naples Pox.'

'He?' cried de Maillé, utterly astonished. 'But I saw him when we slept at Bondy, the other evening, and last night again, at Meaulx. He certainly has not got it. He is as healthy and sound as your dear eyes, my sweet.'

Marie d'Annebault there and then burst into tears, marvelling at de Lavallière's great loyalty, at the sublime resignation of his words and at the lofty sufferings his inward passion had endured, and as she too had her secret, deep in her heart, when de Lavallière fell, at Metz, as elsewhere, in his gossipy book Lord Bordeilles de Brantôme has related, she died too.

IX

The Curé of Azay-le-Rideau

In those times priests no longer took a woman as lawful spouse. They had their own worthy concubines, good-looking if possible. This, later, the Councils of the Church prohibited, as we all know, because not to speak of other abstruse points of doctrine, ecclesiastical adjustments and theoretical views too, of which in this matter of high Roman policy there are many, it is indeed not nice for folk's special confidences to be re-told to some woman or other, to laugh at.

The priest of our part of the country who was theologically the last to maintain a wife in his Vicarage was a certain *Curé* of Azay-le-Ridel. This is a pleasant place, later known as Azay-le-Brûlé, now Azay-le-Rideau. The Castle is one of the wonders of Touraine. However, those bygone days when womenfolk did not hate the smell of a priest were not quite so bygone as some might think, for the Paris See was then occupied by Bishop d'Orgement, son of the previous holder of that office, the serious rebellions of the Armagnacs had not ended, and, to be frank, this particular *Curé* did well to have his living then, for he was cast in a magnificent mould, a fine florid fellow, excellently stout, tall too and powerful, one who ate and drank like a man freshly recovered from an illness. For that matter, he was indeed always in a state of recuperation from a delicious ailment which attacked him regularly. Hence, in a later period, had he tried to observe the continence laid down by canon law, he would have been his own executioner. Add that he was a typical Tourainian, *id est*, very dark, and with eyes containing fire enough to light and water to quench any domestic oven which might require kindling or dowsing.

In short, never had Azay had a *Curé* appointed to it like him. He was a handsome *Curé*, a stalwart *Curé*, ever ready with a blessing, ever ready too to whinny, fonder of weddings and christenings than funerals, a great man for a jape, though all piety in church. An all-round man, in short. There is after all many a *Curé* who has been a fine trencherman and known how to cock his elbow. There are others who have done much blessing. There are even some who have whinnied a great deal. But all put together would still hardly come up to the collective value of this *Curé*. All by himself, moreover, he managed all his benedictions, did it cheerfully too, consoling the afflicted, all so well that he could not show his nose out of doors

124

without somebody wishing to take him to their bosom, he was so popular.

He it was who first said in a sermon that Satan was not as black as painted. He it was too who obliged Lady de Candé by changing partridges into fish, by the argument that since the perch in the River Indre were river partridge, consequently the partridges she had in mind were aerial perch. Nor was he ever a man to indulge in shady legal deals under the cloak of morality, and often teasingly said he would rather work himself into a good bed than a bad will, God had all he wanted, he did not need any more. As for the poor and sundry, there was never a one came to his Vicarage to look for wool went away fleeced, for he always had his hand in his pocket. At the sight of so much poverty and infirmity, he always softened (he who was otherwise so firm!), and would lend himself to stop up any wound.

Thus for a long time there were fine tales told about this King of *Curés*. It was for instance he who at the marriage of Lord de Valênes, near Sacché, made everybody laugh so because the bridegroom's mother had meddled a bit in the victuals, the bakings and other preparations, of such abundance, that there was at least more than enough for a town, though it is, to be frank, quite true that folk came to that wedding all the way from Montbazon, Tours, Chinon, Lageais and all distant places and stayed a whole week. Well, when the good *Curé* was once on his way back to the hall full of its gay company, he came upon a little cook's boy who wanted to inform her ladyship that all the raw materials, all the rich ingredients, the juices and the sauces, were now ready for that super-quality *black pudding* which, to regale the bride's parents, she had vowed she would supervise the mixing, stuffing-in and occult manipulation of, this *Curé* of ours gave the little sauce-messer a gentle clout, told him he was far too foul and dirty to be seen by quality folk, and said he would deliver the message for him.

Then what does the old teaser do? He opens the hall door, clenches his left fist to form a sort of sheath and starts daintily poking the middle-finger of his right hand up and down into it, after which, with a sly squint at Lady de Valênes, he called across to her: 'Come on, dear lady, we're all ready!' Those who did not know what it was all about, at once choked with laughter when they saw their hostess leave her place and go to the *Curé*, for of course to her it only meant that black pudding, not at all what the others thought.

But the way this worthy pastor lost his last concubine, now that is a real tale. Those who had the grant of the living would never hear of a successor to the lady, though as a matter of fact, the *Curé* was never short of the necessary household utensil, there was not a woman in the parish but felt it an honour to lend him hers, the more since he was never a man to do any harm to the pot, he always rinsed them out well, the dear fellow.

However, here is the story.

One evening, the good *Curé* came home to supper, his features most downcast, for he had just laid to earth a good old share-cropper, who had died in a strange way which is still frequently the talk of Azay. Seeing her good man only trifling with his food, just as if he had found gall in a fine dish of tripe cooked exactly as he liked it, his good woman said:

'What's the matter, have you been to see the money-lender' (that is, Master Cornelius, see above), 'have two crows crossed your path, or did the dead man turn in his grave, to make you so out of sorts?'

The *Curé* laughed.

'Has somebody bamboozled you?'

The *Curé* guffawed.

'Then what is it?'

'My dear,' he said, 'merely that I am still very cut up about poor old Cochegrue's death. For twenty leagues round here there's not a worthy housewife or a virtuous cuckold whose tongue is not wagging about it at this very moment. . . .'

'But what happened?'

'Listen. Poor old Cochegrue was on his way back from market, where he had sold his wheat and two store pigs. He was riding that pretty little mare of his, and ever since he left Azay she had been coming on heat without his having the least notion of it. So poor Cochegrue just jog-trotted on his way, reckoning up what he had gained, when just where the old Charlemagne Heath road forks off, there was a stallion which Lord de la Carte was pasturing in a paddock, for fine breeding purposes, this being an excellent animal for hunting, as handsome as an Abbot, an upstanding, powerful horse, so fine a horse that the Lord Admiral has even been out to take a look at it and said it was an upstanding beast indeed—well, this damned stallion smelled the pretty mare. And wasn't he cunning. Not a whinny, nor any other equine euphemism! But when she comes along the road, up he leaps over forty rods of vines and thunders along on his four iron-shod hooves to come down on that little mare trumpeting now like any other amorous gentleman starved of accouplements, snorting trumpetings fit to make the boldest man piss sour, whinnies so loud too that folk heard them as far off as Champy and were scared stiff.

'With his heart in his mouth, old Cochegrue headed across that heath, spurring on his love-sick mare, trusting in her speed, and now, what's more, the good mare heard that stallion, she was all obedience and flew like a bird. But that big lusty clung to them, only a bow's shot off, clattering down the road like a dozen smiths at their anvils, all out, hair on end, answered the nimbler tattoo of the mare's wild gallop with a really frightful *clickety-clack, clickety-clack*.

'Feeling death at his heels, all mixed up with the beast's passion, the good farmer spurred his mare hard and the mare raced, till, pale and half-dead, there was Cochegrue, at his big farmyard, only to find the stable door closed. So he yelled to his wife: "Help, help, wife!" running round and round his mare all the time, hoping to avoid that crazy stallion, whose love appendages were bursting with fire. That stallion was furious now, his lust being all the greater for that long chase, but all Cochegrue's womenfolk were terrified and dared not go out to open that stable door, for they were afraid not only of kicks but also of the unorthodox embraces of that well-furnished lover.

'At last, Cochegrue himself dashed at the door and opened it, but when the good little mare slipped into her stable what did that damned stallion do but attack old Cochegrue, it got him hard up against the door jamb, it got a grip on him too, and it gave Cochegrue the goods all right, with two legs a-straddle of him, holding him and crushing him and treading him, and it had time so to pound and mulch at old Cochegrue's mortar that afterwards all they found of the old man was a shapeless mass as hollow as nut mush when the oil's all out. It was pitiable, they say, to see a man thus pounded to death with his shrieks mingling with the awful love-groans of that stallion.'

'Oh, lucky mare!' cried the *Curé*'s lusty wench.

'What's that you say?' came from the astonished *Curé*.

'Of course she was lucky,' said the *Curé*'s concubine. 'You men couldn't even crack a ripe plum.'

'By God we can!' retorted the *Curé*. 'I'm not the man to let that go unanswered!'

And in a rage he tossed her on to the bed and took his tool and worked her so hard that suddenly she split and came all apart and afterwards she died too, no physician or surgeon ever being able to make out how the dissolution of her links took place, so violently were the intermediate hangings and partitionings taken apart.

Yes, you may take it from me, he was a fine figure of a man, a fine *Curé*, indeed, as stated above, and decent folk in those parts, even the women, were all agreed that he had done no wrong whatsoever, but been well within his rights. And hence, quite possibly, substituting a donkey for a stallion, came the expression so much used in those days: *Que l'aze le saille*—Ass cover him! though the actual verb is as a matter of fact much outspoken than I like to use from respect for the ladies.

However, this great and noble *Curé* was not mighty solely in this respect. Prior to this misfortune he brought off a job such that never after dared any thief ask him if he had an angel in his purse, even when a score or more of them together might have attacked him. One evening, while that good wife of his was still in the land of the living, after supper, when he had been enjoying goose and wife, wine and all else heartily, and was sprawling in his arm-chair contemplating the building of a new tithe barn, there came a message from Lord de Sacché, who was on his death bed and anxious to make his peace with the Almighty and receive and do all the little formalities. You know what I mean.

'Lord de Sacché is a good man and a loyal churchman, I'm going,' said the *Curé*, and, running over to the church, he took the silver casket with all the stock of blessed bread wafers, then, not to get his clerk out of bed, rang the bell himself, and finally in good humour made off across country at top speed, walking. Near Guedroit, which is a beck that discharges into the Indre, on the far side of some meadowland, what did he see but a malandrin.

And what is a malandrin?

A malandrin is a Clerk of St Nicholas.

And what, pray, might that be?

Well, say: a Clerk of St Nicholas is one who sees in the pitch dark. He studies by pressing and turning purses and he usually makes the grade right to the top of the gibbet, before he falls short.

Now do you get it?

Well, as I was saying, there was a malandrin lying in wait for that silver box, which he knew to be of great value.

'Oho!' muttered the *Curé*, depositing the ciborium on a stone at the corner of the bridge. 'Now you bide there till I want you,' he said to it, and he continued straight on towards that thief, when suddenly he made a neat crook to trip the fellow, snatched his iron-shod stick out of his hands, and when the villain scrambled to his feet to tackle him, at his leisure landed him a master thrust straight in his belly appurtenances.

This accomplished, he took up his viaticum again, with the remark:

'Hm, my dear wafers! Had I trusted to your Providence, we would all have been sunk!'

However, uttering such impiety out on the Sacché turnpike was indeed to cock a snook in the dark, since the person he was really

addressing was not God, but the Archbishop of Tours, who had just had him on the carpet and threatened to excommunicate him, admonishing him in Chapter Assembly for having told certain slack parishioners from the pulpit that harvests did not come by God's grace but hard labour and toil, a statement which came near bringing him to the stake. And it was indeed very wrong of him, for the fruits of the earth all need each other. But the *Curé* of Azay died in this heresy for he never would get it into his head that, if it should please God, man could harvest without using the mattock, though scientists have proved such doctrinal interpretation to be true enough, merely by their proofs that wheat used to grow before there were men to harvest it.

I am not going to leave this fine model of a pastor without the addition of an incident in his life which does go to show with what fervour he imitated the saints in the distribution of the goods and mantles which they used to give to the poor and vagrant. One day he was on his way from Tours, where he had been to pay his routine respects to the Bishop, and was nearing Azay, mounted on his mule, when, a step the far side of Ballan, he came upon a girl on the road, making her way on foot. Mortified to see a woman travelling like any dog, the more so since she was clearly tired and sick of heaving her backside along, he whistled softly, whereupon the fair maid turned her head, then paused.

The good priest, a past master at not scaring shy birds, particularly feminine, now suggested with such kindness and so nicely that she should ride on the mule's cruppers that the lass did clamber up, though not without previously making certain fussy conditions, as the sex all do when invited, for instance, to take their place at table or to take anything they want. But once the ewe-lamb had come to an understanding with the good shepherd, the mule plodded on its mulish way with them both, till after a time the lass began to slip first this way, then that, fidgeting so badly in fact that the *Curé* had to reprove her after they had got through Ballan. She really had better hold on to him, he said, whereupon, despite her great timidity, the fair maid at once laced her plump arms about her horseman's breast-plate.

'There!' said the *Curé*. 'Better? Do you bump about now?'

'Oh no,' said the girl, 'I am a lot better now. And you?'

'Yes,' said the priest, 'I'm better too.'

It was true, he was comfortable, soon delightfully warmed in the back by two tangential somethings which rubbed into him till it seemed they were trying to stamp their circular form into his shoulder-blades, which would have been a pity, since that is not the place for such fine white goods. Gradually, however, the mule's motion began to bring the inner warmth of these two fine riders into conjunction and this somehow speeded up the circulation of their blood flow, for the vibration of the mule's motion coincided with their own, so that in the end, though neither knew the mule's thoughts, both lusty lass and *Curé* realized what the other was thinking. Finally, when both got used to that conjunctivity, he to her and she to him, they experienced an inner commotion which came out finally in secret longings.

'I say,' said the *Curé*, turning a moment to his companion, 'now that's a nice thick little patch of wood, isn't it?'

'Too near the road,' said the girl. 'Wood thieves will lop branches. The cattle will eat the young saplings, too.'

'And you're not married?' said the *Curé*, putting the mule at a trot again.

'No,' she said, 'I'm not.'

'Not at all?'

'No, I should think not.'

'Now, that's a shame, at your age . . .'

'Of course, Reverend Sir,' she said, 'it's a shame, but, you see, I have to be careful, if a poor girl makes a baby, she is pretty poor cattle.'

Whereupon, being sorry for such ignorance, and knowing that among other things canon law lays down that pastors should always instruct their ewe lambs and remind them of their duties and responsibilities in this life, the good *Curé* thought he was merely performing his duties by teaching this maid what burden she would some day have to bear. Then gently, so she should not be scary, he popped the question and asked whether she would not trust in his loyalty, saying that nobody would ever know a thing about the trial marriage which he suggested she should make without delay, and as the girl herself had been thinking of this ever since they left Ballan and her desire had been carefully maintained and augmented by the warm motion of the beast, she answered him firmly and said:

'If you talk like that, I'm getting off.'

So the good *Curé* persisted with his gentle pleas, and so well that when they got to Azay Woods, the girl did want to get down and the priest moreover helped her to do so, since to finish this discussion one had to be mounted differently from this mule-riding. Then, to escape the *Curé*, the virtuous girl slipped away into the thickest part of the wood, crying:

'Oh, you naughty man, you won't be able to find me here.'

When the mule reached a clearing where there was a nice patch of grass, the girl stumbled over a root and blushed. The *Curé* at once went to her, and then, already having rung the bells for mass, he went right through the service, and the two together drew a good advance on the delights of Paradise. The good priest's heart really was in it, he instructed her thoroughly and he found his pupil most willing, as sweet of temper as she was of flesh, a real gem, indeed, so that he was most contrite at having curtailed the course so much by only giving her the first lecture too near to Azay, and he would much have liked to repeat the lesson, as all scholarly folk do, for they often tell their pupils the same thing twice.

'Oh, my pet,' cried the dear fellow, 'now why ever did you shilly-shally so long, so that we have come to understanding only here, on the doorstep of Azay?'

'Oh,' she said, 'but I don't live at Azay, I belong to Ballan.'

To cut a long story short, let me tell you that when this good man died there were many people in his parish, children and others, who came most grieved, most upset, weeping, heart-broken to the funeral, and the common lament was:

'Alas, our dear father, now we have lost you!'

And the lasses and widows and the married women and even the little hussies all exchanged glances and lamented him more than any friend and said in concert:

'He was more than a priest, he was a man! And despite all their seminaries, the seed of such priests has gone with the wind and will never produce again.'

Even the poor found that they were the losers, although he left them his savings, and one old cripple whom he had looked after bellowed to the courtyard:

'And me still alive!' by which he meant to complain that death had not taken him in the Vicar's stead, which made some folk laugh, though that would not have annoyed the ghost of that old *Curé* in the least.

X

Last Word

The fair laundress of Portillon-les-Tours, a droll saying of whose appears elsewhere in this book, was a lass so full of spite that she must have filched that of at least six priests or three other women. Hence she never lacked suitors, and if you had but seen them round her you would have said it was so many insects clustering at evening to get into their hive. An old silk dyer who lived in Montfumier Street, where he had a house of notorious lavishness, was one day on his way back on horseback from his vineyard at la Grenadière on the lovely St-Cyr hillside and just going through Portillon to get to Tours Bridge, when, seeing this pretty washerwoman seated on her threshold (for it was a sultry evening), he was kindled with an unreasoning lust. For some time he had had his mind set on that gay piece, but now he was suddenly determined to make her his wife.

Hence, soon, this girl turned from washerwoman to dyer's wife, becoming a handsome burgess of the city now, with her own laces and fine linen and a wealth of furniture, very content, indeed, despite the dyer, since she was well up to pulling the wool over his eyes.

Now, this worthy dyer had a friend who made silk-worker's machinery, a man short of stature, a hunchback for life, and malice through and through. Indeed, what did he say to the dyer on the wedding day but:

"'Twas a good idea of yours, old friend, to marry, now you and I between us have got a nice little wifey. . . .'

To this he added a good number of other spicy remarks, such as it is usual to fire at the newly married.

Moreover, this hunchback did indeed pay court to the dyer's wife, but she, by temperament being no lover of the mis-shapen male, merely laughed at his importunities, teasing him endlessly about his springs and other contraptions, all the bobbins and spindles that she declared his shop to be full of.

However, this great urge of the hunchback's refused to take *no* for an answer, and became so onerous to the dyer's wife that at last she made up her mind to cure the man by a number of shabby tricks. One evening, when he had made many attempts, she told her admirer to come round later to the side door of the house. Towards midnight, she said, all the openings would be flung wide for him. Now this, bear in mind, was in mid-winter, and Montfumier Street abutted on the Loire, and down that street like a funnel even in summer there was a frightful draught, like a hundred needles.

Well wrapped in his cloak, however, the hunchback of course turned up, and began to tramp up and down to keep warm while he awaited his time. Just when he was already half-frozen, stiff, towards midnight, and, furious as thirty-two imps of Satan caught in a priest's stole, was about to abandon this promised fortune, he saw a faint light pass the windows and make its way downstairs to the side door.

'Ah, 'tis she!' he murmured, and his hopes warmed again.

Pressing close to that door, he heard a faint voice.

Yes, it was the dyer's wife.

'Is it you?'

'Yes,' said the hunchback.

'Give a cough, so I know. . . .'

Hunchback coughed.

'It isn't you,' said the voice.

And hunchback cried, quite loudly, too:

'What nonsense, of course it's me. Don't you recognize my voice? Let me in!'

'Alas, you've wakened up my husband,' cried the dyer's wife. 'He came back from Amboise quite unexpectedly this evening. . . .'

Thereupon there was the dyer too! Seeing in the moonlight that there was a man at his door, he tipped a big crock of cold water over the hunchback and yelled: 'Thieves!' at the top of his voice, so that the suitor had no other course but to make his escape. He was so scared, too, that he tripped badly over the chain which barred the end of the street, and fell plump into the stinking ditch which the city magistracy had not yet replaced by a proper culvert to take all the sewerage into the Loire.

The mechanic thought that dip would be his death, and how he cursed fair Tacherette, as this delightful woman was nicely called by the folk of Tours, the reason being that her husband was Tachereau.

Carandas, as the manufacturer of silk spinning, winding and weaving appliances was called, was not quite such a fool as to believe that the dyer's wife was innocent in this, and he swore hell's own hatred of her. But some days later, when he had recovered from his sousing in the dyer's ditch, he came to sup with his friend, and the good wife so well argued the position and put so much honey into her words and so entangled the man in fine promises that his suspicions vanished. He asked for a fresh rendezvous, and with the expression of a woman entirely sold on the idea, Tacherette said:

'Come round tomorrow evening. My husband will be at Chenonceaux for three whole days. The Queen has some old materials to
have dyed and wants to talk over the colours with him, that will be a
lengthy business. . . .'

Carandas decked himself out in his finest and did not fail her.
There he was, at the appointed hour, to find a lovely supper, lampreys and Vouvray wine and well bleached linen, for one certainly
could not reproach the dyer's wife on the colour of her laundry, and
all so well set out that it was a pleasure to see such clean pewter and
smell such a goodly odour of dishes with countless nameless delights
to marvel at, and Tacherette herself in the middle of the room, all
frisky and hot, appetizing as a juicy apple on a sultry day. Indeed, being over-heated by these ardent prospects, the mechanic would now
have started things off at once and leapt on the dyer's spouse, when—
there was Master Tachereau himself, hammering on the street door!

'Oh dear, oh dear!' cried the lass of Portillon. 'Whatever can have
happened? Here, quick, into this chest! I've already had one row on
your account. If my husband found you here now, for two pins he
would kill you, such a violent man is he when he is in a rage.'

In a jiffy she had the hunchback in the said linen chest, then, taking
the key of it, she scurried off to meet her good husband, whom she
had been expecting back from Chenonceaux for supper. There followed a warm kissing of the dyer on both eyes and both ears, while
he, for his part also greeted his dear wife with good smacking nursey-
nursey which resounded far and wide. And then, all jokes, the couple
sat down to table, to end up in bed, and the mechanic heard it all,
forced himself into an erect posture, but unable to cough at all or
make any movement. There he was crushed in among the sheets, like
a sardine in a vat, with no more air than a barbot has sun in the mud
on the river's bottom. No, all he had was the music of love-making to
divert him, with the dyer all sighs and Tacherette all babble. At last,
however, when he thought his great friend was asleep, the desperate
hunchback pretended to be trying to unlock the chest.

'Who's that?' cried the dyer.

'What's taken you, darling?' said his wife, sticking her nose up
above the counterpane.

'I hear scratching,' said the good husband.

'Then we shall have rain tomorrow. It's the cat,' said his wife.

After another little bout of fondling his wife, at last the worthy
husband replaced his head on the pillow.

'Oh, you darling boy,' said she, 'how lightly you do sleep, it's no
use thinking of trying to make a real proper hubby of you. Come
now, do be a good boy. Oh! Oh! Look daddy, your night-cap's on

crooked! Fi! Do put it straight, you cocky darling, you must look your best, you know, even asleep. There, comfy now?'

'Comfy,' he murmured.

'Hushabye!' she whispered, giving him a kiss.

'Hushabye!' he murmured.

When morning came, the fair dyer's wife tiptoed to let the mechanic out. He was paler than a corpse.

'Air, air!' he gasped, and vanished from that house at once, cured of his passion, but bearing away with him as much hatred at heart as a man's pocket could hold black corn.

After this, the hunchback left Tours and moved to Bruges, where some business folk had already been inviting him to set up machinery for making mail tunics. During his long absence in that alien country Carandas, who had Moorish blood in his veins, being descended from an ancient Saracen left half-dead in the great battle between the Moors and the French at Ballan (the Ballan of the preceding tale), where stretch the so-called Charlemagne Heathlands, and nothing grows, all because scoundrels with a curse on them were buried there, and the grass even confounds cattle—Carandas, that is, never once rose from bed or lay down at night without feeding that longing of his for vengeance, and persistently cogitated nothing less than the sudden demise of that good laundress of Portillon. Many was the time he cried:

'I'll eat her very flesh, by gum, I will! I'll have one of her titties boiled, I will, and I'll chew it up, even without any sauce!'

It was unquestionably a genuine, scarlet, dyed-in-the-wool hatred, a cardinal hatred, a waspish hatred, too, the hatred of an old maid. Why, it was all known hates fused into one single hate which was for ever simmering and compounding and transmuting into a very elixir of gallish hate, of diabolical desires all hot from the most glowing of Hell's braziers. In short, it was a mistress hatred.

Now, one fine day this fellow Carandas came back to Tours, bringing with him a fine sum of money from the Flanders country, where he had done good business with his mechanical secrets. He now bought a fine house in Montfumier Street, a house which is standing to this day and is the marvel of passers-by by reason of the really charming hemispherical bosses worked into the stones of its walls.

Back in Tours, hate-mechanic Carandas found very obvious changes in his friend the dyer, for the dear man now had two handsome children, who somehow did not seem a bit like either the mother or the father. However, since children must of necessity resemble somebody, there are always smart fellows who can discern traits of their forbears in them, if they are handsome, the little flatterers. Thus this good husband found his two lads were the very spit of an uncle of his, formerly priest of Notre Dame de l'Egrignolles, though there were other mocking folk who found the two imps the very picture of another charming tonsured head, the one who conducted the services at Notre Dame la Riche, a notorious little parish situated between Tours and Plessis.

Now, there is one thing you may take from me, and get it well into your heads too, and if from this book you do no more than crop, imbibe, extract and exhaust that most reliable principle you may consider yourselves lucky, namely: no man can manage without a nose. In other words, man will always be a snotty brute, that is, he will always be a man, and so throughout all the centuries to come will continue to laugh and to drink and to line his shirt without that making him either better or worse and will always have the same preoccupations, these preparatory digressive considerations being merely in order the better to get into your pates that this two-legged soul, man, will always believe to be true those things which titillate his passions, flatter his hatreds and serve his love affairs. Whence came logic.

Therefore, from the very first day that Carandas set eyes on those offspring of his friend's or the gentle priest's, on the fair dyer's wife, and on Tachereau himself, all together at table, to his own detriment moreover, saw the best slice of the lamprey served by Tacherette with a certain air to that priest friend, the engineer said to himself:

'My good friend's a cuckold, that's what his missus sleeps with, that little confessor! Those kids were made with holy water! And I'm going to show them all that hunchbacks have got a little something in the upper storey that ordinary men have not.'

And that is true, as it is true that Tours is a town that always has had its feet in the Loire, like a pretty girl paddling and playing with the water, splashing it merrily with her white hands too, for this is a laughing, teasing, amorous, frisky, flowering town, a town sweeter-scented than any other in the world. Why, there is not one that's even worthy of combing her hair or fastening her belt. And, let me tell you, if you go there you will find her fent by a lovely gulf which forms a street to delight you indeed, a street down which every man takes a stroll from time to time, a street where there is always fresh air and shade and sunlight, rain and love. Ahah! well you may smile, you just go and see, for it is a street that is ever new, ever regal, ever imperial, a patriotic street indeed, a street with two sidewalks, a street open at both ends, a street well pierced indeed, a street so broad that nobody in it ever had to cry 'Look out!', a street which never wears out, a street which leads to Grand-Mont Abbey and to a channel which slips neatly under a bridge, at the end of which is a fine fair ground. Yes, a street that's well paved, well constructed, well washed, clean as a mirror, a populous street, though it has its hours of silence, a coquette of a street, its pretty blue roofs forming a lovely night-cap. In short, it is the street in which I was born, the Queen of streets, for ever betwixt earth and heaven, a street with a fountain, a street lacking nothing to be celebrated among streets. And in truth it is the true real street, the only street that counts in Tours. There are of course others, but those are dun streets, tortuous streets, narrow and damp streets, and they all lead humbly to salutation of this noble one which dominates them all.

Where now *was* I—for, once in this street, nobody ever wants to leave it, so delightful is it! But I did owe it this filial homage, this descriptive hymn, a hymn sprung from my heart, a hymn to my native street, at the corners of which all that lacks are the brave countenances of my good Master Rabelais and Lord Descartes, unknown though they be to the natives there.

Well, getting back thus from Flanders, this fellow Carandas was fêted by his good friend and by all those who liked him for his jokes, his drolleries and the witty things he said. The good hunchback seemed to have got free now from his former love. He was most friendly to Tacherette and to the priest, and hugged the children, and when he found himself alone with the dyer's wife he even recalled that night in the chest and the night in the midden, and laughed:

'Oh, how you did use to tease me!'

'And how you deserved it,' she replied, with a laugh. 'Had you in your great love but let yourself be diddled and tricked and mocked just a little longer, you might easily have put the trimmings on me like all the others did.'

At these words Carandas laughed heartily, though he raged the more. Then, his eye lighting on the very chest in which he had so nearly ended his days, his rage became still hotter, for in the meantime the lovely dyer's wife had become still more beautiful, as do all women who constantly rejuvenate themselves by dipping in the waters of Youth, which are none other than the springs of love.

The mechanic now, with the aim of avenging himself, made a study of the way his friend's cuckolding was arranged, for there are as many ways of this as there are households, and though all love is as much of the same nature everywhere as human beings are like one another, those who analyse the truth of such things have also shown that, to womenfolk's happiness, every particular love-making has its own special physiognomy, and that though there is nothing so much like a man as another man, there is also nothing so different from one man as another one. That is what confounds it all and also explains the endless fancies of women, who are always wanting, with endless pains and endless delights, to get the best out of the men, and more from one than from another. But however is one to raise objection to their experimentations, their ficklenesses and their contradictorinesses? Why, Nature is never at rest, always switching about, turning this way and turning that, so do you then expect a woman to stay put?

Do you know whether ice is really cold? No. Well, nor do you know any more whether cuckoldom is not also a good trick of life's hazards, producing brains that are better stocked and better fashioned than all others. Under Heaven, do look for more than mere gasbaggery.

This will certainly make for an augmentation of the philosophic reputation of this concentric book. Yes, yes, out with you, the man who cries: *This is rat poison!* is more advanced than those who are engaged in baring Nature's bottom, for she's a proud harlot, a very whimsical one too, not always ready to let you see. Do realize that this is why in all tongues she is of feminine gender, as an entity essentially mobile, fecund and full of sly tricks.

So Carandas soon recognized that of all cuckoldings the best designed and most discreet is ecclesiastical cuckoldry. Here in fact is how the worthy dyer's wife had arranged her affairs. On Saturday evenings she always went out to her Grenadière-les-St-Cyr country cottage, leaving her good husband to wind up his work, do his accounts, check it all and pay his men. He came to join her the next morning, invariably to find a good dinner awaiting him and his wife in a good temper, and she always had the priest in to dine with them.

The truth was that this damned priest would cross the Loire by boat the evening before, to keep the dyer's wife warm in bed, and calm her fancies, so she might have a good night's rest, a task which young men understand rather well. The good fancy-tamer would, however, go back the next morning, getting there in time for Tachereau to call and persuade him to come out to la Grenadière for a day off, the dyer invariably finding the priest snug between his own sheets. And as the boatman was well paid nobody knew anything about this traffic. The lover never crossed but after dark, and always returned on the Sunday very early.

When Carandas had made quite sure of all the details of this arrangement and the regularity of these gallant doings, he waited till one day the two lovers should come together very hungry one for the other, after some unforeseen fast. This happened quite soon, and the curious hunchback watched the manoeuvres of the boatman, down by the quay not far from the St Anne Canal, waiting for this priest, who was a fair-headed young fellow, very slight of build and daintily made, just like that gallant and cowardly hero of love so famous now through the poet Ariosto. Then the mechanic went straight to find the old dyer, who still loved his wife and thought he was the only one ever to have dipped into her lovely stoup.

'Ah, good evening, friend,' said Carandas to Tachereau.

Tachereau doffed his cap, and then the mechanic told him all about these secret love feasts, with many a spicy turn of speech to goad the dyer the more. And at last, seeing him ready to murder his wife and the priest, Carandas said:

'My dear neighbour, I have brought back with me from Flanders a poisoned sword, which kills outright any man at merely a scratch. So you would merely need to touch your tart and her paramour and they would be dead.'

'Come on, and we'll find them,' cried the dyer, and the two good tradesmen hurried away to the hunchback's house, to take the sword and scurry through the countryside.

'But shall we catch them in bed?' asked Tachereau.

'You will,' said the hunchback, ragging his friend.

And he was right. The cuckold had not much need to wait, to see the delights of the two lovers, for the pretty wife and her beloved were busy enough with that pretty snare you all know, netting that bird which always slips out, there they were, laughing and trying again and laughing again.

'Oh, darling,' cried Tacherette, clutching him to her as if to imprint him in her very stomach, 'I love you so I could eat you. No, better still, get you into my own skin so you never left me.'

'I'm ready,' replied the priest, 'though I cannot all of me get inside, you must be content with me bit by bit.'

It was at this delightful instant that the husband came in, his sword bared. The fair dyer's wife, who so well knew her husband's face, saw that this was to be the end of her dear love the priest, but suddenly she rushed half-naked at the burgher, her hair wild, lovely with shame, lovelier still with love, and cried:

'Stop, wretch, will you kill the father of your children?'

At these words, dazzled by the paternal majesty of cuckoldom and perhaps also by the flame in the eyes of his wife, the good dyer let the sword slip. It fell on to the foot of the hunchback, who was following close behind him, and so killed him.

This teaches us not to be haters.

Epilogue

Here endeth the First Decade of these Tales, a cheery batch of the works of the droll muse born in an earlier age in our land of Touraine, a muse who is a good lass and knows by heart the following fine saying of her friend Verville, written in his book, *How to Get on*: *One needs but be bold to get favours*.

Alas, you little madcap, lie down again and sleep, you are worn out with running about! Perhaps you have been far beyond the present. So wipe your pretty bare feet, seal your ears and return to your love-making. If, to complete these comic inventions, you dream any more poetry woven of laughter, you should not give ear to the stupid hullabaloo or the insults of those who, hearing this cheerful Gallic linnet's song, may say: 'Oh, that horrid bird!'

Second Decade

Prologue

Certain gentry reproach the author with no more knowledge of our old-time tongue than hares of tying faggots. Formerly such would certainly have been vilified as cannibals, clots, sycophants or even progeny of Gomorrah. But the author is agreed to spare them the bouquets of such out-of-date criticism, confining himself to the hope never to be in their skins, for the shame and scorn of himself that would cause him, for he would esteem himself the lowest muck-raker thus to calumniate a poor book which is not really in the way of any of his fellow-scribblers. Ah, you wretched fellows, pouring down the drain good bile which you might well use on each other.

Further, the author has found consolation for not pleasing every-body by thinking of an old Tourainian of eternal memory so vilified in his time by like scum that his patience was worn out and in one of his prologues he said he had made up his mind he would never write another stroke.

Tempora mutantur, but behaviour remains the same. Not a thing is changed, neither God on high nor mankind down here below. So the author plods on with his labours, smiling to himself and relying on the future to redeem his exacting toil. For it is certainly no light task excogitating one hundred ribald tales, seeing that, after having mopped up the sniping of men boorish and men jealous, he has also had to suffer that of friends, coming to him in most untimely fashion to apostrophize with him:

'Are you mad? Whatever put the idea into your head, man. There isn't a fellow alive today who can put his hand in the bag of his imagination and draw out a hundred tales up to standard. Come, my dear chap, do strip that bombastic label off your bag, you'll never complete the plan!'

Now, these are neither misanthropical nor cannibalistic. About their manners, indeed, I'm saying nothing. But they certainly are very good friends of mine, are some of those brazen enough all my life to make me the dumping-ground for harsh words, words raspy and prickly as curry-combs, all under cover of being ever one's devoted servant, whether with their tuppences or the toe of their boots, amid all life's sore tribulations, finally to reveal their real worth when one is at one's last gasp.

If only they would limit themselves to such sorry courtesies. But oh no! When their glum prognostications turn out all wrong, what do they do but cry, triumphantly:

'I knew they would! Didn't I say so?'

Nevertheless, in order, however intolerable they may be, to do nothing to put them off such fine sentiments, the author hereby bequeaths to these friends of his certain well-ventilated cast-off footgear of his, plus the assurance (just to console them), that the only movable estate he possesses which has not got a bailiff's seizure on it is that contained in the reservoir of his own nature, namely, the convolutions of his grey matter, to wit, seventy fine tales. By God, and what handsome lads of wit they are, well togged out with fine turn of phrase, painstakingly full of events, lavishly dressed with brand-new gags, cut without a faulty thread from the diurnal and nocturnal roll as woven by *homo sapiens* every minute, every hour, every week, month and year of the great ecclesiastical era inaugurated at that time when the sun could not see its own nose and the moon was still waiting to be shown the way.

These seventy plots (which he gives you full licence to dub bad plots), all tricks and outrage, both lusty and lustful, mocking and jockeying, piebald and ribald, when joined to the two sets of ten recently given to the light of day are, I swear, by the Prophet's Belly, at least a goodish dollop on account of the aforementioned hundred. And were it not a bad time for Bibliophiles, bibliomaniacs, bibliopolists, bibliographers and bibliotecas, which all keeps bibliophagy in check, he would have gushed them full bore out, rather than dribble them in thin trickle as if the kidneys of his brain were blocked. But, *per Braguettam*, of this infirmity he is hardly to be suspected, seeing that he often gives good weight, stuffing more than one tale into a single item, as several in this set show. Further take account that to give good measure he has selected the best and most rascally of them all, so as not to be charged with senile *impotentia*. Come then, a little more friendliness, if you please, in your hatreds, a little less hatred in your friendships.

Now, leaving aside the miserly parsimony of Nature regarding tale-tellers, by which not more than seven in all the seven seas of human scribbling are perfect, there are yet other persons, these too being friends, of the opinion that in an age in which everybody goes about in black as if mourning something, one should concoct only tediously solemn and solemnly tedious works, that from now on your Author can only live by walling his soul up in vast edifices, so that those unable to build cathedrals and vast country houses solid of cement and stone are doomed to die as unknown as the Pope's slippers.

These friends were asked to say which they preferred, a pint of good wine or a barrel of watery wallop, Rabelais's account of how Hans Carvel stuck his finger in a ring or one of our miserable present-day schoolboy stories. And when this plain question left them utterly dumbfounded, it was intimated to them, without a trace of spite, that they might look after their own cabbage patches.

For all other folk one should however add this: The good fellow to whom they are indebted for these fables and yarns of undying authority has merely put his tool to them. The substance he got from others.

Nevertheless, the workmanship lavished on these little sketches has invested them with great value, and although, like good Signor Ariosto, he has been vituperated for giving his mind to such japes and jibes, there are some little beasties of his engraving which have since turned into a far less ephemeral monument than the most solid of masonry. In the special branch of law which covers Bright Erudition the rule regarding precedent is that the merest fragment drawn from the maw of Nature and Truth is more prized than all those tepid volumes which, for all their well-grooming, can never give rise to either a laugh or a tear.

This the Author has the right to say without any incongruity, seeing that he has no intention of straining his insteps to make himself out taller than he is. But, since this concerns the majesty of art, not of himself (poor pen-scratcher whose sole merit is to have a potful of ink), do give an ear to the court bigwigs and inscribe in the record what each of them says. His is the workmanship, Nature's the rest, seeing that from the Venus of Master Phidias the Athenian to that good little fellow Godenot yclept Breloque, Bart., intriguingly drawn by one of the most famous authors of our age, everything has been taken from the unchanging mould of human imitations, at everybody's disposal.

In this fine trade, thieves are in clover, not hanged, but prized and honoured. But he would be a triple boob, what one might call a ten-point boob, who strutted, boasted or vaunted his feathers because of any advantage due to chance concatenation, for real triumph depends solely on the cultivation of one's faculties plus patience and pluck.

As for those mellifluous, sweet-billed little voices which so daintily tickle the Author's ear, murmuring into it complaint of having caught their coiffures or ruined their petticoats in certain places, to them he says: 'What did you dabble in it for?' Regarding which the mischievous insinuations of some persons constrain him to add a declaration, addressed to kindly souls, so these may use it to block the slanders of the Author launched by the aforementioned cacographers.

Everything goes to show that these pithy Tales were written in the days when Queen Catherine of the House of Medici was abroad. Hers was a good period of monarchical dominance, seeing that she always took an interest in public affairs to the advantage of our holy religion. Which period took many by the throat, from the late good Master François, the first of that name, to the Assembly of Blois at which de Guise met his end. Now, every marble-playing schoolboy knows that in that age of soldier princes, when there was much disorder and much peace-making, the French language too was rather turgid, by reason of the private inventions of each and every poet who in those days, just like today, used each to make their own language, apart from all the outlandish words, Greek, Latin, Italian, German and Swiss, with words from oversea and Spanish slang brought in by foreigners, so that your poor scriptophile has ample elbow-room in that Babel of a tongue, come since into the hands of Balzac, Blaise Pascal, Furetière, Ménage, Saint-Evremond, Malherbe and others, who were the first to spring-clean the French tongue, putting foreign words to shame, but giving the freedom of the city to legitimate vocables, words in good usage, words we all know, but of which Milord Ronsard was ashamed.

Thus *explicit*, the Author returns to his lady, and wishes those who like him all the delights in the world, and those who don't—some of those cast-iron black walnuts. When the swallows leave, he will be back again, not without the third and fourth decades which he hereby promises to all Pantagruelians, all good dainty high-cockalorums in all their variety who are not amused by choleographers' gloomy, moony moanings.

I

The Three Students of St Nicholas's

The best food in Tours was to be had at the Three Barbels, seeing that the man who kept this hotel was recognized to be a tip-top cook and used to do wedding breakfasts as far out as Châtellerault, Loches, Vendôme and Blois. This worthy fellow was a cunning hand if ever there was one, perfect at his trade, but he was also a canny man, who never set match to wick while there was any daylight left. He was capable of skinning a flint, he made you pay for beak and bristle as well as meat, and had an eye for everything. Nobody ever sold him a pup, he was ready to tell any man who was a penny short where he got off, even were it a prince.

Such little ways apart, this landlord was a jolly host, a great man for a joke, cocking his elbow too with the best. This all kept him cap in hand with any customer furnished with ample indulgences, claiming *sit nomen domini benedictum* as he led customers into expense, while if needs be always ready with the right word to prove why the wine was dear, and whatever anybody called, he had to take and fork out to the full, since, as he said, nothing was given away *gratis* in Touraine.

In a word, could mine host but have done so without losing face, he would have totted up the good air and the view too on the bill. Thus he built up a good business with other men's money, became well larded, as rotund as a quarter-cask, and 'mistered' too by all and sundry.

Now, when last year's fair came round, three scholarly pupils of the church apprenticed to roguery, with more the making of thieves than saints in them, and already well informed as to how far one could go without getting caught up by levitational exercises on a length of hempen rope, made up their minds they would have a good time and live entirely at the expense of traders at the fair or any other simpleton.

To this end these pupils of Satan had slipped away from their tutors (under whom they were studying gibberish in the city of Angiers), and their first step was to put up at the Three Barbels, where they requested the suite usually reserved for the papal legate. They then proceeded to turn everything upside down. Making themselves out to be fastidious, they earmarked all the lampreys in the market, giving themselves out to be traders in a big way who never carried samples, their presence being enough.

So mine host stirs his stumps, and turns his spits, drawing the best wine and preparing a regular lawyers' feast for these three pernickety fellows, who made a good hundred crowns' worth of fuss, though even under duress they would not have forked out a single crown's worth of the local coppers which one of them kept jingling in his purse. But though lacking the cash, they had wit enough and shared out the parts each was to play as well as any regular thieves at that fair. The piece they put on, moreover, was full of eating and drinking, and in five days they attacked mine host's board so extensively and so intensively too that a troop of German soldiery would have tucked down less than they guzzled.

Well soaked with wine, and gorged like swine, these three wolves in sheep's clothing were off to the fair as soon as they had risen from table, and there with lavish scissors they cut all saps to pieces, filching and pinching, tricking and diddling, switching signs and notices about, so the jeweller turned knick-knacker and the cobbler turned jeweller, throwing sneezing powder into shops, setting the dogs on one another, cutting the horses' hobbles, throwing cats into the crowds, suddenly yelling *stop thief!* or perhaps going up to a stranger and saying gravely: 'Am I addressing Mr Uparse of Angiers?' They jostled folk, they made holes in sacks of wheat, they fumbled in ladies' bags for their handkerchiefs, or, with much lamentation on hands and knees looking for some lost treasure, they plucked up ladies' skirts.

'Pardon me, ma'am,' they cried, 'it must've fallen into a little 'ole.'

They set children astray, they crept up behind gapers and gave them a sudden slap on the belly, in short, they went roistering about, mucking up everything. Indeed, Satan himself would have been a gentleman compared with these rude damned theological students, who would rather have gone to the gallows than done anything decent. One could as well have expected charity from two madmen suing one another. They quitted that fairground not so much fatigued as fed up with their own ill deeds, returning to the Three Barbels to gorge and booze till nightfall, when they resumed in the torchlight. Finishing with the fair-folk, they tackled the city tarts, finding countless devices to give them no more than they gave, here following Justinian's rule: *Cuicum ius tribuere*, or *juice all round*, then, making mock of the poor wenches afterwards, assured them that the *tort* was theirs, what they themselves had was straight enough.

Finally, supper-time come, having nobody else to nark, they set to work on each other, or they complained about the flies to their host, grumbling that anywhere else the landlord caught the things rather than let men of their condition be annoyed.

However, as the fifth day came round, this being the critical day in all fevers, and the good proprietor so far, for all he kept his eyes wide open, not having seen these clients show the royal features of a single crown, and further, being well aware that if all that glittered were gold, that substance would be a lot cheaper, he began to sniff the air and serve these high-class businessmen rather less willingly. Seeing which, the three students, with all the self-confidence of a provost dispatching his man on the gallows, told him he was to serve them a good supper, as they had to leave at short notice.

Their cheerful faces relieved mine host's suspicions, and, thinking that rogues without any money could not be so cheerful, he prepared a dinner fit for canons. He even rather hoped to see the three get tight, with the idea that if things did turn out badly, he could then more easily clap them into gaol. So, at a loss to know how to make good their escape, being now as much at ease in that Three Barbels' dining-room as fish in straw, the three companions ate on and drank on, measuring up the location of the windows, all on the look out for the moment to cut and run. But they never had a chance.

Cursing the situation now, one tried unbuttoning and going outside to let his trousers down on the grounds of colic. Another requested the landlord to go and find a doctor for the third, who did his best to contrive a fainting fit. But that accursed innkeeper darted to and fro between his roasts and his patrons so nimbly and had such a lively eye on those three clients all the time, with now a pace forward to save his dibs, now two paces back not to be too pressing, in case they were real gentlemen—in short, conducting himself like a good cautious innkeeper, fond of his pence but chary of blows, he managed both to pretend to be zealously waiting on them and to keep one ear on the dining-room and one foot in the yard, instead of the bill always presenting his own mug, with:

'Yes, gentlemen, what be your pleasure, gentlemen?'

To this inquiry they would gladly have stuck ten inches of his skewers down his throat, since he looked as if he knew very well what their real pleasure now was, for each would have sold a third share in life eternal to have twenty unclipped crowns. Take it that their benches might have been hot grills, their feet itching frightfully, their backsides so burning.

Mine host had already placed pears, cheese and dishes of compote under their noses, but they now sipped very little sips and merely nibbled at their food with many a sidelong glance to see if the others had not thought of a trick.

In short, their enjoyment began to be rather glum. But when they saw that Rabelais's quarter of an hour had come round, the most wily of them, a Burgundian by origin, gave a smile and suddenly said:

'My dear fellows, we shall have to postpone judgement till next week,' just as if he were in the law courts.

Whereupon, despite the danger, the two others burst out laughing.

'How much do we owe you?' then demanded the possessor of the coppers, rattling them in his pocket as if this might make them procreate.

This fellow was from Picardy, a devilish peppery man, one to pick a quarrel over nothing, could he but have pitched the landlord out of his own window with impunity, hence he uttered these words with the rascally air of one with a revenue of ten thousand doubloons per annum—on the moon.

'Six crowns, gentlemen,' replied the landlord, holding out his hand.

'No, no, my dear Count,' cried the third, quickly—a man from Anjou, this, as crafty as a woman in love—'I'm never going to let you take the whole of this on yourself.'

'Nor shall I,' said the Burgundian.

'Gentlemen, gentlemen,' played up the man of Picardy, 'don't be silly, I am at your service.'

'Tarradiddle!' cried the man of Anjou, 'you're never going to let us pay thrice over. . . . Nor would our good landlord hear of it!'

'Right!' cried the Burgundian, 'then let the man who tells the worst tale settle with our host.'

'Ah, but who's to judge?' asked the man of Picardy, and he let his coppers slip back to the bottom of his purse.

'Heavens, why, our landlord. He must be knowledgeable in such matters, seeing he is a man of such good taste,' said he of Anjou. 'Come now, Master Cuisinier, pray seat yourself there, let's fill our glasses! Lend us your ears! The hearing begins.'

Whereupon the landlord did indeed sit down to table with them, but not till he had filled every glass brimful.

'My turn first,' cried the man of Anjou, 'I begin.

'In our Duchy of Anjou,' he said, 'country folk are very loyal servants of our ancient Catholic faith, and not one would lose his place in Heaven, even though it meant doing penance or killing a heretic. What men ours are! If a minister of shilly-shally ever came our way, he was soon pushing daisies, and didn't even know whence came his untimely demise.

'Well, coming back one evening supposedly from vespers, but in fact from tippling toddy at Pomme-de-Pin, a worthy fellow of Jarzé left his wits and recollective faculties behind him in the pub, and eventually fell plump into his own duck pond, thinking it to be his bed. When a neighbour of his named Godenot found him there, he was already frozen into the ice, for it was mid-winter. So Godenot mocked him and asked him what he was waiting for there.

'"The thaw," said the good drunk, realizing now where he was.

'Whereupon Godenot, being a good Christian, prised the fellow out of his mortice and opened his door for him, all out of profound respect for liquor, which is the sovereign lord of those parts. Upon which, the good fellow slipped straight in between his serving-maid's sheets. She was a decent young filly, whose warm furrow the hard-working old boy, thinking he had got in with his wife, began to plough, thereby liberating her from that remnant of maidenhood which she still possessed. But by now the good wife heard him at it and set up a yell so horrible that the ploughman was made to realize that he was not proceeding up the valley of salvation at all, at which discovery he was most mortified.

'"Ah," cried he, "God has certainly punished me for not going to church to vespers." And he proceeded to blame the liquor for having disturbed John Thomas's memory so, and, getting back into bed, assured his wife that he would rather lose his best cow than have this sin on his conscience.

'"It don't matter," his better half told him, the girl having assured her (when given a pretty fierce drubbing for sleeping so soundly), that nothing untoward had happened, she had only been dreaming she was with her boy. But fully aware of the enormity of his crime, the good fellow wet his bed with many winy tears, from fear of the Lord.

'"My dear boy," said his wife, "first thing tomorrow, you go straightaway and confess, and we'll say no more."

'The good man went and most humbly told the rector of his parish all about it. The rector was one of those old fellows who when they get to Heaven deserve being made God's slipper.

'"Mistakes don't count," said he to his penitent, "you do a fast tomorrow, and I will absolve you."

'"Do a fast? With pleasure," said the good man. "Especially as fasting don't cover drinking."

'"Aha!" said the priest, "it does, it's water only you will drink, and eat nought but a quartern loaf of bread and an apple."

'Lacking confidence in his wits now, the good fellow made his way home, repeating the penance ordered him, but for all that he started out loyally with "a quartern loaf of bread and an apple", by the time he got home, he had ended up with "a quarter of apples and a loaf of bread".

'At once, to cleanse his soul, he set to work on his fast, and when his good housewife had taken a loaf from the crock and unloaded all those apples from the shelf, set sadly to work to ply the sword of Cain. When, reaching the last hunk of bread, he heaved a rueful sigh, not knowing where to stow it, seeing he was absolutely brimful, his wife protested that God could not want a sinner's death, for want of failing to put a mere crust of bread in his belly he was not likely to be reproached for having grazed his tool a bit.

'"Silence, woman," said he, "I must do my fast, if I die of it."

'Well, I've paid my share,' said the Anjou fellow, 'your turn next, Count!' and he gave the Picardian a nasty sly look.

'Our pots are empty,' cried their host. 'Hello there, boy, bring some more wine!'

'And let's drink!' cried the Picardian. 'Tongues slip better moistened.'

Thereupon he tipped down a full glass, without leaving a drop, and after a little choirman's cough, told the following tale:

'Well, you know that in their level-headed way our little Picardy hussies, before they set up house, as a rule earn their gowns, their crockery and their linen-chests, in a word, all the gear they need for marriage. To do this they go out to service at Péronne, Abbeville, Amiens and other towns, where they work as chambermaids, washing up, polishing glasses, folding the linen, serving dinner or what have you. And as soon as they have thus acquired a bit more than what they naturally bring their husbands, they marry. They are the best housewives in the world, since they know it all, and very well too.

'Now, a girl from Azonville, where I shall some day inherit the manor, hearing that in Paris people don't even bother to stoop to pick up silver sixpences, and that you can feed for a day merely on the smell of the restaurants, the air round them is so greasy, conceived the notion of going to that city, in the hope of bringing back with her enough to buy up a whole church.

'After much arduous trudging, there she was, complete with empty basket, at Paris. She happened to come upon the St Denis Gate, and there was a gang of stout soldiers stationed there as temporary guard on account of the disorders, seeing those who profess the new reformed religion seemed like starting their preaching again.

'Seeing this bit of goods in a kerchief coming, the Sergeant in command cocked his hat on one side, put hand on hip, rolled his eyes and stopped this Picardy lass, pretending that he had to see that her ears were properly pierced, for he said it was against the regulations for a girl to enter the city without that being done. Then, gravely, by way of humour, he inquired her business, as if she meant to take the keys of Paris by assault. Upon which the little simpleton told him she was only looking for a good place of employment, she had no evil intentions, if only she could find a steady job.

'"You're in luck's way, my dear," said this joker, "I am a Picardy man myself, I'll find you a place at once where you shall be treated as queens often wish they were, and you can earn well."

'He took her to the guard-house and told her to sweep the boards, scour the pots, poke the fire and keep an eye on it all, adding that she could have thirty sous per man if it pleased her to serve them.

'Well, since this squadron was there for a month, this meant that she could earn a good ten crowns, after which, when they went away, she could make a good arrangement with the newcomers, by all of which honest labour she could take a tidy little sum back home from Paris.

'The lass then cleaned the place out and made it all tidy and prepared meals so well, singing and trilling away all the time, so that when they came in the good soldiers found their burrow like a Benedictine refectory. Hence they were all satisfied, and each gave the good servant a sou. Then, when she had supped well herself, they put her in their captain's bed, he being in town with his mistress, and lulled her with countless pretty, philosophical little soldiers' tricks, since soldiers love all that's decent.

'And there she was, well set up, busy between the sheets too. Now, to avoid quarrels and disputes, these hearty lads drew lots to establish a *rota*, after which they queued up in orderly fashion, and without another word set to work, in good steady Picardy fashion, each in turn taking at least twenty-six sous' worth of her time.

'Taking it that this was a rather hard form of domestic service that she had never tried before, the poor girl did her best, consequently never slept a wink all night. The next morning, seeing the soldiers still sound asleep, she got up, much relieved to find there was not a scratch on the tummy which had moved so many heavy burdens, and, though she was somewhat weary, she set straight off across country with her thirty sous.

'Out on the Picardy road, she came upon a friend who, in imitation of her, was also on her way to try domestic service in Paris, and was most excited about it, so halted the first lass to ask what it was like.

'"Oh, Perrine," she said, "don't you go, you need a backside made of iron, and they'd soon wear that out."

'Your turn, you big Burgundian pot-belly,' cried the Picardian, silencing the natural retort of his neighbour with a hearty sergeant's thump. 'Spit out your tale, or pay up!'

'By the Queen of Antlers!' replied the Burgundian, 'on my faith! God's truth! Damn it, but the only tales I know are tales of the Court of Burgundy, which only suit local currency . . .!'

'Hi, God's bones, are we not in Beauffremont country?' cried the other, pointing to the empty pots.

'Well, I will tell you a happening already well known at Dijon, one which took place when I was in command there, and ought at once to have committed to paper. There was a town bailiff named Franc-Taupin, and if ever there was an old bag of nastiness, he was it, always grousing, always squabbling, cold as ice too, to everybody, never a few gay words from him to comfort those he was leading off to the gallows. In short, he was one of those who would find lice on a bald head, hairs in eggs and faults in God himself.

'Well, this fellow Taupin, with whom nobody would have any dealings, at last took on a wife, and it so happened that he got one as gentle as the skin of an onion, a woman who, when she got to know her husband's nasty make-up, spent more trouble ensuring his domestic pleasures than another would to plant horns on his head.

'But though she took care to obey him in everything, and if it made for peace would have done her best, D.V., to excrete gold for him, this wretched fellow was perpetually sour and no more spared the blows than a debtor his promises to pay. This displeasing treatment continuing, despite the care and angelic labours of the poor woman, she was in the end obliged (seeing she was nohow used to this treatment), to take the matter to her relations, who intervened.

'Well, when they came in, the husband told them that this wife he had married had no sense, he was done every disservice by her, she made life very hard for him. She wakened him from his first sleep, when he arrived home she failed to unlock the door, leaving him to soak or freeze outside, and what was worse still, nothing was ever in order. The linen was mouldy, the wine was sour, the firewood was wet, the bed always creaked horribly.

'The wife's answer to this stream of falsehood was to bring out his wardrobe, and everything was indeed in a state of excellent repair. The bailiff insisted that he was very badly treated, his dinner was never ready, or, if it was, there was no yolk in the broth or the soup was cold, or wine was lacking, or there were no glasses, the meat was ungarnished, there were neither sauce nor parsley, the mustard was curdled, there were hairs on the grill, the cloth smelt stale and killed his appetite, in short, she never gave him anything that suited him.

The wife in astonishment merely denied the amazing shortcomings imputed to her.

'"Oh," said he, "you deny it, you dirty slut? Well, good folk, come to dinner yourselves tomorrow, you shall see how she carries on. And if she can serve me once as I want, I will admit I was wrong in all I have said, and shall never raise my hand against her again, she shall have my halberd and my breeches and I shall leave my command to her."

'"Very well," said she, as cheerful as could be, "then I shall at last be a lady, and mistress in my own house, too."

'Now, sure of the imperfections of his wife and trusting too to nature, the husband asked for dinner to be served out in the vine arbour in the courtyard, thinking that out there he could nag her if she was slow trotting to and fro 'twixt sideboard and table. The good woman put her best into it, and prepared wonderful food. The mustard was fresh and well seasoned, and it was a very well put together dinner, piping hot, appetizing as stolen fruit can be, the glasses beautifully polished, the wine chilled, and all so neat, so white, so gleaming that it would have done honour to any Bishop's Margot.

'But, just as she was lingering at the table, giving yet another once-over as good housewives love to do, her husband appeared in the doorway, and at the very same instant an accursed hen which had conceived the idea of getting up on the trellis-work to fill her gizzard with grapes, let an ample turd plump right into the centre of the cloth.

'The poor woman nearly dropped dead on the spot, so desperate was she, but the only way she could think of remedying that hen's lack of restraint was, regardless altogether of the symmetry of her table setting, to cover the incongruous blotch up with a plate, which she filled with some fruit that she had left over. Then, so nobody should notice, she at once brought the soup in, sat the company down, and called on them to have a good time.

'When they all saw this lovely spread of good things, there was a general outcry of admiration from all except this devil of a husband, who lost countenance altogether and sat there scowling, twitching his eyebrows, scanning it all, seeking the excuse to lay into his wife about. At this instant, overjoyed to be able to tackle him under protection of her own folk, she said:

'"There you see! Your meal is piping hot and well served, the linen is white, the cruets are full, the plates quite clean, the wine cool, the bread golden. What's lacking? What more do you ask? What do you want now? Come on, what else?"

'"Oh—shit!" cried he, in sheer rage.

'Swiftly, the good lady shipped away that plate of fruit.

'"There you are, my love," said she.

'Seeing this, the bailiff was thoroughly done, and thought the devil must be siding with his wife. He was of course now sorely reproached by the relatives, who insisted that he was in the wrong and nagged him no end, teasing him more in a minute than your court registrar writes words in a month. From that day on, the bailiff lived in utter peace with his wife, who, at the least quibble or frown, would ask him if he was perhaps looking for a bit of shit.'

'Well, who has told the worst?' cried the man of Anjou, fetching their host a murderous blow on the back.

'He did, he did!' cried the two others.

The three rascals then began to quarrel like holy fathers at a Church Council, even to the point of fisticuffs and throwing glasses at each other, till they were on their feet and were on the point of utilizing the hazards of battle to get outside and skedaddle.

'Here, I'll settle the question,' then cried the landlord, seeing that now, instead of three good-tempered debtors he had three disputants with not a thought of the real telling to be done, and at his outcry, all three halted, aghast, and waited.

'I will tell you a better one,' cried the landlord, 'then you can give me one-third each.'

'Let's hear our landlord!' cried the man of Anjou.

'In our suburb of Notre-Dame la Riche, on which this inn depends, there was once a pretty girl, who in addition to the trump cards given her by Nature, had a nice little nest-egg. So as soon as she was old and strong enough to bear the yoke of matrimony, she had as many suitors as there are sous in St Gatien's money-box on Easter Day. She chose one who, pardon my immodesty, could ply his business as much by day and by night too as any two monks together. So this suitor and the girl agreed and the marriage went forward. But the delights of the first night did not draw near without causing the bride some apprehension, seeing that by reason of some infirmity of her inner pipes she was prone to excogitate humours which emerged from her like so many bombs.

'Now, loath to let her wild windinesses have free vent while her attentions were on something else on this great night, she had put the matter to her mother and asked her assistance. This good lady then told her that the ability thus to engender explosive wind was in the family, she herself had been much hindered in her time by it, but in the autumn of her life God had been gracious to her and had knit her cruppers together more tightly, so that for the past seven years she had formed no vapours, save one last time, when as a sort of farewell, she had aired her now deceased husband.

'"But," said she to her daughter, "I had a sure method which my dear mother passed on to me by which to reduce those unwanted little words to nothing, and breathe them out soundlessly. Now, seeing that such explosive winds do not smell badly, if you can tame them you completely avoid all trouble. To achieve this all you need do is keep the windy matter simmering for a time. You must bung it back at your vent-hole, then later, heave hard, when, being well cooked, the air slips out without a hint of its passage. In our family we used to call it tenderizing our farts."

'The daughter was glad to learn how to tenderize farts, thanked her mother and on her wedding day danced hard, piling the explosive things up at the end of her back-passage like any organ-blower getting ready for the end of mass. At last, come to the nuptial room, she decided to free herself of it all just as she entered the bridal bed, but that funny stuff was now overdone. It was cooked so hard it just would not come out at all.

'In came the husband. I leave to your imagination how they fenced in that pretty way by which, provided of course that one can, one does scores of things with only two implements. Midway through that night, the young wife got up on a little excuse. She lost no time hurrying back, but, as she was climbing into bed, her back-passage suddenly felt its own belching release and effected such a deliverance of its gunpowder that in my place you would have thought she'd split the window curtains.

'"Ho," cried she, "I've missed fire."

'"Damn it," said I to her, "then save your ammunition, lass, with guns like that, you'd make your fortune in the army."

'For that was my wife!'

'Ho, ho, ho!' cried the students, and roared with laughter, holding their sides and praising their landlord.

'I say, Count, did you ever hear a better one?'

'Oh, what a tale, and what a teller, too.'

'Now, that is an account!'

'A master account!'

'The king of accounts!'

'Oh ho! Our good landlord outdoes all accounts, and the only accounts which count now are innkeepers accounts!'

'On my Christian faith, that's the best account I have ever heard in my life!'

'I assure you, I can hear that fart now.'

'What I'd like to do is give the orchestra a kiss.'

'Yes, upon my word, my dear landlord,' said the Anjou fellow, gravely, 'we would not think of leaving now without meeting our hostess, and if we do not ask to be allowed to kiss her trombone, that is only out of respect for one who has given such a good account of it, ha-ha-ha!'

They praised the landlord so highly, both the instrument she performed with, and his account of his wife's fart, that the dithering old landlord was by now quite deceived by their innocent bonhomie and their lavish praise, and he called his wife to come down. But as she did not do so, the students, not of course without strategic intent, declared they would go up and see her.

Whereupon the whole company left the dining-room, and their host took up a candle and led the way up the stairs, to light the way for them and show them the road, but now through the open door they caught a glimpse of the open road and in a jiffy they were away, light as shadows, leaving their good host free to collect another good fart from his wife as his resounding reward.

II

King Francis's Short Commons

Every schoolboy knows how it came about that King Francis, first of that name, was caught like a silly bird and taken to the city of Madrid in Spain. There the Emperor Charles the Fifth held him in strictest captivity in his own castle, as an object of high value, a fact which caused our deceased sovereign lord of imperishable memory much trouble, seeing that, as a great lover of the open air, of creature comforts and of all that, he was no better at cage life than a cat is at sorting lace.

So it was that he fell into such excessive fits of despondency that when his letters were read out in full Council, his mother (the Duchess of Angoulême), Princess Catherine (the Crown Prince's wife), Cardinal Duprat, Count Montmorency and those responsible for the French Realm, all being familiar with the King's particularly high standard of libertinism, after ripe deliberation resolved jointly to send to him Queen Marguerite his sister, from whom he would be bound to obtain some alleviation of his cares, since he had great affection for that lady, who was a very jocund person, well informed too in all things. But when Queen Marguerite declared that this would put her soul in jeopardy, since she could not share the King's imprisonment with him without grave peril to herself, a secretary with gumption (it was Lord de Fizes), was dispatched to the Court of Rome with instructions to obtain from the Pontiff special letters of indulgence, to include valid absolution for any trifling peccadillo into which, by reason of her consanguinity, the said Queen might find herself involved with a view to curing the King's melancholy.

At this time that Dutchman Adrian VII still wore the tiara, though this by no means made that boon companion oblivious of the circumstance that, despite all the scholastic bonds twixt himself and the Emperor, it was still the eldest son of the Catholic Church who was in question. He was therefore gallant enough to send a special Legate to Spain equipped with full powers to see what, without hurting the Almighty too much, he could do to save both the Queen's soul and the King's body.

This highly urgent matter became a real headache to the gentlemen of the French Court, but made the ladies most itchy. Indeed, so devoted were they all to the Crown that there was scarcely one but would have herself offered to go to Madrid, had it not been for the dark suspicions of Charles the Fifth, who refused to let King Francis be seen by any of his subjects, not even his own family.

Thus it became essential to arrange for Queen Marguerite to go there. Hence the sole topic of conversation became this deplorable fast of His Majesty's and how bad the lack of amorous activity was for a prince who was wont normally to spend so much time on it. Indeed, there was such a to-do about it that these ladies ended up by thinking more about the King's codpiece than the King himself. The Queen was the first to say that she wished she had wings, to which Lord Odet de Chatillon replied that she had no need of wings to be an angel. One dear soul—the spouse of the Admiral of France—thought it a sorry thing of God that they could not send to the King by postal messenger what the poor gentleman lacked so badly, for there was not a lady who would not take her turn lending.

'No,' declared the Dauphine very neatly: 'God did very well to rivet that into us, or when they were away on business our husbands would leave us very poorly equipped.'

So much was said, so much thought, that when Marguerite of Navarre did set out, all the good Christian ladies charged her to kiss the prisoner specially in lieu generally of all the fair sex of the Realm, and had it been feasible to stock up pleasure as one does mustard, Queen Marguerite would have been sufficiently condimented to set up shop in both Castiles.

While, with the aid of countless mules, speeding on her consolatory mission as to a house on fire, Marguerite was fighting her way through deep snows over the Pyrenees, the King came to a worse condition of lumbar pressure than he had ever known in his life. In this extremity of natural pulsation, he at last unbosomed himself to Charles the Fifth, in order to obtain a merciful specific for the cause, arguing that it would be to the undying shame of any king if he let another die for want of exercise of the gentle passion.

The Castilian proved most obliging. Reflecting that he might well make use of his Spanish ladies to extract an advance on the King's ransom, he dropped a sly hint to the fellows charged with guarding his prisoner that they had his tacit consent to meet King Francis in this particular matter, whereupon a certain Don Hiios de Laray Lopez Barra di Ponto, an indigent Captain without a penny to his most genealogical name, who had for some time past been cogitating going to the French Court to make his fortune, conceived that if he furnished the gentleman in question with a soft enough dressing of living flesh, a really fruitful opening would be provided, and there was no doubt about it, those who knew that Court and our Good King could have told you whether he was mistaken or not.

When this said Captain's turn came round to keep the King company in his cell, he inquired with all respect if His Majesty would graciously allow him to put a question or two regarding which he was as interested as in papal indulgences. At which the King of France's hypochondria vanished and, fidgeting on his seat, he told the Captain to go ahead.

Well, said the Captain, the King must not take offence at his freedom of speech, but he, the King, should rest under no doubt but that he had the reputation of being one of the greatest wenchers in all France, and what the Captain wanted to know was whether the ladies of King Francis's Court were really experts in love.

Calling to mind successes he had had, the poor King uttered a profound sigh and said that no women, of no matter what country, including the Captain's own, could know the secrets of that alchemy better than the ladies of France. Why, merely at the memory of the savoury caresses, both gracious and vigorous, of one dame in particular, he felt himself man enough, were she served up to him at this moment, to give her a damn good farriering on a rotten plank over a hundred-foot drop.

As he spoke, ribald-minded if he ever was, the good King flashed such fierce flames from his eyes that though a plucky man the Captain felt intimate trepidation of the bowels at so majestic a conflagration of regal love. But, as soon as he recovered, he took up the cudgels for the ladies of Spain, claiming that it was only in Castile that love was really well practised, the reason being that there was more religion in Castile than anywhere else in Christendom and the more the women there feared eternal damnation because of their compliance with a suitor, the more vigorously did they comply, for they were also aware that it depended solely on them to pile up sufficient enjoyment of it for all eternity. To this the Captain added that if His Majesty would promise him one of the better of the regal estates of France, he would furnish him with a nightful of Spanish love in which, unless he took fine care, his temporary Queen would suck his very soul out through his Kingly cudgel.

'Done, done!' cried the King, leaping up from his chair. 'By Heaven! I'll give you Ville-aux-Dames, a manor in my own home county of Touraine, and I'll throw in fullest hunting rights and jurisdiction high and low.'

Thereupon the Captain, who was acquainted with the mistress of the Cardinal Archbishop of Toledo, requested her to flog the King of France to death with her kindness and show him the great superiority of Castilian fantasy over the simpler movements of

French women. To which, for the honour of Spain, the Marchioness
d'Amaesguy duly consented, though she was also motivated by the
pleasure of discovering of what dough God made kings, a matter of
which she was ignorant, for so far she had only had to do with
princes of Holy Church. So in she came, seething with the super-
abundance of a lioness which has broken the bars of her cage. She
made King Francis's bones creak, and the very marrow of him
squeak, with such frenzy indeed that it would have been the death of
any other man. But the said gentleman was so well equipped, also so
ravenous, so well starved, that he did not really feel her biting jaws
at all, and from the frightful duel it was the Marchioness who
emerged limp, convinced she should now confess to having had
commerce with Satan himself.

Confident his ingenuity of choice would do the trick, the Captain
now called on King Francis to pass the time of day and, as he calculated, pay his first homage for his grant of land, but he found King
Francis most scornful, averring that Spanish women were indeed
warm enough and tough enough, the trouble was, they got too fierce
just where there was need to take things steady, while every time
they came to the point, it was just like the violent spasm of a sneeze
or indeed like rape.

In a word, the King said that French unions did not tire, but made
the drinker more thirsty, with the ladies of his Court love was unparalleled dalliance with a sweetmeat, not like a baker's boy punching
a trough of dough.

The poor Captain was much put out by this talk. Despite the fair
name of gentleman to which the King laid claim, it seemed to Don
Hiios that the monarch was merely trying to cheat him, like any
student winning a spot of love gratis in a Paris clap-shop. But since,
at the same time, he did not know positively whether the Marchioness had not punished His Majesty too much, he begged the
Royal prisoner to grant him another round, giving his word that this
time without fail the King would have an indisputable fairy, while
he himself would get his manor.

This request the King was too courteous and gallant a knight not
to grant. He even added a gentle royal observation that he would
gladly lose the bet. So after evensong, in ardent mood, the sentry
passed into the Royal cell a lady who proved to be most dazzlingly
white and most daintily naughty. Her hair was long, her hands of
velvet, the least movement billowed her gown, for wherever it was
fitting to be so, she was graciously plump. She had laughing lips and
eyes preliminarily misty.

In short, she was a lady compared with whom hell would be tame,

who only had to open her lips for the King's nether garments to burst at the seam.

The following day, when, after the King had broken his fast, this beauty was spirited away, the good Captain again entered the presence, but now happy and triumphant.

The moment he appeared, the prisoner cried: 'My dear Baron of Ville-aux-Dames, may God grant you delights like those I have known! Now I love my gaol! By Notre-Dame, I'm not going to split hairs between the love-making abilities of our countries any more, I pay up.'

'I knew you would,' said the Captain.

'And how did you know?' asked the King.

'Sir, the lady was my own wife,' said he.

And there you have the origin of our French family, the *Larrays de Ville-aux-Dames* for by corruption *Lara y Lopez* in the end came to be Larray. It has, however, proved a fine family, most devoted to the service of the kings of France, and it has multiplied greatly.

Soon after this the Queen of Navarre at last arrived, just in time for the King, for he was beginning to get tired of the Spanish manner and wanted a bit of French jousting.

But what came next is not the subject of my tale. I also reserve till later the right to defer telling how the Legate set about scrubbing out all the sins involved, including a really delightful apophthegm of our Queen of all Marguerites, she who first made such lovely tales. The morals to be drawn from this particular tale are plain enough.

First comes the lesson that Kings should no more surrender in war than their archetype did in Palamedes' great game.* The corollary thereto is that the captivity of a monarch is a very great calamity, a frightful wound for a nation. Indeed, had it been a queen or even a princess, what disaster could be worse? Though I hardly think such a thing could happen, except among cannibals.

Is there ever any sense in imprisoning the flower of a kingdom? I credit Ashtaroth, Lucifer and company with devilry too refined to think that when they were on the throne they would ever have hidden away what delighted everybody—that beneficent fire which warms the hearts of ordinary mortals like ourselves. Indeed, it could only be when there was that most diabolical of devils, *id est*, a malicious old hag of a heretic, on the throne, that lovely Mary Queen of Scots was imprisoned, to the shame of all the knights of Christendom, who should spontaneously all have flocked to Fotheringay Castle and not left a stone of the place standing.

* Draughts. *Translator.*

III

The Edificatory Conversation of the Nuns of Poissy

Poissy Convent is notorious in early authors as a place of pleasure, where indeed nunnish misbehaviour first began, the origin too of so many good stories calculated to make the laity laugh at the cost of our holy faith. Likewise the aforesaid nunnery gave rise to proverbs which in our day for all the academic winnowing and grinding of them mighty small in order to pre-digest them, no scholar can interpret.

Were you to ask one of that breed what 'poissy olives' are, they would respond with gravity that here one had a periphrastic mode of saying *truffles*, hence when formerly, making light of the virtuous virgins of Poissy, folk spoke of 'dressing' such olives, or 'cooking' them, this must have referred to a very special sauce.

This illustrates how such dry-as-dust quill-drivers manage to hit the nail on the head not more than once in a hundred times.

But to get back to the worthy ladies in retreat, it has been said—jokingly, of course—that they would rather find a harlot than a decent woman in their shifts. There are other sly commentators who reproach them with having had their own peculiar way of imitating the life of saintly women of the past, alleging, for instance, that the only thing in which they copy Mary of Egypt is the way she paid the boatmen, whence the mocking phrase: *honour the saints Poissy-wise*.

There is also the *Poissy crucifix*, which is said to have carminative properties for the tummy. Then we have *Poissy matins*. These are said to have ended with choir-boys. Finally, a certain Gallic lady very knowledgeable regarding love's tidbits used to be called *that Poissy nun*. Also, that special tool—you know, the thing a man can never do more than lend—has in its time been called *the key of Poissy Convent*. As for the *porch* of the said institution, well, every donkey knows what that refers to. The said porch or door or gate or hole or gap (so-called because always a-gape), is said to be 'easier to open than to shut' and 'costly of upkeep'.

In a word, there is in this period not one reference to love matters which is not alleged to have derived from this fine nunnery at Poissy. Do not, however, forget that there is a lot of falsehood and wild exaggeration in all these sayings, these taunts, these fibs and squibs. The nuns of the said Poissy institution were good girls.

Admittedly, they diddled the Almighty this way and that, to the profit of old Nick, just like so many others, for our human nature is but weak and for all that these maids were given to the Church, they had their little weaknesses. It was not their fault that there was one spot on their bodies where there had not been quite enough flesh to bridge the gap, whence all the trouble.

The truth of the whole matter is, all these wickednesses were the work of one Abbess only. She had fourteen children, all living too, having been brought leisurely to full term with each. It was the fantastic love affairs and antics of this woman, who was a daughter of the Royal blood, that put Poissy nunnery in the picture for all time. After her there was never a gay tale from a French convent which was not ascribed to the fidgety forks of these poor maids, when in fact they would have been satisfied with a tenth of what was ascribed to them. Later too, as everybody knows, the nunnery was reformed, and the holy nuns were deprived even of that little happiness and freedom which they had been enjoying.

In an old logbook of the Convent of Turpenay near Chinon, which in the recent troubled times found refuge in the Library of Azay, where the present keeper took it in, I came upon a fragment headed: *The Hours of Poissy*. This was evidently the composition of a cheerful incumbent of Turpenay, made for the entertainment of the neighbouring ladies of Ussé, Azay, Mongauger, Sacché and other places in that region. This account I give under the covering of that author's priestly cassock, though, since anyway I have had to translate it from Latin into French, I have somewhat adapted it. Here goes.

At Poissy it was the nuns' custom, when their Abbess, another daughter of a King, had gone to bed. . . . Well, it was she who invented a certain term. She called dalliance in the preliminary details, the prolegomena, the prefaces, the introductions, the forewords, the protocols, announcements, notices, outlines, synopses, prospectuses, arguments, notes, prologues, epigraphs, titles, sub-titles, half-titles, *scholia*, *marginalia*, frontispieces, observations, edge gildings, bookmarks, clasps, reglets, roses, vignettes and the *culs-de-lampe* of love, all, in short, that is done without ever actually opening the glorious book to read, re-read, to study and to browse in, to master and to construe the contents—it was she who called it *playing goosie-goosie*, herself moreover establishing a complete systematization of all those little out-of-court rogueries of that lovely language, which though they certainly proceed from the lips, yet make no noise whatsoever, and all this she practised so neatly that when she died her virginal body was still utterly untapped.

This glad science of goosie-goosie was subsequently made much more profound by the ladies of the Court, who took lovers merely to look after their goosies, though there were also others who took them for the honour of it and also cases of men who were general practitioners acquiring jurisdiction at all levels, a condition which many ladies preferred.

I resume. When this virtuous Princess-Abbess was mother-naked between the sheets, without shame of anything, these maids (those whose chins were still smooth and hearts gay), crept soundlessly from their cells, to cluster and cloister in that of a sister whom they all adored. There they had lovely talks, complete with sweetmeats, sugar-balls, liquor, and girlish squabbles, making mock of their seniors, monkeyishly mimicking them, all with absolute innocence, telling stories till they laughed, laughing till they cried, and up to countless games. At one moment they would measure feet, to see whose were the daintiest, or they would compare the roundness of their arms, or see whose nose went red after supper, or count their freckles, or tell each other where they had birthmarks, or judge whose skin was the best, or who had the best colour or the finest figure. For, mark you, among these figures belonging to God there were slim ones and plump ones, flat ones and hollow-bosomed ones, stout ones and lissom ones and fragile ones, all sorts. They would thus argue as to who needed the least material for a body-belt and the one who spanned the least was pleased without knowing why. Next they told their dreams and what they had seen. Often one or two of them, but sometimes the whole band would have dreamt that she had had firm hold of that famous key.

Then they described their ailments. One had scratched her finger, another had a whitlow, a third had wakened with a blood-streak in her eye, a fourth had strained her forefinger telling her beads. There was never one but had some little thing wrong.

'Ah!' said one to her neighbour, 'you have lied to our Mother Superior, look, white lines on your nails.'

'You were a long time at confession this morning, Sister,' said another, 'had you so many little sins to declare?'

Then, just as nothing is more like a cat than is a female of our species, they would swear eternal friendship, they would squabble, they would sulk, they would argue, would be jealous, would agree, would make it up, they would pinch each other from sheer high spirits and they would laugh till they had to pinch themselves, and they would play tricks on the novices.

Another frequent game was to ask: 'If a soldier had to take shelter in a storm, where should we put him?'

'In Sister Ovide's cell, hers is the biggest, he could get in there with his helmet on.'

'Whatever do you mean,' cried Sister Ovide, 'all our cells are the same size!'

At this, the girls all laughed like ripe figs.

One evening they added to their deliberations a pretty novice of seventeen who seemed as innocent as a new-born babe, a child who could have gone straight to communion without confessing. These secret confabulations, these little drinking-parties, these little tournaments by which the young nuns sweetened the sacrosanct captivity of their bodies had for some time been making her mouth water, till she had wept bitter tears at not being admitted.

'Well, my pretty little doe,' said Sister Ovide to her, 'have you slept well?'

'Far from it,' she replied, 'I was eaten alive by fleas.'

'What, fleas in your cell? Oh, but you must get rid of them immediately. Did you not know that the rules of our order enjoin us to chase all fleas away and make sure no sister even sees the tail of one in all her life in our convent?'

'I did not,' replied the novice.

'Then let me tell you now. Can you see any fleas in my cell? Can you see any traces of any fleas? Can you smell the stink of any fleas? Is there any sign at all of fleas? Look and see.'

'No, I can't see one,' said the little novice, who was a de Fiennes, 'I can't smell anything but ourselves.'

'Do as I tell you, then, and you will no more be bitten by fleas. The moment you feel the prick, my girl, strip, lift up your shift and sinlessly examine your body all over. Doing so, you must have thought of nothing else but the accursed flea, and must genuinely search for it, thinking only of it and of its capture, which in itself is a difficult job, since you are liable to be misled by little black spots which are natural birth-marks. Have you got any birth-marks, my pet?'

'I have,' said she, 'two purple blemishes, one is on my shoulder and the other on my back, rather low down, as a matter of fact, it is hidden in the crack . . .'

'However did you see it then?' inquired Sister Perpetua.

'I didn't know about it at all, it was young Lord de Montrezor who found it.'

'Ha-ha!' cried all the sisters, 'and is that all he saw?'

'He saw everything,' replied the novice, 'I was very little at the time. He was nine and a bit, we used to play together.'

When the nuns, now reflecting that perhaps they had laughed too hastily, were silent again, Sister Ovide continued her homily.

'Now, it's no use,' she said, 'that flea jumping about from your legs to your eyes, trying to hide in all the ravines and all the little forests, in the ditches, down the valley, up on the little hill, trying to escape from you, the rules of the house order you to say *aves* continuously while you pursue it. Usually at the third go you get the brute . . .'

'The flea?' asked the novice.

'Yes, I'm still talking about the flea, of course,' retorted Sister Ovide. 'But to avoid the dangers of this hunt, wherever you happen to set your finger on the beastie you must take care not to get hold of anything else. . . . Then, without taking any heed of his cries, his laments, his groans, his efforts, his wrigglings—if, for instance, he is rebellious, which is often the case—just pin him down with your thumb or any other finger of the hand set apart to hold him, then, with the other hand, find a ribbon with which to blindfold the flea and keep it from hopping, for when the creature can no longer see it does not know where to go. However, as it might still bite you and be liable to become mad with rage, you should open its beak a bit and slip in a bristle of the blessed brush which hangs above your pillow. If you do that, the flea is bound to behave.

'But don't forget that the discipline of our Order forbids us to own anything on earth, so the little brute may not belong to you. You must also remember that it is one of God's creatures, therefore try to make it comfortable. Hence, before anything else you must make sure about two points, namely: whether the flea is male or female, and if it is a virgin.

'Suppose she is a virgin—which is very rare, since brute things have no morals, they are all very vicious creatures, yielding to the first come—you should take firm hold of her feet from behind, pull them under her little caparison, tie them in that position with one of your own hairs, then take her trussed to the Mother Superior, who will then consult the Chapter and decide what to do with her. If, on the other hand, she is a male . . .'

'But however can one tell if a virgin flea is a she at all,' asked the inquisitive novice.

'First,' resumed Sister Ovide, 'by the flea's being sad and melancholic, by the flea's not laughing like other fleas, by the flea's not dying so stubbornly, by the flea's mouth being less open and finally, by the flea's blushing when you touch it you know where . . .'

'If that's so,' said the novice in reply, 'they were all males that bit me. . . .'

At this the sisters all burst out laughing so violently that one of them let out a bass clef fart with such a sudden bang that it made her rather wet, Sister Ovide pointing out the fresh little pool on the floor, and remarking that as usual the wind had blown up rain.

The novice laughed too, but thought the laughter was caused by Sister Ovide's exclamation.

'Well,' resumed Sister Ovide, 'and so, if she is a male flea, you take your scissors, or your lover's dagger, if perhaps he gave you one as a memento before you entered the convent—in short, arming yourself with a cutting instrument, with great care you slit open the flea's loins. You must expect to hear the creature yap and cough and spit and implore your pardon. You will also see it wriggle and sweat and cast imploring glances at you and do all it can think of to avoid the operation. But don't let that surprise you, just pull yourself together and reflect that you are thus acting in order to put a perverted creature on the road to salvation.

'Neatly now, take the gizzard, the liver, the lights, the heart, the guts and the noble parts and dip them all several times in holy water to wash them and purify them, not without begging the Holy Ghost to sanctify the creature's interior.

'Finally, put all the innards quickly back into the flea. It will be rather impatient about getting them back again.

'Thus baptized, the creature is turned into a Catholic. You should now at once go and get needle and thread and sew the flea's belly up with the utmost care, with due regard to the task, with all possible attention, indeed, such as you owe to your sister in Jesus. You pray for it at the same time, and from genuflections and keen looks the dear thing will give you, you will see it quite touched by this attentiveness.

'In a word, the flea will no longer cry or want to bite you. There are even quite a number which die of pleasure at thus being made converts to our holy faith. You must treat all you catch in the same way, for when they see this a few times, others, after a good look at the convert, will clear off, for they are most perverse creatures and are very afraid fearsome of becoming Christians.'

'That is certainly a great mistake on their part,' said the novice. 'Is there any happiness greater than being in the bosom of the Church?'

'Indeed there is,' declared Sister Ursula, 'here we are sheltered from the dangers of the world, but also from love, in which one finds so much . . .'

'Is there any other danger but that of having an untimely child?'

'Since the new reign began,' replied Sister Ursula, tossing her head, 'love has inherited leprosy, St Anthony's fire, the Ardennes' fever, the red blister, and piled all possible fevers, anguishes, drugs and suffering into its pretty mortar, to produce therefrom a frightful sickness for which the devil gave the recipe, luckily for convents, for a tremendous number of womenfolk enter such places in terror, becoming virtuous from fear of such love.'

Here, terrified by these words, they all pressed close to one another, yet still wanted to know more.

'Does one always suffer if one loves?' asked one.

'Sweet Jesus, yes, I should think one does!' cried Sister Ovide.

'All for one miserable little bout of love with a fine gentleman,' went on Sister Ursula, 'you risk seeing your teeth drop out one by one, your hairs fall out one by one, your cheeks lose their colour, your eyebrows peel with frightful stabbing pains, and this good-bye to all your nicest parts costs you dear. There are some poor women who get a raw wound on their noses, while others end up with a frightful millipede always rooting and eating at their tenderest parts. In a word, the Pope has had to excommunicate that sort of love.'

'Oh, how lucky I am not to have caught all that!' cried the novice, sweetly.

At this bare reference to love, the nuns all got the impression that after all the said maid must have limbered up a bit under the warmth of one of those *Poissy crucifixes* and all this time had been pulling Sister Ovide's leg, and they were delighted to find her such a boon companion, so sprightly (as indeed the filly was). So they asked her straight what adventure it was that had brought her in to take the veil.

'Alas,' said the novice, 'I let myself get bitten by a monster flea which was not baptized.'

At this reply the diapasonal nun could not hold back a second profound gasp.

'Aha!' cried Sister Ovide, 'now you'll have to give us a third. If you could only trump like that in the choir, the Abbess would put you on Sister Petronilla's diet. Do pray stick a mute on your little instrument.'

'Is it true?' asked Sister Ursula, 'is it true, for you knew Sister Petronilla before she died, is it true that God had endowed her with the gift of going but twice a year to the counting-house?'

'That is so,' declared Sister Ovide. 'And one evening she had to squat all night through till matins, when she cried out: "I be here, and by God's will!", to be delivered at the very first canticle, so she should not miss service. And yet our late Abbess never would agree that this dischargement was by special favour from above. She maintained that God could not see so low down.

'Here is the truth of it: our late Sister, for whose canonization our

Order is at present supplicating the Papal Court (and would have been granted it by now, had it been able to find the application costs), our later sister, Petronilla that is, always had wanted to get her name into the Calendar, which could do our Order nought but good, and to that end she began to live a life of constant prayer, standing ecstatic at that altar of the Virgin over on the meadow side, making out she could clearly hear the angels fluttering about in Heaven, so well, in fact, she could note down the music of it. But everybody of course knows that she just pinched that nice tune in which nobody could find a dull note out of the *Adoremus*.

'Sister Petronilla spent whole days with her eyes as set as fixed stars fasting hard, eating a mere eyeful. She had taken a vow never to touch meat, cooked or raw, and she never ate more than a crust of bread a day, though on two-bar feasts she did take a scrap of salt fish, but never a trace of sauce. On that diet she turned really thin, as yellow as saffron and as dry as a gravedigger's bone, and as she was in any case hot by nature, had any man had the fortune to bump into her he would have struck fire as from a flint.

'Nevertheless, however little she ate, Sister Petronilla could not entirely avoid that weakness we are all more or less subject to, for good or ill, since, without it, we should certainly be most out of countenance, that weakness I mean being the obligation after food, just like all other animals, to perform the messy task of expelling from ourselves a substance of greater or less lack of sweetness according to the person. Now, Sister Petronilla differed from other nuns in shitting hard and dry, turds that anyone might have declared to be those of a doe on heat, which are the hardest concretions any gut ever produced. Perhaps you have happened on them along a ride in the woods. In high venerial circles they are known as knobbles.

'In other words, this stuff of Petronilla's was in no way super-natural. It was merely that those fasts of hers kept her nature constantly a-simmer. According to senior sisters, it was so scorching that if you put it into water it sizzled like a hot coal. There were sisters who averred that Petronilla cooked eggs on the sly at night between her toes, so as to bear her deprivations. But those I take to be malicious inventions, made merely to tarnish this great sanctity which made other convents jealous. Our dear sister was guided on her path of salvation and divine perfection by the incumbent of St Germain des Près of Paris, a holy man, who always wound up his good counsel with another piece of advice—to offer God all our tribulations and submit to his will, being that nothing happens without his express command, though, for all its sensible appearance, that doctrine did give rise to great controversies. It was finally condemned on the advice of Cardinal de Châtillon, who held that were the doctrine true, there would be no more sin, and that would cut the Church's revenues down so.

'Sister Petronilla however lived on permeated with that opinion, without knowing how dangerous it was. After one Lent, with its great fasting, for the first time in eight months, she felt a need to go to the golden closet, and go she did. When she got there, she hitched up her skirts well and set to work in the proper posture for producing what we poor sinners produce a bit more often. But she got no greater easement than the emergence of the beginning of the solid matter, after which it kept her panting, without the rest once emerging from the container. For all that she wriggled her bum, and scowling, compressed this and that spring of her inner works, her eight-months' tenant tenaciously preferred to stay in that beatified body, doing no more than poke his head out of the natural window like a froggie taking the air, devoid of such sense of vocation as might prompt it to tumble among all the others in the vale of wretchedness and alleging that there it would not have the same odour of sanctity. And considering that it was only a lump of common muck there was some sense in this.

'When the good saint had exhausted every method of coercion, including dilation of the gluteal muscles beyond measure and distension of the facial tendons till her cheeks bulged purple, she realized that there was no worse suffering in the world and when her pains reached the apogee of sphincterial discomfort, "Dear Lord!" she cried (heaving harder still), "but I'm making a gift of it to ye!"

'Upon which lament the calcareous substance broke off clean, at ground level of the orifice, and clip-clopped like a pebble down the privy walls, after which, my dear sisters, you may well imagine there was no need for arse-wiper, while expulsion of the rest was postponed to the week after.'

'Did Sister Petronilla then see angels?' inquired a sister.

'And have they got backsides too?' asked another.

'Of course not,' replied Ursula. 'Have you never heard how one conference day, when God told everybody to sit down, the angels cried: "And on what?"'

At this they all went to bed, some of them alone, some almost so. They were good girls, you see, doing no wrong except among themselves.

I cannot leave them now without relating a little thing that happened in their convent when the 'reforms' swept through it and, as mentioned above, they were all sanctified.

At this time, the See of Paris was occupied by a really saintly man who never blew his own trumpet and whose only care was for the poor and the suffering, for whom his good old episcopal heart had always room, forgetting himself for the sake of the grieved and always on the look-out for misfortunes to assuage them by words and assistance, care and money, according to circumstances, at hand when the rich as well as the poor came to bad times, patching up their souls, calling them back to God, leaving no stone unturned to guard his flock, the dear shepherd.

This good man did not give a care what state his cassocks or his cloaks or his breeches were in, provided only that the nakedness of his Church was well covered. He was charitable to the point of pawning his own self to help a poor wretch in trouble. His servants were forced to keep a sharp eye on him. Many's the time he reproved them when without a word from him they substituted new clothes for his old ones, for he would have had them patched and darned to the very last thread.

Now, this old Archbishop knew that the late lord of Poissy had left behind him a daughter without a penny or a stitch, for he himself had eaten and drunk away her heritage. This girl was living in a hovel without firing in winter or cherries in spring, doing odd jobs, unwilling either to make an undesirable marriage or to sell her virtue. Till such time as he might hit upon a young husband to provide her with, it occurred to the prelate that as stand-in he might as well send her his old breeches to mend, a job the young girl, having nothing to do, would be very glad of. And, his next thought being to go to the Convent at Poissy to inspect those reformed nuns, he handed those old tights of his to his man. 'Saintot,' he said, 'take these old bags round to the Poissy girls,' instead of saying, as he intended, 'to the Poissy girl'. And, having his mind so much on nunnish affairs, he quite forgot to add where the girl was living, another reason being that he was discreet enough to keep her desperate condition dark.

So Saintot took those tight breeches, codpiece and all, and off he goes to Poissy, cheerful as a grasshopper, halting on the way there with any friends he came across, cocking his elbow in the inns and letting those intimate garments of the Archbishop's see many a thing on this journey which was instructive for them. At last he reached the Convent and told the Abbess that the Archbishop had sent these 'for her to have mended'. Then off he hurries, leaving the Reverend Mother with this garment accustomed to assume the three-dimensional contours of the continent nature of the good old man (as breeches did at this epoch), including the configuration of those parts which the Eternal Father has not granted his angels, but which did not fall short of grace in matter of amplitude in the Archbishop.

When the lady Abbess had intimated to the sisters that she had a precious message from the Archbishop, they came in haste, as inquisitive and busy as ants in whose republic a chestnut has fallen. But when they had undone that codpiece, which gaped shockingly, they shielded their eyes with their hands, fearing they saw Satan himself. They stared aghast, with the Abbess crying:

'Cover your eyes, my daughters, this is the habitation of mortal sin.'

The Mother of the novices, however, did peep through her fingers and that restored the pluck of that sacred wenchery, for she swore by an Ave that there was no living beastie at all in that particular codpiece. They thereupon all blushed at their ease and investigated the said habitation, thinking perhaps the Archbishop intended them to discover some wise admonition or gospel parable in it. But despite the fact that the sight caused certain ravages in those virtuous maids' hearts, they took no heed of such fluttering of their own appurtenances, but instead sprinkled a drop of holy water down into the abyss. Then, as first one touched it, then another stuck her finger right into the sheath, they all found sufficient courage to look. It has even been maintained that when the first wave of excitement died down the Abbess herself asked quite calmly:

'What can be at the bottom of it? Why ever has our Father sent us this thing that is women's ruination?'

'Mother,' cried one girl, 'I haven't had a chance to see the devil's purse these fifteen years.'

'Silence, girl,' cried the Abbess, 'you prevent me thinking clearly what is best to be done.'

Upon which the said archiepiscopal codpiece was so much turned about, sniffed over, so much weighed in the hand, stared at and admired, so much turned inside out, discussed, talked about, thought about, and dreamed about all night and all day, that in the morning, after singing matins, from which they completely dropped a whole canticle and two responses, a little one suddenly cried:

'Sisters, I have seen through the Archbishop's parable. He has given us his nether garments to mend so as to mortify us. It is a sacred lesson in avoiding laziness, which is Mother Superior of all the vices.'

Upon this everybody wanted to get at the Archbishop's pantaloons, but the Mother Superior used her high authority to reserve for herself what she termed the meditation of this task, and hard did she work with the under-prioress for more than ten days, drawing

threads in that codpiece, then working it with silks and double hem-stitching it thoroughly in great humility. Then the Chapter assembled and it was resolved that as kindly memento the Convent should bear witness of its gratitude to the Archbishop for thus thinking of his daughters in the Lord. So all the nuns down to the most novitial of all had to put in some work on those edifying drawers and thus do honour to the virtue of the dear man.

Meanwhile, the prelate had so many irons in the fire that he had forgotten all about his breeks. This is how it was—he had made the acquaintance of a court gentleman who, having just lost his wife, who had been vicious and sterile too, told the Archbishop that he would like a good wife now, one given to the Lord, with whom he might stand a chance of not getting into trouble, also one having fine, good offspring, and would like the Archbishop to find her, as he had confidence in his choice. The worthy Archbishop thereupon praised that daughter of Lord Poissy's to this courtier, and the fair young thing was soon enough Lady de Genoilhac. The wedding was celebrated at the Archbishop's cathedral in Paris, and there was a feast of notables with a table full of the highest ladies in the land, fine Court folk, among whom the bride was the loveliest, especially as the Archbishop guaranteed she was a virgin.

When they came to the sweetmeats and fruit, which included all sorts of dainty things, ornamenting the table, Saintot whispered to the Archbishop:

'My Lord, your dear young ladies of Poissy have sent you a special dish as centre-piece.'

'Then put it in the centre,' cried the good Archbishop, and a moment later eyed with admiration a tall erection of velvet and satin, heavily embroidered with gold and silver braid and worked bobbles, rather like an ancient *pithos*. The lid of this object exhaled the sweetest of odours, and at once the bride opened it, to find all sorts of sweets and dainties and marzipans and what have you, with which the ladies were regaled. Now, however, one of them, being rather pious and also inquisitive, observed a little silken tassel and gave this a tug, whereupon what did she expose to the gaze of them all but the masculine compass, to the great discomfiture of the Archbishop, since the tittering soon grew into a great guffaw of laughter up and down the table, all ways.

'And a fine centre-piece they have made, My Lord,' cried the bridegroom. 'Those young ladies certainly know a thing or two. Those are the sweets of marriage indeed.'

IV

The Building of Azay Castle

John, son of 'Sim' or Simon Fourniez, burgher of Tours, native of Moulinot, a village near Beaune, whence the surname which, in imitation of some purveyors, he assumed when he was made treasurer to the late King Louis XI, one fine day flitted, with wife and all, to Languedoc, because he had fallen into disfavour, and behind him in Touraine he left his son without a penny. This youth, without a thing in the world beyond his own person, complete with bonnet and sword, but whom old men whose John Thomas had expired would have esteemed a rich man indeed, got the notion firmly into his head that he would both rescue his father and make his own fortune at Court, which was at that time in residence at Tours. So as soon as the sun was up, this good Tourainian sallied forth from his dwelling, empty-bellied, completely enveloped in his cloak, only his nose thrusting out into the wind.

Thus he roamed the city, without being greatly troubled by his digestive processes. He poked that nose into the churches and thought them fine. He examined every item in the Cathedral chapels, he even brushed the dust off the pictures, and he paced every one of the aisles like any sightseer who doesn't know what to do with his time or his money. He would even pretend to recite the Lord's prayer, though really making mute prayers to the ladies, as they left the church, offering them a sprinkling of holy water, then following them a long way. Altogether by various little services he tried to strike lucky, and at risk of his life find a gracious mistress to keep him. In the purse in his belt he had two doubloons, of which he was more careful than of his own skin. After all, his skin would mend, but never those doubloons. Every day so far he had taken from the kitty the price of a crust of bread and a few measly apples, and kept himself going on that and the Loire water which he drank at will and discretion, a steady, prudent diet which, apart from being good for the doubloons, kept him as frisky and agile as a young hare, encouraging limpidity of wit and warmth of heart, for of all elixirs the Loire is the most heating since, rising afar, it is well warmed up by sandy shallows by the time it reaches Tours.

Thus you may be sure my poor hero conceived countless lucky encounters which for want of a hairsbreadth never came true. Upon my word! What a fine time he did have, till one evening Jacques de Beaune (as he styled himself, though he really had no title to that name), was lounging along the embankment, cursing his stars and his everything else, when, at the corner of a side alley, he nearly bumped into a veiled lady who flooded his nostrils with a goodly whiff of superfine odour of woman.

This foot-passenger, neatly perched on the neatest of pattens, was attired in an elegant gown of Italian velvet with full, satin-lined sleeves. What was more, through her veiling, evidence of her wealth, one could see a rather large white diamond which glittered in the setting sun on her forehead, and brought out a coiffure so delightfully and so neatly coiled and tiered and plaited that her women must have taken three hours over it. Her gait, too, was the gait of a lady normally accustomed to being carried in a litter. She was followed by only one armed page. She must be the light o' love of some high-ranking lord, or else she was one of the Court ladies, to judge by the nice way she lifted her skirts, with a lissom wriggle of the haunches which also betokened a lady of some style.

Lady or tart, this person suited Jacques de Beaune, he was not going to turn up his nose. Indeed, so desperate was he now that he resolved to attach himself to this dame at all costs and let only death part them, so, his mind made up, he decided to follow and find out where this would take him, whether to Heaven or to Hell, to the gallows or to a love nook. He was so down and out that he was all hope.

The lady began to stroll down the Loire embankment, towards Plessis, breathing the lovely freshness of the waters like a carp, trotting and tripping along, frisky as a mouse abroad, out to see everything and taste it all. But when the page I have mentioned saw that Jacques de Beaune was following them persistently, halting whenever they rested and quite barefacedly watching the lady's trifling, as if this was quite permissible, he suddenly swung round and showed a viciously fierce jowl, just like a dog saying: 'Keep off, gentlemen.'

The good Tourainian, however, was determined. Holding that if a cat may look at a King, a baptized Christian like himself might also contemplate a pretty woman, he continued straight ahead, pretending to give the page a smile and maintaining a position now a few paces in front of them, now a few behind. All this time, the lady said not a word, merely stared her fill at the sky, which was already beginning to be wrapped in a night with many stars. Things were shaping well.

To cut the story short, opposite Portillon the lady at last halted and then, as if to get a better view, threw her veil back on to her shoulders, as she did so shooting her escort a well-bred look as if to ask if there was any danger of being robbed. Bear in mind here that not only could Jacques de Beaune do the work of three husbands, but he also had that gallant, resolute air which pleases the ladies, fit to accompany a princess without causing her shame, while, if he was a trifle sunburned by all the trotting about of the past week, his complexion would doubtless appear somewhat less florid under the curtains of a four-poster. That needle-sharp glance, which the lady gave him certainly looked livelier than she would grant her prayer-book.

The consequence was, de Beaune at once built up on that glance hopes of a nightful of love, and resolved to push forward with the business to the very hem of her skirts, risking, if he went any farther, not his life (for that he now valued little), but his ears, and perhaps also another protuberance of his.

So our gentleman followed the lady back to the city, where she turned down *Trois-Pucelles* (Three Virgins) Street, leading the gallant through a network of alleys to the square where today stands the *Crouzille Hotel*. Here she halted at a handsome mansion, and the page knocked on the door. A servant opened, the lady slipped quickly in, and there was the door, closed again, leaving milord de Beaune a-gape, dumbfounded, as big a ninny as Saint Denis before he found how to pick up his head.

He tipped his nose skywards, to see if there were not some favour dropped, but saw no more than a single light. This mounted the stairs and appeared in one room after another, but it halted at last at a fine casement window, and there no doubt the lady was. You may imagine how sadly our lovesick young man stood there dreaming, at a loss to know what to do next. Then the window suddenly creaked and broke into his reverie. Thinking that the lady was going to call him up, he stretched his nose out still farther, and had it not been for the balcony, which served him as shelter, would then have received a sound dowsing with a cold liquid and also the vessel which had contained it, for only the handle of the slop-pot remained in the hands of the person now trying to shower-bath the loiterer.

Jacques de Beaune, however, was delighted with this mishap. Not for an instant losing his presence of mind, he dropped at the foot of the wall and in a stifled voice cried: 'I am dying.' Then he stiffened his muscles and waited patiently for whatever was to come. He now heard a great commotion in the house. The front door opened, and out came the servants, fearful of their lady, to whom they confessed their apparent error, and they carefully picked up the victim, who nearly burst out laughing when he was thus carried in and up the stairs.

'He is quite cold,' said the page.

'He's all blood,' said the butler, who, feeling Jacques, lay his hands where the liquid had soused him.

'If he recovers, I shall endow a mass at St Gatien's,' cried the guilty one, quite tearful now.

'Madame takes after her late father,' said another. 'If she does not have you strung up for this, she's at least sure to kick you out of her service. I am sure this Knight is dead, he's so heavy.'

'Well, it's certainly a lady of condition,' thought Jacques.

'No, tell me the truth,' demanded the fellow who was responsible for the accident, 'does he really feel dead?'

Then, as with great difficulty they heaved the young man of Tours up past the balusters, and his doublet caught on a projecting knob, the corpse muttered: 'Damn it, that's my doublet gone.'

'He groaned,' cried the culprit, heaving a sigh of relief.

The servants of the Regent, for this was the mansion of none other than the daughter of King Louis XI of France, of virtuous memory, carried Jacques de Beaune into the living-room, and left him lying all stiff on a bench, never thinking he might recover.

'Run and fetch a master surgeon,' cried the Princess, 'find one, no matter where!'

And before you could say *Our Father* the servants were down those stairs. Next the kind-hearted Princess-Regent sent her women for ointment and linen to bind de Beaune's wounds, then for some lead lotion and so many other things, that she was left quite alone. Then, examining the handsome fellow lying lifeless there, she admired his parts and thought how excellent he looked, even in death.

'Alack,' cried she, 'it is God's intention to punish me! For the first time in all my life tonight, a naughty thought boiled up out of my nature and made me wicked. Now my patron saint is angry with me and has taken away the handsomest young man I ever saw. God of Easter, by the spirit of my father, I shall have all those responsible for his death strung up by the neck.'

'Madame,' cried Jacques de Beaune, springing up from the boards on which he had been lying at the feet of the Regent of France, 'I live but to serve you and I am so little damaged that for this one night I promise you as many delights as there are months in the year, in good imitation of that grand pagan, Lord Hercules. In the past three weeks,' he ran on, suspecting that he ought to lie a bit to contrive the situation, 'I have met you countless times, till I am out of my mind, yet from great respect for your person have never dared approach you. But do take note how intoxicated I must be by your regal beauty to have thought of the trick to which I owe the fortune of being at your feet.'

179

Here he kissed the said feet so very lovingly and gazed at the dear lady with ruinous passion. The Regent, on account of the normal passage of years, which is no respecter of royalty, was, as everybody knows, in that second maidenhood that womenfolk know. Now, in that critical, brutal season, women who have been well-behaved and lived without lovers do long here or there secretly to find, God please grant, at least one nightful of love, so they do not pass to the other world with hands, heart and everything else empty through lack of knowing those particular things—well, you know what I mean.

Therefore this lady showed no astonishment when she heard what this young man proffered her, it is proper for Royal personages to be accustomed to everything by the dozen, and she kept that ambitious speech under her bonnet or under her love registry, should one say, a region already swollen with anticipatory heat, and helped the young man to his feet, and despite his misery he contrived to smile at her. She had slipper-like ears, all the majesty of an antique tea-rose, and the skin of a sick cat, but on the other hand she was so well dressed, so dainty of figure, so queenly of gait and so lively of loin, that there was still a chance in this ill-fortune to find unsuspected springs by which Jacques de Beaune could parse that word he let slip.

'Who are you?' asked the Regent, assuming the stern air of her late father.

'I am your very faithful subject, Jacques de Beaune, son of your treasurer, who despite his loyal service has fallen into disgrace.'

'Very well,' replied the lady, 'now you lie back on your bench again, I hear someone coming, and it is far from seemly for my household servants to know I am privy to this farcical game.'

The good lad saw from the soft tone of her voice that the kindly dame had most graciously forgiven the enormity of his declaration of passion. So he lay back on the bench and reflected how before this many a lord had ridden to Court on an old mare, and this thought entirely reconciled him with his good fortune.

'It is all right,' said the Regent to her maids. 'I don't need anything. This gentleman is better. Thanks be to God and the Holy Virgin, my house has not been the scene of a murder.'

Saying this, she passed her hand through the hair of this admirer fallen from heaven in the nick of time, then, taking the Bonhomme water, rubbed de Beaune's temples with it. Then she unfastened his doublet and under pretext of seeing how the victim of the accident was recovering, better than any officer of court performing an examination took the measure of this young man who so boldly promised a fine time.

Although it never is unseemly for royal persons to show humanity, it made everyone present gape to see the Regent behaving like this. Jacques now got to his feet, made a pretence of being puzzled to be there, thanked the Regent most humbly, dismissed the physician, the surgeon and certain black-robed devils, and declared himself recovered. He then loudly made known who he was and made as if to withdraw, bowing deeply to the Regent, and as if quite in awe of her, because of the disgrace his father was in, though doubtless terrified by his own terrible vow.

'But I cannot possibly let you go,' she said. 'No visitor of mine should receive what came to you. Milord of Beaune shall sup here,' she told her major-domo. 'And if he confesses, the man who treated him so unworthily shall be at M. de Beaune's discretion, otherwise I shall have him rooted out and hanged by my Provost.'

Hearing this, the page who had followed him on her stroll declared himself the guilty one.

'Madame,' said Jacques, 'on my plea, may he be both pardoned and rewarded, since it is to him that I owe the fortune of beholding you, the favour of supping in your company and perhaps also that of seeing my father restored to the charge to which it once pleased your illustrious father to appoint him.'

'Well spoken,' said the Regent. 'D'Etouteville,' she said, turning to her page, 'I grant you the command of a company of archers. Only take care in future not to throw things out of windows.'

Her appetite gingered up by young Beaune, the Regent offered him her hand and conducted him very nicely to her room. Here by dint of elegant conversation they now mutually took each other's measure very nicely while awaiting the announcement of supper. Jacques made good use of the occasion to display all his points and both justified his father and suited the lady's wit, for, as everybody knows, she had developed into the very spit of her father and always acted on impulse. Inwardly, however, Jacques de Beaune told himself that it was going to be frightfully difficult to sleep with the first lady of France. Such business is not accomplished like the marriage of cats, who have always a gutter up on the roofs to receive their suitors in, undisturbed by any eye.

Hence in conclusion he patted himself on the back for merely getting known to her at all, without having to deliver her that promised dozen. That would require having all the servants, male and female, well out of the way, so that my lady's honour should not be in jeopardy.

Nevertheless, having a shrewd notion of the good lady's ingenuity, he did now and then feel himself, wondering if he would even have enough spunk to rise to the occasion.

On which question, under the shield of conversation, the good Lady Regent also pondered. After all, she had contrived many a stickier piece of business. And indeed, she now thought of a very good device. Sending for one of her secretaries, a man well up in all the ingenuities apt to keep the machinery of government oiled, she instructed him covertly to send her a false message during supper.

The meal was now served, but she did not touch a thing. Her heart had swollen like a sponge, to the parallel diminution of volume of her stomach. All her thoughts were on this handsome, desirable young man, all her appetites reserved for him. Jacques for his part did not fail to do justice to the food. There were a variety of reasons for that. The messenger turned up on time and delivered his secret message. The Regent of France then rose to her feet and began to storm, scowling just like her late father the King.

'Is there never to be peace in this country?' she cried. 'God of Easter, cannot we have one quiet evening?'

Up and down the room she stamped.

'Hi there!' she cried suddenly, 'bring my horse! Where is my groom de Vieilleville? Absent? In Picardy? D'Etouteville, you come on later and bring my household to Amboise Castle. . . .' And she turned, as on impulse, to Jacques. 'My Lord de Beaune,' she said, 'you shall be my groom. Are you willing to serve your King? You have a good opportunity, God of Easter, come on! There is a rebellious plot to quell, I shall need faithful assistants.'

In the time it would have taken an old beggar to mouth a hundred *Aves*, horses were saddled and ready, Madame was mounted and our Tourainian at her side, and they were galloping madly to Amboise Castle, with men-at-arms following. To cut a long story short and get to the kernel without further commentary, at Amboise Lord de Beaune was lodged within easy reach of the lady, and far from prying eyes.

The courtiers and all the soldiers meanwhile ran about in much astonishment, trying to find out whence the attack would come, but the young gambler had no doubts, he was nicely caught. The virtue of the Regent in any case was a preservative against suspicion. She was said to be as impregnable as Péronne Castle.

When curfew came and all was shut up for the night, ears and eyes too, and the castle was silent, the Regent dismissed her maid and called for her groom. The groom came. Under the hood of the vast fireplace, side by side on a bench well upholstered with velvet, lady and adventurer then conned each other. At once, in cosseting tones, the inquisitive Regent asked if Jacques had truly suffered no damage?

'It is very bad of me,' she said, 'to make so charming an attendant, who had just been attacked by one of my men, ride horse twelve miles. I was so worried that I could not go to bed till I had seen you. Does nothing hurt you?'

'Only my impatience,' declared Lord Dozen, calculating that in this situation there was no point in hedging.

'I see clearly,' he added, 'noble, loveliest mistress mine, that your servant pleases your eye.'

'Now, now!' she cried, 'were you not fibbing when you said . . .'

'When I said what?' he demanded.

'Why, when you said that a dozen times—er—you had followed me in the churches and other places I have been?'

'Of course I was not,' he said.

'Then,' the Regent replied, 'I am indeed astonished that it was only today that I should notice a noble young man whose pluck is so clearly expressed in his features. I am not unsaying what you heard me say when I thought you were hurt. You suit me, with your dozen intentions.'

Whereupon, the hour of the diabolical sacrifice having struck, Jacques knelt before the Lady Regent and kissed her feet, her hands, indeed, it is said he kissed everything. Then, kissing and making ready, by many an argument, he demonstrated to the long-standing virtues of his sovereign that when a lady is gravid with the State she has every right to disport herself a little. Such licence, however, the Lady Regent in question would not admit, insisting on being forced, so she could lay all the blame on her lover. Nevertheless, one must point out that in preparation she had well perfumed herself, making ready for the night, and was indeed aglow with eagerness to be coupled, the heightened colour which resulted being a perfect make-up for her which well brought out her complexion.

So, despite the feeble resistance she made, she was borne as unceremoniously to the bed like any young flibberty-gibbet, and once there grand lady and young gambler were well married in all conscience. There was first gentle play, then play less gentle, after which some ribaldry, the Lady Regent protesting that she believed in de Beaune's dozen as much as she believed the Queen of Heaven had been a virgin.

As it turned out, between the sheets Jacques de Beaune missed this great lady's age. Night-lights indeed change much, many women of fifty are twenty at midnight, others who are twenty at midday are centenarians after evensong.

Thus Jacques de Beaune was more content with this encounter than the King on a hanging day, and he kept his part of the bargain, whereby his lady was also astonished, though she vowed she would do her best to help—apart from the Azay-le-Brûlé estate and all its tithes, which she undertook to make over to her man as well as pardoning his father, if, that is, she was defeated in this jousting bet about a dozen encounters.

Whereupon the faithful son in turn cried:

'And here's to save my father's rights! And here's for the land! And now for the rents and the revenues! And here's again for the isles of the Indre! And now let's win the pastures! Now let's get my father back his lands he so dearly bought! And here's for a post at Court!'

Without mishap reaching this score, he thought he had saved his codpiece's dignity, as if, with France in this wise under him, the honour of the Crown was also at stake. In short, in discharge of a vow he now made to his patron saint to build him a church at Azay, he offered up to his sovereign lady his allegiance and loyal manhood cast in eleven unequivocal, quite distinct, lucid, eloquent periphrastic assertions. As far as the final epilogue of this low down dialogue goes, the man of Tours had a self-confidence that was swollen—swollen enough to propose to do the Lady Regent really well, by ensuring that she should have a final encounter in the form of a fine accolade when she eventually came back to consciousness, and thereby Jacques would give his sovereign his real thanks as the new Baron Azay.

This was all duly agreed. But when Nature wants to be sly she is much like a horse. She—or he lies down and instead of stirring, just flounders, however much he is flogged, and lies there till at last his charger restocked, it pleases him of himself to stand up. Hence when, at daybreak, the young falcon of Azay wished to assay to assail the daughter of Louis XI with a mighty aubade, for all his good intentions he was constrained to do so more in the normal manner of saluting royal personages, that is, merely by blank charges of gunpowder. Hence, after rising, while breaking her fast with Jacques, who claimed to be the legitimate lord of Azay, she took due note of his morning's short fall to contradict him, saying that as he had not won the bet he had not won the estate.

'By Saint Paterne's belly!' he cried, 'I was jolly near, anyway. But, dear lady and noble sovereign, it is surely not fitting either for you or for me to be judge in our own cause. Since the matter concerns freehold land, it should come before your Council, for Azay is in the gift of the Crown.'

'God of Easter!' cried the Lady Regent, with a smile (though it was only a very watery one), 'what I'll do is give you the position of Lord of Vieilleville in my household, I won't prosecute your father, and I give you Azay. Further, I will appoint you to a Royal office *if without damage to my reputation you can put your case successfully to the full Council.* But if a single word sullies my name as honest woman . . .'

'I choose the gallows,' cried the young gambler, turning it all into a great joke, though his bed companion of the night before thought she detected a suspicion of anger on his cheeks.

The truth is, Louis XIth's daughter was more anxious about the royal name than any dozen naughty acts, to which now she paid no heed, seeing that, as she reckoned she had had a good nightful without so much as loosening her purse-string, she would rather have him tackle his difficult plaint than give her the last one of the dozen which he was already offering.

'Very well, Madame,' said our boon companion, 'I certainly shall be your groom.'

Every jack-man of the Captains, Secretaries and others with offices under the Regency were astonished at the sudden departure of their mistress, then, learning the alleged reason for her concern, they rallied to Amboise Castle, in a hurry to learn whence had come the disturbance. Consequently, when her majesty was dressed they were all ready for a Council. She certainly made a point of convening them, too, not to be suspected of having tricked them, and she offered them certain lies to mull over—which they duly mulled. At the close of the sitting the new groom entered to escort his mistress. Seeing the Councillors risen, the bold Tourainian asked them if before they left they would settle a dispute which concerned him and a Royal domain.

'Hear him,' said the Lady Regent, 'he is quite right.'

Without blenching at this high court, Jacques de Beaune then spoke as follows (or approximately so):

'Noble Lords, although I am going to talk about walnuts and their shells, be attentive to my case, I beg you, and forgive me the apparent frivolity of my language. A certain lord was strolling with another in an orchard, when they noticed a fine specimen of the Jove walnut, well planted, well developed, lovely to look at, lovely to keep, even if a bit hollow, a nut-tree that was always fresh and sweet-smelling, a nut-tree you would never tire of, had you seen it a real pet of a nut-tree which might well have been the tree of good and evil which our Lord God forbade us and on account of which our mother Eve and her noble husband were turned out of the garden.

'Now, my lords, this tree became the subject of a certain tendency to contention between these two lords, in the form of one of those delightful wagers we are all of us accustomed to make between friends. The younger of the two, as any of us might, strolling in his orchard, declared he would fling a stick he had in his hand at that

G

moment right over that leafy tree a dozen times and each time knock off a walnut.

'Is this the kernel of the case?' he added, turning slightly towards the Lady Regent.

'It is, my lords,' she replied, astonished at the gumption of her groom.

'The other lord,' de Beaune resumed, 'held the opposite. So this worthy gambler started throwing his stick and he did so with skill and pluck, so featly and so neatly that both of them enjoyed it. Moreover, by the glad protection of the saints, who no doubt enjoyed the sight too, every cast of the stick brought down a nut, and at the close there were certainly a dozen of them. But it so happened that the last nut brought down was a dud, in-so-much as it lacked that nourishing inner cream which, if a gardener chooses to plant it, produces another nut. Now who won, the one with the stick? Or the other? That's all. Judge!'

'You have put it well,' said Sir Adam Fumeé, a man of Tours, who was then keeper of the seal. 'There is only one way out for the other lord.'

'And what is that?' asked the Lady Regent.

'To pay up, Madame.'

'He is far too clever,' she said, patting her groom's cheek. 'He'll get himself strung up one of these days.'

She meant to joke, but these words were the treasurer's true horoscope. What is more, he mounted the fatal ladder when at the peak of Royal favour, and all by the vengeance of another middle-aged woman, together with the base treachery of a man from Ballan, his secretary, whose fortune he had made for him, a fellow named Prévost, and not René Gentil, as some have erroneously suggested. That rascally, faithless servant Prévost is said to have given the Countess of Angoulême a receipt for money which Jacques de Beaune advanced him when he had become Baron de Semblançay and Lord of La Carte and Azay, one of the topmost men of the State. Of Azay's two sons, one became Archbishop of Tours, the other Chancellor and also Governor of Touraine. But that is not the subject of our present tale.

No, what touches on this yarn about the good man's youth is that the Lady who was Regent of France, come to the delightful sport thus rather late in life, also very pleased to find this fortuitous lover so wise and so understanding in public affairs, made him Lord of the Privy Purse, in which post he was of such good conduct and so intriguingly multiplied the Royal *dozens* that his great renommé one day won him the charge of the state's finances, which he controlled and supervised the judicious use of, not without making a pretty penny himself, which was fair enough. The good Regent certainly paid her gambling debt, handing to her groom the estates of Azay-le-Brûlé, the castle of which, as everybody knows, had well before this been brought to ruin by the first cannon to be brought to Touraine, for which dusty wonder, had the King not stepped in, the engineers in question would have been condemned to death as criminals and satanical heretics by the Ecclesiastical Chapter Court.

At this juncture, it happened that the Castle of Chenonceaux was being built by Lord Bohier, Minister of Finance, who, as fantasy and curiosity, built his mansion straddled over the River Cher. Now the Baron de Semblançay, wishing to outdo this Bohier fellow, decided to build his at the mouth of the Indre, where it still stands, the ornament to that lovely green vale, so solidly is it built on its piles. On it Jacques de Beaune spent thirty thousand crowns, apart from the forced labour of his men.

Do not forget that this castle is one of the really handsome, really graceful, really exquisite, the best built castles of all our delightful Touraine, constantly washed by the Indre waters like a princely tart, all decked out with turrets and built-out windows with fine stone work, and handsome soldiers as weather-cocks, turning as the wind blows like all military men.

But before he completed his mansion, good Semblançay was hanged, and since his death nobody has ever had enough money to finish it off. And yet his master, Francis I, King of France, the first of that name, had been his guest there. Indeed, you can still see the room he slept in. And when the King went to bed, Semblançay (whom the said King used to call 'dad', in honour of his white poll), hearing his master (to whom he was most attached), say: 'Your clock, dear father, has just struck twelve,' replied: 'Ah, Sire, indeed it gives twelve strokes of a hammer, which is getting old now, and to twelve good strokes well struck at this same hour I owe my very title, all the money spent on this castle, and the happiness of serving you into the bargain.'

The good King then wanted to know what his courtier meant by that strange declaration. So, while the King lay in bed, Jacques de Beaune told the story you now know. Francis I, a glutton for such yarns, found it delightfully spicy, and was the more tickled by it when, at the change of life, his own mother, the Duchess of Angoulême, ran after the Constable of Bourbon to get a dozen from him. Bad love of a bad woman, that was, for it brought the whole kingdom into jeopardy, through it the King was captured and poor de Semblançay put to death, as just recorded.

In this tale I have been concerned to relate how the Castle of Azay came to be built, since it is unquestionable that here was the beginning of the great fortune of Semblançay, who did much for his native city, which he embellished, also spending considerable sums on the cathedral towers. This edifying narrative was handed down from father to son and one lord to another, in this same place, Azay-le-Ridel, where it still frisks about behind the Royal Four-poster curtains, which have most intriguingly been respected to our day.

Hence it is falsehood of falsehood to attribute that Tourainian dozen to a German knight alleged in this way to have won the Austrian domains and the Hapsburg House. The author who in our day has been responsible for putting that story about, however learned he may be, allowed himself to be duped by certain chroniclers, for the Chancellory of the Holy Roman Empire makes no mention of any such manner of acquisition. I hold it against him to have thought any beer-fed codpiece could ever have endowed the great alchemy with the pride of those Chinonian codpieces which Rabelais so prized.

Consequently, for the good of the country, the renown of Azay, the conscience of the Castle and the fame of the House of Beaune, whence sprang the Sauves and the Noirmoustiers, I have narrated what actually did happen in all its historical and delectable sweetness. If any ladies come to see the castle they can still find a few dozens left in the district, though only retail.

V

A Courtier's False Wife

What some folk do not know is the truth about how the Duke of
Orleans, brother of Charles VI, met his death. That was a murder
due to a number of causes, one of which will be the subject of this
tale.

There can be no doubt about it, that Prince was the greatest and
hottest wencher of all the royal line of saintly Louis, in his time King
of France, and that not excluding by handicap even the most debauched of that fine family, which has been so well matched to the
vices and specialities of our fine, rascally people, so that one could
as well think of hell without Old Nick as France without those
courageous, rampageous, outrageous, lecherous kings of hers. So
you might as well make fun right away of those dealers in fine
thoughts who will tell you: 'Our fathers were better men,' as also of
those lover-of-man bunglers who make out that our human race is
on the road to perfection. They are all of them purblind, they see
neither how oysters feather or birds grow shells, for the ways of
these no more change than human ways.

Right you are then, sow your oats young, fill your skins and
above all, don't slobber; an ounce of hilarity is worth many a ton
of gloom.

Well, the deeds of this Prince, lover of Queen Isabella, to whom he
was wildly attached, brought him into many a delightful adventure,
for he was a great rascal by nature, like Alcibiades, a true piece of the
old French block. He it was who first thought of having relays of
girls, so that whenever he went down to Bordeaux from Paris, the
moment he dismounted anywhere he was sure of a good meal and of
a bed complete with a pretty line in nightgown-linings.

Lucky prince, he died in the saddle. Riding was his customary
posture, even between the sheets. Our worthy King Louis XI added
an obituary tribute about his entertaining delights to the Hundred
New Tales written under his eyes while he was in exile at the Court
of Burgundy where, in the evening hours, to while away the time,
his cousin Charles and he used to relate the great deeds of those times,
and when they lacked true ones, there was always one of the courtiers
to do his best to invent a better one. Nevertheless, out of respect for
the royal blood, the Dauphin of France ascribed what happened to a
certain lady of Cany a citizen of that town, under the title of *The
Other Side of the Medal*, which anybody may read in the collection, in

which it is one of the best told stories in the whole book, and inaugurates the series. Here is my contribution:

There was a gentleman attached to the Duke of Orleans' court, a baron of the province of Picardy named Raoul d'Hocquetonville, who to the future misfortune of the said Prince took to wife a bride with a lot of land who was related to the House of Burgundy, this girl however standing out from most girls due to inherit estates, by being of such dazzling beauty that when she was present all the ladies of the Court, even the Queen and Lady Valentine, were put quite into the shade. Yet in this Lady d'Hocquetonville it was not those Burgundy connexions, it was not her heritage, it was not even her beauty and her charm that were the most striking features, but the fact that these rare assets had been given a religious polish by her supreme innocence, her fine modesty and her chaste upbringing.

The result was that the Duke did not waste much time merely sniffing at such a flower dropped from Paradise, but became simply enfevered with passion for her. He fell into a dire despondency, gave up all thought of brothels, all available light-o'-loves, merely, at long intervals, pecked at his own enchanting royal portion (that is, Isabel the German), then, losing all control, swore that, be it by sorcery, force or trickery, he would lie with that so lovely female who, by the mere sight of her exquisite form, even forced him to handle himself during nights now become empty and miserable.

First, he pursued her straight, pressing hard with gilded speeches, but soon seeing, by her unconcerned air, that as far as she went he was condemned to good behaviour, for without the least indignation or anger such as less innocent ladies would have shown, she replied:

'Sire, I must inform you that I do not wish to involve myself in a love relationship with anybody else but my husband. This is not out of any scorn for the delights therein to be found, for they must be very lively, since so many women lower themselves to them, yes, lower themselves, their homes, their good name, their future, their all. It is from love for the children for whom I am responsible. I do not want to give myself the slightest cause to blush, for I intend to din into my daughters the basic principle that woman's true happiness is to be found in being virtuous.

'Indeed, Sire, since we all of us have more old age than youth, it is our old age we should think of. From those who brought me up I learned to take a sober view of life, and I know that all except the security of natural affection is transitory. Therefore I crave everybody's esteem, above all that of my husband, who is my whole world. For that reason it is my wish to remain honest in his sight, and

I beg you to let me attend to my domestic affairs in peace, otherwise without question I shall tell my lord and master and he will withdraw from your service.'

This spirited reply merely made the King's brother still more amorous, so he decided somehow to trap this noble woman, to possess her so to speak, dead or alive, and did not doubt he would get her in his grasp, trusting to his experience of that sort of hunting, the most delightful of all, one in which one has to use the devices of all other forms, seeing that one's pretty game is to be taken running, if you can only get it in your sights, by torchlight or daylight, in town or country, in wood or by river, netted or caught with hoodless falcons, with dogs or with decoys, with guns or with horns, with lime or with bait, in short, with any one of all the many traps devised since Adam was turned out of the garden. After this come a thousand different ways of killing it, though the usual way is to ride it.

So the good crafty fellow did not utter another word about his cravings, but contrived to have Lady d'Hocquetonville given a position in the Royal household. Then, when one day his wife Isabel had gone to Vincennes to see the King, who was sick, leaving him alone at his St Paul mansion, he ordered his cook to prepare the most lavish of regal suppers and said it was to be served in the apartments used by the Queen. Then he issued his unaccommodating lady an express command to be present and sent this by one of the household pages.

Thinking it was the Duchess Isabel who wanted her on something connected with her office, or that some impromptu party was in question, she hastened to respond. Now, this treacherous admirer of hers had made such arrangements that there was nobody to tell the unfortunate lady that the Princess had gone away, so she went straight in to that lovely room in the St Paul mansion which is next to the Queen's former bedroom, and there she found the Duke of Orleans, alone. At once suspicious of some shabby design, she hurried through to the bedchamber. But of course, there was no Queen, only a gay laugh from the Prince.

'I am done,' she cried and would have escaped, but this excellent skirt-chaser had posted loyal men all about, and they, without a hint of knowledge of what it was all for, had shut the place up, bolting and barring the doors, so that there was our lady of Hocquetonville in that mansion, which must have been a quarter the size of Paris, as if in the midst of a desert, her only succour her patron saint and God. Now that she saw through the whole design, for the purpose of this trap which had been so ingeniously planned was now made quite clear by the beaming countenance of her admirer, the poor lady began to shiver terribly and sank to a chair. When now the duke made as if to approach her, she rose and took up her first weapon, her tongue, while her eyes flashed a thousand curses.

'You may have your pleasure of me,' she said, 'but only of my dead body. I mean what I say, Sire, do not venture to force me to a struggle which will have a certain end. Otherwise, I could leave you and Lord d'Hocquetonville need never know what a black moment in my life you have caused.

'Duke, you spend too much time looking into women's faces to study those of men, and you simply do not know what a loyal servant you have. Lord d'Hocquetonville would let himself be hacked into pieces for your sake, so devoted is he to you, in memory of your kindnesses and also because he likes you. But he is as good a hater as he is a lover, and I think him quite capable without fear of finishing you off with one blow of his mace merely at the rumour that you had compelled me to submit. Do you wish for your death and mine, wicked man? Have no doubts that my honest cheeks could never conceal the truth, good or evil. Now will you not let me go?'

The rogue just let out a whistle, hearing which, the good lady went straight into the Queen's bedroom and took a sharp-pointed iron which she knew to be there. And, as the Duke followed, to find out what this withdrawal might mean, 'Set foot across that floorboard,' she cried, pointing to the floor, 'and I kill myself.'

Unabashed, the Duke took a chair, placed it up against the join of the flooring and then began to bargain and reason with her, still hoping, by kindling this wild woman's imagination and upsetting both heart and head and the rest of her too, by his depiction of the matter he intended, to bring her to the point of seeing nothing to make a fuss about. So, with the charming graces of manner customary in princes, he set to work to explain to her that virtuous women purchase their condition at very high price, since in order thus to lay claim to the uncertain goods of a future life they lose the loveliest delights of the present, for from lofty reasons of conjugal policy husbands are obliged not to open love's treasure chest to them, for its jewels glow so in the heart and offer such spicy pleasures, such ticklish enjoyments, that if once informed of them no woman would be able to keep to the chilly realm of the household any longer.

This wretched way of husbands, he argued, was very base indeed, for merely as recognition of the steady way of living of a well-established woman and her so expensive qualities, any husband ought to put himself out, work himself to death indeed, to serve her in every way with the billings and the cooings and the rogueries, the dainties and the fine confections and sweet tidbits of love, and he added that if she would but taste a little of the seraphic sweetness of those dainty ways of which she was so far quite ignorant, the rest of life would seem dull indeed to her. If that was agreed, he added, he for his part would keep mum about it better than any dead man, and no breath of scandal would ever damage her reputation. Then, seeing that this lady now was certainly not stopping her ears, the wily rogue began a description, rather in the style of those oriental drawings then much in fashion, of the delectable love inventions of the initiated.

Now his eyes certainly did shoot flame and there were a thousand hot coals concealed in his words, making his voice melodious, as he revelled in recollection of all the various positions beloved of his many mistresses, and told Lady d'Hocquetonville all the things they did, down even to the little Lesbianic tricks, such as the pussy-kissings and charming caresses by which Queen Isabel herself made love, and he then made use of a little word which was of itself so charming and so ardently tempting that it seemed to him that this lady even relaxed her grip of that menacing spiky bar, and he at once made as if to follow in, but so ashamed was she at thus being caught dreaming things that she shot a furious glance at the diabolical Leviathan tempting her and cried:

'My fine Prince, thank you indeed, you have made me love my noble husband more, for what you tell me shows that he esteems me highly, having such respect for me that he never dishonours our mutual bed by such animalities and villainry of men and women of evil life. I should hold myself shamed for ever and contaminated for eternity were I to set foot into the muck-pits to which such hussies descend. There is a dictinction between a man's wife and his mistress.'

'And I'll bet,' cried the Duke, grinning broadly, 'that from now on you will at least urge my lord of Hocquetonville to a little more dalliance.'

At these words the good lady cried out:

'You are a scurrilous man. What talk is this? Unable to sully my honour, you now think to befoul my soul? Sir, you do me grave harm in this. Were you yourself not the author of the lines:

> 'Though I may give you pardon, yet
> God Almighty'll not forget?'

'Madame,' cried the Duke, changing colour, 'I could have you bound . . .'

'Not a bit of it,' she replied, desperately waving her weapon, 'I have made sure of my freedom.'

The scoundrel now began to laugh.

'Fear not,' he said, 'I shall find a way to plunge you into the same muck-pit as those hussies whom you scorn.'

'Never, on my life!'

'And right in, too,' he said, 'in with your two feet, your two hands, those two ivory titties, that other pair of rotundities white as snow, your teeth, your hair, every inch of you. . . . You'll go in too of your own free will, with all the naughtiness in the world, and what's more you'll be the breaking of the man who rides you like any mad un-broken mare breaking her harness, snorting and bucking and lashing about, you'll be right in, on St Castud I swear it!'

He whistled at once for a page and secretly instructed him to go and fetch Baron d'Hocquetonville, also Savoisy, Tanneguy, Cypierre and some other ruffians of that ilk, inviting them all to supper there, also telling the latter to make a point of bringing with them some pretty skirts nicely lined with fresh meat.

He then returned to his chair, ten paces from the lady, off whom he had not taken his eyes once all the time he was whispering instruc-tions to his page.

'Raoul d'Hocquetonville is a jealous man,' he said, 'so therefore, Madame, I owe you a preliminary word of good advice. In this little closet'—he indicated a secret door—'are all the Queen's creams and superfine perfumes. In that other little room she performs her ablu-tions and attends to the things a woman should. From much ex-perience I know that every one of your sweet beaks has its own special scent, by which one can know it. Well, if, as you say, Raoul is choked with jealousy, which, by the way, is the worst possible thing, you will now make some use of those muck-heapers' scents, because you're certainly in a mucky hole now.'

'Oh, Sire, whatever do you mean to do?'

'You shall know—when the right time comes for you to know. I wish you no ill, and give you my word as loyal knight that I shall show you every respect and shall never breathe a word about how you turned me down. But you shall instead learn that the Duke of Orleans is a good-hearted fellow, and takes a noble revenge of ladies who scorn him, doing so by putting the key of paradise into their hands. All I ask is that you should give ear to the roisterous talk you will soon hear in the next room. And, above all, if you so love your children, please, no coughing.'

Since there was no way out of the Queen's bedroom and the win-dows of it scarcely opened enough to put your head through, the

rascal could lock the door and be quite sure of keeping her captive there, and his last word to her was again, to keep mum. Now the roisterers came hurrying in, to find a lavish supper smiling from silver platters on the well-laden, well-lighted table, lovely with all its silver tankards and pots of the Royal wine.

Then their Lord and Master said:

'Come, come, be seated good friends! I was wondering whatever I could do to amuse myself, when into my mind came the idea of banqueting with you in ancient style as the Greeks and Romans when they said their Lord's Prayers to Master Priapus and the horned god known in every land as Bacchus. True, it will be a two-partite feast, since as dessert we shall have some pretty triple-beaked jays, the best biller among whom I know from great experience.'

As there was no question but that he was their master in everything, they were all much heartened by this fine speech, all, that is, save Baron Raoul d'Hocquetonville, who now came forward and addressed his prince.

'Gentle Sire,' he said, 'I will gladly support you in any battle but that of petticoats, or face you in single combat, except with a tankard. The boon companions I see here all have no wife at home, but I have. I have married one so worthy that it is to her that I owe my company and account of all I do.'

'Is this then to signify, Baron, that I do wrong since I too have a spouse?' demanded the Duke of Orleans.

'Oh no, my dear master,' replied d'Hocquetonville, 'you are a prince, you do as you find fit.'

As you may imagine, these fine words made the lady closeted fast in the inner room go both hot and cold.

'Ah,' she murmured, 'Raoul, my dear one, you are indeed a noble man.'

'D'Hocquetonville,' now said the Duke of Orleans, 'you are a man I like and whom I count the most faithful and reliable of my followers. We others,' and he turned to give the remaining company a dark glance, 'are bad. But pray be seated a moment, Raoul. When the linnets come—and they are, by the way, also linnets of high rank —you may go to your housewife.

'God's death, I always did assume you to be a man of good behaviour, completely ignorant of the delights of extra-marital love, so, as a matter of fact, in that room there I have taken good care to have ready the Queen of all daughters of Lesbos, a sheer devil who has known how to combine all the devices of womenkind. Now, I really would like you, who never have had much taste for the spices of love, and only dream of war fighting, to be provided for once an opportunity at least once to know the wonderful devices of the gallant sport, the more so since it would be a shame for one of my men to ill-treat so charming a lady.'

Upon these words, d'Hocquetonville sat down to table to please his Prince as far as he thought he legitimately could, so everybody was very gay, with merry tales all round and bawdy talk of womenfolk. In this, as was customary, there was much confession of adventures and lucky encounters, and no woman was spared, even the best loved of them all, the special little tricks of each were betrayed, which led to some very nice, but also very shocking avowals. These in fact, grew in falseness and roguery as the company drained their tankards. The Duke was as gay as if he had inherited the world, egging on his companions, telling more lies to winkle out more home truths, and the company all made inroads on the meats and the wines as they poured forth their merry tales.

Now, as he listened to all this, and his wine went to his head, even d'Hocquetonville too unbuttoned little by little, and despite his strict standards gave himself a bit of head in these matters, till he was as deep in the mire as a saint can be bogged down in his prayers.

Seeing which, the Duke of Orleans, out to satisfy his rage and his spite, started to jockey him.

'Oho, by St Castud,' he cried, 'Raoul, my boy, I see that we are all tarred with the same brush, all discreet till we are at table. Don't fear, we won't tell your good lady. Well, by God's belly, tonight I'm going to introduce you to the delights of heaven. In there,' and he tapped on the door of the bedroom where Lady d'Hocquetonville was hidden, 'in there is a lady-in-waiting and friend of the Queen's, but she's the greatest priestess of Venus there ever was, there's not another to touch her, not even a tart, not a whore, in any brothel either, no, not one to touch her. . . . She must have been begot in a gay moment of Paradise, when Nature was originally spliced and the plants were first making love, with the animals whinnying and bucking all around them and everything afire with love.

'But there's only one thing I should tell you: though she would sleep with a man on the altar, that goddess would, she is far too great a lady to let herself be seen, and too well known to utter any other sound but the inarticulate little cries of love-making. Besides, you won't need any light, her eyes spurt fire enough, nor any speech, for she can tell you the story by hitches and wriggles livelier than those of wild creatures caught in the thickets.

'Only, my dear Raoul, with such a bucking mount, do take care to hang on to the wretch's mane, ride her real hard and see you keep your saddle, or with one heave she'd stick you up on the rafters, if you had only a lump of resin on your backside. She lives on her back, she's always hot and she always wants a man. Our poor late friend young Lord de Giac died smitten by her, for she whipped the marrow out of him in one springtime. By the true God, what man would not sacrifice a quarter of his days to know a feast like that of which she rings the carillon and initiates the delights. The man who has known her would give all eternity without regret for another night of it.'

'But,' said Raoul, 'in unions which are such natural things, how can there be such great divergences?'

At this Orleans roared with laughter, and all the company joined in. Then, at a wink from their master, lit by the wines, they all began relating refinements and niceties of love, ad infinitum, shouting each other down and denying each other's stories, but yet licking their chops with enjoyment, and so, totally ignorant of the fact that it was an innocent schoolgirl on the far side of the inner door, these rascals, who with liquor had by now drowned any trace of shame in themselves, went into details fit to make the faces carved or cast on chimney, wall and ceiling blush.

Then the Duke took the next step. Declaring that the lady shut in the bedroom, awaiting a gallant, should be made the Empress of these lurid fantasies, and adding that she added devilish spicy ones of her own every single night, the Duke took advantage of a moment when all tankards were empty, to push d'Hocquetonville (not, it must be admitted, against any great resistance, so heated up was he) into that bedroom where, in this way, Orleans forced the unwilling courtier's wife to make her choice by which pointed iron tool she would live or die.

Halfway through the night, Lord d'Hocquetonville emerged from the inner closet, very pleased with himself, though still with a shadow of remorse for having deceived his wife. And, later, the Duke of Orleans let Lady d'Hocquetonville out of the grounds through a side door, so that she could get home before her husband. As she passed the postern she whispered in the Prince's ear:

'This will cost us all dear.'

One year later, in the old Temple Street, Raoul d'Hocquetonville, who had left the service of the Duke of Orleans for that of Jehan de Bourgongne, got in the first blow and delivered this Duke, the King's brother, a stroke on the head with his battle-axe which finished him off. Within a year, Lady d'Hocquetonville was dead, having faded like a flower deprived of air or gnawed by a worm. On her tomb in a convent of Peronne her husband erected a fine marble tablet to her memory, the wording being:

DROLL STORIES

HERE LIES
BERTHA OF BURGUNDY
NOBLE AND LOVELY WIFE
OF
RAOUL, BARON D'HOCQUETONVILLE
ALAS, PRAY NOT FOR HER SOUL
SHE
HAS BLOSSOMED AGAIN IN PARADISE
JANUARY 11TH, IN THE YEAR OF
OUR LORD MCCCCVIII
AT THE AGE OF XXII YEARS
LEAVING HER TWO SONS AND HER LORD SPOUSE IN GREAT
MOURNING

This epitaph was written in lovely Latin, but should, for the convenience of all, be turned into our modern tongue, even though the word lovely is a poor rendering of *formosa*, which means *of gracious figure*. The Duke of Burgundy, nicknamed the Fearless, to whom, before dying, Lord d'Hocquetonville confided the sufferings cemented for ever in his heart, used to say, despite his fierce rigour in such matters, that this epitaph made him unhappy for a month and that, among the abominations of his cousin Orleans there was one for which, were he not already murdered, he would re-murder him, and that is for having put vice into the most divine virtuousness in the world and thereby prostituted two noble hearts one to the other. When he said this, he was thinking of Lady d'Hocquetonville and of his own wife too, for without any apparent reason her portrait too had been placed in the room in which his cousin kept a gallery of paintings of the women he had made his lascivious mistresses.

This story is so profoundly shocking that when it was told by the Count de Charolois to the Dauphin, later King Louis XI, he refused to have his secretaries give it to the light of day in his Collection. This was out of regard for his Great-Uncle, the Duke of Orleans, and his old friend Funois, son of the Duke. Yet the character of Lady d'Hocquetonville is so brightly virtuous and so gloriously sad that for her sake one can excuse the tale being told here, despite the devilry of ingenuity and the revenge of the Duke of Orleans. The just termination of that rascal's life did however have its bad side. It caused a number of serious wars which at last, losing patience, Louis XI ended by more blows of the axe.

This is clear proof that in all things there is a woman at the bottom of it, whether it is France or some other land. It also shows that sooner or later we have to pay for our follies.

VI

The Danger of Being Too Much
of an Innocent

That good soldier of Touraine, Lord Moncontour—the one who in memory of the battle won by the Duke of Anjou, now our most glorious monarch, built Vouvray castle—it was because he bore himself so valiantly in that affair, conquering the greatest of heretics, that the Court was authorized to assume the name—well, this said illustrious warrior had two sons who were both good Catholics, the elder of them standing very well at Court. But it happened that just after the armistice which was concluded before the Saint Bartholomew plot, this worthy man returned to his manor, which was not then as elaborate as it is today, only to receive the sad news that his son had just lost his life, killed in a duel by de Villequier. The poor father was the more grieved by this since he had just arranged a fine marriage for this son with a girl of the male branch of the Amboises.

Now, this most pitiable and lamentably untimely death swept away all that fortune and also those advantages by which Moncontour had hoped to make his family great and noble. To the same end he had early entered his other son as a monk under the guidance of a man who, renowned for his sanctity, was bringing him up in a most Christian way as the father desired, aiming (so ambitious was Moncontour), to develop the lad some day into a meritorious cardinal.

To this end the good Abbot had kept the said young man in private residence, so no foul weed should take root in his mind. He was bringing him up pure of soul and truly contrite, as all men of the church should be. Thus it happened that this young clerk thereby had reached the age of nineteen without knowing any other love but that of God, or any other nature but that of the angels, who are fashioned without those carnal appendages of ours, so they should stay very pure, seeing that otherwise they would make much use of them. Which, since he wanted his attendants always to be spruce, was what the monarch of the upper world feared. And a very good idea of his this was, too, because his excellent young men are not able to go dibbling about in taverns or potting about in brothels, like ours. Thus the Almighty is well looked after. Apart from this, however, do not forget that he is lord of everything.

So now, in his misfortune, the Baron de Moncontour resolved to

199

get his second son out of the cloisters, and equip him with military and courtly purple, instead of that of the church. Further he made up his mind to marry him to the same girl to whom the dead one had been affianced which was a sensible idea, for, swaddled with continence and plugged up all round as the young monk was, the bride ought to be better served and happier with him than she would have been with the elder one, by the ladies of the Court, who had already been well harvested, well stooked, well flailed and well winnowed.

First befrocked, then now defrocked, this younger son, who was by birth rather a sheepish fellow, acquiesced in his father's sacred wishes and agreed to the marriage without a clue to what a wife meant, let alone, which was indeed much worse, what a woman was. And now, his journey hindered by the marching and clashing of rival factions, this dim creature (much dimmer than even the dim should be), only reached Vouvray Castle on the eve of the wedding, which was to be celebrated there by special dispensation bought of the office of the Archbishop of Tours.

Now a word about the bride and what she was like. Widowed long since, her mother lived with Lord de Braguelogne, Civil Lieutenant of the Chatelet Ambit of Paris, while, to the great scandal of people at the time, the wife lived with Lord de Lignières. But in those days these people had so many beams in their eyes that they had no claim to see the motes of others. Thus in every home folk were going to perdition without thought of what their neighbours would say, some slowly, some cantering, but many at the gallop, though, since the road was in any case downhill, there was also a smaller number who just ambled their way to hell. Hence at the time Old Nick was doing very well all round, and frisky behaviour was quite the mode. Poor old Madame Virtue meanwhile sat shivering in some shelter, nobody knew exactly where, just managing to keep body and soul together with a mere handful of wives whose conduct was proper.

In the most noble Amboise mansion meanwhile the Dowager Lady of Chaumont was still on the active list, a woman of long standing, well-tested virtue, in whom whatever religion or civility existed in that illustrious family were concentrated. She had taken charge of the little maid who plays the principal part in this story when the girl was only ten years old. This left Lady Amboise free to come and go as she wished, with no need to worry, and since then she had dropped in only once a year, when the Court was passing, to have a peep at her daughter.

Regardless, however, of that high degree of maternal reserve, Lady Amboise was invited to the offspring's wedding, and so was Lord Braguelogne, for good old soldier Baron de Moncontour knew

who was who and what was what. Only the dear dowager did not
attend, because her frightful sciatica would not let her, nor her
catarrh, nor her poor legs, which no longer permitted tripping about.

This caused the good lady many tears. It much irked her in any
case to abandon that gentle young virgin her pupil to the hazards of
Court and life generally, especially as this was as pretty a maid as a
pretty maid could be, but there was no possibility of preventing her
thus taking flight, though she did not let her go without a promise
of constant prayer and masses every evening for her good fortune.

By this the good lady was somewhat comforted, reflecting too that
the support of her old age was being taken over by a demi-saint,
whom the above-mentioned Abbot had trained to virtuous acts, the
Abbot in question being a man of her acquaintance, a circumstance
incidentally which had done much to ease the last-minute switch
over of bridegrooms.

At last, kissing the young bride and with tearful eyes, the virtuous
Dowager gave those final words of advice which married women
give to brides, such as to be respectful to her mother-in-law and
obedient in all things to her husband. Thus with great to-do the
maid reached Chaumont Castle, with such a train of maids and skiv-
vies, grooms and gentlemen and valets, that you would have thought
it was a Papal Legate arriving. It thus happened that both groom and
bride only got there on the eve of the ceremony.

At last, the feasting over, the two young people were made man
and wife in great splendour, on the Lord's Day, at a mass conducted
in the Castle by the Bishop of Blois, who was a great friend of the
Baron de Moncontour. In short, there were celebrations, with feasting and merry-making of all sorts till break of day. But before midnight, after the fashion of Touraine, the bridesmaids took the bride
to her room, while the poor innocent of a husband was subjected to
all manner of japes aimed at keeping him up, away from his innocent
half, and such an ignorant fool was he that he actually aided and
abetted them, till at last the good Baron insisted on putting a stop to
the practical joking and leg-pulling, for it was high time his son got
to work.

So our gentle innocent went to his bride in the bedroom, when he
thought more highly of her than even the painted Virgins, in the
Dutch, Italian and other pictures to which he had said his *Our Fathers*
so many times. Bear in mind that the principal hindrance to his proving himself a husband was his sheer ignorance of the task which now
confronted him. He merely knew that there was some sort of job to
be done, but what it was exactly, he had been far too shy to ask anybody, even his own father, who had merely grunted:

'You know what you've to do, make a good job of it, boy.'

Now that he beheld the delightful maid vouchsafed him, she was tucked well down between the sheets, and, though devilish curious, was sternly turned away from him. Her glance, however, was as sharp as the point of a halberd, and inwardly she kept telling herself that what she had to do was obey. She was, you see, also utterly ignorant, so merely waited on the desires of this gentleman of rather ecclesiastical appearance to whom, after all, she now belonged.

Seeing the situation, young Moncontour went to the bedside, scratched behind his ear, then knelt down, at which exercise he was expert.

'Have you said your prayers?' he whispered, as if butter would not melt in his mouth.

'No,' she replied, 'I forgot. Do you think I should?'

So the young couple began their conjugal life by calling on God for aid, which was in itself not unseemly, except that it was not God, only Old Nick who heard them and replied, God at the moment being completely preoccupied by that abominable new Protestant faith.

'What did they tell you to do?' inquired the husband.

'Love you,' said she, in all simplicity.

'They didn't tell me that,' he said. 'But I do, all the same. Moreover, I am ashamed to say, I love you more than I used to love God.'

These words did not seem to worry the bride too much.

'If it won't disturb you too much, I should awfully like to get into bed with you,' resumed the husband.

'I will be pleased to make room. I am anyway supposed to be under you,' she said.

'All right then,' he said, 'only please don't look. I am going to undress and get in.'

At this virtuous announcement, the maid most expectantly turned the other way, for this was the first time she had found only the thin partition of a girl's shift between herself and a young man.

In due course the booby comes and slips cautiously into the bed. In this way husband and wife found themselves indeed united, though not at all in the way you are thinking of.

Have you ever seen a monkey freshly brought from overseas first given a walnut? Knowing by monkey imagination how tasty the food hidden inside the shell is, he sniffs and turns it about a thousand monkeyish ways, muttering I know not what between his teeth. Oh, how lovingly he examines it, how studiously, how he holds it and pulls it about and turns it over and angrily shakes it, and often, if it is a monkey of no great breed or sense, in the end he leaves it alone.

Just so our poor innocent who, as day was breaking, was compelled to confess to his darling wife that as he had not a notion how to accomplish his duty, nor even exactly what the duty was, nor even where to find the office, so to speak, he would have to make some inquiries about it, seeking assistance and, as he put it, a supporting hand.

'You must,' she said, 'since, unfortunately, I shall not be able to teach you.'

Indeed, despite all their devices, all manner of attempts and the countless extraordinary things which boobs will try, things which would never even occur to anybody who knows what love is, the young couple fell asleep, quite despondent at not having succeeded in cracking their conjugal nut. However, at least they had sufficient gumption to agree both to profess to having been very satisfied with their first night.

When the young wife rose, still a virgin, totally unqueened, she boasted valiantly about it all and said she had the king of husbands. But, when it came to being ragged and teased about it, she was like anyone else who knows nothing, she piled it on a bit too much. Everybody indeed found that she was a bit too free with her tongue, for when a certain Lady de la Roche-Carnon prompted a young girl named de la Bourdaisière, who was also ignorant of such matters, to ask the bride 'how many loves her husband put in the oven', she overdid it again and cried: 'Twenty-four.'

Now, as the young husband went droopily about, which hurt his wife very much (for she was following him out of the corner of her eye all the time, hoping to see his innocence come to an end), the ladies of the company got the idea into their heads that the pleasures of the first night had cost him a little too dearly. They also thought that the bride must already be feeling rather rueful at having exhausted him already.

Now came the wedding breakfast, with all the prickly wisecracks which in those days were so much in taste. Somebody for instance, made the remark that the bride looked very open, another that somewhere in the castle during the night he had heard a lot of knocking, a third that somebody's loaf had come out of the oven very soft, and yet another that after such a night there were two families that had lost something they would never get back again, and there were countless other salty observations and sly references which, unfortunately, were all Greek to the young groom. However, on account of the wealth of the families and their neighbours and other guests, nobody had really been to bed at all, there had been dancing and rollicking and roistering all night, as is usual at weddings with the nobility.

All this satisfied the said Lord de Braguelogne, while Lady d'Amboise, well primed by the thought of the nice things happening to her daughter, was with a view to a gallant encounter eyeing the Civil Lieutenant of her own Ambit with eyes as sharp as a kestrel's. But the poor Civil Lieutenant, so knowledgeable about court bailiffs and sergeants, and quick to seize all the rogues and pickpockets of Paris, made out he did not perceive the opportunity offered him, especially as it came from a mistress of so long-standing. For the love of this grand lady was getting rather burdensome to him. Indeed, it was only from a lively sense of what was proper that he stuck to her at all. It was, he thought, not seemly for a Lieutenant of the police to change his mistresses like a gentleman-in-waiting. After all, he was in charge of public decency, police and religion.

Nevertheless, there would have to be an end to his rebellion. The day after the wedding, most of the guests left, and this meant that Lady d'Amboise, Lord de Braguelogne and the grandparents could go to bed at last. Hence, as supper drew nigh the good Lieutenant was the recipient of summonses so nearly explicit that it was no more seemly than it would have been, had they come from the magistrates' court, to oppose any procrastinatory arguments.

Before supper, therefore, Lady d'Amboise made signs (more than a hundred), aimed at extracting good old Braguelogne from the room where he had settled down to entertain the bride. But in place of the Lieutenant it was that innocent of a bridegroom who emerged. He thought he would like to take a stroll in the air with his dear young wife's mamma. The reason was that the innocent had suddenly conceived an idea which had grown like a mushroom, namely, he would make inquiry of this good lady (since he thought her of most circumspect behaviour), about the task before him. Yes, recalling the saintly precepts of his spiritual pastor, who had always told him to seek information on any matter from 'elderly folk with experience of life', he proposed to entrust his situation to Lady d'Amboise.

Being all timidity and shyness, however, before he could find how to put the matter, he took a few turns up and down the garden. Lady d'Amboise for her part was extremely glum, being shockingly put out by the blindness, deafness and apparently deliberate paralysis of the senses of Lord de Braguelogne. Hence, as she paced at the side of this delectable morsel, this innocent of whom she thought nothing, unable to conceive that a tom so well provided with young bacon would be thinking of elderly folk, she mused in this wise:

'Silly old ass, with his daddy-long-legs of a beard, his floppy grey gappy rotten old beard, his dim-witted, shameless beard, lacking respect for a woman, his beard that makes out it can't feel or see or hear, his debearded beard, his beaten-down beard, his be-draggled beard, his gutless beard, may the Italian Pox deliver me from the rascally old wretch, with his thrashed-out nose, his snotty-snitchy nose, his frozen nose, his godless nose, his nose as dry as the sounding-board of a lute, his bloodless, soulless, shadowless, dripless nose, his nose shrivelled as a dead vine-leaf is, oh, how I hate that nose of his, that antique of a nose, that wind-stuffed nose! . . . That *dead* nose! Whatever was I thinking of to attach myself to such a truffle nose, to an old bolt like that that doesn't know where it's proper hole is! Old Nick can have my share of that dishonourable old conk, that desiccated old braddle, that grizzled old topknot, that marmoset of a headpiece, that old bag of rags, that limp rag of a man, that whatever it is! What I ought to do is find me a young fellow who would husband me well . . . and often . . . every day . . . one who would . . .'

She had reached these condign reflections when the young innocent of a bridegroom at last brought himself to pipe up his *introit* to this most pepperishly worked-up female. The result was that the very first circumlocution caught fire in her mind like a hot spark on tinderwood in the soldier's musket, and it at once occurred to her that she might do far worse than try her own son-in-law as stop-gap, and so now she murmured to herself a very different response: 'Oh darling young beard, how sweet you do smell. . . . Oh, pert pretty nose, all dewy and fresh. . . . Oh untried beard, oh silly beard, oh virgin beard, oh nose full of delight, oh springtime beard, oh master key of love!'

She had to keep this up the whole length of the garden (and it was a large garden too) before she had connived with the booby that when night fell he should leave his room and slip into hers, where she promised to teach him more than his father knew. The novitiate husband was very pleased with this and thanked Lady d'Amboise, only begging her to keep it secret.

Meanwhile old Braguelogne had been swearing and cursing, saying to himself:

'The silly old jenny, may whooping-cough choke you! May cancer corrode you! You toothless old currycomb! You down-at-heel old slipper, that won't stay on a man's foot! You antiquated old cross-bow! You ten-year-old cod! You old spider, the only time you can move is when you make your web at night! You pop-eyed old corpse! You old Nick's cradle! You old town-crier's lantern! You old hag whose very look is a man's death! You old whiskers of a treacle-seller, hoary enough to make death weep! You old organ-pedal! You old sheath with a hundred blades! You old church porch worn hollow with knees! You old poor-box everybody's dropped his mite in! I'd give my whole fortune to be free of you!'

Just as he was concluding this nice line of thought the young bride, full of thought of the worry it must be to her young husband not to know the way to accomplish this matter essential to marriage, but completely at a loss to guess what it might be, conceived the notion of saving him perhaps considerable worry, shame and trouble by finding out for herself. In this it was her intention to make him a pleasant surprise and please him and when night came, teach him his duty, and be in a position to say: '*This is what it is all about, dear love!*'

So, having been brought up by the old dowager with great respect for elderly folk, she thought she might discourse gracefully with the good Lieutenant of Paris and in so doing extract from him the sweet mystery of coition. At this moment, full of shame at thus being entangled in agonizing reflections on the night's task before him without saying a word to his sportive companion, Lord Braguelogne remarked bluntly to the pretty young bride how lucky she was to have such a nice young husband.

'Yes,' said she, 'he is very nice indeed.'

'Too nice, perhaps?' murmured the Lieutenant, with a smile.

To cut a long story short, things went so smoothly between these two that Lord de Braguelogne suddenly struck up a very different canticle, one trilling with delight and also with promises, regarding the matter under discussion, to spare nothing to disobfuscate the understanding of Lady d'Amboise's daughter, that young person engaging to call on him for her first lesson.

Take account too that the said Lady d'Amboise after supper dinned a shrill music into Braguelogne's ears about his scant recognition of the benefits she had brought him, her estate, her money, her loyalty and all that, and even after half an hour of it she had not spilled one quarter of her wrath. They brandished a hundred blades against each other, yet kept the sheaths on them all.

Meanwhile the young couple, nicely gone to bed, each cogitated inwardly how to slip away, in order to delight the other. At last our dim one declared that he felt all of a flutter, he did not know why, he would have to go out for a breath of fresh air. Immediately, his unqueened spouse suggested that perhaps a little moonlight might do him good. Then the good innocent said how sorry he was for his little one, being left all alone for a moment.

In short, both of them, one after the other, quit the bridal bed, in

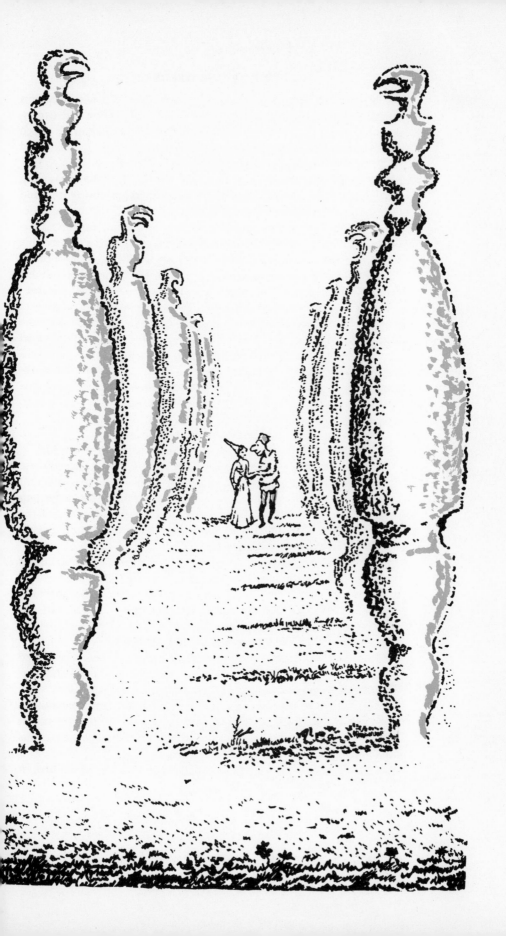

great haste to acquire wisdom. They visited their authorities, who also, as you may imagine, were most impatient. Thus they acquired excellent instruction. What sort, exactly?

I cannot say, because in this matter everybody has his own education system and his own practices. Of all the sciences, this is the one in which the basic principles are most fluid. You may however count on it that there never were pupils who more eagerly acquired the teaching in any tongue, in any form of conjugation or any other discipline. And when at last the two spouses returned to their nest, they were delighted to communicate to each other what they had discovered during their scholarly peregrinations.

'Why, darling,' suddenly cried the bride in astonishment, 'you already know better than my teacher.'

From such fascinating experiment, delight entered the young couple's home and with it went perfect fidelity, for at the very outset of their marriage they each found by experience how much better equipment their partner had than any of their mentors, even including their special subject masters. Hence for the remainder of their days they stuck to the legitimate substance of each other's bodies. Hence too it was that in his old age Lord Moncontour used to say to his friends: 'Take my advice, be cuckolded green, not ripe.'

Which is the true morality for married codpieces.

VII

An Expensive Night of Love

In each winter in which the gentlemen of religion first shed each other's blood (the incident known as the Conspiracy of Amboise), a lawyer named Avenelles lent his dwelling in Marmouzets Street to the Huguenots for their meetings and conventions, since, though utterly unsuspecting that de Condé, La Reg-naudie and others were already plotting to kidnap the King, he was one of their supporters.

This Avenelles was really a nasty piece of work. He was as slippery as a stick of liquorice, and, like all these men of law entombed in the black hole of the high courts, devilishly pale—in fact, he was the most vicious old lawyer that ever lived, sniggering at hangings, a man who would sell his grandmother's shirt for twopence, a regular Judas of a man. According to some authors knowledgeable about such wolves in sheep's clothing, in this Huguenot business he played a very double rôle, as the following story should abundantly show.

He had married a very charming Parisian girl, about whom he was so jealous that he could have killed her had he found an unfamiliar crease in the bed-sheets that she could not explain, which would have been a bad thing, since sheets can get rucks in them honestly. However, the lawyer's young wife as it happens was great at folding her linen, and that was that.

At the same time you may also be sure that, being well aware what an evil nature her husband had, indeed, what a born cut-throat he was, she was very true to him, was this Parisienne lass, always, so to speak, the ready candlestick, always prepared to do her duty, as dumb as a linen-press which never stirs except to open at command.

All the same, to make quite sure, the lawyer had placed her under the sharp-eyed surveillance of an old servant, a duenna as ugly as a cracked old pot. But this duenna had wet-nursed master Avenelles and now in her old age was very much attached to him.

The poor wife, meanwhile, whose only solace in life was her chilly home, used to attend divine service at St John's Church in the Place de Grève, where, as every schoolboy knows, the quality used to meet. There, while mumbling *paternosters* to her maker, she could feast her eyes on all the frizzled, frilled and starched gallants, tripping here, tripping there, flitting about like real butterflies.

This relaxation of hers finished up with her picking out one particular one, a young nobleman who was a friend of the Queen Mother, and to this handsome Italian she quite lost her head. The reason for this no doubt was that he was a man in his Maytime. He was well built, he bore himself finely, he was frank of countenance and he was indeed all a lover should be to fill with love the heart of any woman who, however respectable, felt too tightly laced in marriage, a condition which always irks and prompts a woman to kick over the conjugal traces.

Now you must learn that this young nobleman for his part was equally badly smitten by the good wife, for her tacit love whispered its secret language to him, without either Old Nick or they themselves knowing how. Thus now began a mutual exchange of unspoken love. It started with all the lawyer's wife's concern for her toilet being bestowed on church-going. She was constantly devising new and sumptuous outfits. Next, instead of giving thought to the Almighty, she outraged her Maker by giving thought to her handsome gentleman. Abandoning prayer, she gave herself up to that fire which not only singed her heart, but also moistened her eyes, her lips, indeed, every part of her, seeing that this particular fire always produces moisture. Many a time she told herself that she would give her life to make the acquaintance of that 'handsome lover' who was clearly attracted by her.

What is more, instead of saying her litanies to that lady who was a virgin, her heart now mused in this fashion: *'If only I could feel this handsome lover's wholesome youth and have full enjoyment of love, tasting it all in one moment, a lot I care for the eternal fire into which heretics are cast.'*

After this, observing the good woman's fancy dressing and twigging the way her colour would mount whenever he looked at her, the Italian invariably passed close to her pew and made some of those remarks which the fair sex grasp so well, thinking the while: *'By my father's horns, I swear I'll have that woman, if it costs me my life.'* And when the duenna was looking the other way, the two lovers, by glances calculated to light the fuse of a musketeer (had there been a musketeer present), squeezed and pressed each other, breathed and sniffed each other, mouthed and devoured each other.

Inevitably, a love so deeply thrust into the heart took root. The Italian rigged himself out in the garb of one of Montaigu's pupils and set himself to treating the lawyer's secretaries and rollicking in their company, all in order to find out the husband's habits, when he was absent, when he was away on business and so forth, all on the look-out for the day when to stick horns on his head.

And here is how, to his perdition, the opportunity was arranged. The lawyer, being compelled to follow the Huguenot plot through (particularly as he had made up his mind when the time came to betray it to the de Guises), resolved to go to Blois, where the Court then was, in great danger, of course, of being kidnapped. Getting mind of this, the Italian reached Blois first, and there engineered a master trap into which despite his astuteness, Master Avenelles was bound to fall, and not get free till scarlet with cuckoldom.

Heady with love-yearning, the Italian nobleman summoned all his pages and serving-men there and posted them all over the place, so that when the lawyer arrived, complete with wife and duenna, all the inns where he tried to get rooms told him that, owing to the Court's being in residence, they were full, so they would have to try elsewhere. Further, the Italian gentleman had made an agreement with the man who kept the Soleil Royal by which he took the whole place, installing his own servants in place of the innkeeper's. To make doubly sure, he also dispatched this hotelier and his men away into the country, and further posted his own men so that the lawyer should not get to know anything about it. He then filled the inn with his own friends, newly come to Court, keeping for himself one room above those in which he proposed to establish his fair mistress, the lawyer and the duenna, and in the floor of this room he had a trap-door made leading through to the lawyer's apartment.

Now his chief cook, who was to play the role of innkeeper, and his pages all dressed up like valets and his maids were also suitably rigged out in disguise, and he waited for his scouts to bring him in the chief actors in the play, namely: the wife, the husband, the duenna and their retinue. They were sure to turn up, for, owing to the great influence of the nobles, the merchants, and the army men, the servants and others brought thither by the residence of the young Monarch, the two Queens, the Guises and all the Court, nobody had any right to show astonishment or reveal the plot or the change-about at the Soleil Royal.

Therefore to his discomfiture, Master Avenelles with wife and duenna, pushed around from inn to inn, till he thought himself very lucky to be accommodated at the Soleil Royal where our gallant was installed ready, warming up and maturing his passion.

When the lawyer had settled in, the gentleman began strolling in the yard, on the look-out and search for a glance from his lady. Nor did he have long to wait, seeing that Milady Avenelles soon peeped out herself (as a woman will), whereupon, not without some fluttering of her heart-strings, she saw and recognized her gallant, much beloved gentleman. And was she not happy! Had they by good fortune been alone together for a jiffy the good fellow would not have had a second to wait, so fevered was she from tip to toe.

'How warm it is in the rays of this lord!' cried the lawyer's wife, meaning to say 'sun', for it was shining brightly.

The moment he heard this, the lawyer bounded to the window, when he saw the Italian.

'Ah, so it's lords you want, is it, my popsie?' he cried, then seizing her arm, drew her back, and flung her on the bed as if she had been one of his pouches of papers.

'Don't you forget that even though at my side in place of a sword I have only a writing-set,' he declared, 'in that writing-set there is a pen-knife, and that pen-knife shall certainly plunge into your heart at the least sign of sullying of our marriage. For methinks I have seen that man before somewhere!'

The lawyer was indeed so spitefully angry that getting to her feet, the young woman cried:

'Well, then kill me! I should be ashamed to hide from you that, after being threatened like that, by you, you shall never touch me again. From now on my only thought will be to go to bed with a more civilized lover than you are.'

'Ah well, my little lambkin!' cried the lawyer in surprise, 'perhaps I did go a bit far. Kiss me, pet, and forgive.'

'I won't kiss you and I won't forgive either,' she said, 'you are a bad man.'

Now Avenelles tried to take by force what his spouse refused him, whence ensued a struggle from which he emerged rather scratched about the face. The worst, however, was that at this juncture, well initialled by her nails, the lawyer had to leave her in the care of his old nurse, for the conspirators were in council and waiting for him.

Seeing Avenelles leave, the Italian gentleman at once placed one of his men on guard at the street corner, and went to his room, where, opening that lucky trapdoor soundlessly, he gave his lady a *Psst! Psst!* which though very muffled was audible to her heart, an organ which usually hears everything. She looked up at once and saw her fine lover no more than four flea-hops above her. At a sign from him, she grasped two ropes of coarse silk, to which were attached rings through which she could pass her arms, and in the twinkling of an eye she was hauled up on pulleys from her bed into the upper room. The trapdoor closing at once, the old duenna down below was in a great state when, turning her head, she could no longer see either clothes or lawyer's wife, and grasped that a certain robbery had taken place. But how? By whom? By what? Whither? It was indeed a *hey presto* of a job. Alchemists over their crucibles reciting *Her Trippa* could not better it.

However, the old woman at least recognized the nature of the crucible and also what was stirring in it. The one was the most de-lightful asset of the lawyer's wife, the other was a fine fricassee of cuckoldry. She awaited her lord and master dumbfounded. Indeed, it was like awaiting death, because in his fury he was capable of razing everything to the ground and it would only be with great prudence that the duenna could escape with her life, since the lawyer had left her locked in with the wife.

The first thing Madame Avenelles saw up above was a delightful supper, with the hearth well aglow, though her lover's heart was even fiercer in heat as he took her and kissed her, with tears of delight, first on the eyes, to thank them for those lovely glances during services at St Jean's in the Place de Grève. After that the well-fired lawyer's wife did not stint her kisses, and was delighted to be well worshipped, well pressed, well caressed, in the style of famished lovers. After the first bout, they fully agreed about being one another's all night. They were utterly careless of what might come. She counted the future as nought in comparison with the pleasures of this immediate night. He trusted to his credit and his sword to repeat the pleasure *ad lib*.

In short, neither of them thought much about their lives provided that together they could put behind them a thousand lives, enjoy a thousand delights, each giving the other double what they got. They felt as if they plunged headlong down a chasm, glorying thus to fall closely clipped together, piling all the fury of their love into this one time.

How lustily they loved! Poor little middle-class folk who go to bed coyly with their housewives never know such love as this, for they remain ignorant of what fierce heart thrills, what hot gushes of life, what lusty engagements are feasible when two young lovers first come together all a-glow with desire and coupled under pain of death. Thus the Italian and the young wife paid little heed to food and were soon in bed, and we must leave them to it, since no speech save that of Paradise, of which we are ignorant, could describe the delicious pangs their writhings brought them.

Meanwhile, the lawyer husband, so well cuckolded that any memory of his marriage was swept away by love, this fellow Avenelles, that is, found himself in sore difficulties. With all his captains and bigwigs, the Prince de Condé had come to that Huguenot consilium, and at this meeting the decision was taken to kidnap the Queen Mother, the Guises, the young King and the young Queen, and effect a *coup-d'état*.

With this grave turn of events, seeing he was risking his neck, the lawyer became quite insensitive to the said horn-implantation, but busied himself, instead of thinking about his wife, with hurrying to the Lord Cardinal of Lorraine to betray the plot. The Cardinal at once took the lawyer round to his brother the Duke, when all three put their heads together, the two brothers making fine promises to Master Avenelles, whom only with difficulty would they let go somewhere about the middle of the night, when he slipped secretly from the castle.

At that moment the Italian gentleman's pages and other men were making a sorry din, in honour of their master's adventitious nuptials. Thus, arriving back at the hotel in the thick of it, through a forest of merry hiccups, Avenelles was assailed all round by roistering, rollicking rapscallions, and when he entered his room and found only the duenna there, their ribald laughter took the colour from his cheeks.

The poor duenna would have explained, but the lawyer gave her no time to do so. Taking her by the throat, he ordered her with warning gestures to keep a still tongue in a wise head. Then, rummaging in his trunk, he took from it a good dagger.

Just as he was slipping this from its sheath to hone it up, an unrestrained, blatant, joyous, charming, amorous, heavenly burst of laughter, followed by certain speech only too easy to understand, descended from the rafters above. The wily lawyer immediately extinguished his candle, and in default of the keyhole customary in legal matters, now through the cracks between the boards saw a light which revealed the mystery to him, being that he had further recognized both the voice of his spouse and that of the Italian with whom she was fighting a very pretty duel.

Taking his old servant by the arm, Avenelles now crept up the stairs, feeling for the door of the room which contained the lovers, and indeed succeeded. It must now be recorded that with a frightfully legal unceremoniousness he flung that door open and in one bound was on that bed, where he surprised his wife half-naked in the arms of her gentleman.

'Ahhhh!' cried she.

Dodging the first stroke, the lover tried to snatch the dagger from the lawyer's hands, but the lawyer held on like grim death. But, feeling that in the struggle he was hampered by his assistant, who now had him in a terrible iron grip, and also bitten by his wife, who was rending his flesh from his bones with her fine teeth, gnawing him like a dog with a bone, he suddenly conceived a better way of assuaging his anger. In his local patois this newly be-horned legal devil wickedly ordered his servant to tie the lovers together with those silk ropes which had been used to haul the lady up there and then, throwing down his dagger, he helped her accomplish this. This being achieved in no time, he gagged them with the sheets to stifle their cries, and without a word ran across the room for his good dagger.

At this moment, however, a number of the Duke de Guise's men burst into the place, for during this scrimmage nobody had heard them sacking everything around the inn. These men, now demanding Master Avenelles, were warned by a cry of one of the pages of the trussed-up, half-dead Italian gentleman. Flinging themselves between the man with the dagger and the lovers, they disarmed the lawyer, then did their duty by arresting him and taking him to the castle prison, together with his wife and the duenna, whereupon the de Guises' men, recognizing a friend of their masters', with whom at the moment the Queen was anxious to take counsel, and whom they were under instructions to take to the Council, they asked him to go with them.

The gentleman was soon untied, and while he dressed, on the quiet told the man in charge of the escort that for love of him he was to see that he kept the husband apart from the wife. The Italian promised the man his favour, good promotion, even a good sum of money, if he took care to obey him in this matter. Indeed, to make more sure, he revealed why he made this request, adding that if the husband found himself within reach of that charming young woman, he would be sure to give her a blow in the belly from which she would never recover.

In the end, what he told this officer to do was to put the woman in a pleasant part of the gaol, on a level with the gardens, but the lawyer in a good dungeon, and also keep him well fettered and chained. This the officer in question both promised and did, while the Italian himself went with his lady as far as the castle yard, feeling sure that the upshot of this move would be her widowhood, so he might even take her as his own married wife.

Master Avenelles was indeed now thrown into an airless back dungeon, while, out of consideration for her lover, who was Lord Scipio Sardini, a nobleman of Lucca, a very rich man who, as we have already said, was a friend of Queen Catherine de Medici, at the time hand in glove with the Guises, his charming wife was placed in a little closet over his head.

Now, hurrying up to the Queen, in whose chamber a secret grand council was in progress, the Italian learned what was afoot, and the peril in which the Royal Household stood. He found the privy councillors very disconcerted and astonished by the plot, but he brought them all to agreement, telling them they would find it all to their advantage. It was indeed due to his advice that the wise measure was taken of lodging the King at Amboise Castle, so as to be able there to bag all the heretics and put them to death. (Actually, we all know, of course, how the Queen and the de Guises dilly-dallied and how the Conspiracy of Amboise really ended, but that does not concern us here.)

When morning came, they all left the Queen Mother's chamber, with everything arranged, Lord Sardini was not forgetful of his passion for that citizeness, though he was at the time badly smitten also by Fair Limeuil, a girl of the Queen Mother's household (a relative of hers, in fact, through the Tour de Turenne family), and he inquired why the old Judas had been put behind bars. When the Cardinal of Lorraine then assured him that he had no intention whatsoever of harming the lawyer, but had merely put him temporarily out of the way, out of fear of his remorse, and to be sure of his silence till it was all over, and added that he intended to liberate him when time and place warranted.

'Liberate him?' cried the man of Lucca. 'Not on your life! Stuff the blackbeetle in a sack and tip him into the Loire. First of all, I know the man. He would never forgive you for gaoling him. He will take up his preaching again. So it would be pleasing to the Lord to get rid of a heretic. Then nobody will know your secrets and none of his confederates will bring himself to ask what happened to him, because he is a traitor. Release his wife for me and I'll fix the rest, I'll get him out of the way.'

'A first-rate idea!' laughed the Cardinal. 'But before taking advantage of your advice I'll run along and have them put under stricter guard. Hallo there!'

A police officer ran up and was ordered not to let anyone whatsoever have dealings with the two prisoners. Next, the Cardinal asked Sardini to make it known at his mansion that the lawyer had left Blois to go back to his briefs in Paris. The men charged with Avenelle's arrest had been strictly ordered to treat him as a man of importance, so they did not strip him or rob him.

Thus the lawyer still had thirty crowns in his purse, and he resolved to spill them all, if he could but satisfy his vengeance and with solid arguments prove to his gaolers that it ought to be permissible for him to see his own wife, for he doted on her and desired her legitimate embrace.

Fearing for his mistress that if that red-bearded old lawyer got near her, he must gravely fear misfortune for her, Sardini now decided he should spirit her away that very night and get her to a safe place, so he hired some boatmen and their boat with them and hid them near the bridge, after which he instructed three of his nimbler men to file through the bars of the lawyer's wife's cell, and take her and bring her to the outer garden wall, where he would be waiting for her.

Good files were bought, and all these preparations were carried out, while he secured himself a morning interview with the Queen Mother, whose rooms were above the dungeons where the lawyer and his wife were held, for he relied on the Queen's ready agreement to the flight. He was indeed received by her and asked her not to find it bad of him if, unknown to the Cardinal or de Guise, he freed the lady. Then he persuaded her very vigorously to tell de Lorraine to throw the husband in the river, to all of which the Queen murmured: '*Amen.*'

The lover then sent his lady an urgent note hidden in a dish of pickled cucumbers to inform her of her impending widowhood and the hour of her escape, of all of which she was very pleased, was this Parisienne.

Therefore, when dusk fell, and the soldiers on guard had been got out of the way by the Queen, who sent them to see a ray of moonlight which had frightened her, there were men speedily removing the cell bars and calling to the lady, who, ready enough, was thence taken to Lord Sardini on the wall.

But, once the postern gate was closed, the Italian, outside, as he thought with his lady, now saw her throw off her mantle and turn into none other than the lawyer, who at once seized his cuckolder's throat and tried to strangle him, dragging him to the water's edge to tip him into the Loire, with Sardini fighting back, shouting, writhing, but unable despite his stiletto to get free from that gowned devil. Then he was silent, and as he fell back into a sewage ditch at the lawyer's feet, through the confusion of this frightful wrestling match, in the moonlight, he saw that Avenelle's cheeks were splashed red with the blood of his wife.

Thinking the Italian dead, the infuriated lawyer left him, another reason being that the serving-men with torches were now rushing to the scene. Just in time he leapt into the boat and got quickly away.

Thus poor Mistress Avenelles was the only one to die, seeing that Lord Sardini, though badly throttled, was found lying there still alive, and recovered, later, as everyone knows, to marry the lovely Limeuil girl—after that lovely one had given birth to a child in the Queen's room, a great scandal which from great affection the Queen Mother tried to conceal and which further Sardini's marrying her from great love, covered, Catherine in return giving him the lovely estate of Chaumont-sur-Loire, with the Castle thrown in.

However, Sardini had been so furiously nipped, trodden and poked by that lawyer husband that he never made old bones, and thus still in the springtime of her age the Limeuil girl became a widow. In spite of his misdeed, however, the lawyer was not prosecuted. On the contrary, after returning to the Huguenots, for whom he worked in Germany, he actually had the ingenuity to get himself included in the list of those pardoned by the Edict of Nantes.

Poor Mistress Avenelles, pray for her salvation. Nobody knows where her body was thrown, she never had any prayers said over her dead body, nor Christian burial. Alas, all you ladies whose love affairs go well, do give a thought to her!

VIII

The Sermon of the Merry Incumbent of Meudon

When Master François Rabelais finally came to the Court of King Henry, the second of that name, it was that winter in which, by force of Nature he was to relinquish his bodily form, to be resurrected and live again for ever in his writings, all a-glow as they are with that kindly philosophy to which man will again and again be bound to have recourse.

The grand old man when he died had counted, or nearly so, seventy broods of swallows. His Homeric skull was almost bare of hair, but he still had a beard expressive of his immense dignity, and in that sly smile of his, springtide ever breathed, just as wisdom dwelt in that ample forehead. He made an imposing old man, say those who had the fortune to behold that countenance in which Socrates and Aristophanes, once such enemies, now mingled their features in friendship.

It was indeed because he could hear his last hour tolling that he decided to go and greet the King of France, for this sovereign of ours, having repaired to his Castle of Tournelle, the veteran had the Royal Court within a stone's throw, since he then lived at Jardins-de-St-Paul. When he arrived there were gathered in the Royal Chamber Queen Catherine, Lady Diana (whom for reasons of high policy the Queen received), the King himself, the Constable of France, Cardinals de Lorraine and du Bellay, Lords de Guise, also Lord de Birague and a number of other Italians, who were at this juncture, under the Queen's protection, taking a front place at Court. There were also present the Admiral, Montgomery, various gentlemen in waiting, and a bunch of poets, as Mellin de Sainct-Gelais, for instance, Philibert d'Orme and Lord Brantôme.

When he caught sight of Rabelais, the King, who thought the veteran a great *farceur*, with a broad grin and after a few introductory words, said:

'I suppose, by the way, you've never coughed up a single sermon to those Meudon parishioners of yours?'

Master Rabelais assumed the King to be joking, for he had never concerned himself with his living beyond collecting the emoluments of the Meudon sinecure, so he replied:

'Sire, my flock is universal and all Christendom has heard my sermons quite well.'

Then, casting a glance at all those courtiers, who, save for du Bellay and de Châtillon, generally considered Rabelais to be merely a clown with a little book-learning (whereas he was the King of all Minds and a better king too than him of whom the courtiers merely respected the crown), there came into the worthy fellow's head the malicious desire, before stripping off the outward apparel of this world, for once to piss his fill on all their courtly heads, in a philosophical sense, of course, exactly as good Gargantua was pleased to drench the gentry of Paris from the high tower of Notre Dame. So he added:

'If you happen to be in a good mood, Sire, I could regale you with a nice little sermon, one which will always come in useful, too, one which I have been storing up under my left ear-drum for delivery in some good place, to serve like a parable of old.'

'My lords,' cried the King, 'I pray silence for Master François Rabelais, and as it apparently concerns our salvation, *oyez*, gentlemen, *oyez*, our author is pregnant with some sort of hot-gospel witticisms.'

'Sire,' said good old Rabelais, 'I commence.'

All the courtiers were at once silent and formed a ring, pliant as withies before the man who had engendered Pantagruel, and Master François then burbled out the following Tale in words the distinguished eloquence of which is unmatchable. But as the Tale in question has not come down to us verbatim, the Author may be pardoned for retelling it in his own style.

In his old age, Gargantua had queer ways which surprised his domestics greatly, but were indeed forgiven him, seeing that he was then seven hundred and four years old—whatever, in his *Stromates*, Saint Clement of Alexandria may say alleging that at this point Gargantua was about six hours younger, which matters little.

Well, this paternal master, seeing everything in his home going widdershins, everybody grabbing as he could, he fell into great fear of being utterly penniless in his last moments, so he resolved to think out some more efficient way of running his estates. And did so well. To the end that in the cellars of the Gargantuan mansion he tucked away a fine pile of red wheat, twenty jars of mustard and many another tasty morsel, such as Tourainian dried plums and apricots, wheaten bannocks, pork scraps and goose scraps, Olivet cheeses, goat's milk cheeses and other cheeses famous from Langeais to Loches, jars of melted-down butter, hare pasties, ducks in white onion sauce, pigs' trotters in white crocks and tubs of split peas, pretty little boxes of Orleans quince cheese, kegs of lampreys, jars of green sauce, river game, such as francolins, teal, sheldrake, herons, flamingoes, all preserved in sea-salt, dried raisins, tongues smoked according to the recipe of his famous ancestor, Happe-Mousche, stocks of sweetmeats of all kinds for Gargamelle when good and countless other things, the details of which are to be read in the *Collections of Riparian Laws* and certain scattered folios once part of the *Capitularies, Pragmaticals* and *Royal Establishments, Decrees and Institutions* of the period.

To cut a long story short, good fellow Gargantua clapped specs to nose, so to speak, or nose to specs, and set about the search for a good winged dragon or unicorn to whose care he might consign this most valuable store. Much preoccupied with this, he paced and paced about his gardens. He would have nothing of your Cockserons, being that, as the hieroglyphs apparently assert, the Egyptians were let down by them. He also rejected any of the vast cohorts of Coke-morrhahs, seeing that the Emperors had had more than enough of them (also the Romans, according to what that dour fellow Tacitus has to say of them). Next he rejected the united senatorial of Pichro-choliers, shovelfuls of Magi, skepfuls of Druids, legions of Papi-manians and cohorts of Massoretians, who sprouted like spear-grass and empested every patch of ground, as his son Pantagruel had assured him when he came back from his travels. And thus, mulling over classical Gallic tales, the old man lost confidence in every breed and had such a bounty been vouchsafed him, would there and then have demanded from the Creator of all things one utterly new.

Gargantua, however, was diffident about troubling God concerning his own petty troubles. Indeed, he just did not know what to choose. He was beginning to wonder whether such a goodly store of comestibles was not going to be rather a burden, when what should he see toddle across the path in front of his nose, but a nice little shawcrop (or shrew) of the noble race of shawcrops, whose device is *all gules in a field azure*. By the Belly of Mahomet, take due note that this was a fine buck shawcrop, with the finest tail in the family, and he was preening away there in the sunshine like any one of God's good shawcrops, proud to be in this world in post-diluvian reinstatement by letters patent of incontestable nobility, moreover, duly recorded in the Central Court of the Universe, for it has been established by Oecumenical Investigation that there was such a shawcrop in Noah's Ark.

At this point Master Alcofibras raised his bonnet a trifle and made the pious observation that it was incidentally also Noah who planted the first vines 'and first acquired the boon of having a skinful of liquor. And there is no doubt about it, there was a shawcrop in Noah's famous vessel,' he continued, 'from which we have all descended. But it was man who subsequently miscegenated, not the shawcrop. For shawcrops are more jealous of their coat of arms than any other animal and will not admit even a field-mouse to be one of themselves, even were such a field-mouse to have the special gift of transmuting grains of sand into fresh hazel-nuts.'

This fine flower of shawcroppian nobility having pleased good Gargantua, he had breadth of vision enough to grant this particular one the Lieutenancy of his storeroom with the widest powers of Justice, including the right of *Committimus*, that of *Missi Dominici*, jurisdiction over the Clergy, over Men-at-arms and indeed over everything else. The shawcrop promised that he would fulfil his charge well on condition he might make his home on that heap of wheat. This Gargantua found reasonable.

So there was our shawcrop capering about in his fine purple, happy as a Prince is when happy at all, trotting round to reconnoitre his immense territories of mustard, his landscapes of sweetmeats, his provinces of hams, his dukeries of raisins, his counties of chitterlings, and all his baronies of this, that and the other, scrambling his way into heaps of corn, whisking this and whisking that with his tail. It will be sufficient here further to record that everywhere the shawcrop was accorded full honour by the pots, which maintained a silence and profound respect, all except a couple of golden goblets which jangled against each other like church bells clashing out a salute, with which however Lord Shawcrop seemed very pleased, for he thanked them, right and left, by nodding his head as he paraded down a sunbeam which made his purple glow, the tanned hue of his pelt gleaming so well that you would have thought it a King of the North in sable fur.

Then, having made and re-made his rounds, having gambolled and capered, the guardian nibbled a couple of grains of wheat, seated on the heap like a King in full Court, and now believed himself the finest shawcrop that ever was.

At that very moment, by their customary orifices, there appeared the gentry of the Nocturnal Court, those whose little tootsies trip over the boards, namely, the rats and the mice and every other kind of the hordes of gnawing, thieving, idle beasts of whom good citizens and housewives also complain. But, seeing this shawcrop, all of these were now afraid and held back timidly on the threshold of their holes.

However, one among all these little heads, despite the danger, came well forward, an elderly rascal of the trittotrot-grittogrot race of mice. Cocking his snout skew-wise, this pert little squirt had guts enough to quiz Lord Shawcrop, haughtily poised there, tail in the air on his backside.

In the end the mouse convinced himself that the thing was a devil from whom he might expect nought but scratches. For this reason, jolly old Gargantua, in order that the elevated authority of his Lieutenant should be universally known to all other shawcrops, and all cats, weasels, martens, field-mice, house-mice, rats and other bad characters of the same sort, had lightly dipped his muzzle, pointed as a skewer, into oil of musk, whence shawcrops since have drawn a musky heritage, Gargantua's aim being that when, notwithstanding Gargantua's sound counsels, his Lieutenant rubbed his nose against other predatory creatures, the odour might repel. Whence came all the troubles of the shawcrop world, which I would give you a good account in a history manual, did I not lack the time.

However, an elderly mouse (or else a rat, the Talmudic rabbis are still not quite of one opinion on the species), grasping by the said perfume that the shawcrop was appointed to watch over Gargantua's grain and had to that end been sprinkled with essential virtues, invested with ample powers and armed from head to foot, was most alarmed, fearing he might now easily be deprived of all sustenance, since according to the ways of all rodent gentry, he had been used to live on the crumbs, the grits, the crusts, the drips, the scraps, the morsels and portions, and all the countless other tidbits which falling from the great Gargantuan table constituted the milk and honey of all mice and rats' promised land.

Faced thus with this terrible problem, the good mousey, as wily as any old courtier is who has seen through two regencies and the reign of three kings, determined that he would assay the mettle of Master Guardian Shawcrop, thus consecrating himself to the relief of all musomorphic masticatory parts. This would have been laudable enough in a human being, but was the more so here by reason of the egotism of mice, who live each for themselves without disgrace or shame, and to achieve that end would never hesitate utterly shamelessly even to gnaw the stole of a priest, or to drink from a chalice without a thought of God, or even ease nature on a communion wafer. Therefore this mouse now advanced, executing pretty curvettes, and the shawcrop allowed it to approach quite near, for I should explain that by nature the breed of shawcrops do not see very far. Thereupon, this Curtius of nibblers said his piece, not in mouse jargon either, but in good shawcroppian Italian.

'My lord,' he said, 'I have heard much talk of your illustrious family, of which I am one of the most devoted of servers, and I am acquainted with the whole legend of your ancestors, once revered by the Ancient Egyptians, who held them in great awe and together with other sacred birds worshipped them. Nevertheless, your furry proboscis is so regally perfumed and its colour so superconscientiously stained that I am not quite sure whether I should assume you to be of the said race at all, for I have never before seen one of your kind so finely attired.

'Nevertheless, I presume that after the ancient fashion you too have guzzled grain, your snitch is a scholarly snitch, like a shawcrop of great wisdom you too have rooted, further, you really must have, I do not know exactly in what part of your ear but certainly somewhere, a superauditory canal, closable by I know not what miraculous valve, nor do I know precisely at what hours, by your occult behest, to afford you, since the perfection of your sacrosanct, capable, all-sensitive hearing, renders you liable to wounds, I know not why, licence to remain utterly deaf to I know not what things which are distasteful to you.'

'True,' said the shawcrop. 'Look, I close my little door, and I hear naught.'

'Let's see,' the wily old rat resumed, plunging straight into the heap of wheat, and at once beginning forthwith to spirit away enough for his winter store.

'Can you hear me?' he cried.

'I hear my own heart's rise and fall. . . .'

'Coo-ee!' cried all the mice, 'then we can easily diddle him!'

But, thinking that he had come upon a faithful servant, the shawcrop at this point opened the trapdoor of his musical orifice, and at once heard the gritty rattle of the grain into the rat's hole. Whereupon, without any recourse to the worthy justice as administered by magistrates, he leapt on to the old fellow and forthwith strangled him.

What a glorious death that was, seeing that this hero fell into the heart of that mountain of wheat, further to be canonized as a martyr! But the shawcrop took the corpse of the rat by the ears and tipped him out through the granary trapdoor, as Panurge was all but tipped by the Ottoman Porte.

At the cry of the dying rat all the mice and all the rats and others of the mob had flicked away into their holes in great terror. But with the onset of night, they all came to the cellar, rallied there to hold council and investigate public affairs, to which assembly, in pursuance of the law entitled *Papiria* and of other laws, legitimate wives were admitted. The rats then wished to take precedence of the mice and a grand dispute about order of seniority nearly ruined everything. But a big rat suddenly took a little mousey on his arm and with papa rats thus pairing off with mamma mice, there they were all in a twinkling seated in a ring on their rumps, tails erect, snouts outstretched, chins a-quiver, eyes as bright as those of falcons. There then began a debate which terminated in mutual abuse and a hubbub worthy of any fine council of the Oecumenical Fathers. Some cried yes and others cried no, till a passing cat was frightened and, hearing those strange noises, ran away: Boo boo! Froo-oo-oo! Wick Wick! Briff! Briffnacknack! Fouicks fouicks! Trrr trrr trrr trrr! Razza za-za-zaaah! Brrr brrr! Raa! Ra-ra-ra-ra-fouicks! all so well blended together in vocal dinnery that no councillors in a Town Hall could have done better.

During this storm, a little wench of a mouse who was not of age to sit in Parliament also came. She thrust her inquisitive little snitch through a crack in the wall. The hair of her pelt was as silky fine as that of any other mousey wench who has not yet been taken. As the tumult of the adult assembly increased, this little hussy gradually pushed forward body following snout, till soon enough there she was on a barrel so well clinging to one of the hoops that you might have taken her for a nice piece of engraving of an ancient bas-relief. When now a certain old rat raised his gaze heavenwards to supplicate a sensible remedy for the public woe, and caught sight of this charming maiden, so feat of line, he abandoned the public woe and declared that the Public Weal should be retrieved by her.

All snouts at once turned towards this Maiden of Kindly Succour and became silent, and they agreed to offer her up to the shawcrop. Notwithstanding the envy of certain jealous mice of female kind, she was triumphantly paraded the length of the cellar, when, seeing her dainty little feet trip with automatic springy oscillation of her rear parts and how she tossed her crafty little head, wiggled her diaphanous ears, and with her pink little tongue licked at her chaps and the nascent beard of her busser, all the old rats fell straightaway in love with her and with their wrinkled, white-whiskered bussers set up a monocordic baritonic buzz much as in ancient time did the old Trojans, admiring fair Helen as she returned from her morning dip.

Thus this virgin mouse was turned loose into the granary entrusted with the diversionary task of seducing Chief Constable Shawcrop and thereby saving the grain-guzzling race, as in former time the fair Jewess Esther as writ in the master book (seeing that the word Bible comes from Greek *biblos* as if to say, *the* book), saved the chosen people of God under that Sultan named Ahasuerus. The little virgin for her part undertook to set the grain free, for it so happened that she was the very Queen of mice, and oh so dainty, oh so blondie, oh so bosomy, oh as sweet a little dame as ever bounded blithesome over the rafters or lightly skimmed the friezes, uttering, as she found nut or crumb or scrap of bread, the daintiest of cries. A

regular fairy of a virgin mouse, in fact, a pretty little mouse, a harum-scarum little lively mousey, with eye limpid as a white diamond, head small, skin of satin, her body naughty, her paws of pink, her tail of velvet, a highly-born mousey indeed, a finely spoken, by nature loving a lie-a-bed life, a *dolce far niente life* mousey, a glad little virgin mousey, wilier far than any old Sorbonne doctor who knows his Decretals by heart, a lively, a white-bellied, a striped-backed little mousey, each dainty titty as pert as a suspicion, each fine tooth of mother-of-pearl, a mousey moreover full of pep, in short, a mousey morsel fit for any King.

This description was so indiscreet (for in it everybody at once recognized a true portrait of 'Lady Di', who was present), that all the courtiers were aghast. Queen Catherine, of course grinned broadly, but the King was far from wanting to laugh. And there was good old Rabelais plunging on, deeper and deeper, without paying any heed to the warning glances shot him by Cardinals du Bellay and de Châtillon, who were most apprehensive as to what might now happen to him.

'This pretty little mousey,' said Rabelais, continuing, 'made no very lengthy circumbilivaginations. From the very first evening that this Court Lady trotted past Lord Shawcrop, she had him at her apron-strings for ever, by reason of her coquetries, her mincings, her cossetings, her Lesbian niceties, her exciting little refusals, her slippery glances, all that fiddle-faddle of your virgin who would like to but dare not, all those love darts, those half caresses, those preparatory antics, those haughtinesses of a mousey who knows her price, those amusing little annoyances and annoying little amusements, those caprices and those feminine devices and contrivals and nice ensnaring devices, all those traps which the female of the species in every country makes use of.

'And when, after many a curvet, many a tap, many a nuzzle, many an amorous mousey trick, many a frown, many a sigh, many a serenade, many a tidbit, many a supper and dinner in that heap of wheat and other tasty roguish places besides, the superintendent of the grange apparently triumphed over the scruples of this maiden he so admired and they acquired great taste for their love both illicit and incestuous, and as moreover the mousey now led Lord Shawcrop firmly by his John Thomas wherever she wanted, she became the Queen of it all, whereupon she felt a desire to season her wheat with that mustard, and set the mixture off with sweetmeats, in short, stick her muzzle in everywhere.

'All this, the shawcrop allowed the empress of his heart to do, for all that he took a poor view of his own miserable betrayal of his shawcropic duties and the oaths he had taken to Gargantua. Finally, pursuing her Christian enterprise with all the pertinacity of a woman, during one of their nights of frolic together, she suddenly thought of her dear old dad, and expressed a wish that he might now and then have a nibble of grain. Indeed, she even threatened Lord Shawcrop she would leave him to mope by himself in his domain if he did not give daughterly piety full licence to expand, upon which, in the twinkle of a paw, the said Lord Shawcrop issued letters-patent sealed with a big green seal of green wax, over ribbons of crimson silk, to the father of his mistress, to the end that the Gargantuan mansion should be open to him and he might at any hour see his kind, virtuous daughter, plant a kiss on her forehead and eat his fill, provided this was accomplished in a corner.

'Shortly after this there then came to Lord Shawcrop a white-tailed veteran rat, a venerable fellow weighing twenty-five ounces, with the gait of a High-Court President Judge, wagging his head, and followed by fifteen to twenty nephews, all toothed like saws, and by fine talk and interlocutory phrases of all sorts they argued to Lord Shawcrop that they, relatives of his, were most loyally attached to him and would assist him to make his inventories of the goods in his charge, put them in apple-pie order, and label them properly, so that when Gargantua did come to inspect it all he found the balance-sheets and store of those victuals in the best possible order.

'This seemed to be a genuine offer, though, despite this conclusion poor Lord Shawcrop was still much harassed by certain counsel from on high and by grave perturbation of his Shawcropian conscience. Seeing that because of this worry he now turned picksome about everything, doing nothing but mooch disconsolately about, much harassed by concern about his master, who was now liable to mort-main him, one morning his fair Mistress Mousey, as she sat roosting, so to speak, being as she was then in the family way by reason of Lord Shawcrop's labours, conceived the notion of allaying his alarm and easing his mind by calling a Universitarian Consultation.

'Indeed, she did send for learned men of academic ilk. Thus, in the course of the day, she brought him a certain Dr Evegault, who issued forth from a cheese in which he was living a life of hermetic absti-nence, a veteran confessor indeed, well lined with lofty fat, a comical character to a degree, but an upstanding type, in fine black robes, solid as a keep, his head slightly tonsured by a cat's claw. He was a solemn rat, with a cloistral paunch, one who had studied scientific authorities and eaten many an administrative parchment, many a Clementine document, not to speak of all manner of books, parts of which had blotched his grey beard.

'This is why, from great honour and respect for his eminent qualities, his wisdom and his modesty of cheesy living, he was accompanied by a band of black rats paired off with darling dainty private
mousies (seeing that the Canons of the Council of Chezil had not yet
been adopted, and rats were still within their rights to have ladies of
substance for concubines). Which prebendary rats and mice were
strung out in two ranks, so that you might have thought the sight
was of a university procession going to some common convocation.
And all together, they at once sniffed at those victuals.

'When each of them had assumed his proper place for the proceedings, the veteran Cardinal of Rats spoke up, and in mouse Latin delivered an address to make clear to Lord Shawcrop that there was
nobody but God over him, it was to the Almighty alone that he
owed obedience, after which came many fine phrases, all tricked out
with quotations from the Gospels to twist principles inside-out and
fiddle-de-daddle those present—in a word, fine argumentation well
larded with slices of common sense, this address leading up to a
peroration amply drummed home with much bumbling about the
glories of the shawcrop breed, among whom this specimen was the
most worthy and the finest ever extant under the sun, by all of which
the good granary guardian was greatly flattered.

'This good worthy's turn was thus headed or his head thus turned
and he installed these rats with the gift of the gab in his domain,
where now night and day there were to be heard incessant gilded
words of praise and many a fine anthem in his honour, not without
due respect being paid his lady, every jack man there planting a kiss
on her paw and sniffing at her delightful cruppers.

'Finally, knowing that there were young rats which were still
going hungry, Mistress Mousey desired to crown her good work,
and so, with much able tongue-work, lovingly lamenting with endless coy tricks, one alone of which would have melted an animal's
heart, she remarked to her good Lord Shawcrop that he was losing
time precious to their love in all that beating of the bounds and
watchman business of his, he was always out and about, she never
had her full meed of pleasure from him, so that just when she craved
attention from him, he would be mounted on a gutter and chasing
cats away, whereas she would like to have him otherwise mounted,
billing and cooing, and with lance erect. In her sorrow she now
plucked out a grey hair and said she believed herself to be the most
unhappy female mouse there ever was, and burst into tears.

'Thereupon, Lord Shawcrop of course expostulated that she was
mistress of it all, and would have argued, but after the regular downpour of tears which followed he desisted from this, craved an armistice

and gave ear to her request. Her tears then dried very quickly. Giving him her paw to kiss, she advised him to arm some soldiers, good well-tried rats, old campaigners, reliable men, to go the rounds and keep watch.

'Everything was then sensibly arranged. Lord Shawcrop had the rest of the day for dancing, playing about, enjoying himself, listening to rondeaux and ballades composed for him by poets, playing the lute and mandoline, devising acrostics and tipping the pot and eating.

'One day, his mistress, rising from after having given birth to the loveliest of little mousified shawcrops, or the loveliest of little shaw-croppized mousies, for I do not know exactly what to call that product of love's alchemy, which as you may well imagine, those wolves in sheep's clothing legitimized'—here Lord de Montmorency, Constable of France, who had married his son to the legitimized bastard of the said lord the King of France, lay his hand to his sword and clenched the hilt terrifyingly—'there was a banquet in those store-rooms the like of no banquet or Court gala you ever knew, save that of the Field of the Cloth of Gold. In every corner there were mice hugging their sides, they laughed so.

'There were dances of all kinds all over the place, concerts and drinking parties, with much good fare and sarabands and orchestras and gay songs and epithalamia. The rats broached pots, uncovered jars, unsealed demijohns, unlaced every parcel, there were rivers of mustard to be seen, hams in shreds, piles of food spread about, every-where overflowing, streaming, trickling, rolling, baby rats paddling in streams of green sauce, mice forging their course through sweet-meats, old boys diverting the pasties. There were weasels straddling salt tongues of beef, there were field-mice swimming in crocks, while the more cunning were carting away corn to their special hide-outs, making good use of the din of the junketing to stock up amply. And not one once passed by the Orleans quince cheese without tak-ing a nibble, and often a second.

'In short, it was a non-stop Roman carnival, and anyone with a keen ear might have heard the frizzling of frying-pans, the cry and clamour issuing forth from the kitchens, and frizzling and crackling in the ovens, the clang-clang of pestles in mortars, the gurgle of casseroles, the squeak of turnspits, the whinnying of skeps and bas-kets, the rustle of pastries, the clicking of brochets and little feet trotting about the boards like hail.

'These were businesslike celebrations, a constant coming and go-ing of all persons with household duties, footmen and stablemen and mouthmen too, not to count the musicians or the antics of acrobats, with endless toasts of the company and whirling about of the soldiery and utter inter-confusion of the three orders of society.

'In short, the merrymaking reached such a pitch that everybody took part in it and added to the general hullabaloo to make that lovely nightful a memorable one. But at the height of it what should be heard but the terrible tread of Gargantua descending the stairs of his house to make his way to his storehouses and shake the rafters, flooring and all. Certain elderly rats immediately made inquiry about that noise, but as nobody was aware what this lordly tread might signify, some made off in great fear, and did well, seeing that the lord suddenly entered.

'Then, seeing what this ratty gentry had done by way of disorder and finding his preserves and stores all pillaged, his mustards streaming about, and everything full of turds and all ripped up, Gargantua simply stamped on that merry-making vermin, to rout them, without even a chance to cry out, and thus spoiled their lovely silky coats, their pearls, their velvets, their trappings, and that was an end to the feast.'

'And what happened to that shawcrop?' demanded the King, emerging from a deep reverie.

'Well, Sire,' replied Rabelais, 'there's a matter in which Gargantuan folk were unjust. He was put to death, but, being a nobleman, not by the rope, but decapitation. This was bad, seeing that he too had been duped.'

'My good fellow, you go rather far,' said the King.

'Not so, Sire,' retorted Rabelais. 'I only go rather high. Have you not pushed up the pulpit above the crown? Moreover you it was asked me to deliver a sermon. I have but complied, though it was a most gospel true sermon, you know.'

'My fine Court Vicar,' whispered Lady Diana in his ear, 'what if I were to be a bit spiteful?'

'My lady,' replied Rabelais, 'is there then no need to warn your master the King against the Queen's Italian hangers-on, who are as plentiful here as cockchafers?'

'My poor preacher,' whispered Cardinal Odet in his ear, 'get away abroad quick.'

'Oho, my Lord Cardinal,' replied our good friend, 'I shall soon be in a very foreign country, anyway.'

'God's truth, Mr Scribbler,' cried the Constable of France, whose son, as everybody knows, had treacherously deserted Mademoiselle de Piennes, to whom he had been engaged, to marry France's Lady Diana, daughter of the King by an ultramontane lady, 'who made you so bold as to tackle such eminent personalities? Ho, you wretched versifier, you choose to elevate yourself. Very well, I give you my word, I'll soon set you up very high.'

'Where we all get in time, My Lord Constable,' replied good Rabelais. 'However, if you are a friend of the State and the King, you will thank me for having warned His Majesty of the hosts of Lorrainians, for they are all rats capable of ruining everything.'

'My good fellow,' whispered Cardinal Charles de Lorraine in his ear, 'if you happen to need a few gold crowns to bring out the Fifth Book of your Pantagruel, my treasurer will be pleased to find the cash, seeing you have put the matter straight to that old bitch who has put a spell on the King, and also to her crowd of hangers-on.'

'Well, Gentlemen,' asked the King, turning about him, 'what do you all think about this sermon?'

'Sire,' said Mellin de Sainct-Gelais, 'seeing that everybody was quite pleased, I must say that I never heard a better Pantagruelian prognostication. Just what one might have expected of the man who made the following noble *carmina* at *Thelema Abbey*:

> '*Come, enter here! who Holy Writ*
> *Interpret, live howe'er men scold,*
> *Here you shall have your true stronghold.*
> *From enemies who, twisting words,*
> *By style that's false befoul the world.*'

Every courtier having thus agreed to lick up to his neighbour, all together now lauded Rabelais, who withdrew, escorted with great respect by the Royal Pages, who by express order torch-lighted his path.

Some have accused François Rabelais, the imperial glory of our land, of apish naughtinesses and of buffooneries, unworthy of so philosophic a Homer, so great a prince, also of wisdom so fatherly, and a fount of so many admirable compositions. Shame on those who have cast dirt on that divine head! May those who fail to recognize his wise and edifying food grit sand between their teeth all their lives.

Dear drinker of clear water, faithful observer of monastic restraint, twenty-five carat scholar, how interminably and ebulliently you would laugh if, grown green again for a moment near Chinon, it were given you to read the incongruous wafflings, the dilapidation and misuse of language of idiots in B-flat and B-flatulent who have interpreted and commented, hacked and sullied, misunderstood and betrayed, betrayed and twisted and embroidered your incomparable work! As many dogs as Panurge found busying themselves with the skirts of that dame of his in church have we found two-legged academic pups, with heads devoid of grey matter, busy without stint at befouling that lofty marble pyramid of yours in which, apart from fine instruction in all things, has been cemented every possible kind of fantastic and humorous invention. Though pilgrims with the breath to follow your ship in its sublime peregrination through the vast ocean of ideas, methods, smoke-clouds, religions, sciences and human deceits are still rare, at least their incense is unadulterated, pure and genuine, while your own omnipotence, your omniscience and your omnilinguistic powers are grandly recognized by them.

Thus, you see a poor son of gay Touraine has here endeavoured to do justice to you, however triflingly, to enlarge your countenance and praise your never-to-be-forgotten inventions, so cherished by those who love writings which all converge to a point and embrace a moral universe in which one finds close packed all manner of philosophical ideas, all sciences, arts and all eloquence too, not to speak of dramatic fun.

IX

The Succuba

Certain persons of the noble land of Touraine, being duly edified by the Author's enthusiastic researches into the antiquities, strange happenings, valorous deeds and kindly acts of that beatific land, got the idea into their heads that he must know everything about it, so after a libation to Bacchus, let it be said, made inquiry of him as to whether he had not also elucidated the etymology of the street of Tours called then *Chaulde*, or Hot, Street; why, that is to say, this particular passage should be said to be hot.

The answer he gave was that he had been most astonished to find that old inhabitants had forgotten the large number of monasterial establishments (male and female) once there situated, for those were precincts within which the arduous continence of monks and nuns alike must have heated the very walls, for it was observed that certain ladies of standing were put in the family way merely by walking down that street too slowly after dusk.

A country squire, however, out to score off a man of letters, maintained that formerly all the clap-shops in the town had been located there. Another fellow, getting much entangled in the petty details of that field of knowledge, spoke incomprehensibly of gold, and played with words, juggling tunes ancient and modern, comparing usages, extracting verbs, alchemizing languages of the postdiluvian Hebrews, Chaldeans, Egyptians, Greeks and Latins and finally also of the Turnus, who founded Tours, all of which was to lead up to this fellow's assertion that if you subtracted the *H* and the *L*, from *Chaulde* you got *caude*, and in the last resort *cauda*, being a tail—of sorts—had something to do with it all. But all that the ladies could make out of his rigmarole was this final reference.

Further, there was an elderly person who stated that this street had once been the site of a hot spring, the water of which his great-great-grandfather had drunk.

In short, in less time than it takes one fly to ride another, there was a whole bunch of etymologies in which it was harder to find a grain of truth than a louse on the miserable chin of a shaven-skulled Capucin monk.

Finally, a learned man, known to have set foot in various monasteries (and convents), also to have burned much midnight oil, gutting many a volume and accumulating more fragments, tags, deed-boxes, charter-rolls and registers bearing on the history of Touraine than a gleaner can straws in August, put in his spoke. Aged, doddering, gouty, this worthy veteran had all this time been tippling steadily and silently in his corner, grinning a scholarly grin and knitting his brows till the grin and the brow-knitting ended suddenly in a loud cry of 'Bosh!' uttered so clearly that the Author caught the sound at once and grasped that the greybeard was pregnant with a yarn historically so sound that he would be able to disclose its charms in this pleasant collection.

Well, the following day this gouty old man said to him: 'By that poem of yours entitled "A Venial Sin" you have won my eternal esteem, for that story is true from top to toe, which I reckon is praiseworthy full measure in such matters. Yet I doubt whether you know what happened afterwards to that Saracen woman whom in your tale Lord Bruyn de la Roche-Corbon converted to our faith. But I do. So if the origin of this street name interests you as well as your gypsy nun, I will lend you a very intriguing ancient document which I acquired by accident in the Olim of the Archbishopric, the libraries of which were rather shaken up at a moment when we none of us knew whether we should wake up the next day with our heads on our shoulders or not. Now tell me, would such a document not delight you?'

'Certainly it would,' the Author said.

Thereupon the worthy collector of truth handed the Author a number of lovely dusty parchments which, not without considerable effort, for they consist of very ancient minutes of an ecclesiastical trial, he has now translated. It has seemed to him that nothing could be quainter than the effective resurrection of that ancient business so revealing as to the simple ignorance of the good old days.

Very well then, now give ear. Here is the sequence of these writings, used indeed by the Author in his own fashion, seeing that the original language was diabolically gawky.

I. Concerning a Succuba

In the name of the Father, and of the Son, and of the Holy Ghost, Amen.

In the year of Our Lord one thousand two hundred and seventy-one, before me, Jerome Cornille, Grand Penitentiary and Ecclesiastical Judge, appointed by the Lords of the Chapter of St Maurice, the Cathedral Church of Tours, having heard the matter in the presence of our Lord Archbishop Jean de Monsoreau, relative to the complaints and allegations of burghers of the city (whose application will be given in an appendix), certain nobles, burghers and villains of the

Diocese appeared before me and made deposition of the following facts regarding the outrages committed by a demon suspected of having assumed female form, to the considerable affliction of the souls of the Diocese, and at present held fast in the Chapter gaol, and, to attain the truth of the said complaints, we have instituted the present judicial inquiry, this Monday, December 11th, after mass, in order to put to the said demon the statements of each and every man and cross-examine the said demon regarding those said acts imputed to it and then to judge it in pursuance of the relevant statutes *contra daemonios*.

In this inquiry I have been assisted by Guillaume Tournebousche, as clerk, a scholarly man and chronicler of the Chapter.

First came before us Jean Tortebras, a burgher of Tours, who under licence holds the *Cigogne* or Stork Inn in the Place du Pont, and who has sworn on his soul, laying his hand on the Holy Gospels, to say nothing but what he himself saw and heard. Whereupon he made the following deposition:

'I declare that, about two years before the Feast of St Jean, when festive fires are lit, a nobleman whom at first I did not know, but certainly a subject of our Lord the King, and at the time returned to our country from the Holy Land, came to me to ask me to lease him an out-of-town house which I built on chapter land, near the place called St Etienne and I did so on a nine years' lease for three sovereigns of fine gold.

'In the same house the said nobleman established a beautiful concubine which he had, with the outward look of a woman, dressed in the outlandish Saracen or Mohammedan manner, and he would not allow anybody to come within an arrow's flight of her, while with my own eyes I saw strange feathers on her head, an unnatural colour in her skin and eyes more glowing than I can tell, from them sparked forth the fires of Hell.

'This nobleman, now deceased, having threatened with death any person showing intention of examining the said dwelling, from great fear I abandoned the house completely and to this day have in my innermost mind cherished certain conclusions and suspicions as to the ill appearance of the said alien female, who was pleasing to the senses as no other woman I have ever seen.

'Numerous persons of all sorts having at the time reported the said nobleman to be deceased but by certain charms, philtres, spells and diabolical acts of sorcery kept on his feet by that apparent woman, who wished to take up domicile in our country, I further declare that I always saw the nobleman in question so terribly pale that I used to compare his countenance to the wax of a Paschal candle, and to the

knowledge of all the men of the *Cigogne Inn*, this nobleman was laid to earth nine days after his arrival.

'According to his groom, the deceased man was hotly coupled close in my house with the said Saracen woman for seven whole days, without coming forth once, of which I heard him make his monstrous declaration of on his death-bed.

'Other persons at the same time said that this she-devil kept the said nobleman fastened on her by her long hair allegedly possessing heating properties by which Christians were imbued with the fires of hell in the form of sexual desire making them toil at this till in such wise their soul was sucked from their bodies and delivered to Satan.

'I declare, however, that I saw nothing of this except that the said deceased lord, exhausted, de-bowelled, unable to move, despite his confessor still craved to go to his woman, and was then recognized to be Lord de Bueil, a Crusader, said by some persons of this city to be under the spell of a demon which he met in the Asiatic parts of Damascus or some such place.

'Therefore I abandoned my house to the said stranger woman under the clauses stated in the lease agreement. When Lord de Bueil died, I did nevertheless go to my house in order to learn from the said stranger female whether she wished to remain in my dwelling, and with great difficulty at last gained admittance to her led by a foreign man who was half-naked, black of skin with white eyes.

'Then I saw the said Saracen woman in a closet glittering with gold and precious stones, lighted by many lights, on an Asiatic rug, where she sat, very lightly attired, with another lord, who was already losing his soul, and I had not courage enough to look at her, since her eyes would at once have stirred me to abandon myself to her, for already her voice alone gnawed at my vitals, made my brain turgid and debauched my soul.

'Realizing this, from fear of the Lord and also of hell, I immediately stepped therefrom, abandoning my house to her for as long as she chose to keep it, so dangerous was it to look upon that Saracenish complexion in which was engendered demoniacal heat, not to speak of her having a foot smaller than it is right for a real woman to have, and also hearing that voice which penetrated to the heart, and from that day on I have lacked the courage to go to my house, in great fear of falling into Hell. I have spoken.'

We then showed the said Tortebras an Abyssinian, Aethiopian or Nubian person, who was black from head to foot and found to be devoid of the virile parts with which as a rule Christians are equipped, who, having persevered in his silence after having been put to torture and tormented a number of times, albeit that he groaned much, is stubborn in not knowing how to speak the language of our country. And the said Tortebras recognized this heretical Abyssinian as having been in his house in the company of the said demoniacal spirit and is suspected of having aided and abetted the acts of sorcery.

Further the said Tortebras confessed his great Catholic faith and declared he knew no other matter except certain rumours known to everybody else but of which he had in no way been witness except in having heard them repeated.

Under the summons served on him one Mathieu then came forward, *alias* Cognefestu, a day-labourer on the St Etienne land, who, having sworn on Holy Gospel to speak the truth, confessed to having always seen a powerful light in the dwelling of the said foreign woman and heard much wild and diabolical laughter by day and by night on working days and holy days alike, particularly during Holy Week and Christmas, as if there were many people in that house.

Further he said he had seen in the windows of the said dwelling green vegetation of all kinds in winter, growing by magic, especially roses, even during frosty weather, and other things which required heat, but was not at all astonished seeing that the said foreign woman did give out such great heat herself that when in the evening she walked down her garden wall the next morning her lettuce seed was up and sometimes by the rustle of her petticoats she had made trees gush sap and brought forth new buds.

Finally the said Cognefestu declared he knew no more, as he worked mornings and went to bed with the hens.

Next the wife of the said Cognefestu was called upon by us to state likewise on oath what events she knew of in this matter and she limited herself to admitting nothing but praise of the said foreign woman because since she came her husband treated her better by reason of having that kind lady near who she said spread the feelings of love in the air as the sun does its rays and other unseemly twaddle not here committed to paper.

We confronted Cognefestu and his wife with the said unknown African, who had been seen by them in the gardens of the house and this was reputed by them unquestionably to be the said devil.

Thirdly, the Lord of the Manor of Maillé, Harduin V, came forward, who, when respectfully requested by us to enlighten the religion of our Church, replied that he was quite willing to do so, and further also gave his word as knight of honour to say nought else but that which he had seen.

He then declared that in the Crusading Army he had known the demon in question. Further, in the city of Damascus he had seen the late Lord de Bueil fight a duel to be the sole possessor of the demon. The aforesaid female or demon at this time had belonged to Lord Geoffrey IV, Duke de la Roche-Pozay, who used to maintain that although she was a Saracen woman he had brought her from Touraine, which surprised the French knights exceedingly, as much as her beauty did, this being much renowned and causing many scandalous scrimmages in the camp.

During the journey home he alleged this said female to have been the cause of a number of murders, for la Roche-Pozay had already in single combat defeated a number of crusaders who wanted her for themselves alone, because, according to certain knights rewarded by her, she offered delights like none other.

At last, however, de Bueil, having killed Geoffrey de la Roche-Pozay, became the lord and master of this mortally dangerous sheath and put her away in a convent or harem in the Saracen manner. Before this was done she used to be heard chattering at her gay parties in many a foreign lingo, Arabic, Greek of the Romish Empire, Moorish and much French as none other knew the tongues of France better in the Christian forces, whence this belief that she was largely diabolic.

The aforesaid Lord Harduin has confessed that the reason he did not duel for her in the Holy Land himself was not fear or anything else but that he thought he was to be favoured to bring away a portion of the True Cross and also had himself a noble lady of the Greek lands of his own who saved him from that danger with the Saracen by draining him herself of love night and morning, for she took from him more or less all he had, leaving his vitals void, nothing left for any other woman.

Further, the said Lord affirmed the woman lodged in the country house of Tortebras indeed to be this said Saracen woman come from the land of Syria, for he had been invited there by the young Lord Croixmare to a junketing exactly a week before that knight departed this life after, as Lady de Croixmare, his mother, asserted, having been ruined in every way by the said female, whose couplings had consumed all his vital spirits while the same extraordinary fantasies spent all his sterling.

Thereupon, questioned, as a man of sound judgement, and of wisdom and of authority in this land, as to what opinion of this said female he held and enjoined by us to unburden his conscience, seeing that it was a most abominable case touching the Christian faith and divine justice, the said Lord Harduin V made the following reply:

That there were men in the crusading army who had said that this she-devil was always a virgin to any who rode her, and that there was no doubt about it, she was full of Mammon, whose work it was to fashion her a new maidenhood for each new lover of hers and a thousand other wild words of intoxicated men certainly not fit to make a fifth Gospel.

It was however indubitable that an elderly knight at the change of life who was totally ignorant of the allegations had felt himself a young man again at the last supper at which Lord de Croixmare had regaled him, that the voice of that demon had struck straight to his heart before it even reached his ears, thereby imbuing his body with such glowing lust that all his being flowed to that limb by which lust is outpoured and in the end, without the aid of the Cyprus wine of which he had drunk much to close his eyes so he might put himself under the table, that he might no longer see the flaming eyes of that devilish hostess and not exhaust himself in her, there was no doubt but that he would have slaughtered young Croixmare merely to have one enjoyment of that supernatural female.

Subsequently he took pains to confess the evil thought, then, by counsel from on high, had taken back to his spouse his portion of the True Cross and remained close in his Manor where, notwithstanding his Christian precautionary measures, the said voice on occasion still whipped his brain up to frenzy so that when morning came he found his mind full of memory of that female devil, and her breasts seared into him with points of flame. And since the sight of this female was so enflaming that it made him hot-rooted as any young one, for all he had one leg in the grave, and since all this cost him much loss of vital humours from his body, the said lord begged that we should not now confront him with that empress of passion, to whom if she were not a demon God the Father had consigned strange jurisdiction over the natural parts of a man.

Then, having made these statements, Lord Harduin retired, but not without having recognized the aforementioned African to be the body-servant and page of the woman.

In the fourth place, on our guaranty, in the name of the Chapter and our Lord Archbishop that he would not be put to torture, pressed or harassed in any thing or any way, nor anything he said repeated elsewhere, and with assurance that he would be at liberty to withdraw at will, a Jew came before us of the name Solomon al Rastchild, who, despite the infamy of his name and his Judaism, was heard by us, to the sole end of learning all concerning the behaviour of the aforesaid demon. Therefore the said Solomon was required to give no oath, being outside the Church, cut off from us by the blood of our Saviour (*trucidatus Salvator inter nos*).

Interrogated as to why he appeared before us without the green cap on his head or yellow circle in place of a heart on his clothing, as ordered by Ecclesiastical and Royal edicts, the said al Rastchild showed us letters patent giving him dispensation granted by our Lord the King countersigned by the Seneschal of Touraine and Poitou.

The Jew then deposed that he had carried out big business for the lady lodged in Innkeeper Tortebras's house, selling her golden candlesticks with fine engraving, platters of silver-gilt goblets inlaid with precious stones, emeralds and rubies, bringing from the Levant for her expensive materials, Persian rugs, silks and fine linens, in short, things so magnificent that no Queen of Christendom could claim to be so well equipped with jewels and household goods, and that for his part he had received three hundred thousand pounds (Tours exchange) for the rare purchases he had been engaged to make, such as flowers from the Indies, parrots, birds, feathers, spices, Greek wines and diamonds.

Requested by our Judge to state whether he had furnished any ingredients for magical charms, such as blood of new-born babes, black books or any thing whatsoever in general such as is used by witches, giving him licence to make such a statement without any process being subsequently made against him or any trouble caused him, the said al Rastchild swore on his Hebrew faith that he never dealt in such things. Then he added that he was involved in interests too high to lower himself to such petty things, being treasurer to certain very powerful lords, such as the Marquis of Montferrat, the King of England, the King of Cyprus and Jerusalem, the Count of Provence, various Lords of Venice and other Germanic lords, having his own merchant galleons of all kinds trading with Egypt under licence from the Sultan and being in the trade in precious gold and silver articles, which frequently took him to the Tours Mint.

Furthermore, he said he considered the said lady to be a very loyal ordinary woman, the most gracious in form and the most charming that he had ever seen. That by reason of her fame as a diabolical spirit, moved by wild fantasy, and also because he became enamoured of her, one day, when she had been widowed, he had offered to be her gallant which she was ready to agree to.

But though that night left him for a long time with the feeling that his bones had been dislocated and his loins broken, he had not had the experience of which some spoke, that any who fell once never recovered, but were melted like lead in an alchemist's crucible.

Then the said Solomon, whom following our guaranty, we left at liberty, despite this declaration, which was ample proof of his own commerce with the devil, since he emerged whole where Christians had succumbed, submitted to us an agreement regarding the said demon, namely, he offered the Cathedral Chapter to give for the same seeming woman a ransom large enough, if she be condemned to burn at the stake, to complete the largest of the towers of Maurice's church, under construction at this present moment.

This we made note of for discussion at an opportune moment when the Chapter meets. Then the said Solomon withdrew, refusing to say where he was lodged, telling us the decision of the Chapter could be communicated to him by a Jew of the Tours Ghetto named Tobias Nathaneus.

The said Jew Solomon was before he left confronted with the African, whom he recognized to be the demon's page, and said it was the Saracen practice thus to denude their slaves of their masculine appendages so as by ancient custom safely to put them to watch the women, as shown by the profane histories of Narsez, the Constantinople General and others.

Fifthly, the following day, after mass, there appeared before us the most noble and illustrious Lady de Croixmare, who swore on her faith and the Holy Gospels and said with tears that she had interred her eldest son, dead by the fact of his extravagant embraces with a female devil. The young nobleman had been twenty-three years old, of perfect complexion, very virile, with dense beard like his deceased father. However, despite his great spunk, in ninety days he had gradually lost colour, ruined by his couplings with the succuba in *Chaulde* or Hot Street, as it is called by ordinary folk, and she added that she had had no maternal authority over her son.

At the end, in his last days, he had been more like a poor desiccated worm found by a housewife when spring-cleaning her rooms, but still, so long as he could walk, had willed to continue living with that cursed female creature on whom he thus squandered his substance. Then, when at last brought to bed, he saw his last hour come, swore, declaring on oath, and with menaces, too, to everybody, sister, brother and her his mother herself, a thousand insults, then rebelled to the chaplain's face, denied God and insisted on dying in perdition, whereby, above all, the servants of the family were heartbroken since to save his soul and snatch him from Hell-fire they had already endowed annual masses in the Cathedral.

Subsequently, for giving him Christian burial in holy ground, the Croixmare family had undertaken to supply all the chapels of the church with wax for Easter Sunday candles for a century.

Finally, excepting the evil things heard by that reverend personage Dom Louis Pot, a monk of Marmoustiers, who came at the eleventh hour to aid the said Baron de Croixmare, the said lady affirmed never having heard the deceased utter a word concerning the demon that had caused him such tribulation.

The noble and illustrious lady then withdrew, in deep mourning.

Sixthly, after the adjournment, Jacquette, known as Vieulx-Oing, or *Old Grease*, a kitchen skivvy, now domiciled at la Poissonière, appeared before us and she, after having taken the oath not to say anything but what she held to be the truth, made the following declaration, namely, that one day she had come to the kitchen of the said demon, of which she was not at all afraid, because it never devoured anything but males, and she had the opportunity to see this female demon in the garden, superbly dressed and strolling in the company of a knight with whom she was laughing like any other woman. That then in this demon she recognized a resemblance to the Saracen woman converted and placed in the Convent of Notre Dame de l'Egrignolles by the late Seneschal of Touraine and Poitou, Lord Bruyn, Count de la Roche-Corbon, the Saracen woman being left there in place of the icon of Notre Dame Our Lady the Virgin, mother of our blessed Saviour, stolen by the gypsies about eighteen years earlier.

In these days of which, because of the disturbances which arose in Touraine, there is no record, this loose female, namely, aged about twelve, was saved from the stake where she was to be burnt, by being baptized, and the said deceased Seneschal and his deceased Spouse had been god-father and god-mother to her, this daughter of Hell. At this time, being washerwoman in the Convent, the witness re-called how twenty months after her acceptance of the faith the said gypsy female had escaped from the nunnery so cleverly that nobody had known where or how she had been removed. It was at the time thought by everybody that with the assistance of Satan she had flown, seeing that despite searches being made no trace of her riding any broom had been found in the convent, where everything re-mained in its customary place.

The African man having been brought before the said skivvy, she said she had never seen him, though she had been curious to do so because he was put on guard at the place where the Saracen woman had her pleasure with those she drained dry through the water-tap.

In the seventh place was brought before us Hugues du Fou, son of Lord de Bridoré, who, aged twenty, had been placed in the hands of his father, under penalty of his estates, and is by him represented in this inquiry, on which he depends, to be properly attained and con-victed for that, in the company of a number of unknown lads of ill conduct, he besieged the Archiepiscopal Chapter gaol in an attempt to influence and disturb the course of ecclesiastical justice by securing the escape of the demon concerned. Despite his ill intent, we ordered the said Hugues du Fou to give true witness concerning the things he must know about the said demon, with whom he is most positively reputed to have had commerce, it being put to him that his salvation and also the life of the said demoniacal creature were in question. Whereupon, the oath taken, he said:

'I swear by my eternal salvation and by the Holy Gospels, here held in my hand, that I hold the woman suspected of being a demon to be an angel and a perfect woman, even more in soul than in body, living with absolute decency, full of charms and refinements of love, in no way evil, but generous, greatly aiding the poor and suffering.

'I declare that I saw her weeping real tears at the death of my friend Lord de Croixmare. Moreover, on this account on that day she vowed to Our Lady the Virgin never more to receive the gift of love of young nobles too feeble to serve her, and she steadfastly and with great courage refused me the enjoyment of her body and granted me but the love and possession of her heart, of which she made me sovereign.

'Since that gracious gift, in spite of my ever greater ardour I remained by myself in her house, where I spent the greater part of my time, happy to see her and hear her. Yes, indeed, I took all my meals close to her, sharing the air which entered her lungs, the light which lit her lovely eyes, finding in that occupation more delight than the lords of Paradise can know. Elected by me for ever to be my lady, chosen to be one day my dove, my spouse and sole love, I, poor simple man, have received from her no earnest of the joys to come, but, on the contrary, many a virtuous counsel, such as that I should gain fame as a good knight, and become a strong and handsome man, fearing nought but God, honouring womenfolk, but serving only one, loving them all in the name of that one, then, when I may be hardened by the labours of war, if her heart still delighted mine, only then would she be mine, for she would be able in her great love for me to wait for me. . . .'

Saying this, young Lord Hugues wept and, weeping, added: That, thinking of the gracious and frail woman, whose arms had formerly seemed to him too weak to bear the weight of her gold bangles, he had been unable to bear the thought of the irons which now chafed her flesh or the miseries she was being so wrongly forced to suffer, and that he had rebelled because of this, and that he had a right to declare this to the law outright because his life was so closely linked with that of this delicious mistress and love that he would certainly die if harm came ever to her.

Further the said young man uttered a thousand other praises of the said demon, all of which were evidence of the powerful charm wrought against him, proving copiously the abominable, outrageous, incorrigible and treacherous sorcery to which he was then subject, of all of which Our Lord the Archbishop will judge in order to save this young soul from the snares of Hell, if the devil has not too firm a grip on it, by exorcism and penances.

Thereupon we handed the said young man back to the keeping of the noble lord his father, after the said Hugues had recognized the African to be the manservant of the accused woman.

In the eighth place the yeomen of Our Lord the Archbishop in great honour brought before us the MOST ELEVATED AND REVEREND LADY JACQUELINE DE CHAMPCHEVRIER, ABBESS OF THE CONVENT OF OUR LADY, under the invocation of Mt Carmel, in the charge of whom the late Lord Seneschal of Touraine, father of my lord the Count de la Roche-Corbon, present lawyer of the said convent, had placed the Egyptian female, described in the baptismal records as Blanche Bruyn.

The said Abbess was informed briefly of the present inquiry, which concerns the Holy Church, the glory of God, the eternal salvation of the people of this Diocese afflicted with a demon, and also the life of a creature who may be quite innocent.

Then, the case outlined, we requested the said Lady Abbess to give evidence of what she knew of the magical disappearance of her daughter in God, Blanche Bruyn, bride of Our Lord under the name of Sister Claire.

Thereupon the very noble, very elevated and very powerful Lady Abbess gave evidence as follows:

Sister Claire, of unknown origin to her, though suspected of being issue of parents heretical and enemies of God, had indeed been converted and entered at the Convent the government of which had fallen to her lot, unworthy though she felt herself.

The said Sister Claire had fully completed her novitiate and taken her vows according to the holy rules of the Order, but when she had taken her vows she had fallen into a profound melancholy and grown very pale.

Interrogated by the Abbess regarding her melancholy sickness, the said sister had replied with tears that she had no notion of the cause thereof, that tears endlessly welled out of her now she no longer felt her lovely hair on her head, that apart from this she felt a need for air, that she could not restrain her longing to climb trees and do acrobatics out of doors as she used to, that she passed her nights weeping, dreaming of woodlands and sleeping under the shade of their leaves, and that when she recalled this she abhorred the conventual air which harassed her breathing, that in her lurked evil humours and that sometimes in the church she was inwardly absorbed by thoughts which made her lose control.

'I then drilled the holy teachings of the Church into the poor child and reminded her of the eternal happiness which women void of sin would enjoy in Heaven and how transitory earthly life was and how certain the kindness of God who for a few bitter pleasures lost kept endless love for us.'

In spite of this sensible motherly advice, the evil spirit persisted in the said sister, and she was always looking at the foliage of the trees and the grass of the meads through the church windows during services and prayers, then she took it into her head to go as white as a sheet from viciousness only in order to be able to stay in bed and on other occasions went loping about the convent like a goat off its tether.

'Finally, she grew thin, lost her very great beauty and shrank to a mere shadow.

'When she came to this state we, her mother, the Abbess, fearing she was about to die, had her placed in the sick-room. But one winter morning the said sister was gone, without leaving any trace of her passage, without opening a door or unfastening a lock, or any window opened, or anything to show how she went, a terrible happening which was held to have taken place with the aid of the devil which was torturing her and tormenting her. For that matter, the authorities of the Metropolitan Church concluded that this daughter of hell had been sent to turn aside our nuns from their holy vows but had been so dumbfounded by their pure lives that she had returned through thin air to the sabbath of sorcerers which had sent her to the precincts of the Virgin Mary in mockery of our holy religion.'

Having deposed, the Lady Abbess, in pursuance of strict orders of our Archiepiscopal Lord, was escorted with great honour all the way back to Mount Carmel Nunnery.

In the ninth place, on our summons delivered to him, there came before us Joseph surnamed Leschalopier, a money-changer living at the sign of *The Golden Bezant* above the Bridge, who, after taking the oath by the Catholic Faith to say nothing but the truth as known to him concerning the matter before the Ecclesiastical Tribunal, gave evidence as follows:

'I am a lamentable father, sorely afflicted by the sacred will of God. Before that succuba came to *Chaulde Street*, I had a son and he was all I had in the world, handsome as a nobleman, as learned as any clerk, who had made more than twelve journeys into foreign lands, also a good Catholic and one who kept away from the stings of love, for he avoided marriage, knowing himself the support of me in my old age, the love of my sight and constant delight of my heart, a son of whom any King of France would have been proud, a good, courageous man, the light of my business, the joy of my home, hearth and in short of incalculable value seeing that I am all alone in the world, having had the evil fortune to lose my partner and being too old to find another for myself.

'Now, My Lord, this treasure without equal has been taken from me and brought to Hell by the demon. Yes, Lord Judge, the moment he saw that sheath with a thousand blades in it, that female demon in whom everything is a workshop of perdition, a tangle of pleasure and bodily delight, which nothing can assuage, my poor boy got caught in the lime of her passions and since lived only betwixt the pillars of Venus and that not for long, because that is a place whence issues such great heat that nothing can slake the thirst of that chasm even were you to pour into it the spunk of the whole world.

'Alas then, for my poor boy, alas for his chances to engender, alas for his privy purse, alas for his eternal salvation, all of him and more than him was sucked down into that crack like a grain of millet into the jaws of a bull. Hence the man who is now before you was made an orphan in his old age, the only hope left him the pleasure of seeing that demon which fed on blood and gold, that Arachné who has drawn and sucked more marriages, more green grass, more hearts, more Christians than there are lepers in all the leper houses of Christendom, burned at the stake. Burn this ghoul, torment her, this vampire feeding on souls, this tigrish nature that sucks blood, this crucible of lust in which the venom of all the vipers seethes! Seal that abyss of which no man has ever found the bottom.

'I offer all I have to the Chapter to build the pyre, I offer my labour to stoke the fire. Lord Judge, keep good watch not to let the demon escape, for she has hotter coals in her than any earthly fire, she has all the conflagration of Hell in her lap, all the strength of Samson in her hair and the semblance of heavenly music in her voice. She charms so she may kill body and soul in one, she smiles to murder, she kisses to consume, in a word, she would cast her petticoats over a saint and make him deny God.

'My son, oh my son! Where now is the flower of my life, snipped off by that female thing as by foul shears. Oh, My Lord, why have you called on me? Who will give me back my son, whose soul has been engulfed by a belly which gives death to all and life to none? Only the devil thus copulates, but engenders never.

'This is my evidence, which I would beg Master Tournebousche to set down without omitting a jot of it, then give me a note of it so

I may tell it to God every evening in my prayers and thus din into his ears this story of innocent blood and by his infinite mercy win forgiveness for my son!'

Twenty-seven other persons followed, the full transcription of whose detailed evidence, at full length, would be too fiddling and lengthy and confuse the thread of this intriguing inquiry, the story of which, according to ancient precept, should go straight to the point like a bull at his principal task. Therefore here in summary form is the substance of the remaining evidence:

A large number of good Christians, burghers and burghesses, inhabitants of the noble city of Tours, alleged that this demon made every day into a Royal banquet and orgy, that she had never attended any church, that she had cursed God, that she had mocked God's priests, had never made the sign of the cross anywhere, that she spoke all the languages of earth, a thing permitted by God only to the Holy Apostles, that she had many times been seen about the countryside mounted on an unknown animal and as high as the clouds, that she did not age, but had a countenance which was always young, that she had unbuckled her belt to father and son on one and the same day, declaring thereto that it was not her door that did the sinning, that there were clearly visible humours of a malevolent nature issuing from her; for a marzipan-maker seated on a bench outside his house, seeing her pass one evening, had received such a breath of hot lust that he went straight indoors, took to his bed, coupled in a state of frenzy with his wife and the following morning was found dead, still coupling; that at her call elderly citizens squandered their remaining days and all their money, merely to taste with her the delight of the sins of their youth and died like flies, all against Heaven, some of them turning black as Saracens as they perished, that this demon never allowed any eye to see her at dinner or supper, but ate alone, because she lived on human marrow; that many had seen her during the night go to the graveyards and grub out the corpses of men died young, being that she had no other way of assuaging the devil that writhed in her bowels and raged tempestuously therein, whence came those seething, acrid, mordant, piercing, thrusting and devilish jerks, strainings and writhings of love and lust from which many a man had returned bruised, all a-wry, gnawed and battered and flaccid, and that since the coming of Our Lord there had never been seen in any place on earth such an ill-doing, such a poison-oozing, such a gryphonous beast as she was, to such immodest extreme that were the entire city of Tours thrown into that paddock of Venus, she would there and then turn it into the mere dust of a city which the demon in her would gobble up as if a dish of ripe strawberries.

There were further innumerable other statements, assertions, depositions, which in all clarity brought out the infernal engendrance of this woman, this wench, this sister, this ancestress, spouse, whore or brother of Satan, not to speak of the abundance of evidence of her evil doing and the calamity she had spread in every home. Indeed, were one at liberty here to include all that the good fellow to whom this revelation is due had listed, it would be a specimen of the awful cries uttered by the people of Egypt on the day of the Seventh Plague.

This court record further is much to the honour of Master Guillaume Tournebousche, by whom all the registers were drawn upon.

Thus was this inquiry terminated in the tenth vacation, having reached a sufficiency of proofs, supported by authentic depositions, all amply supported with details, plaints, denials, counter-allegations, charges, asseverations, recantations, controversies and confrontations, to all of which the demon was to make reply. Thus to a man the burghers maintained that, were she indeed a female demon, furnished with interior horns, hidden in her privy party, with which she both drank men's substance and broke them, this woman would swim long through this ocean of scribble, at long last, safe and sound, reaching Hell.

II. The Trial of the Said Female Demon

In nomine Patris, et Filii, et Spiritus Sancti, Amen.

In the year of Our Lord one thousand two hundred and seventy-one, before us, Jerome Cornille, Grand Penitentiary and Ecclesiastical Judge, canonically appointed, have appeared:

Sir Philippe d'Ivré, City Constable of the City of Tours and the Province of Touraine, domiciled at his own house in Rôtisserie Street at Chateauneuf; Master Jean Ribou, Provost of the Confraternity and Master Guild of Drapers, domiciled on the Quai de Bretaigne at the sign of St Pierre-es-Liens; Master Antone Jahan, Alderman, Master of the Guild of Money-Changers, domiciled in Place du Pont at the sign of St Mark counting Tours sovereigns; Master Martin Maupertuis, Captain of the City Archers, domiciled at the Castle; Jean Rabelais, Caulker and Boat-builder, domiciled at St Jacques' Island port, and Treasurer of the Confraternity of Loire Mariners; Marc Jerome, surnamed Maschefer, hosier at the sign of St Sebastienne, President of the Goodfellows; and Jacques, surnamed de Villedonner, Masters Teverner and Vineron, domiciled in the main street at the sign of the Pine-Cone; to which Sir Philippe d'Ivré and to which burghers of Tours we have read the following

Solicitation by them drawn up, signed and deliberated for submission to the Ecclesiastical Tribunal.

SOLICITATION

'We, the undersigned, all citizens of Tours, have come to the mansion of our lord Sir Philippe d'Ivré, Chief Constable of Touraine, our Mayor being absent, and have requested him to hear our plaints and representations concerning the following facts which we urge upon the Tribunal of the Archbishopric, judge of ecclesiastical crimes, to which should be relegated the pursuit of the cause we lay bare.

'A long time since there came to our city an evil demon in the guise of a woman, who dwells now in the parish of St Etienne, in the house of Inn-keeper Tortebras, situated on the glebe-land of the Chapter, and under the temporal jurisdiction of the Archbishopric. The said foreign woman pursues the trade of prostitute in prodigal and outrageous fashion, and with such power of evil conduct that she threatens to ruin the Catholic faith in this city, since those who go to her come away with their souls in every sense lost, and with innumerable shocking pronouncements reject any assistance of Holy Church.

'Now, considering that a great number of those who have abandoned themselves to her are dead and that, being come to our city with no other goods than her sex, according to popular report she now has untold wealth, regal treasures the acquisition of which gives serious rise to the suspicion of witchcraft or if not of theft committed with the aid of the magic of the attractions of her supernaturally amorous body;

'considering further that it concerns the good name and security of our homes and that in this land there never was seen a woman prodigal of her body or any such light-o'-love plying her whorish task to such general harm and so openly and poignantly menacing the life, the savings, the morals, the chastity, the religion and all of the inhabitants of this town;

'considering further that there is need for an examination of her person, her goods and her conduct, in order to verify if these effects of love are legitimate and do not, as her behaviour suggests, proceed from the malevolence of Satan, who often comes to pester Christendom in the guise of woman, as may be seen in Holy Writ, where it reads that our Blessed Saviour was carried up to a mountain whence Lucifer on Ashtaroth showed him the fertile domains of Judaea and in many places were seen succubas, that is, demons with female faces, which, not wishing to return to Hell but being ever devoured by insatiable fire, ever try to find refreshment and substance by sucking men's souls;

'considering too that the case of the said woman is borne out with much evidence of diabolical acts, of which certain burghers speak openly, and that it is meet for the peace of the said woman that the matter should be examined so that her peace should not be infringed by any persons ruined by the course of her evil doings,

'for these reasons we beg you to be pleased to submit to our Spiritual Lord, the Father of this Diocese, the most noble and holy Archbishop Jehan de Monsoreau the trials of his afflicted sheep, that he may pronounce in the matter.

'Doing this, you will fulfil the duties of your charge as we do that of guardians of public security in this city, each man caring for the things in his charge in his own ward.

'We have further signed this present in the year of Our Lord one thousand two hundred and seventy-one, on All Saints Day after Mass.'

When Master Tournebousche completed the reading of this solicitation, we, Jerome Cornille, said to the supplicants:

'Gentlemen, do you today still maintain these things, have you any other proofs than those brought to our knowledge so far, and do you undertake to sustain the truth of all this before God, before men and before the accused woman?'

All except Master Jehan Rabelais persisted in their belief, but the said Jehan Rabelais withdrew from the prosecution, declaring that he held the said Saracen female to be an ordinary woman and a good wench too who had no other fault than to maintain a remarkably high temperature of love.

Therefore we, as appointed Judge, after due deliberation, have found there is a matter to investigate on the solicitation of the said citizens, and we hereby Order that proceedings shall be instituted against this woman placed in the Chapter gaol by all the legal procedures laid down in canon law and the decrees *contra daemonios*.

The said Order shall in the form of a Writ be published by the Town Crier in all wards and at the sound of the horn, so it may be made known to all, and so that everybody may bear witness according to their conscience and be confronted by the said demon and finally that the said accused person shall be furnished with a defending counsel according to custom and then the interrogation and trial may be conducted according to law.

(signed) Jerome Cornille
(countersigned) Tournebousche.

In nomine Patris, et Filii, et Spiritus Sancti, Amen.

In the year of Our Lord one thousand two hundred and seventy-one, on the Tenth Day of February, after mass, by Edict of ourselves, Jerome Cornille, ecclesiastical justice, the woman taken at the house of the Inn-keeper Tortebras, situated on Chapter land of the Cathedral of St Maurice, was taken from the Chapter Gaol and brought before us and thus subjected to the temporal and seignorial jurisdiction of the Archbishopric of Tours, apart from which, by the nature of the crimes imputed to her, she is subject to the tribunal and under ecclesiastical jurisdiction, which we have informed her of so that she may not be ignorant of it.

Then, after solemn reading in toto and well comprehended by her, first of the Solicitation of the Burghers of Tours, then further the statements, plaints, charges and proceedings inscribed in twenty-two notebooks by Master Tournebousche, all of which are above narrated, we counselled her to speak the whole truth, praying God and the Church to aid her, being charged to elicit the truth, first by cross-examination of the said accused woman.

As first question we required the said woman to tell us in what country she was born. By her who spoke the reply given was:

'In the Moorish country.'

We then inquired whether she had father and mother or any other relations. By her who spoke the answer was that she had never known them.

We then required her to declare her name. By her who spoke the answer given was:

'Zulma, in the Arabic tongue.'

We asked her why she spoke our language. By her who spoke the answer was:

'Because I came to this country.'

We asked:

'When?'

By her who spoke the reply given was:

'About twelve years ago.'

By us the inquiry was made how old she then was. By her who spoke the answer was:

'Fifteen, or nearly.'

By us it was then said:

'So you admit to being twenty-seven years old?'

By her who spoke the answer given was:

'Yes.'

By us it was said to her that this would mean that she was the Saracen girl found in the alcove of the shrine of the Virgin Mary,

then baptized by the Archbishop, held over his font by Lord de la
Roche-Corbon and Lady d'Azay his spouse, then entered by them in
the Mont-Carmel Convent, where she had made vows of chastity,
poverty, silence and love of God, under the divine assistance of St
Claire. By her who spoke the answer was:

'That is so.'

By us it was then asked whether she accepted as factual the assertions
of the Most Noble and Reverend Lady Abbess of Mont Carmel, and
also of Jacquette known as Old Grease, kitchen skivvy. By her who
spoke the answer given was that what they said was true in the main.

Then by us it was put:

'So you are a Christian woman?'

And by her who spoke the response was:

'Yes, Father.'

At this point she was requested by us to make the sign of the cross
and take holy water from a stoup placed within reach of her, by
Guillaume Tournebousche, which she doing, by us witnessed, it was
admitted as proved fact that Zulma the Moor, in our country known
as Blanche Bruyn, nun of the Convent known as Mt Carmel, there
named Sister Claire, but now suspected of being a false appearance of a
woman concealing a demon, had in our presence made the act of faith
and thereby recognized the jurisdiction of the ecclesiastical tribunal.

Then the following words were spoken by us:

'My daughter, you are strongly suspected of having had dealings
with the Devil in the manner in which you left the Convent, which
was in every way supernatural.'

By she who spoke the reply made was that on this occasion she
reached open country in a perfectly natural manner, through the
street door, after evensong, under the cassock of Dom Jehan de
Marsilis, Visitor of the Nunnery, who subsequently housed her, her
who spoke, in a hut which he had situated in Cupid Alley, near one
of the city keeps. There this said priest had further at great length and
very thoroughly initiated her who spoke into the delights of love,
which, she who spoke said, she hitherto had known nothing of, and
she had found those delights very much to her taste, moreover, they
had been most useful to her. For then Lord d'Amboise, having
noticed her, her who spoke, at the window of the priest's secret
dwelling, he straightaway fell passionately in love with her. Then she
who spoke, loving him genuinely more than the friar, escaped from
the hovel where this Dom Marsilis held her to the advantage of his
own pleasures. She then went at all speed to Amboise, the castle of
the said lord, where she had countless amusements, hunting and
dancing and fine regal clothes.

One day, Lord de la Roche-Pozay, being the guest of Lord d'Amboise, drinking and merrymaking, Baron d'Amboise let Lord de la Roche-Pozay see her without her knowledge as she left her bath, naked. Now, at this sight of her, this Lord de la Roche-Pozay fell passionately in love with her who spoke and the following day in duel he killed Lord d'Amboise, and by great violence, notwithstanding her tears, had taken her to the Holy Land, where she who spoke had led the life such as lead much-loved women, held in great respect because of her beauty.

Then, after many trials, and despite her misgivings of ill-fortune, she who spoke had come back to France, which she did because this was the desire of her lord and master, Baron de Bueil, who was dying of homesickness in foreign parts and wished once again to see his ancestral manor. But he promised her who spoke to protect her from any danger, and she who spoke had great belief and faith in him, the more so since she now loved him very much. But when he reached this country Lord de Bueil fell ill of an illness and lamentably passed away without any recovery, and saw no doctor despite the fervent requests which she who spoke had made him, without success, for he detested physicians, master surgeons and apothecaries, and this was the whole truth.

It was then put to the accused woman by us that this meant that she accepted as true what good Lord Harduin and the Inn-keeper Tortebras had said. By her who spoke it was answered that in the main she admitted those statements to be true, but in other parts they were false, they were lying and stupid.

Then by us it was requested of the accused woman to state whether she had had love and carnal union with all the men, nobles, burghers and others as stated in the deposition of the people of Tours. At which she who spoke said very impudently:

'Love, yes, but about carnal union, I don't know.'

By us it was then said that these had all died by her acts. By her who spoke it was replied that those deaths could not be due to her, because she had always refused those particular men, but the more she avoided them, the more they came to her, pestering her who spoke with endless frenzy of love, but then, she said, she who spoke, that when in the end she was taken by those men, by God's grace, she went at it with all her force since she felt joy like none other in that act of love. Then she added, she who spoke, that she had thus unbosomed her inmost feelings solely because we had required her to speak the truth in all things and that she who spoke was terribly afraid of the torments of the torturers.

Then she was required by us to declare, under pain of torture, what her state of mind was like when a certain nobleman was dying as a consequence of his couplings with her. Then by her who spoke the reply was made that she was left utterly desolate and wished then to do away with herself, she prayed to God, to the Virgin and to all the Saints to receive her in Heaven for ever, for, as she who spoke said, she had met but kind and gracious hearts in which there was no vice, so that when she had seen them dead she had fallen into great grief, believing herself to be a malefactory creature or subject to an evil fortune which was passed on to others like a disease.

Then by us the question was put as to where she offered up her prayers.

By her who spoke it was replied that she prayed in her own oratory, on her knees before God, who, the Gospel said, saw and understood everything and was in all places.

Then by us the question was put why she never went to churches either for services or on feast days. At this by her who spoke the answer was made that those who used to come to love her used to choose holy days for their delights and that she who spoke did everything to please them.

By us the Christian remonstrance was made that this would mean that she was more subject to the orders of men than the commandments of God.

Then by her who spoke the reply was made that for the sake of those who had loved her well she who spoke would have thrown herself on to burning faggots, had she ever in her love followed any other course than that of her nature and for the weight of the world in gold she would not have given her body or her love even to a King, if she did not really love him in her heart, her feet, her head, her hair, her forehead and every part of her. In short she volubly averred, she who spoke, never having performed any act of prostitution by selling a scrap of love to a man she had not chosen for herself and that the man who held her in his arms an hour or even as much as touched her lips with a kiss, possessed her for the rest of his days.

Then by us she was requested to state whence came the jewels, gold vessels, silver, precious stones, regal furnishings, rugs *et caetera* according to expert opinion to the value of two hundred thousand doubloons all found in her dwelling and given now in charge to the Chapter Treasury. By her who spoke it was said that she placed all her hopes in us as much as in God himself, but she dared not make answer to this, because it concerned the choicest things of love by which she had always lived.

Then, interpellated anew, she who spoke said that if we, the judge, only knew how fervently she regarded any man whom she loved,

how studiously she submitted to him, with what gladness she heard
his wishes and hung on the sacred words with which his lips gratified
her, in what adoration she held his person, no sum of money could
recompense that great affection for which all men crave. Then she
said, she who spoke, that from no man she had loved had she ever
solicited any present or recompense, but had always been utterly
content to find a place in their heart, that there she snuggled with
imperishable, inexpressible delights, thinking that heart the greatest
richness there could be, and never thought of aught else but to
afford them as much delight and happiness as she received from them.
Nevertheless, despite her insistence on this, her lovers always insisted on showing her their gracious gratitude. One would come, to
her who speaks, with a necklace of pearls, saying: *'This is to show my
love that the satin of her skin did not deceive me in seeming whiter than pearls!'*
And place it round her neck, with ardent kisses.

She who speaks had been angered by such silly things, but could
not refuse to keep a jewel which it so pleased these men to see where
they laid it on her. Every man had a different fantasy. There had been
one whose whim it was to tear up the costly clothes which she wore
to please him, another liked to dress her who spoke with sapphires
on her wrists and long wrappings of silk or black velvet, and would
for days on end be ecstatic about the perfect features of her who
spoke, who was delighted without end by the things her admirers
desired because those things made them all so happy.

Then she said, she who spoke, that just as we do not like anything
so much as our own delight, and love to have everything ablaze with
beauty and harmony outwardly as well as inwardly in our hearts,
likewise they all liked to see the purple she wore ornamented with
fine things, and in that thought all her admirers delighted as much as
she did in smothering her with gold, silk and flowers.

Further, seeing that such lovely things spoiled nothing, she who
spoke was powerless nor had any right to prevent a knight or even a
rich commoner who loved her doing his will, and so she was forced
to accept precious perfumes and other satisfactions with which she
was overwhelmed and this was the origin of those gold plates, those
rugs and those jewels seized by the authorities in her dwelling.

Here ended the first interrogation of the said Sister Claire, suspected of being a demon, for we the judge and Guillaume Tournebousche were exceedingly fatigued by the sound of the voice of the
said woman in our ears and now found our understanding utterly
befogged.

By us as judge a second examination was fixed for three days hence,
to ascertain the evidence of the obsession and the presence of the

demon in the body of the above-mentioned female, who, by orders of the judge, was taken back to her gaol under guard of Master Guillaume Tournebousche.

In nomine Patris, et Filii, et Spiritus Sancti, Amen.

The Thirteenth Day of February following, before us, Jerome Cornille, *et caetera*, was brought the above-named Sister Claire for the purpose of being interrogated regarding facts and deeds imputed to her and to be convicted of these.

By us, as judge, it was put to the accused female that, in view of the various answers given by her to the preceding interrogations, it was established that it was not within the power of an ordinary woman, even were she authorized, supposing, that is, such licence even to be given, by living the life of a woman loose with her body furnishing pleasure to all, to effect so many deaths and accomplish such perfect spells without the aid of some special demon being lodged in her body to which demon furthermore her soul must have been sold under a special pact.

It was therefore clearly proved that under cover of her body there resided and acted a demon which was the author of these evils. She was therefore now called upon to declare at what age she had received this demon and to state the conditions agreed between the said demon and herself, then confess the whole truth regarding their joint malefactions.

By her who speaks the response was made that she wished to answer us, as man, as she would answer God Almighty, who should be the judge of us all. She then made out, she who spoke, that she had never seen any demon or spoken to any such one or in any way even desired to set eyes on one. Nor had she plied the trade of courtesan, for she who spoke had never once indulged in the multifarious delights which love devises otherwise than on the prompting of that pleasure with which the sovereign Creator has imbued these acts, and she who spoke had always been prompted to this rather by the desire of being gentle and kind to a knight dearly beloved by her than by any constant urge of bodily desire, but if she had had such bodily desire, she who spoke implored us to reflect that she was a poor African girl in whose veins God had implanted very hot blood and in her mind such easy understanding of the pleasures of love that when a man looked at her she at once felt a great turmoil in her heart. If then a lusting knight having intent to couple with her but touched her who speaks in any part of her body and caressed her there she was in spite of everything in his power, for her heart at once faltered. By such touch, remembrance and awareness of all the lovely delights of love was awakened in her middle, there generating a fierce heat, which made upward passage through her body, glowing in her veins and imbuing her with love and delight from head to foot.

Hence, from that day on which Dom Marsilis first, in her who spoke, opened up understanding of these things, she had had no other thought than this, perceiving from that time on that love was in such perfect concord with her particular nature that since then it had been proved to her who spoke that had she not then at last known a man and a man's natural moistening of her body, she would in the said Convent have died of desiccation. In witness of this, she who spoke affirmed to us with complete conviction that since her flight from the said Convent she had not been for one day or any morsel of time downcast or gloomy, but had ever been, she who spoke, happy, and thereby considered that she had but pursued the sacred will of God regarding herself, from which further she maintained that she had been wrongly diverted during all that lost time she had been in the Convent.

To this, by us, Jerome Cornille, it was objected to the said demon that by this reply she had openly blasphemed against God, because we had all been made for His great glory and placed in this world to honour and to serve Him, to have under our eyes His blessed commandments and to live in sanctity so as thereby to attain eternal salvation, and not to be on our backs all the time doing what even the animals only do at certain seasons.

Then the same female replied that she who speaks had honoured God abundantly, that in every country she had cared for the sick and suffering, giving them much money, and clothing and weeping at the sight and knowledge of their miseries, and that when the Last Judgement came she who spoke hoped to have about her a goodly company of holy works pleasing to God, which would cry mercy for her.

She then said that, were it not for her humility, her fear of being reproved and fear of displeasing the Lords of the Chapter, she would with delight have spent her worldly wealth on the completion of the Cathedral Church of Saint Maurice and on endowments in this for the salvation of her soul, sparing neither her joy nor her person, and that in this thought she would have found a double delight in her nights of love, seeing that every act of love would then add another stone for the beautification of that Basilica. Likewise, to that end and for the eternal salvation of her who speaks, all those men who loved her would have gladly and largely have given their worldly goods.

Then it was said by us to this demon that she was unable to justify her childlessness, in that despite so much copulation no child had been born of her, this proving the presence of a demon in her body.

What was more, only Ashtaroth or one of the Apostles could speak all languages, and she spoke in the fashion of each and every country, which witnessed the presence of the devil in her.

To this by she who spoke it was said that as to various languages, the only Greek she knew was *Kyrie eleison!* of which she made much use, and of Latin she knew nothing, lest it be *Amen!* and this she said to God, hoping from him to obtain her freedom. Further she said that as for the rest of our argument she who spoke had been greatly grieved never to have conceived and if ordinary housewives had children she thought that this was perhaps because they only found little pleasure in the act whereas she who spoke found a little too much, but that this was no doubt God's will, who thought that the world would be in danger of perishing if there were too much happiness.

Hearing this and a thousand other arguments which sufficiently established the presence of a devil in the body of this sister, for it is the property of Lucifer always to find heretical arguments plausible as truth, we ordered that in our presence the said accused female should be put to torment and greatly tortured, for the purpose of reducing the same demon by suffering and submitting it to the authority of the Church. We therefore sent for François de Gangest, Master Surgeon and Chapter Physician, to assist us and by the Order given below required him to investigate the qualities of the female parts (*virtutes vulvae*) of the aforesaid woman, to enlighten our Religion on the methods made use of by this demon to capture souls in her privy passage and find out if any device was to be perceived therein.

Then the said Saracen female wept and groaned sorely in anticipation, and despite her irons fell to her knees, with great outcry and clamour begging the revocation of this order, pleading that her limbs were so weak and her bones so tender that she would break like glass, then finally offering to buy herself out of this torture by the free gift of all her goods to the Chapter and her undertaking forthwith to leave France.

Upon this she was required by us of her own free will to admit that she was and always had been a demon of the type of a *succuba*, which things are female devils, charged with corrupting Christian men by the blandishments of flagrant pleasures of sex. At this she who spoke made answer that such an affirmation would be an abominable lie, seeing that she had always felt herself a very natural woman.

Then, her irons having been struck off by the torturer, the said female suddenly cast loose her clothing and purposely and maliciously confused, disturbed, and obfuscated the understanding by the vision of her body, which certainly exercises supernatural power on a man.

At this point Master Tournebousche by reasons of nature dropped his pen and withdrew, pleading that he was unable without unbelievable temptations which harassed his brain, to witness this torture, being that he felt the devil taking violent possession of him.

Here ended the second interrogation, and as the Bailiff and Janitor of the Chapter had declared Master François de Hangest to be absent in the country, the torture and interrogation were postponed till tomorrow at midday, after mass.

This last has been entered in the protocol by me, Jerome, in the absence of Master Guillaume Tournebousche, on whose behalf it is signed.

Jerome Cornille,
Grand Penitentiary.

SOLICITATION

Today, the fourteenth day of the month of February, in the presence of myself, Jerome Cornille, the aforementioned Masters Jehan Ribou, Antoine Iha Iahan, Martin Maupertuis, Jerome Maschefer, Jacques de Ville d'Omer and Sir Philippe d'Ivré in place and stead of the Mayor of the City of Tours, appeared before me, all being plaintiffs designate in the act of inquiry made at the Town Hall, to whom, on the request of Blanche Bruyn, presently confessed nun of the Convent of Mont Carmel, under the name of Sister Claire, was made known the appeal made to the Judgement of God by the said woman accused of demoniacal possession and her offer to undergo trial by ordeal of water and of fire in the presence of the Chapter and of the City of Tours, for the purpose of proving she was innocent and her real nature to be that of a woman.

To this Solicitation for their part the said accusers agreed and on condition the City be security therefor have undertaken to prepare the site and a suitable wood-pile to be approved by the godparents of the accused woman.

Thereupon by us, as Judge, was appointed the date for the ordeal as the first day of the New Year, which will be next Easter, and indicated the hour of midday, after saying of mass, every one of the parties having agreed that this period was ample.

Therefore the present decision shall be cried on the urgency of each of them in all the cities, towns and castles of Touraine and of the other lands of France at their application, cost urgency.

Jerome Cornille.

III. What the Succuba did to Suck out the Soul of the Venerable Judge and what Came of that Diabolical Pleasure

This is the act of special confession made on the First of March in the Year One Thousand Two Hundred and Seventy-one after the coming of our BLESSED SAVIOUR, by Jerome Cornille, priest, Canon of the Chapter of the Cathedral Church of St Maurice, Grand Penitentiary, with full admission of his unworthiness, who, come to his last hour, and repenting his sins, trespasses, shortcomings, misdeeds and wickednesses, desired his confessions to be given to the light, to serve the affirmation of Truth, of the glory of God, of the justice of this Tribunal, and to be for himself an alleviation of his punishments in the world to come.

The said Jerome Cornille, being on his death bed, there were convoked to hear his declarations Jean de la Haye (de Haga), incumbent of the Church of St Maurice, Pietro Guyard, Treasurer of the Chapter, appointed by our Lord Jehan de Monsoreau, Archbishop, to record his words, further Dom Louis Pot, of the *maius monasterium* (Marmoustier), by him chosen as spiritual father and confessor, all three assisted by the great and venerable Doctor Guillaume de Censoris, Archdeacon of Rome, at present sent to our Diocese as Legate by our Holy Father the Pope. Finally, in the presence of a large number of Christians come to witness the passing of the said Jerome Cornille, upon his known desire to make an act of public repentance, seeing that he is dying in Lent and his word is further likely to open the eyes of Christians likewise in the process of bringing themselves eventually to Hell.

And then, being that he was very enfeebled, and unable to utter a word, Dom Louis Pot read to Jerome Cornille the confession which ensues, causing much commotion in the hearts of the said persons present:

'My brothers, up to the seventy-ninth year of my life, that in which I now am, save for minor sins for which, however holy he be, a Christian becomes guilty before God, but which we are permitted to redeem by penitence, I maintain that I led a Christian life and merited the praise and renown accorded me in this Diocese, where I was elevated to the very eminent responsibility of Grand Penitentiary, of which I am unworthy. Now, seized by realization of the infinite glory of God, horrified by the pains which in Hell await all wicked persons and deceivers, I think to diminish the enormity of my crimes by the greatest penance I can make in the extreme hour to which I am come. Hence I have requisitioned of the Church which I have deceived and betrayed, selling its rights and the fair name of justice, the great boon of charging me publicly in the manner of the Christians of antiquity.

'I would crave, in order to manifest greater repentance, still to have in me sufficient life to be spurned by all my brothers at the Portal of the Cathedral, there to spend a whole day on my knees, holding a candle, with a noose round my neck, barefoot, seeing that I have greatly served the divagations of Hell against the sacred interests of God.

'However, in this great shipwreck of my fragile virtue—and may this teach you to shun vice, and the snares of the demon and find refuge in the Church which is your only succour—I have been so frightfully enchanted by Lucifer that by that intercession, by that aid and those prayers which I crave of you all, our Lord Jesus Christ may have pity on me, poor misled Christian, whose eyes now melt in tears.

'I would also crave another life, to spend it in penitential toil. Therefore now give ear and tremble in great fear! Chosen by the assembled Chapter to conduct, to guide and to effect the proceedings begun *vis-à-vis* the demon which has substantiated itself in the female form of the person of a relapsed nun of such abomination that she denies Almighty God, by the name of Zulma in the infidel land whence she came, which demon is known in the Diocese under the name of Claire of the Convent of Mont Carmel, and has caused much affliction to the city by laying herself under an infinite number of men, to win their souls for Mammon, Ashtaroth and Satan, Princess of Hell, by bringing them to spill out this world in a state of mortal sin and causing them to pass away in the part which should produce life, I, I the Judge, in the autumn of my days, fell into this trap and lost my senses, miserably falling short of the duties committed by the Chapter in its great truth to my cold body in its hoary old age.

'Hear how cunning the demon is and be steadfast against the artifices of Satan. When I heard the first response made by the said succuba, I observed with terror that the fetters on her ankles and wrists left no trace, and I was astonished at the occult strength possessed by her in apparent frailty. Next my mind was suddenly troubled at sight of the natural perfection with which the devil in this instance was clad. I listened to the music of her voice, which warmed me from head to foot and made me wish I were young, to give myself to this demon, finding that for one hour spent with her my eternal salvation was a feeble gift compared with the pleasures of love tasted in those delightful arms.

'I then put aside that rigour with which judges should ever be armed. The demon, questioned by me, argued back with such words that at her second interrogation I became firmly persuaded that if I fined or tortured such a poor little thing which wept like an innocent child, it would be to commit a crime. Then, warned by a voice on high to do my duty, and that those golden words, that music of celestial seeming, were but diabolical pretence, that this body so fine, so disarming, would suddenly turn into a beast with disgusting hairs and sharp claws, those eyes which were so soft into fiery irons, and those haunches would sprout a scaly tail, the gracious pink lips of that lovely mouth become crocodile jaws, I returned to my purpose of putting the said succuba to the torment till she should confess her mission after the mode in which this has hitherto been done in Christendom.

'Then, when this demon was revealed to me in her nudity, to be put to the torture, I was by magic enchantments all at once subjected to her power. I felt my old bones creak. My brain was filled with hot light. My heart brimmed over with young, seething blood. I felt inwardly glad, and by virtue of the philtre which had been cast in my eyes, all the snow of my forehead was melted. I lost consciousness of my Christian life and thought myself a lad wandering about the countryside, escaped from his classes, stealing apples. I had not even the strength to make the sign of the cross, and forgot all about the Church, about God the Father, and even about the Sweet Saviour of mankind.

'In prey to that vision, I made my way through the streets, recalling the delights of that voice, the abominable beautiful body of that demon, telling myself countless evil things. Then, smitten and drawn on by a prod of the Devil's prong, planted in my head already like a crowbar in an oak, I was driven by that sharp iron towards the gaol, despite the efforts of my guardian angel, who from time to time plucked at my arm and bade me disregard these temptations, but notwithstanding his holy words of counsel and his aid, I was drawn by a million claws that caught in my heart, and soon found myself in that gaol.

'When the door was opened to me, I no longer saw any outward sign of its being a prison, for by the help of evil genies or fairies the succuba had there built a tent of purple velvets and silks, full of sweet scents and flowers, where she lounged in superb attire, with neither iron on her neck nor chain on her ankles. I allowed my ecclesiastical clothing to be stripped from me and was placed in a sweet-scented bath. Then the demon wrapped me with a Saracen gown and served me a feast of rare dishes in precious vessels, with golden goblets, wines from Asia, singing and marvellous music and countless words of praise which, titillating my ears, reached my soul.

'All this time the said succuba stuck to my side and her hateful but winsome touch distilled fresh fire in my members. My guardian angel abandoned me. Then I lived by the frightful luminosity of the eyes of that Moorish woman and craved for the warm embrace of that fair body, longing for ever to feel the pressure of those red lips which now I believed to be natural, and was without any fear of the bite of her teeth, which drew me to the very bottom of hell. I found delight in the feel of the unparalleled softness of her hands, without any thought of these being monstrous claws.

'In a word, I was all a-quiver like a bridegroom impatient to go to his bride, without heed that that bride was eternal death. I cared naught for the things of this world nor the interests of God, dreaming solely of love, of the lovely breasts of that woman, which made me burn with lust, and of that hell-opening of hers into which I thought to plunge myself.

'Alas, my brethren, for three days and three nights I was constrained thus to labour without being able to exhaust that which gushed forth from my loins, into which like two pikes were thrust the hands of the succuba, imparting to my poor senile flesh, my desiccated old bones, an unbelievable perspiration of lust.

'At first, to draw me to her, that demon made something of the gentleness of milk course through me. Then came sharp delights which pricked hard like a hundred needles, into bones, into marrow, into brain, into nerves. Then, in this play, the secret parts of my head became enflamed, my blood, my nerves, my flesh, my bones, till I verily smouldered with the true fire of hell, which excited griping agonies in my joints and an unbelievable, unbearable, insufferable, flaying delight of love which wore away the bonds of my life. The hair of the demon, with which my poor body was enveloped, wrapped me in a mist of flame and I felt each single tress like the red-hot bar of a grill.

'In this state of mortal voluptuousness I could see the glowing features of the said succuba and they were laughing and uttering a thousand teasing words to me, telling how I was her knight, her lord, her lance, her day, her delight, her thunder, her life, her good, her best rider, craving either to be in my skin or for me to be in hers, hearing which, under the pricks of that tongue which sucked my soul, I plunged deeper and pressed yet further into her hell without finding any bottom.

'Then, when at last I had not another drop of blood in my veins and my soul no longer beat in my body, when I was in every way a ruined man, the demon, ever fresh and white and glowing and luminous and smiling, addressed me and cried: "Poor fool, to think

I was a demon! Tell me then! If I asked you to give your soul for a kiss, would you not give it me?"

'"I would," I told her.

'"And if, in order for ever to labour thus at love, you had to drink the blood of newborn babes, so as ever to have fresh life to spill in my bed, would you not suck that blood gladly?"

'"I would," I told her.

'"If, ever to be my knight, riding me, gay as a man in the spring of his youth, feeling full life, drinking delight, thrusting to the depths of joy, like a swimmer in the Loire, you had to deny God, would you not spit in the face of Jesus?"

'"I would," I told her.

'"If you were granted twenty more years of monastic life, would you not barter them for two of this love which scorches, and to indulge in this lovely motion?"

'"I would," I told her.

'Then I felt a hundred sharp claws which tore at my diaphragm as if a thousand birds of prey's beaks were rending me and shrieking. Then, borne on this alleged succuba which I rode, I was elevated suddenly above the earth, for she had spread out her wings and she cried:

'"Ride on, ride on, my riding manikin, cling firmly to the cruppers of the mare you straddle now, cling to her mane and ride, ride on, my riding manikin! Everything rides!"

'Thus elevated I saw the cities of the earth like a fog and there, by a special gift, beheld every couple with a female demon all copulating and engendering with great lust, all uttering countless words of love-lust, all manner of exclamations bursting from them as, mortised close in mutual embrace, they jiggled and they joggled. Then my mare, with Saracen's female head, as she flew on and on, galloping through the clouds, showed me the earth fornicating with the sun in a coitus whence burst a germination of stars and every female world made love with a male world, only in the stead of words as spoken by living things, the worlds exuded the din of tempests, shooting lightnings and yelling in thunder.

'Then, ever riding higher, I saw above all the worlds, and there was female nature such as it is in all things that love, coupling with the Prince of Motion. Here, to taunt me, the succuba placed me in the midst of that monstrous and incessant leaping, where I was lost as if a grain of sand in the oceans. And all the time, my white mare kept crying to me:

'"Ride on, ride on, my fine rider, ride on! Everything rides!"

'Then, aware what a trifling thing a priest was in that flood of the semen of all the worlds, where everything was perpetual accoupling and coitus of the metals and the rocks, the waters and the airs, the thunders and the fishes and the plants and the animals and the men and the spirits and the worlds and the planets, all of them at their coupling, I denied the Catholic faith.

'Whereupon, the succuba, showing me that vast belt of stars which is to be seen in the heavens, told me that Milky Way was not of milk but of celestial semen spilt from the great fluxion of the copulation of the worlds. At which words I rode that succuba still more fiercely in a fever of passion of the light of a thousand million stars and longed, thus copulating and riding, to sense the very nature of those thousand million creatures in universal copulation.

'Then, by this terrible effort of love, I fell, in universal impotence, to the sound of a vast infernal laughter, when at last I saw my bed surrounded by my menservants who had had the courage to fight the demon by casting over the bed where I lay a full bucket of holy water, amid fervent prayers to God.

'Even so, despite that assistance, I had to bear a frightful battle with the said succuba, the claws of which rent at my heart, causing me untold suffering. Even when, at last, restored by the voices of my men, my relatives and my friends, I could force myself to make the sacred sign of the cross, the succuba, perched on my bed at its head, at its foot, everywhere, strove to make my nerves taut, grinning, grimacing, thrusting countless obscene pictures under my eyes and engendering in me a thousand evil cravings.

'Nevertheless, having pity on me, My Lord the Archbishop sent for the Holy Relics of St Gatien, and when the casket touched my bed the said succuba was forced to take flight, leaving behind an odour of sulphur and Hell, which for a day stifled my menservants, my friends and others about me.

'Then, the Heavenly light of God having lit my soul, I saw that by reason of my sins and my battle with the evil spirit, I was in great peril of death. Therefore I implored special grace to live a little longer, to pay tribute to God and to His Church, to declare the infinite merits of Jesus on the cross, who died for the salvation of Christians.

'By that prayer I obtained the grace to regain strength and accuse myself of my sins and insist on all the members of the Church of St Maurice giving their aid and assistance to get me out of Purgatory, where I shall have redeemed my sins by infinite misfortunes.

'Further, I declare that my proclamation, which appeals to the judgement of God for the sake of the said demon to be given in ordeal by water and fire, is a trick due to the malevolent power instilled in me by the said demon, which thus would be able to escape the justice of the Court of the Archbishop and his Chapter, for the demon secretly told me that it had the jurisdiction necessary to call up a demon used to those ordeals to go through them in its stead.

'Finally, I give and bequeath to the Chapter of the Church of St Maurice my goods of all kinds, to found a Chapel in the said Church, to build this and decorate it and place it under the joint tutelage of St Jerome and St Gatien, one of whom is the Patron, the other the Saviour of my soul.'

This being heard by all present was placed before the Ecclesiastical Court by Jehan de la Haye (Johannes de Haga).

'We, Jehan de la Haye (Johannes de Haga), elected Grand Penitentiary of St Maurice by the General Assembly of the Chapter, according to the usage and custom of this Church, and appointed to prosecute anew the trial of the demon succuba, at present in the Chapter Gaol, have ordered a fresh inquiry in which shall be heard all those of this Diocese who have known any facts relative to this.

'We declare null and void any other proceedings, interrogations, declarations, and quash them in the name of the members of the Church assembled in General and sovereign Chapter, and declare that the appeal to God infamously made by the Demon is likewise null and void, by reason of the base treachery of the devil in this matter.

'And the said judgement shall be cried to the sound of the horn at all points of the Diocese where the false edicts of last month were published, all notoriously due to the instigation of the Demon, as shown by the confession of the late Jerome Cornille.

'Let all good Christians aid our Holy Church and obey its commandments.

Jehan de la Haye.'

IV. How the Saracen Female whisked so Quickly Round about and Out of Chaulde Street that it was with Difficulty She was put to the Stake and Burned in Preparation for Hell

The following was set down in the Month of May in the year 1360 in the form of a Last Will and Testament.

'My dearest, well-beloved son, when it shall be lawful for you to read this, I, your father, shall be sleeping in the tomb, craving your prayers and begging you so to conduct yourself in life as advised in these presents which I bequeath to you for the wise management of your family, for your property and for your security, for I pen this still fresh from the blows and the grievous impressions of the ruling injustice of humankind.

'In the vigour of my youth, my son, it was my great ambition to rise high in the Church and attain the highest dignities in it, for no life seemed to me finer. It was therefore with that solemn intention that I learned to read and write, till by dint of great effort I was fit to take Holy Orders. And, seeing that I had no powerful patron, nor any sound counsellor to guide my steps, to achieve my ambition I contrived to get myself appointed registrar, scribe or clerk of the Chapter of Saint Martin, which then included among the highest and most wealthy personages of all Christendom, for in it the King of France himself was a mere Canon, so that I was sure there more than anywhere else to have various opportunities of rendering little services to certain lords, hence to gain myself masters or patrons, and in due course be crowned with the mitre as well as any other man and appointed to a Diocesan see.

'But that first project was much too hopeful a one, and a trifle too ambitious, which indeed God made manifest to me, for it was Jehan de Villedomer who later became cardinal who was appointed, whereas, to my great discomfiture, I was turned down.

'It was then, at that setback, that my anxieties were relieved by good old Jerome Cornille, that veteran Cathedral Penitentiary of whom I often spoke to you. Out of his kindness of heart that dear man prevailed upon me to go as penman to the Chapter of St Maurice and Archbishopric of Tours, which I did in all good faith, for I was by now accounted a fine calligrapher.

'In the year in which I was finally to take Orders, however, that notorious case of the Chaulde Street demon arose. Older folk indeed still talk about it and during winter evenings tell the tale to the younger generation. Indeed, over the years it has been related round every hearth in the land of France. Thinking that this would suit my ambitions and that in return for such aid the Chapter would push me up a few rungs, my good master had me serve as Clerk to the Court and copy out all that was to be committed to writing about the sorry business.

'At the very outset, however, Monseigneur Jerome Cornille, a man of great wisdom, justice and clarity of thought, then in his late seventies, suspected something dirty about that case. For all that he had himself never favoured loose-living females, nor indeed had ever polluted himself with any woman in all his life, which had throughout been of an adorable saintliness, which indeed had earned him the position of Judge, it became obvious, as soon as the charges had been heard and the poor wench interrogated, that though the girl was certainly a rather wild hussy who had broken the rules of her Convent, she was innocent of any Satanic act. It was merely that her great wealth was coveted by many enemies, and others whom out of prudence I refrain from naming.

'At the time it was indeed generally assumed that she had so much money and gold that according to some accounts, had she so pleased, she could have bought up the whole Province of Touraine. Hence there were a thousand lies and slanders set into circulation about her, and she was also much envied by honest women, and all those lies went the rounds till they were regarded as gospel truths.

'In this situation, recognizing that there was no demon in the girl but the demon of love, Jerome Cornille made her agree to retire to a Convent for the remainder of her life. Then, informed by certain gallant knights who were great fighters and owners of considerable estates that they intended at all costs to rescue her, he called on her secretly to have recourse to God's judgement, not without giving her worldly goods to the Chapter, so as to silence evil tongues. By this means was to be saved from the stake the daintiest flower that Heaven ever let fall to earth, her only fault being that from excessive tenderness of heart and obligingness she yielded to the love which her eyes shot into the hearts of her suitors.

'The real devil, however, then meddled in the matter in the guise of a certain monk. In the following wise. A great enemy of the virtue, decency and holiness of My Lord Jerome Cornille, a man called Jehan de la Haye, having learned that in her gaol the poor girl was being treated like a Queen, maliciously laid a charge that the Grand Penitentiary was conniving with her and had become her agent, because, so this evil-minded priest averred, she made him young, passionate and fortunate again, of which accusation the poor old man died from grief in a single day, knowing therefrom that Jehan de la Haye had sworn to ruin him and lusted after his appointments.

'True enough, our Lord the Archbishop visited the gaol and found the Saracen girl in a pleasant room, well bedded, without irons, this being because, having hidden a diamond in a place where nobody thought it could have been held, she had purchased the gaoler's goodwill. At this time, indeed, some also claimed that the gaoler too was smitten by her and that by love, or else perhaps in great fear of the barons who were this woman's lovers, he was plotting her flight.

'Poor old Cornille lay dying and through all the fuss made by Jehan de la Haye, the Chapter considered it essential that the trial conducted by the old man and also his decisions should be annulled, while the said Jehan de la Haye, at the time a mere Vicar of the

Cathedral, made out that all that was needed to achieve this was for the good old man to make a confession on his death bed.

'Thereupon the dying man was tortured by the lords of the Chapter, together with those of St Martin and men of Marmoustiers Monastery, the Archbishop and also the Papal Legate, to make him retract as the Church desired, to which at first the worthy man refused to agree.

'However, after endless torture a public confession was at last drawn up and the leading townsfolk attended the event and this confession spread such horror and dismay that it is indescribable. The churches of the diocese offered public prayers about the grievous wound and every man began to wonder if at any moment the devil would appear at his own fireside. The truth however is that my poor Master Jerome was in a state of fever and saw visions when they forced this retraction from him, and when the so-called confession had been made, learning of the trick from me, the poor saintly man wept greatly. Indeed, in the presence of his doctor, he passed away in my arms, in desperation at the mummery of it all, and told us that when he finally passed over he would go straight to fall at God's feet to beg him not to allow such iniquity to be accomplished, for that poor Saracen girl had touched his heartstrings very sorely by her tears and her repentance, for, before persuading her to rely on God's judgement, he had given her special confession, which had freed the heavenly soul locked in that body, and he spoke of it as a precious stone worthy to adorn the Holy Crown of God Almighty, when after having made her penitence she wished to do away with herself.

'Then, my dear boy, knowing from the talk of the town and the unaffected replies of the poor dear girl all about it, I decided, on the advice of Master François de Hangest, Chapter Physician, to pretend I was ill and to leave the service of the Church of St Maurice and the Archbishopric, not wishing my hands to be stained with innocent blood which still cries out and will cry out to the last day of God's Judgement.

'The gaoler was then banished and in his place was put the torturer's second son and he threw the Saracen girl into a dungeon and inhumanly forged on her arms and legs irons weighing fifty pounds, and a strait-jacket of hardwood. The gaol was then put under guard of the city musketeers and the soldiery of the Archbishopric. The wench was stretched on the rack and tortured. Defeated by pain, she confessed all that Jehan de la Haye wanted and was shortly condemned to be burned in the St Etienne ground after exposure in the Church porch in a brimstone shirt. Her worldly goods were to go to the Chapter and so forth.

'This decision gave rise to great disturbance and scrimmaging in the city, for three young Knights of Touraine swore to give their lives in the service of the poor girl and somehow to liberate her. To this end they came to the city with a thousand suffering folk, labourers, old soldiers, soldiers, artisans and others whom the said girl had assisted or saved from misfortune and hunger and misery. They raked out of the city slums all who had been done good to by her, and then, all of them in riot and assembled under St Louis's Hill, under the cover of the soldiers of the said knights, they were joined by all the rapscallions of twenty leagues around and one morning all came in to besiege the Archiepiscopal prison, demanding the delivery to them of the Saracen girl, pretending they would put her to death, but actually meaning to save her and get her secretly to a swift horse so she might get well away, seeing that she rode like a jockey.

'Then, in that terrible rush of folk between the Archiepiscopal buildings and the bridges, we saw more than ten thousand people fighting, not to speak of those on the roofs of the houses or at the windows on all floors, watching this rebellion. In a word, you could have heard the noise on the far side of the Loire, out beyond St Symphorien, with the frightful yells of good-intentioned Christian folk and all those who were closing in on the gaol to free the poor girl. The crush and pressure of bodies was so great in that wild mob crying for the poor girl's blood, who would have fallen on their knees to her had they had the fortune of sighting her, that seven children, eleven women and eight men were crushed to death, so trampled underfoot that they were unrecognizable, just lumps of mud.

'In brief, so wide gaping was the mouth of that Leviathan of the people, a frightful monster indeed, that the din could be heard as far away as Montils-les-Tours. They were all yelling:

'"*Death to the succuba! Give us that demon! Ha, I want a quarter of her! I want her hair! I want a foot! You can have her mane! The head for me! I want her parts! Are they red? Shall we see them? Shall we toast them? Kill her! Kill her!*"

'Every man had his cry, but the yell of: "Alms to God, death to the succuba!" burst from them simultaneously so harshly and so cruelly that ears and hearts bled and the other cries were scarce audible in people's houses.

'To calm this storm which threatened to upset everything the Archbishop had the ingenuity to issue from the church in full canonicals, holding aloft the Host. This act saved the Chapter from ruin, seeing that the rapscallions and the knights together had sworn to destroy and burn the cloisters and kill all the Canons.

'Thus by a stratagem were they all compelled to break up and go home empty-handed. Then the Monks of Touraine, the Lords spiritual and temporal and the Burghers of Tours, greatly fearing further rioting the next day, held a midnight assembly and accepted the advice of the Chapter. In their assiduity the soldiery, archers, burghers and lords, an indefinite number of them, mounted guard, slaughtering a band of herdsmen, old soldiers and beggars who, hearing what a turmoil Tours was in, flocked in to augment the number of malcontents.

'Lord Harduin de Maillé, an elderly nobleman, now harangued the young knights who were the admirers of the Saracen woman and put it reasonably enough to them, whether they wished to put all Touraine to blood and fire for the sake of one trifling woman, and asked whether, even if they won, they thought they could afterwards master the scoundrels they had assembled, for it was put to these young knights that these pillagers, once they had despoiled the castles of their enemies, would turn on those of their leaders too. In any case, since the rebellion they had started had not succeeded in its initial assault, seeing that so far the walls had nowhere been breached, were they likely to be able to master the Church of Tours, which would now call in the aid of the King? And so on and so on. To which argumentation the said knights replied that it would be easy for the Chapter to get the girl out during the night, whereby the cause of the uprising would be removed. To which sound and humane suggestion Lord de Censoris, the Papal Legate, replied that it was essential for Religion and the Church to triumph, which meant that the poor wretched girl must foot the whole bill, the more so since it was now agreed that there should be no action of prosecution undertaken regarding this seditious enterprise of the said knights.

'The Chapter was thereby afforded full licence to proceed to the torture and death of the girl, to which ecclesiastical ceremony folk came in from twelve leagues around. So on that day on which after due worship of God the succuba was to be handed over to secular justice to be publicly burned at the stake, not only a commoner, but not even an abbot could for a pound of gold have hired a night's lodging in the city of Tours. The eve before the event many people camped in tents or bedded themselves down on straw outside the city precincts. Food supplies fell short. Many who came full-bellied went empty-bellied home, having seen no more than flames flaring in the distance. Ne'er-do-wells then brought off many a robbery on the high roads.

'The poor courtesan was by now almost dead. Her hair had turned white. Truth to speak, she was but a skeleton with a skin drawn over it and her irons weighed more than she did. For whatever happiness she had known in life she certainly paid dearly now. Those who saw her pass said she wept and lamented so that the hardest heart was moved. Indeed, in the Church she had to be gagged and she bit at that gag like a crocodile at a stick. Finally, the executioner lashed her to a pile to keep her up straight, as at moments she slumped lifeless to the ground.

'All at once, however, she recovered considerably, and despite her enfeebled condition, so it was said, contrived to cast off her ropes and escape into the church, where, recalling her one-time profession of acrobat, she climbed with great agility to the upper galleries, flitting like a bird along the little columns and minute friezes, and went up on the roofs to escape, where however a soldier got her in the sights of his cross-bow and planted an arrow in her heel. Despite her foot being rent open the poor girl ran on, nimble still, over the church roof, paying no heed to her wounds, but treading on splintered bones, blood streaming behind her, in such fear of the flames of the fire was she.

'At last, however, she was captured and bound, then thrown into a tumbril and taken to the stake, without anybody hearing another cry from her.

'The story of her behaviour in the church helped lesser folk to believe she really was the devil. Some now even alleged that they had seen her fly through mid-air. At last, the city executioner threw her on to the fire, where, after two or three horrible leaps, she fell back into the flames, which burned for a day and a night.

'The next evening, I went out to the place to see if anything was left of that girl who had been so kind, so sweet, so loving, but found no more than a miserable fragment of the belly bone in which, despite the great fire, there was still a trace of moisture, and some averred it quivered still like a woman in the transports of love.

'My son, I cannot recount all the countless and unparalleled misfortunes which for about ten years bore me down. I was utterly unable to forget that angelic life snuffed out by wicked men. I could always see her eyes swimming with love. In a word, the supernatural gifts of that innocent young girl glowed night and day before me and I prayed for her in the church in which she was brought to her martyrdom, till I no longer had strength or courage to look without trembling on the Grand Penitentiary, Jehan de la Haye, who eventually died eaten by lice, leprosy taking just toll of that executioner of a man, and his house was burned down by fire and his wife and all who had had a hand in that burning at the stake thus got good return for themselves from the flames.

'This, my dear boy, gave rise to much thought which I am here now committing to writing, so it may for ever govern our family's behaviour.

'I quit the Church service after that and married your mother, from whom I received infinite kindness and with whom I shared my life, my goods, my soul, my all. She was also my way of seeing things in these following precepts, namely:

'*first*, to live happily, one should keep as far as possible removed from ecclesiastics, show them due respect but keep them from your door, as also any others who are by law, whether rightly or wrongly, considered to be superior to us;

'*secondly*, assume a modest position and maintain it, without desiring in any way ever to appear rich. Take care to excite no man's envy or to offend any man in anything, for to crack envious skulls one needs be as strong as the oak which kills the weeds at its roots. Besides, to risk this would be one's downfall, for human oaks are particularly rare and no Tournebousche should flatter himself on being one, provided he is a real Tournebousche;

'*thirdly*, never depend on more than one quarter of your income, keep mum about your possessions, keep your profits dark and get into no debt, go to church like other folk and invariably keep to yourself what you think, for your thoughts are always your own, not other men's, though other people like to take them and put them on and wrap themselves in them, but also to twist them in their own way into slanders;

'*fourthly*, always stick to the present state of the Tournebousches, being now, as they always were, cloth-merchants. Marry your daughters to good cloth-merchants, send your sons to be cloth-merchants in other towns of France, equipped with these wise precepts, and bring them up to glory in the cloth trade without leaving any ambitious idea in their minds. *Sell cloth like a Tournebousche* should be their pride, their motto, their coat of arms, their life. For if they always stay cloth-merchants they will thus always be Tournebousches, persons indistinguished, living comfortable little lives like good little beetles which, once they establish themselves in a beam, make their good burrows and live safely there till the end of their ball of thread;

'*fifthly*, never speak any other language but that of the cloth trade, never discuss religion or government and even when the government of the State or that of the province or of religion or of God swerve from the true path and waver to left or right, stick, as good Tournebousches should, to your cloths.

'That way, unnoticed by anybody in the town, the Tournebousches will live peaceably with their little Tournebouschekins, paying their tithes and their taxes and all they are obliged to give, whether to God or King, city or parish, with which regiment of things you should never quarrel. Hence the need always to maintain a family nest-egg, to have peace, to buy peace, never to owe anything, always to have a full larder and always to make merry behind closed doors and windows.

'Living that way, nobody will have a handle against the Tournebousches, neither the State nor the Church, nor even the nobility, to whom, when they fall on bad times, if you have to, you can lend a few crowns, without ever cultivating any hope of seeing them again, I mean the crowns. Thus everybody at all times will like the Tournebousches. The Tournebousches may be ridiculed as little folk, those unenterprising Tournebousches, those dim Tournebousches, but let the fools chatter, the Tournebousches won't be burned at the stake or hanged on gibbets to suit King or Church or any other, and those level-headed Tournebousches will always have a silver penny tucked away and a jolly home with a warm family hearth snugly hidden from all envious eyes.

'Therefore, my dear son, take this advice and pursue a mediocre little life, keep this device in your family like a map of your county and when you are on your death-bed let your heir take it over as the sacred Gospel of the Tournebousches, till it be God's will for there to be no more Tournebousches in this world.'

This testamentary letter was found when an inventory was made in the house of François Tournebousche, Lord of Vertez, Chancellor of the Crown Prince of France, who was condemned at the time of the rebellion of this same lord against the King to be decapitated, and all his worldly goods to be confiscated by order of the Parliament of Paris, which letter was handed to the Governor of Touraine as an historical curiosity and laid with the records of the Trial at the Archbishopric of Tours by me, Pierre Gaultier, Sheriff, President of the Trades Council.

Having now completed the decipherment and transcription of these parchments, reconstituting them from their strange tongue, the Author was further informed by their owner that according to some people *Chaulde Street* at Tours was so called because the sun lingers longer there than elsewhere. Nevertheless, despite that practical suggestion, men of high discernment are still of the opinion that it was the hot passage of the said succuba that gave rise to the said name. With which the Author agrees.

This teaches us not to abuse our bodies but to use them wisely to our own salvation.

X

Desperate Love

At the time when King Charles VIII conceived the idea of embellishing Amboise Castle, a number of Italian master workers who were sculptors, painters and masons or architects came with him and did fine work in the galleries which by neglect have since undergone much dilapidation.

The Court was therefore then situated at that delightful spot, and as everybody knows, the good young King took much pleasure in watching his master men at their ingenious work. Among these foreign gentry there was a Florentine called *Messer* Angelo Cappara, a man of great parts, who made sculptures and works of low relief like none other, and this despite his age, for there were many amazed to find him still in his springtide, yet already so capable. Indeed, those hairs which stamp a man with his full virile majesty were only just frizzling out over his physiognomy.

Nevertheless, all the ladies were quite smitten by this fellow Angelo, for he was as handsome as a dream and melancholy too as any dove left alone on its nest by the death of its mate. And here is why: this young sculptor suffered from the great disease of poverty, which makes hell of all a man does in life. He certainly lived hard, eating little, for he was ashamed of being thus without substance, and he gave himself up to his gifts out of great despair, anxious whatever it cost to earn himself a leisurely life, which for those whose soul is engaged is the sweetest of all.

From bravado, however, the Florentine used to come to Court finely dressed, but then, from the great shyness of youth and from his misfortune, dared not ask the King for his money, while seeing him dressed like that the King of course thought him well off. Courtiers and ladies all alike used to admire his lovely works and also the maker of them, but that did not bring in a penny. And everybody, particularly the ladies, thought him naturally rich and well away with his glorious youthfulness, his long black hair, and his bright eyes, so that thinking of these things and the rest they never gave a thought to money. Indeed, they were largely right, seeing that the assets this young man possessed had already provided many a rascal at Court with fine properties, money and all else he needed.

Despite his youthful exterior, *Messer* Angelo was twenty years old and no fool. He had a warm heart and lovely poetry in his head, and was also a man of great imagination. But being humble about himself and akin to all poor, suffering folk, he was eternally astonished at the sight of the success of ignoramuses. So he got the idea that he must himself somehow be faulty in mind or body. However, he kept these thoughts to himself, though that is not quite true, for in his wakeful night hours he did tell them to the shadows and also to God, to Satan and to the whole world.

In such moments he lamented possessing so hot a heart that there was no doubt but that because of this the women avoided him like a red-hot iron. He further told himself how ardently he would regard a lovely mistress of his own, what a place of honour she should have in his life, how faithful he would be to her, with what love he would serve her, how studied her every commandment would be, and by what delights he would be able to disperse those fragile clouds of his melancholy when the skies darkened.

In short, with his eloquent imagination depicting to himself a mistress, he grovelled at her imaginary feet, kissing and fondling them, stroking and nibbling them and sucking them with all the reality of a captive seeing the open meads through a hole in the wall. Then to soften her heart, he addressed her and with great enterprise crushed the breath out of her and, despite his respect for her, finally violated her just a little, biting his bedclothes from end to end in his frenzy, for lack of the non-existent lady. He was all pluck when alone but an absolute ninny the moment a woman came his way.

Nevertheless, aflame as he was with his imaginary love commerce, he chipped away all the harder at his marble statues, shaping breasts so dainty that those lovely love fruits would make any man's mouth water, not to speak of the other parts to which he gave luscious curves, chiselling in with persistent chisel, smoothing away with caressing file, till he had so fashioned everything that the most utter simpleton would know what it was all for and de-simpleton himself in broad daylight.

Moreover, in those beauties, the ladies used all to imagine they saw themselves and they all fastened on *Messer* Cappara, with *Messer* Cappara's eyes roving over them, swearing that the day any one of those gave him her finger to kiss he would have the whole.

Among these ladies of high lineage one day one did corner and engage the charming Florentine all for herself, asking him why he pretended to be so wild and was there no woman in that Court could tame him?—after which she graciously invited him to call on her in the evening.

Messer Angelo set to work with scents and with purchase of a fringed velvet cloak lined with satin, and further borrowed from a friend a tunic with billowing sleeves, a slashed doublet, and silken hose, and there he was, come to her house at dusk and hot-foot up the stairs, drinking in great gulps of hope, not knowing what to do with his heart, which was hopping and skipping like a goat, in a word, so full of love in advance from top to toe that his back was streaming with perspiration.

Here take due note that the lady in question was indeed beautiful, which *Messer* Cappara knew the better since because of his trade he was so well-informed regarding armpits, and body's curves, the secret enfoldings of the callipygous regions and other mysteries, and this lady satisfied all the special rules of his art, and in addition was slender and white with a voice that awakened vital spirits wherever she was, striking thunder to the heart, the brain and all, in short, she filled one's imagination with all the loveliest depictions of the act without seeming to be thinking of it at all, which is the nature of these damned females.

The sculptor found her seated in a tall chair in the inglenook, and at once she began the easiest conversation, whereas in French *Messer* Angelo could say no more than *yes* and *no*, and now found no other words in his gullet or other thought in his brain, and would have banged his head against the hearth-stones, had he not so enjoyed seeing and listening to that fair mistress, vibrant there as a midge in a ray of sunlight.

Since, despite the muteness of this admiration, they both spent till half through that night moving inch by inch deeper into the boggy but flowery channels of love, the good sculptor departed very happy. On the way back he came to the secret conclusion that if a noble lady kept him so close in to her petticoats as that for four hours of the night it needed but a trifle more for her to keep him there till morning. So now, from these premises drawing certain pleasing corollaries, he made up his mind to ask of her you know what, even determined to commit general slaughter, kill them all, husband and wife and himself too, for want of spinning an hour of delight with his spindle. Indeed, so seriously was he charged now with passion that he deemed life itself a trifling stake in such a matter of love, seeing that a single day of it was worth a thousand lives.

The Florentine chiselled away at his stone, thinking of the night to come, till, by too much thought of another part of the body, he had damaged a number of noses. Seeing how things were going, he decided to quit work, perfumed himself well and went round to taste his lady's charming babble again, with some expectation of turning all the word-play into acts, but when he found himself in the queenly presence, her female majesty again performed its radiation and poor Cappara, who on the way had been such a killer, when he beheld his victim, turned again into a sheep.

Nevertheless, when the moment came in which desires heat mutually, he had wriggled forward till he was almost on top of his lady and held her fast. He had bargained at least for a kiss and he took it, much to his delight for when they grant it readily, the womenfolk retain the right of subsequent refusal, but when they let it be stolen brusquely, the lover can count on stealing a thousand more. This is why they are all so used to letting themselves be taken. And the Florentine had stolen a fair number of kisses, and things were already fitting in perfectly when this lady who was so sparing with her cloth, suddenly cried:

'Here comes my husband!'

Indeed, there was milord, back from his game of tennis, and the sculptor had to quit his niche, not without an eloquent glance from the lady thus interrupted in her enjoyment.

This was all the Florentine could sculp, his only instalment, his only comfort, for a whole month, seeing that whenever he was on the brink of his delight the good husband would always turn up, always, moreover, just between a blank refusal and those sops with which the ladies season their refusals, little concessions which revive love and make it stronger. And when at last, growing impatient, the sculptor set to work at that battle of the skirts as soon as he arrived, so that he might complete his mortising work before the husband came (to whom these domestic excitations otherwise were no doubt quite profitable), our pretty lady, seeing longing writ clear in her sculptor's eyes, always began some silly quarrel.

First, she would pretend to be jealous, quite without reason, just to hear her own voice uttering those barbed words of love, then she would assuage the dear fellow's rage with the water of a kiss, then would not let him get a word in edgewise, babbling all about how she insisted on her lover's being a good boy and doing exactly what she told him, or she would not be able to accord him her soul and her life, it was rather a poor gift that he offered his mistress, no more than his mere lust, she was more courageous, she was, for, loving him more than he really loved her, she was making the bigger sacrifice. Then, just in the nick of time, she would rap out: 'Drop that!' pronouncing the words with regal tones, after which for a time she would assume an offended air and when Cappara began at last to reproach her, would say: 'If you are not what I want you to be, I shall not love you any more.'

In short, rather late in the day, the poor Italian saw clearly that this was no noble love, one of those loves which do not measure out their delights like a miser with his coins, but that this lady found her pleasure precisely in keeping him thus hopping up on to the fence, master of everything so long as he did not actually set foot in the pretty garden of love.

Reduced to this trade, Cappara got murderously angry, and the next time he visited the lady he took some good companions with him, friends of his, charging them with the job of attacking the husband when he was on his way back to bed after his game of tennis with the King, while he visited his lady at the usual hour.

When the sweet love play in which the lady indulged with Cappara was in full swing, this love play meaning well tongued kisses, well entangled hair, hands and ears furiously nibbled and nubbled, in short, all the works save that particular one which with reason good authors find shocking, here was our Florentine, between two rather excessively drawn-out kisses, to cry:

'My love, do you not love me any more?'

'But of course I do!' cried she, since words are cheap enough.

'Then,' said he, 'be wholly mine.'

'But my husband will be here any moment,' she objected.

'Is that all that prevents it?'

'That's all.'

'Ah, well, I have friends who are going to seize him,' said the Florentine, 'and they will not let him go till I put a light in that window. Then, if he complains to the King, they will say they meant to play the trick on one of us.'

'Oho, my love,' said she, 'very well, but let me just see if everybody in the house has gone to bed.'

And, getting up, she put the light in the window for a moment, seeing which, *Messer* Cappara quickly blew the candle out, then took his sword, and, facing this woman whose scorn and shabbiness of soul he now knew well, said:

'I am not going to kill you, Madame, but I am going to mark your face so as to stop you coquetting like this with poor amorous young men with whose lives you play. You have tricked me shamefully, and you are not a good woman. You shall now learn that a kiss is never wiped from the heart of a true lover, and a kiss on the lips deserves the rest. You have made my life sour and wretched for ever, so I am going to give you something you shall for ever remember my death with, for you are its cause. Upon my word, you shall never more look in your mirror without also seeing my features.'

With those words, he raised his arm and brought his sword swishing down, as if to slice a nice chunk from those pretty cheeks on which there were still traces of his kisses. The woman told him he was unloyal.

'Silence!' he cried, 'you have told me that you loved me more than all else. Now you talk otherwise. Every evening you have drawn me a little nearer Heaven, only at one blow to cast me down into Hell. Do you think then that your petticoats will save you from a lover's anger? Oh no!'

'Oh, Angelo mine,' she murmured, 'I am really thine,' for she was bedazzled by the sight of this man in a furious rage.

But, drawing three paces back, *Messer* Cappara cried:

'Oh, you Court chattel and evil heart, so you love your own face more than your lover, do you? Take this!'

She turned very pale and humbly offered her face, understanding that in this instant her past perfidy gave the lie to her present love. With a single cut Angelo then slashed her face, after which he left the house and the country. The husband, meanwhile, having never been troubled by the Florentines, because of that light shown in the window, arrived home to find his wife minus her left cheek. But despite the pain, she did not utter a word, for after this blow she loved her Cappara more than life or all else. Nevertheless, the husband insisted on learning the origin of the wound, and as nobody had come to the house except that Florentine, he complained to the King, who at once sent his men after that master-workman with orders to seize him and hang him.

The Italian was captured at Blois, but on the day of the hanging a certain noble lady, thinking him a lover of good tempering, decided to save that lucky young man, and begged the King to grant him her, which Charles VIII gladly did.

Cappara, however, declared himself completely preoccupied by his own lady, memory of whom he could not expel from his heart, and he entered a monastery. Later he became a cardinal and a great scholar, and in his old age used to say that he had lived by the memory of the delights he received in those miserable hours of anguish in which he was at one and the same time well treated and foully treated by that lady of his. There are, however, authors who say that in ensuing years he did get beyond the petticoats with the same lady, whose cheek had healed, but that I cannot credit, since he was a man of heart who had a very lofty idea of the holy delights of love.

This story teaches us nothing that is good, unless it is that in life one has unlucky meetings, for the story is true in every detail. If in other places the author may perchance have exceeded truth, this one will earn him privileges where there is any talk of love.

END OF THE SECOND DECADE

Written at the d'Arcy Hotel at Eaux-Vives, Geneva,
February, 1834

Epilogue

While a note at the end of this Second Decade states that it was completed when it was cold and snowy, it comes out in the lovely month
of June, when all is green. That is because the poor muse to whom
the Author is subject has more whims than a Queen's love has fancies, and mysteriously insisted on dropping her fruit among the
flowers. No man can boast himself the master of that fairy creature.
Just when solemn thought preoccupies the mind and worries the
brain, there the hussy is, laughing, purring her delightful suggestions
into an author's ear, tickling his lips with her wings, sarabanding
away and disturbing the whole house. If by chance, quitting learning,
the penman answers back with: 'Wait, my pet, a moment, I'm coming!' however quickly he rises to play with the madcap, she's gone,
back in her hole, sulking, coiled up, groaning! Take a poker, a church
staff, a cudgel, a lady's stick, raise it and strike the hussy, shower her
with epithets, and she groans. Strip her, she groans. Fondle her,
caress her, she groans. Kiss her, cry: 'Come, darling'—she groans.
She feels cold. She's on the point of death. Farewell love, farewell
laughter, farewell delight, farewell good stories! Put yourself in full
mourning for her, bewail her, count her dead, till you too groan—
and then up pops her head, she bursts into laughter, spreads her
white wings, flies all over the place, curvetting and cavorting in the
air, showing her Old Nick's tail, her woman's breasts, her powerful
loins, her angelic countenance, shaking loose her sweet-scented hair,
rolling in the sunlight, glowing in all her loveliness, all scintillating
with colour like the breast of a wood pigeon, and laughing till the tears
come, to spatter in the sea, where fishermen find them transmuted
into pretty little pearls to deck a queen's brow. In short, she performs
a thousand evolutions like any young colt broke loose, revealing
virginal cruppers and such dainty parts between that at mere sight of
them a Pope would be ready for damnation. And while all this domestic
disturbance of the untamed wretch is going on, what does one find
but ignoramuses and middle-class individuals pestering the poor poet
with: 'Where's your stock? What about those other ten tales? You are
a heathen prophet. Yes, you are constantly on the tiles, but between
one junketing and another, you are bone idle, where's the work?'

Although my very name reveals me to be a lover of gentleness, I
would like to see one of those gentry impaled à la Turque. Mounted on
that pole, I would tell him now he could ride and go hunting rabbits.

Here ends the Second Decade. If Old Nick would but give it a lift
with his horns, a smiling Christendom would welcome it.

Third Decade

Prologue

Certain persons have inquired of the Author as to why there was such interest in these stories of his that never a year passed without his unloading his forkful of them, and asking for the reason and explanation of this production of so many commas (showing up among bad syllables, all making the ladies blush in public), and countless other barren chestnuts.

The Author must say that these treacherous words put in his path like so many boulders have touched him to the quick. Apart from what has already been said, he is well enough aware of his duty not to omit in the present Prologue to give his readers certain instruction, since one always needs to edify the young till, with riper years, they understand things themselves and curb their tongues, and also since among the countless loud-mouthed ones he can see quite a number of malicious fellows who deliberately ignore what these stories are really about.

In the first place, you must know that though some virtuous ladies, I say virtuous because those who are not virtuous and women of the people do not read these tales at all, prefer to live original, unpublished yarns, there are on the other hand those ladies, whether of the nobility or the middle-classes, who are double-sleeved and, being full of religion and without question revolted by what the tales are all about, do read them, assiduously too—to satisfy the Old Nick in them and thereby keep good.

Clear, my good horn-gatherers? Better be cuckolded by a tale in a book than the tail of a gentleman-at-leisure. You poor bastards save yourselves the damage, not to speak of the advantage you get from your love-sick lady's fruitful jiggling, all prompted by that of this book. And thus these stories bring the country's nurseries good harvest, which keeps the land happy, honourable and healthy. I say *happy* because much happiness is to be derived from these stories. I say *honourable* because by them you may preserve your nest from the claws of that sempiternally youthful demon called in Celtic tongue Kuckuldun. I say *healthy* because when menaced by cerebral plethora this book prompts that little act prescribed by the Salernian Church.

Go and find like advantages in other volumes blackened with printer's ink! Aha! Is there any other book that makes babies? You can't find it. But you will on the other hand find hosts of babes making books which engender much boredom.

I resume. Take note then, that if certain ladies, virtuous by nature but over-free with their tongues do lay public complaint about these tales, there are on the other hand a sufficient number of the sex who, far from reproaching the author, confess they like him very much indeed, accounting him a fine fellow, worthy of being an alumnus of Thelema Abbey and holding that for as many reasons as there are stars in the heavens he should not lay aside the pipe with which he dispenses the said tales, but instead let such persons vituperate him, going his own way. For our noble land of France is a wench who always says no to you-know-what, lamenting, wriggling, crying out: 'No, no, never! Oh, Mr Balzac, whatever are you doing? No, I won't let you, you will ruin me,' and then, when the tales are all told and the set of ten is perfect in every lissom line, come back with: 'Oh, Mister Author, isn't there any more?'

Therefore, be assured that the Author, boon companion, is not in the least bit scared by outcry, tears or writhings of the lady you know as Fame, or Fashion or Public Favour, for he knows her to be really a very naughty girl, ever ready for a good rogering. He knows that in France her battlecry is *Mount Joy!* A fine cry too, take it from me, for all that certain scribblers have misrepresented it, a cry which means that there is no delight without a fight, but if you only look quick, it is there waiting for the taking, otherwise it's *bye-bye!* An interpretation which the Author acquired in Rabelais, who passed it on to him.

Indeed, just probe into history and tell me if France ever really complained when ridden with real pleasure, boldly ridden, tempestuously ridden, quickly ridden. She is a real madwoman, and loves being mounted thus above all drinking. Why, cannot you see that these tales are essentially French in their delight, French in their riding, French fore and French aft, French all over?

Stand back, you mongrels! Let there be music! Silence, hypocrites! Forward, my merry fellows, come, my dear fellows, slip your gentle hands into those of the ladies and tickle them—in the middle, of the hand, of course. Oh ho, here are rumbling, peripatetic arguments, or the Author is an ignoramus in the rumblings of Aristotleianism. On his side he has the Crown of France, the Oriflamme of the King and that of Lord St Denis, he who even headless cried out Mount my Joy.

You quadrupeds, are you going to say that cry was false? No, it was certainly heard by many of the time, but in these days of great abjection you no longer believe the good saints.

The Author has not yet said all. Take note then, you who read these tales with eyes and hands, feeling them solely by the head, but loving them in your hearts for the delight they give, which mounts to that organ, take note that the Author, having in an evil hour lost his cleaver, *id est*, his heirloom (never since come to light, either), finding himself smooth from top to toe, set up a hullabaloo, just like the woodsman in the prologue of the book of his dear master Rabelais, in order to be heard by the gentleman on high, the sovereign lord of all things, and get another cleaver from him.

The said Very Important Person, still preoccupied at that instant with congresses, at once had Mercury toss him down a double inkstand. On this, as motto, were engraved three letters: A V E. Seeing no other interpretative help to hand, the poor child was at great pains, turning that inkstand about this way and that, to find the obscure meaning of it, construe those strange letters and discover their spirit. The first thing he saw was that God, great lord as he was, by possessing the world and being dependent on nobody, was courteous. But since, recalling the doings of his youth, he could find no particular service that he had rendered God, the Author began to be dubious, suspecting the courtesy might be rather a hollow one.

He thought a great deal, indeed, without extracting any concrete profit from the celestial tool. Then, by dint of turning the said inkstand about all ways, examining it, studying it, filling it, emptying it, thoughtfully tapping it, cleaning it, standing it upright, on its side upside-down, at last he chanced to read those letters backwards, and got: EVA. And what is that but the sum total of all women? And it meant that here was the Voice of Providence saying to the Author: 'Think of woman, man! Woman will heal your wound; woman will fill your pouch, woman is your wealth; draw on woman; woman is everything. She has her own ink-pot, dip your pen in that, it's bottomless. Woman adores love-making, love her then with your ink-pot! Only take care to tickle her fancies well and make her a thousand jolly pictures of love in millions of pleasant ways! Woman is generous, and women, all for one or one for all, will both pay the artist and provide the hair for his brush.'

After all, think on what is writ there: Ave—salute; Eva—woman. Or: *Eva* is woman, *ave*—to greet her or look out! Upon my word, indeed, it is so. Woman makes and woman unmakes. So pass the ink-pot please!

What does woman like most? What do women want? They like and want all the particularities of love! And right they are, too! Giving birth, producing, is to emulate Nature, and always be in childbed. So give me woman, give me Eva!

At once the Author began to dip in this fruitful pot of ink, in which he found a brainy purée compounded of supreme talismanic essences. From one pot came solemnities. These set themselves down in dun ink. From the other came titillations which made the very leaves of the notebook gayer. From inattention, however, the poor Author has often got his inks mixed, dipping first in one, then the other. But as soon as any ponderous phrase worked in the contemporary taste, so hard to plane smooth, to varnish and to polish was complete, the Author in his eagerness for a little light relief, notwithstanding the shortness of laughing ink in the left-hand pot, did from time to time make passionate theft of a dip comporting endless delights. It is, indeed, those latter penfuls which constitute these present *Droll Stories*, the authority of which is beyond suspicion, since they are issued from a heavenly source, as may be seen from this unequivocal confession of the Author.

There are persons of malice who will rail at this too. But is there to be found on this mud crumb of ours one single man who is entirely content? And is that not shocking? In all this, however, the Author has conducted himself with circumspection, as directed by the Almighty. He proves this by an *atqui*. Is it indeed not clearly proved to men of great science that though admittedly the Great Lord of the worlds has made an infinite number of heavy, cumbersome and ominous machines with monster wheels and chains, terrible cogs and frightful complicated revolution of screws and weights (like turnspits), he did also engage in dainty little matters, things fanciful and airy as the wind that blows, and that he further did also create some simple, pleasing things which make you laugh the moment you see them? Is that not so?

Ergo: in any concentrical work of art such as this most ample edifice of the Author's engineering, one must, if one is to base oneself on the laws of the said Almighty, also design a few dainty flowers, a few delicate little insects, even a few handsome dragons all well imbricated, contorted and over-painted (not to mention being gilded, even though they may often lack gold), and those one cannot but deposit too at the foot of mountains with their awful snows, the grim piles of rocks and all the highbrow philosophies, the long drawn-out frightful works, the marble columns, and also the genuine porphyrian sculptures of thought.

By God, you shameless beasts that scorn and would reject the flights of fancy and imagination, the nonsense-babble, the harmonies and all the grace-notes too of the lovely Muse of Drollery, will you now not file down those claws of yours lest from now on you scratch that fair white skin with its azure network of veins, those amorous loins, those graceful thighs, those feet kept so modestly between the sheets, those satin cheeks, those lustrous forms, that heart in which there is never a trace of gall? Oh, you numbskulls, what are you going to say now, now that here you see that that good lass sprung from the very heart of France, attuned to all the humours of woman-kind, to be welcomed by the angels with a kindly *Ave*! in the person of Mercury the gift-bearer, for in the last resort, what is she but the very quintessence of all art?

In this work meet necessity, courage, fantasy and woman's avowal as well as that of a Pantagruelian in full cap and gown. In short, everything.

Silence then, cheers for the Author, and do let that double ink-pot of his get on with his work of endowment by the Laughing Wisdom of the Hundred glorious *Droll Stories*.

Stand back then, you mongrels! Let there be music! Silence, hypo-crites! Chuck out all ignoramuses, and forward, my merry fellows! Come, dear lads who serve me, slip your soft hands into those of the ladies and tickle them in the middle, nicely too, saying as you do so: 'Read and thou shalt laugh.' Then say something more lively to them, to make them roar with laughter, for when the ladies laugh their lips part and their resistance to love is low.

I

Persistent Love

Approximately in the opening years of the thirteenth century after the advent of our Divine Saviour, there occurred in the city of Paris an event of love caused by the doings of a man from Tours which were such that they astounded the town and also the Royal Court.

As for the clergy, you will see from what follows what part they played in the story. Indeed, it is to them that we owe preservation of any record of it.

The person in question, known by lesser folk as the Tourainian (seeing he was born in our happy land of Touraine), was properly surnamed Anseau. In his old age the worthy fellow went back to his native parts and became Mayor of St Martin, or so the chronicles of the Abbey of that town record. But at Paris he was an outstanding goldsmith. By reason of this, when he was in his prime, his great sobriety, his industry and all that won him the citizenship of Paris. He also became King's liege, purchasing Royal protection according to the customs of the age, and then had a house built, free of any ground rent, near St Leu's church, in St Denis Street, where his workshop was well known by all connoisseurs of fine jewellery. Despite being a Tourainian and on the near side of forty, he had notwithstanding the blandishments of that city remained as modest as any saint, and got through all his salad days without once loosing his breeches in a claphouse. There's many a man avers that this exceeds those powers of credulity which the Lord planted in us to aid us in the faith which we owe the mysteries of holy religion. One must therefore needs furnish ample justification of the mysterious cause of this restraint on the part of the goldsmith.

Well, first note down that he arrived in Paris on Shank's mare, poorer, as old acquaintances of his said, than ever Job was. But, in distinction from all the men of our parts, who have but one vital fire, he possessed a will of iron and kept to the straight and narrow path like a monk bent on vengeance. As improver, he was ever at work, then, as master man, still worked on, ever seeking out new devices, ever acquiring new secrets, and as he sought, so he came upon all manner of new ideas. Any man returning home late, or a watchman or marauder, could always see a discreet light burning behind his windows and the good jeweller tapping, bending, sculping, engraving, filing and polishing, with him some apprentice, doors fast closed, their ears alert.

Poverty prompted work, work prompted that outstanding sobriety, and the sobriety engendered great wealth. Mark this, oh children of Cain, you who gobble doubloons but piss water: if this goldsmith did feel those wild yearnings which now and then rack any poor man who is alone, when the devil suggests inveigling him on to a Poissy cross, the Tourainian hammered his metal and drew those seductive humours up to his brain as he bent himself over the fashioning of delightfully delicate work, dainty engravings, gold figurines and exquisite silver forms, with all of which he quenched the fires of his Venus.

Add to this that the Tourainian was a simple sort of fellow, limited of intelligence, fearsome (in this order), of God, thieves and aristocrats, but above all these, of riot.

Though he had two hands, he never did but one thing at a time. When he spoke, he lisped like a bride at the altar. But though the priests, the soldiery and others accounted him rather ignorant, in fact he had learned his Latin from his mother well and spoke the language correctly and readily. In course of time the Paris gentry had taught him to look neither to right nor left, never to beat the bushes for others and to eke out his passions in proportion to his income, never to give any man permission to shoe anybody else with his hide, but to keep his weather eye open, not to believe any window-dressing, never to say what he was doing, but always to do what he said, not to spill anything but water, though to have a better memory than flies usually possess, to keep to himself his fists, but also his purse, not to pay attention to public crowds, and, finally, to sell his jewellery much dearer than he bought it; all of which things, wisely observed, afforded him enough wisdom to sell his wares at will and to satisfaction. And so he did, without pestering anyone. And, observing this little fellow going his way, many remarked when they met him:

'Upon my word, even if it meant splashing knee-deep in Paris mud for a hundred years, I wish I were in his shoes!'

They might as well have wished they were King of France, for the goldsmith was a massive man, with hairy, sinewy arms, so wondrous hard that when he clenched his fists, no pincers wielded by the toughest of men could have opened them. So you can be sure that whatever he got hold of there was no mistaking to whom it belonged. What is more, he had teeth he could have masticated iron with and stomach to dissolve it, guts to digest it too, and a sphincter fit to discharge it without a scratch. He had shoulders to bear the whole world on, like those of a pagan noble to whom this task was once committed, but whom in a lucky hour the advent of Jesus Christ released of that burden.

In short, the goldsmith was indubitably one of those cut solid, and the better for it too, since those who need patching are never worth much thus botched and endlessly reconditioned. Master Anseau was thus a true man, leonine of countenance, under his brows a smouldering glance which would have melted the gold for him if his forge fire had ever gone out. However, a limpid humidity implanted by the Moderator of all things tempered the great ardour therein residing, or the man would have scorched everything about him. Was he not then a fine piece of humanity?

After this list of his cardinal virtues some may want to ask why the good goldsmith remained a bachelor, as tight-knit as an oyster, especially since these natural properties of his could serve well in anything. But do such pigheaded critics really know what loving means? Fiddlesticks, of course they don't! Being a lover involves a man in much coming and going, listening and peeping, silence and babblement, retirement and exhibition, making himself small and even making himself nothing at all. He has to be pleasing, he has to pipe the right tunes, he has to find Old Nick where Old Nick is, he has to be able to gather peas in dovecotes, flowers under the snow, he has to pray to the moon, make a fuss of pet cats and dogs, greet the family friends, condole with the aunt's gout or catarrh and at the right moment tell her how well she looks and that she'll outlive everybody. He has to guess what pleases all the family, he must never tread on any of their corns, never drop a brick or say anything extravagant, but mince all his words well, say pretty nothings, hold butter in his mouth without melting, and marvel at rubbish, crying: 'But how lovely!' or 'Ah! Madame, how wonderfully that suits you!' What is more, he must play a hundred variations on that.

Further, he must wear a ruff and starched linen like any lord, be quick of tongue yet sober, endure with smiles the devil's own misfortunes, always swallow his anger, keep his temper on the snaffle, have the finger of the Almighty and the tail of Satan, with presents for the mother, presents for the cousins and presents for the maid. He must invariably present a smiling phiz, or the wench may slip out of his grasp and leave him on the plate, without any Christian reason given.

In short, the man who courts the most benevolent wench that God in a moment of good humour ever made, even though he talk like a good book, hop like a flea, whirl like dice, make music like King David and perform a hundred thousand monkey tricks, yet if he fail in a certain thing, that which is kept hushed but often (without her knowing it, though she needs to know it) most pleases his lady, she quits him like a red leper.

Quite right too. Nobody can blame her for doing so.

In such case, some men become morose, angered, enraged more than you can imagine. Indeed, there's many a one has done away with himself on account of such feminine change of mind, whereby the human species is distinguished from the animals, since no animal ever gets depressed by unrequited love, which is abundant proof that they have no soul.

Thus the task of suitor of a woman is that of a trickster, a soldier, a charlatan, a buffoon, a prince, a ninny, a king, an idler, a monk, a dupe, a rascal, a liar, a boaster, a sycophant, an empty-head, a wind-chaser, a bibbling, babbling boob of a man—a calling which Jesus eschewed and which, in imitation of him, men of any great intelligence likewise avoid, a calling in which a man of any worth is required above all to squander his time, his life, his blood, his finest words, not to speak of squandering heart, soul and brains, of all of which all females are cruelly greedy, because the moment their tongues begin to wag they assure one another that unless they have the whole of a man they have nothing. Bear in mind that one can come upon hussies who even when a man goes the whole hog for them, frown and grumble, merely to see if there is a wholer hog he could go, for in everything they want the most, from sheer spirit of conquest and tyranny. And this supreme law of things has always ruled over Parisian life, where the women are more salted at their christening than anywhere else in the world and hence malicious from very infancy.

Thus the goldsmith, ever busy working, burnishing gold and casting silver, was utterly unable to heat love or burnish his imagination and make that shine, nor had he any time for finery or parade or any monkey business of that sort or for chasing after any flibberty-gibbet. Now since in Paris virgins are no more likely to drop into bachelors' beds than roast peacocks into the streets (even though that bachelor be a Royal goldsmith), the Tourainian had the advantage of having his particular shirt, as explained above, lined with innocence. But, this good citizen could still not utterly fail to see the natural points possessed and amply displayed by the feminine world, including those burgesses with whom he debated the value of his pieces of jewellery.

Hence, frequently, after hearing delightful suggestions from ladies out to beat him down, and all sweetness merely to get a favour out of him, the good Tourainian many a time wended his way back through the streets as dreamy as any poet and even more anxious than any nestless cuckoo, and would on such occasions tell himself that he really ought to acquire a wife. 'She would sweep out the house for me, she would have a hot meal ready for me, she would press my clothes for me, she would mend and do for me, and she would sing delightfully all about the house, and to get me to do all she wanted, she would be all over me, saying (as they all tell their husbands, when they want a piece of jewellery), "Oh, darling, do look here, isn't this just sweet?" And everybody in the quarter would have his mind on my wife and think what a happy man I am.'

It was not long from that point that the goldsmith was getting married, having a lovely wedding, petting Milady Goldsmithess, dressing her finely, giving her a gold chain, adoring her from head to foot, placing in her hands all the domestic arrangements (save the cash-box), giving her an upstairs room with big windows, a really pretty room, hung with tapestry, with a fine carved linen chest and an extra-large bed with twisted pillars and head and tail boards of sandalwood. He would buy her plenty of fine mirrors and whenever he came back there would of course be a dozen little ones, all theirs, about the place.

However, once he reached that point, wife and children used to be sublimated into the tip-tap of his hammer as he sadly translated his fantasies into fanciful designs, fashioning his love thoughts into quaint pieces of jewellery which greatly pleased his customers, who never knew what a host of wives and babies were engulfed in the filigree work of this worthy who thus fretted himself away to the measure of his artistic skill. Indeed, had the Almighty not taken pity on him, he might have departed this world without ever knowing what love was at all, though, of course, in the next he would have known it, and incidentally without that fleshly transformation which spoils it—that is, according to Plato, an authoritative fellow, who, however, not being a Christian, did sometimes go astray.

Heavens, but all this preparatory talk is most tedious digression, all this niggling commentary that villains insist on a man's wrapping his tale in, like a baby in swaddling clothes, whereas it ought to go around mother naked. May the leading imp of Satan enclyster them with trident red-hot, I am now going to tell the whole story without equivocation!

Well, here is what befell that goldsmith in his forty-first year. One Sabbath Day, taking a walk along the left bank of the Seine, pursuing matrimonial meditations, he wandered as far as that meadow later known as the *Pré aux Clercs*, then part of the lands of the St Germain Abbey, not the University estate. And when, continuing his walk, he reached that point, at which he found himself out in open country, the Tourainian came upon a poor girl, who, noticing he was well dressed, greeted him with: 'God save, My Lord!' When she pro-

nounced these words, her voice revealed such warm melodiousness
that the goldsmith felt his mind ravished by the feminine music of
it, and conceived love for the girl, the more easily since, itching as he
was for marriage, everything now pointed to that business.

However, once he had overtaken the wench, the goldsmith could
not at first even bring himself to turn back, being as shy as any maid
who would rather die in her petticoats than raise them for her pleasure. But when he had gone on a bow-shot, he told himself that a
man accepted these ten years as a master goldsmith, now become a
citizen of Paris, and with twice the years of a hound behind him,
might at least, if that was his whim, contemplate a woman's front
elevation, the more so since his imagination was now itching him
considerably. So Master Anseau turned sharply about as if he had
changed his mind about his stroll, and so reviewed this girl, who on
a rope was pasturing a wretched cow which was cropping the grassy
bank of the ditch which at that point bordered the road.

'Well, my dear,' said he, 'you must be very poor to be pasturing
your cow like this on the Lord's Day. Are you not afraid of being
taken to prison?'

'My Lord,' replied the girl, lowering her eyes, 'I have nought to
fear, because I belong to the Abbey. And the Lord Abbot has given
us permission to take the cow out after evensong.'

'So you love your cow more than the salvation of your soul, do
you?'

'Indeed, My Lord,' she replied, 'our beast is almost half our poor
living.'

'But I am astounded, my girl,' he said, 'to find you so poor and
ragged, tousled as a faggot of brushwood, out in the fields barefoot
on a Sunday, when you have on your person more treasure than
could be routed up on the whole Abbey land. Surely the townsmen
pursue you and torment you with love.'

'Oh no, My Lord, I belong to the Abbey,' she replied, now showing the goldsmith on her right arm an armlet, just like the collars
which beasts of the field carry, except that it was without a bell. She
then cast so wretched a glance at the good burgher that he was rendered utterly melancholic, for when they are powerful the infections
of the heart may be caught through the eyes.

'I say, what on earth is this for?' he inquired, and anxious to find
out about everything, he lay his hand on the armlet, on which were
quite clearly engraved the arms of the Abbey, which however he
appeared not to notice.

'My Lord,' replied the girl, 'I am the daughter of a serf. So whoever joins with me in marriage would become a serf too, even were

he a burgher of Paris, and would belong to the Abbey, body and all chattels with him. Even if he loved me without marrying me, the children he had by me would still belong to the estate. Because of this I am shunned by everyone and neglected as if I were only a miserable field animal. But, which angers me gravely, be it the pleasure of My Lord the Abbot, I stand to be mated when and where it pleases him with another serf, for, even were I less displeasing than I am, at sight of my armlet the most loving suitor would flee me like the Black Death.'

As she spoke she began to tug at the rope, to force her cow to follow her and go on her way.

'But how old might you be?' inquired the goldsmith.

'I do not know, My Lord, but our Lord Abbot has a note of it.'

This utter degradation touched the good fellow to the quick, for he himself had once eaten the bread of misfortune. He matched his stride to the step of the girl and thus they proceeded beside the waters of the Seine in a very profound silence, the good burgher peeping at her handsome forehead, her fine sunburnt arms, her queenly lines. Though dusty, this girl's feet were fashioned like those of the Holy Virgin, while her sweet features were a true picture of Saint Genevieve, patron saint both of Paris and of all girls who live in the fields. Also bear in mind that though so innocent, mint-new from head to foot, this good man had a shrewd suspicion what a lovely white boon of breasts this lass could offer, though at present with coy grace these beauties were concealed most carefully by foul rags. And he suddenly craved for them as a schoolboy might for juicy pippins on a hot summer's day.

From this you may well assume that there were excellent hints of ripeness which here suggested a lass fashioned, like all else that these monks possess, to real perfection, and the more the burgher was prohibited from touching, the more his mouth watered after these love fruits, till his heart mounted to his very gullet.

'That's a pretty little cow you've got,' said he, all at once.

'Would you like a drop of her milk?' was the response. 'May has come in so hot this year, hasn't it? And you have a long way to go back to town.'

The sky was indeed limpid, glowing like a forge, not a cloud in sight. Everything shone with youth, foliage, fresh air, girls—and innocents. Everything was ablaze, everything green, everything sweet-scented as balm (and this ingenuous offer, made with no eye to recompense, and even a gold bezant would not have defrayed the charm of her speech), together with the modesty of the gesture with which the poor girl looked back at her cow's udder, gripped the goldsmith's heart, and he would gladly have implanted that serf-girl in the skin of a queen and put all Paris at her feet.

'Oh no, my pet, I do not thirst for milk,' he said, 'but for you, and would like to have permission to set you free.'

'That cannot be, and I shall die belonging to the Abbey,' she replied. 'It is a long time that we have lived, from father to son, from mother to daughter, in this condition. Like my wretched ancestors, I shall spend my whole life on this land, and so will my children, for the Abbot never lets any of us get away without progeny.'

'What?' cried the Tourainian, 'for the sake of those lovely eyes, has no gallant ever tried to purchase your liberty, as I did mine of the King?'

'Indeed, no, for it would cost too dear, so those who like me at first sight always depart as quickly as they came.'

'And have you never thought of getting to some other part of the country with a lover mounted on a good steed?'

'Certainly I have. But, My Lord, were I to be captured, I should at least be hanged, and were he a nobleman, it would cost my gallant more than his estates, not to speak of other pains. So much I do not ask. Besides, the arms of the Abbey are longer than my legs are swift. Therefore I live on in complete subservience to God, who planted me here.'

'And what does your father do?'

'He prunes the Abbey vines.'

'And your mother?'

'She does the washing.'

'And what is your name?'

'My dear Lord, I have no name. My father was christened Etien, my mother therefore is Etienne, and I am Tiennette, at your service.'

'My dear,' said the goldsmith, 'never did any woman please me as you do, and I suspect your heart to be full of sterling riches. Therefore, since you presented yourself to my eyes just when in any case I was definitely making up my mind to take a wife, I take this as an intimation from on high, and if I am not displeasing to yourself I beg you to accept me as your suitor.'

The girl now became still more bashful, for this speech was made in such a way, so precisely and so penetratingly, that the said Tiennette was prompted to tears by it.

'No, My Lord,' she replied. 'I should be the cause of endless unpleasantness and of your ill fortune. A little chat is sufficient for a poor bond-girl.'

'Ah!' cried Anseau, 'my child, you just don't know your man!'

The Tourainian thereupon made the sign of the cross, lay his two hands together and said: 'I hereby swear to Saint Eli, under whose jurisdiction do we goldsmiths stand, that I will make two shrines of silver-gilt with the finest workmanship I can put into them, one to be for a figurine of Our Virgin Lady Mary, as token of thanks for the liberation of my dear wife, and the other for a figurine of my own patron saint, if I succeed in my enterprise of liberating Tiennette, bond-girl, here present, to whom in St Eli's presence I make this solemn vow. What is more, I swear by my eternal salvation to persist courageously in this enterprise and to spend on it all I possess and not to abandon it while I live. Now, God cannot fail to have heard that well,' he concluded. 'But what about you, my pet?' And he turned to the girl.

'Oh, just look, my dear Lord, please! . . . My cow, she's got away!' she cried, with tears, at her man's knees. 'I shall love you all my life, but you must take back that vow.'

'Let us first go and look for your cow,' retorted the goldsmith, lifting her to her feet, but still not daring to kiss her, for all that the girl was quite ready.

'All right,' she said, 'or I shall get a beating.'

So there was the goldsmith bounding away after that confounded cow, which never gave a thought to these love negotiations. However, soon enough her horns were gripped as in a vice by the Tourainian's hands, and for two pins he would have tossed the animal up into the air like a truss of straw.

'Fare-thee-well, my pet,' he said to Tiennette. 'If you ever come into the town, call at my house, it's next to St Leu's Church. I am called Master Anseau and I am Goldsmith to our Lord the King of France, at the sign of St Eli. Promise me to be out in the fields next Sunday. I shall not fail to come, even if it rains javelins.'

'Very well, my good Lord, I myself would leap any wall to do so and out of gratitude would like to be yours without any trouble and cause you no damage on account of my future well-being. While I await that blessed hour next Sunday I shall pray hard to God for your sake.'

Then she stood there, like a saint carved in stone, and did not budge till the burgher was quite out of sight, and he went very slowly too, every now and then turning round towards her to gaze at her. Even when he was far away and quite out of sight, still there she stood, lost in thought till night fell, not sure whether or not she had dreamed what had just taken place. Thus she arrived home late, to get a beating for it, but without feeling the blows at all.

The good burgher meanwhile went quite off his appetite for food or drink. He closed his workshop, so in love with the girl was he.

His only thought was of her, seeing her everywhere, in everything, and the very next day he set off to go to the Abbey, terribly anxious to speak to the Lord Abbot. But on the way there it occurred to him that it would be prudent to place himself under the protection of one of the King's courtiers, so with this in mind he doubled back to the Court, which was then at Paris.

Now, since he stood high in everybody's consideration for his decency, and was liked for his dainty work and obliging ways, the King's Chamberlain (for whom once he had at short notice made a unique jewelled gold casket for a lady of that gentleman's heart), promised him his aid, and had his horse saddled and a hack for the goldsmith, and at once went with him to the Abbey, where he asked for the Abbot, who was Hugo de Sennecterre, then in his ninety-fourth year. Thus entering the hall, with the goldsmith who could scarce bear wait for the verdict, the Chamberlain asked Abbot Hugo if in advance he would accord him something it would be both easy and pleasant to accord. To which My Lord Abbot replied by shaking his head and declaring that the Canons forbade and prevented his thus engaging his word.

'This, my dear Father,' then said the Chamberlain, 'is the Court Goldsmith, who has conceived a great love for a bond-girl belonging to your Abbey, and I request you, in return for satisfying whatever wish you like to make, to free the girl.'

'Who is she?' the Abbot asked the burgher.

'She is called Tiennette,' said the goldsmith, timidly.

'Ho! Ho!' cried good old Hugo, with a grin. 'So the bait has hooked a fine fish, indeed! This is a serious matter. I simply can't decide a matter like that by myself.'

'And I, Reverend Father,' said the Chamberlain frowning, 'know what that means.'

'My dear Sir,' said the Abbot, 'do you realize what that girl is worth?'

The Abbot then ordered Tiennette to be sent for, telling his man to dress her in fine clothes and make her as fine as he could.

'Your match is in danger,' whispered the Chamberlain to the gold-smith, taking him aside. 'Look here, drop this fancy of yours. Everywhere, even at Court, you can find well-off women, young and pretty too, who would gladly marry you. To that end, if needs be, I am sure the King would assist you with the grant of a title which, in time, would enable you to get up a fine establishment. Is your treasury not well enough lined to provide the wherewithal for a noble line?'

'I simply could not do such a thing, My Lord,' replied Anseau, 'I have set my heart on this.'

'Then you must contemplate paying a price for the manumission of the girl. I know these monks. With them, money does everything.'

'My Lord,' said the goldsmith to the Abbot, coming back to him, 'you have the responsibility and charge here on earth of representing the bounty of the Almighty, who in his mercy towards us frequently has infinite treasures of charity for our wretchedness. For the remainder of my days I will include you in my prayers night and morning and never forget having received my good fortune by your charitableness, if only you will assist me to have enjoyment of this girl in holy wedlock without the children that issue from the union being in bondage. And for this, I can make you a shrine to hold the Holy Eucharist, so well worked and enriched with gold, precious stones and figures of wingèd angels, that there will not be its equal in all Christendom, it will be unique and a delight to the eyes, so greatly to the glory of your altar that the folk of Paris and foreign lords too will all hasten hither to see it, so magnificent will it be.'

'My son,' replied the Abbot, 'have you taken leave of your senses? If you insist on having this girl for legitimate spouse, your goods and your person too will be transferred to the Abbey Chapter.'

'Yes, My Lord, I am mad for this poor girl, and more affected by her poverty and her utterly Christian heart than I am by her perfection of form. But,' he added, with tears in his eyes, 'I am still more astonished by your hardness of heart, and tell you so straight, although I know my lot is in your hands. Yes, My Lord Abbot, I know the law. But yet, though all my goods must fall to your estate, though I myself must become bondsman, though I shall lose my house and my burgherdom, still shall I keep a contrivance acquired by my work and my studies, a contrivance, My Lord Abbot, which resides here,' he added, tapping his forehead, 'in a place where no person save God himself can be master. Nor could your whole Abbey ever pay for all the unparalleled creations which issue therefrom. You shall have my body, my wife, and my children, but nothing will ever give you my ingenuity, no, not even torture, for in myself I am stronger than iron is hard and more patient than pain can be great.'

Having spoken, the goldsmith, put to anger by the Abbot's impassivity (for the Abbot seemed determined to annex to the Abbey the good fellow's doubloons), thumped an oak chair with his fist so hard that it smashed to matchwood, splitting under his fist as under the blow of a sledge-hammer.

'There, My Lord, see what a servitor you will have, turning a maker of divine objects into a mere beast of burden.'

'My son,' replied the Abbot, 'you are wrong to break my chair like that and your assessment of my soul is most frivolous. This girl belongs to the Abbey, not to me. I am merely the faithful servant of the rights and the customs of this glorious monastery. Even though I could give this woman's belly free licence to engender babes, I still owe God and the Abbey due account of the transaction. Now, ever since there was an altar here, with bondsmen and monks, *id est*, since time immemorial, there never has been an instance of a burgher becoming Abbey property by marrying a bond-girl. There is therefore need to exercise that right and make use of it, so it should never be lost, never become enfeebled, obsolete or defunct, which would be the cause of many troubles. And this right is of much greater advantage to the State and the Abbey than your shrines, however lovely they be, seeing that our treasury enables us to purchase fine *objets-d'art*, but no treasury can ever establish customs or laws. I appeal to My Lord the King's Chamberlain to bear witness to the infinite trouble to which Our Lord Sovereign goes every day of his life to fight for the establishment of his Decrees.'

'This is said to shut my mouth,' declared the Chamberlain.

The goldsmith, who was no great student, became very thoughtful at this. At this point, Tiennette entered, clean as a pewter platter freshly polished by the mistress of the house, her hair done up and herself dressed in a gown of white woollen cloth with waistband of purple, on her feet white stockings and dainty shoes, in a word, so regally lovely, so nobly got up, that the goldsmith was petrified with ecstasy and the Chamberlain himself admitted he had never seen so perfect a creature. But then, considering that in this sight there was too much danger for the poor goldsmith, he bustled him off to the city, charging him to think the matter well over, since the Abbot was never going to let go such a good bait for fishing both burghers and noblemen in the waters of Paris.

The Abbey Chapter now definitely informed the poor love-sick goldsmith that if he married this girl he would certainly have to resign himself to abandoning his worldly chattels and his house to the Abbey and admit himself a serf, and his children likewise, if there were issue of the said marriage, though, as special favour, the Abbot would lease former Master Anseau his own house against an inventory of the furniture and the goldsmith's spending one week every year in a bothy on the Abbey lands as act confirmatory of his servitude.

The goldsmith, who was spoken to by each and all concerning the pigheadedness of monks, clearly saw that the Abbey was going to stick irrevocably to its decision, and he was worried to death. He contemplated setting fire to the place at five points, he got the idea of inveigling the Abbot somewhere outside and torturing him till he signed some sort of charter of liberation for Tiennette, but in the end all his many dreams evaporated one by one, till, after much lamentation, he resolved to abduct the girl and take refuge in some sure place from which nothing would extract him, and made preparations to that end, since if he were outside the Kingdom his friends or the King could better deal with the monks and get some sense into them. But the worthy man counted without his Abbot, for when he next went to the pasture he found no Tiennette, and then learned that she was so strictly locked in the Abbey that to have her he would have to lay siege to the place. Then did Master Anseau spread himself in complaints and threats and supplications, till all over the city burghers and their housewives were talking of the matter, and it became so notorious that the King, seeing the old Abbot at Court, tackled him as to why in this matter he would not yield a little to the goldsmith's great love, why indeed he made no practice of Christian charity.

'Because, Sire,' replied the man of God, 'all rights are interlocked like the pieces of a suit of chain mail, and if one link goes, the whole thing collapses. If this girl were taken against our will and this custom of serfdom were not observed, soon your subjects would take away your very crown and rise everywhere in riot and sedition in order to abolish the taxes and rates which plague people so.'

At this, the King kept his lips tightly closed, so that every man was anxious how the matter was going to end. The curiosity was so lively that there were lords betting that the Tourainian would abandon his love, and ladies betting the contrary. With tears the goldsmith complained to the Queen that the monks had robbed him even of sight of his beloved. This she found hateful and oppressive, and on her representations to the Lord Abbot the Tourainian was then permitted to make daily visits to the Abbey parlour, where Tiennette too came, but always under the tutelage of an old monk, and always magnificently attired, like a real lady, so that the two lovers could do no more than see each other and speak to each other, without snatching even a mere handful of delight, which merely made their love so much the greater.

One day, Tiennette addressed her beloved as follows:

'My dear Liege, to relieve you of suffering, I have decided to make you a present of my life. Like this. Thinking it all over, I have devised a plan which will cheat the Abbey of its rights and give you all the delights you expect to gather from me. The Ecclesiastical Judge has said that since you only become a serf by accession to that state and not by being a bondsman by birth, your servitude would cease with the cause which made you a serf. Therefore, if you love me more than all else, sacrifice your chattels to acquire our happiness and marry me. Then, when you have had your pleasure of me and embraced me to the full I shall before I have progeny put an end to myself and thereby you will become free again. At least that would be an enterprise in which you will have our Lord the King on your side, for I am told he wishes you all good, and there is no doubt but that God will pardon me for dying such a death, at my own hand, to deliver my Lord Spouse.'

'Beloved Tiennette,' cried the goldsmith, 'it is all settled! I shall be a serf, and you shall live to make my fortune as long as I live. In your company, the most massive chains will never weigh heavy, and little I care if I am without a penny of my own, when all my wealth is in your sweet earthly dwelling. I put my trust in good St Eli, who in this misfortune will vouchsafe to see us with pitying eyes and preserve us from all ills. I am now going straight to a scribe, to have him draw up charters and contracts. At least, dear flower of my life, you shall be well clothed, well lodged and served like a queen all your life, since the Lord Abbot does at least allow us to enjoy my chattels.'

Weeping and laughing, Tiennette fought off her good fortune, anxious to die in order not to reduce a free man to bondage, but good Anseau spoke such gentle words to her and so well persuaded her to follow, not precede him to the grave, that at last she agreed to their marriage, thinking secretly that she would always be able to put an end to herself after she had had her taste of the delights of love.

When the news of the Tourainian's submission and the fact that he was abandoning his possessions and his liberty for his dear one swept through Paris, everybody wanted to see him. The ladies of the Court mounted all their jewellery to speak to him and in revenge for the time he had been without the fair sex, there now descended on him whole coveys of it. But though there were some that approached Tiennette in beauty, not one had a heart equal to hers.

To cut a long story short, now that the hour for him to know both servitude and love had sounded, Master Anseau melted all his gold down and cast it in one single Royal crown, into which in enamel he worked all the pearls and diamonds he possessed, then went in secret to hand it to the Queen, with these words:

'Madame, I know not to whom else to entrust this fortune of mine. Tomorrow, all that is found in my dwelling will be the property of those damned monks, who are pitiless towards me. Here is a

small token of gratitude for the delight which I had by your intervention, seeing the woman I love, though no sum is equal to one of
her glances. I know not what will now become of me, but if one day
my children are freed, I shall have faith in your Queenly generosity.'

'Well spoken, good man,' said the King. 'The day will come when
the Abbey will need my assistance, and I shall certainly not forget
this.'

There was a tremendous crush in the Abbey at the wedding of
Tiennette, to whom as present the Queen gave a wedding gown,
while the King gave permission to wear gold rings in her ears every
day. When the handsome couple reached the house of Master Anseau,
now become a serf, near St Leu's church, there were torches in all
windows to see them pass, and the streets were lined with people as at
a Royal entry. The poor husband had forged for himself a silver arm-
band which he wore on his right arm, in token of his belonging to
the Abbey of St Germain. But now, despite his servitude, people
shouted to him 'Noël Noël', as at a new King. And the good fellow
greeted them magnificently, happy as a lover and very pleased too
with this respect which they were all rendering to the grace and
modesty of Tiennette. Reaching his house, the good Tourainian
there found green branches and corn-flowers crowning the doorway,
with the leading folk of the district all present, greatly in his honour
making music and crying:

'Despite the Abbey monks, you will always be a noble man!'

You may be sure the spouses fenced together to exhaustion, and
count that the burgher thrust grand strokes into his dear one's dol-
lar, while she, as a fine country virgin, was well capable of giving as
good as she got, and they lived finely for a whole month, as merry as
doves in the spring building their nest by straw. Tiennette was delighted with her fine dwelling, as also were the goldsmith's customers
who came and departed amazed by her.

This month of flowers over, one day there was the good Abbot
Hugo, their lord and master, in great style at their door. Entering the
house, which no longer belonged to the goldsmith, but the Chapter,
he addressed them both and said: 'My children, you are free, clear of
all obligations, for I must tell you now that at the very start I was
greatly struck by the love which joined you both one to another.
Further, once the Abbey's rights were recognized, I for my part was
resolved to afford you complete delight, testing your loyalty in a
Divine test. Nor will this manumission cost you a penny.'

Delivering himself of this news, the Abbot patted their cheeks,
while they fell on their knees before him, weeping for joy, and for
good reason. The Tourainian then told all the folk of his district,

now gathered in the street outside, about the generosity and blessing of good Abbot Hugo, and then, to do the Lord Abbot great honour, Master Anseau held the bridle of his mare as far as the city gate. As they went, the goldsmith, who had taken a bag of silver with him, scattered coin to the poor and suffering, crying:

'Largesse! Largesse to God! God save and Guard the Abbot! Long Live Lord Hugo!'

When he returned home, Anseau feasted his friends and celebrated his wedding anew with festivities lasting a good week.

You may be sure that the Abbot was sorely reproached by his Chapter for his mercy, for they had all had their jaws ready to gobble up their fine prey. And when, a year later, that good man Hugo fell sick, his Prior told him it was Heaven's punishment and that he had betrayed the sacred interests of the Chapter and the Lord.

'If I judged that man aright,' replied the Abbot, 'he will not forget what he owes us.'

Indeed, this day happening to be the anniversary of Anseau's marriage, at this very point a monk entered the room to announce that the goldsmith begged his benefactor to receive him. When he appeared in the hall where the Abbot lay, he placed before him two wonderful shrines, of such workmanship that since that time no worker has surpassed them in any part of the Christian world, and which were therefore said to be the *Vow of a persevering Love*. As everybody knows, those two shrine treasures were placed on the main altar of the church, and are accounted incomparable, for the goldsmith spent all his wealth on them. And yet, instead of emptying the goldsmith's purse, that piece of work filled it to overflowing, for his fame now grew so greatly and his profits with it that he was able to purchase nobility and much land, to found the House of Anseau, which subsequently brought great honour to the glad land of Touraine.

The moral of this is always to have recourse to the Saints and to the Almighty in life's undertakings and in anything admittedly good to persevere in, further, most emphatically it shows that a great love triumphs over everything, which of course is an old moral, but the Author has written it anew, because it is a very, very pleasing one.

II

Of a Justiciary who did not Recall Certain Parts

In the good town of Bourges, at the time when it was the scene of the high-spirits of that Sovereign of ours who later on abandoned the search for satisfaction in favour of that of mastering the Kingdom (and did indeed so do), there was once a Lord Provost appointed by him to keep order and known as the Royal Provost. This was the origin under the glorious son of that same monarch, of the appointment known as *Provost of the House*, in which Lord de Méré (otherwise Tristan), mentioned, despite his being not at all a merry fellow, here and there in these stories, behaved rather harshly.

This tale is addressed to friends who plunder old folios so they may piddle something fresh, also to show how learned, without appearing so, are these collections of mine.

Well then, this Provost of whom I speak: he was called Picot, that is, 'pick', or 'wedge', otherwise written Picault, whence *picottin* (peck), *picoter* (peck at) and *picorée* (a pecking or pilfering), though some made it *Pitot*, otherwise written *Pitaut* (whence *pitance* or pittance). Others, however (for instance, the southern dialect), said *Pichot*, whence came nothing any good, while yet others said *Petitot* and *Petinault* or even *Petiniaud* (as in the Limousin country).

At Bourges, however, he was plain *little*, that is, *Petit*, which name finally became that of the family, a brood which spawned greatly, for you will find Petits everywhere. So, in this tale let him be Petit—I add the etymological notes merely to illustrate the French tongue and show how middle-class folk and others finally got their surnames.

Enough of erudition. Well, this Provost, who had as many names as the estates to which the Royal Court went in turn, was actually in the flesh a rather little squirt, badly finished off by his mother, so that whenever he made to smile, he opened up his plaster-mug much as cows do their hind-quarters when about to drain off, a grimace which became known as 'a Provost's grin'. One day, however, hearing certain lords use the term, the King laughingly said:

'Wrong, gentlemen, Petit's not grinning, he's merely a bit of hide short at the bottom of his jib.'

However, that deceitful grin of his was no drawback, it suited Petit the better for his police job of winnowing out the bad grain, and there's no gainsaying that he was worth whatever gasp he cost

in the producing. His only shortcoming was being a bit of a cuckold; his only vice, going to evensong; his only wisdom, obeying God whenever he could; his only delight, having a wife at home; his only amusement, finding a man to hang when required to furnish one and never failing to find it. However, when he was hushabye, with the bed-curtains tight drawn, he never fashed himself about thieves. Now, in all justiciary Christendom, could you find a less harmful Provost than that? Indeed not! All provosts hang either too much or too little, whereas this one hanged just as many as required to justify the title.

So this good 'petit' justiciary, or good justiciary Petit (whichever way round you like), had acquired one of the prettiest women of Bourges all for himself in lawful wedlock, which amazed him as much as it amazed everyone else. Hence often, on the way to a hanging of his, he would in thought put to the Almighty a question which frequently came to the lips of others at Bourges, namely: why was it that he, Petit, Justiciary and Royal Provost, had all to himself, namely, to Master Petit, Provost Royal and Justiciary, a woman of such fine form and so perfectly compacted of charms that a moke would bray with pleasure at sight of her passing by?

God never made any answer to this question. No doubt he had his reasons. Malicious tongues in the town, however, have responded for him. They said that when she became lawful wedded wife of the said Petit the girl there was a span less of the girl than would make a proper virgin.

Others averred that she was not only Petit's wife. The glib response to this was that you may often find an ass in the best of stables. Everyone indeed produced his own quip about it. For anyone interested, there was a skepful for the gleaning. One should, however, subtract almost four-quarters of them, seeing that Madame Petit was in fact a discreet burgess who had only one lover (for pleasure) and her one husband (for duty). See if you can find many in the town as reserved of heart or lip. If you can, I will give you a bob or a lob, whichever you prefer. Some women you will find who have neither husband nor lover. Some have a lover and no husband. There are further ugly wenches with husband, but no lover. But— find women who, having a husband and a lover, stick to the *deuce* and never try for the *trey*, there's the miracle, don't you see, you ninnies, you greenhorns, you ignoramuses? So mark down Madame Petit with approval in your diaries and go your ways, and I will mine.

Good Madame Petit was thus not of that ilk always on the go, all over the place, unable to keep still, ever a-fidgeting and a-twitcheting, ever running round, ever seeking distraction, with nothing to hold them or stay them, so frivolous that any will-o'-the-wisp will bait them as if 'twere reality. No, quite the contrary, Madame Petit was a sober housewife if ever there was one, always in her chair upright or tucked in her bed on her back, a candle-stick ever ready for its candle to be inserted, ready for lover when Provost was out, accepting Provost when lover was not there.

Nor did this invaluable woman ever dream of decking herself out merely to spite the neighbours. Fiddlesticks! She had found a better use for her young days and indurated her joints with life so they should go the farther.

Well, so you are acquainted with both the Provost and his good spouse. Now a word for Provost Petit's adjutant in the matrimonial task, which as a rule is so arduous that it takes two men to accomplish it thoroughly. Well, all we need say of him is that he was a leading member of the landed nobility who detested the King. This however should be well noted, for it is an important point in this tale.

Now, the Constable of France (an uncouth lout of Scots origin), happening by chance to see the wife of this fellow Petit, said he wanted to see her, though some say *la voir* has been misconstrued, and should be written *l'avoir*, that is, what he wanted was not *to see her*, but *to have her*, and this at leisure, in the small hours, long enough to tell his beads, Christianly frank or frankly Christian beads, that is, together with her to probe into certain parts of knowledge, or knowledge of certain parts.

No doubt believing herself very knowledgeable, Milady Petit would not countenance the Constable's suggestion, being, as stated above, a decent, sober and virtuous housewife. After a number of probings and expostulations, turns and returns, messages and messengers, none of which were accepted, the Constable swore 'by his big black cockdowel' that for all his being a man of some status he would disembowel that lover, saying nothing, however, about the lady, which rather suggests a good Frenchman, for in such situations there are some unrequited persons who attack the whole bag of tricks and out of the triangle concerned slaughter four. No, My Lord the Constable, in the presence of the King and Agnes Sorel, Lady de Beauté (who were having a round of cards before supper), confined himself to staking that big black cockdowel of his that he would deal with only the lover, which was all right by the good Sovereign, since thereby, without it costing him a *Pater*, he would get rid of this nobleman, who greatly displeased him.

'And however will you accomplish it?' demanded Agnes Sorel, daintily.

'Oho!' replied the Constable, 'you can rest assured, My Lady, that I have no intention of losing my big black cockdowel!'

Now whatever, in this age, was this object, this 'big cockdowel'? Ah! Now, that's a point obscure enough to ruin a man's sight in ancient books, though it must have been an object or part of some importance.

However, let us don our spectacles and probe. In Brittany a dowel (or *douille*) becomes a young female, while a *cocque* is a round pan with a long handle, a frying-pan, in short, a *coquus*, in Latin patois, whereas in French the word *cocquin* stands for a rogue who is always nibbling and nosing, trussing and guzzling, lipping and lapping, frittering and frying, feasting and snick-snacking, always eating, in fact, so that between meals he is incapable of anything, useless, impoverished, thereby prompted to stealing and beggaring, whence the really learned have been forced to conclude that 'a big cockdowel' meant a household utensil rather like a fish-kettle, used for frying. Frying girls, of course!

'Well, if you want to know,' resumed the Constable, otherwise Count de Richemonde, 'I shall have it intimated to this justiciary fellow that he should make a twenty-four hour trip out of town, in the King's service, to round up certain peasants suspected of contriving treacherous dealings with the English. Thereupon my two love-birds, knowing their man absent, will be as happy as a soldier on a twenty-four hour pass, and if they indulge in a snack, I shall unsheath the Provost by next dispatching him in the name of the King back to town to search the house where the couple are a-bed, so that there and then he goes on with the dispatching by dealing with this friend of ours who thinks he is going to have this particular bit of tonsuring all to himself.'

'And who's the monk involved?' demanded Lady de Beauté.

'Oh, that was a cunning one,' said the King, with a grin.

'It's time we had a bite of supper,' said Lady Agnes. 'You are both very naughty men, equally disrespectful to good citizens' wives and holy men.'

True, for a long time good Madame Petit had been longing to take her time at it for at least one night through, and slip off on her capers to the said nobleman's dwelling, where she might cry out to her heart's content without wakening the neighbours, for at her own home she was always afraid of being overheard, so had but scraps from love's buffet, snippets snatched in a hurry, crumbs gobbled quickly, never daring to take things steadily, at the same time itching to know what it would be like for once to have a really hell for leather ride.

So, the following day, towards noon, the pretty citizeness's maid trotted round to the nobleman's house to acquaint him with the worthy Provost's departure and inform the good lover, from whom she too had received many presents, so she was far from hating him, to get ready for a little diversion for without fail the Provost's clerk would be there, both hungry and thirsty.

'Fine!' said the nobleman, 'tell your mistress that she shall not go hungry or thirsty long.'

Now that the lads of that damned Constable, who had been keeping watch all round the nobleman's house, saw him ordering drinks and meats, and getting ready for a gay time, ran to their master to inform him that all was going according to plan. Hearing this, and thinking of the blow the Provost was sure to deal, the fine Constable rubbed his hands. So now he at once instructed him on express orders of the King to come back to town, there at the house of the nobleman in question, to capture an English *milord* with whom it was strongly suspected a very dark plot was being hatched. Before executing this order, however, he was to call on His Majesty for instruction regarding certain niceties to be observed in the matter.

As happy as a sandboy at this injunction to call on the King, the Provost was so speedy that he was in town by the time the two lovers were just tinkling the bells of their evening service for the first time. The Lord of the Realm of Kuckuldun and the Limitroph Lands, an unruly gentleman, distributed the parts so well that Madame Petit was engaged in a fine ding-dong discussion with her beloved lord just when her lord spouse was busy talking to the Constable and the King, which resulted in his being very pleased with himself and his wife very pleased with herself too, a rare thing in marriage.

'I was saying to His Majesty,' said the Constable to the Provost, when that worthy entered the Royal presence, 'that anywhere in this Kingdom any man has the right to draw his sword and slay both his wife and her lover if he catches them mounted. But our Sovereign, who is a clement man, reasons that it is licit only to do the rider to death, but not the mare herself. That being so, tell me, my good Provost, what would you do if perchance you yourself came upon a nobleman sauntering in that pleasant paddock in which by laws both human and divine it is reserved to you all by yourself to water and to fork over the flower-beds?'

'I should kill them all,' said the Provost, 'I would make mincemeat of the five hundred thousand demons of their parts, I would cut down flower and seed too, the whole bag of skittles and the balls, the pips and the apple too, herbage and soil, woman and buck.'

'And you would be doing wrong,' said the King. 'That would be contrary to the laws of the Church and of the Kingdom, for it might rob me of a subject—of the Church, because you might thereby dispatch to limbo an unchristened babe.'

'Sire, I respect your profound knowledge and see clearly that you are the centre of all justice,' said the Provost.

'So we may only kill the cavalier? Clear? Amen then!' said the Constable. 'So, cut the rider down! Quick, off to your suspect, but take care, don't let anybody throw dust in your eyes, and do not fall short of what the Lord in question deserves.'

Our Provost, thinking himself now sure, if he brought this job off well, of being made Chancellor, arrives at the nobleman's town house, sets his men all round, blocking all the house exits with sergeants, forces an entry into the house in the King's name, but without making any noise. He mounts the stairs, he puts them all under arrest, finds out from the servant where the nobleman is abed, he goes up to the door alone and knocks, just when the two lovers inside were fencing—with you know what weapons—and calls on them to open up 'in the name of His Majesty'.

Madame Petit at once recognized her husband's voice. Her first act was to grin, seeing that she had already opened up without waiting for any royal command. After the laughing, however, came alarm. The nobleman meanwhile snatched up his cloak to cover his nakedness, and went to the door. Here, quite unaware that his life was at stake, he told the interrupter that he was himself a member of the Court, one of His Majesty's household.

'Taradiddle!' said the Provost. 'I am here on His Majesty's express instructions and on a charge of insurrection. You must let me in without delay!'

The nobleman then came out, but keeping his hand on the door behind him.

'What exactly are you looking for here?' he demanded.

'An enemy of our Sovereign, whom I hereby order you to deliver to me, otherwise you too will have to come with him to the Castle.'

This, the nobleman told himself, is a plot of Master Constable's, whose advances my dear lady has refused to countenance. I must find a way out of this wasps' nest for us! Then, turning to the Provost, he risked doubling the stakes, by arguing with his good cuckolded husband in the following wise:

'My friend, you know that I consider you a model of chivalry, as far as any Provost in his office may be chivalrous. Then perhaps I trust you? I have here with me in bed the loveliest of the ladies of the Royal entourage. As for the English, I have not even sufficient of them even to make Lord de Richemonde, who sent you here, a breakfast. To be plain, this descent on me is all the result of a bet between the Lord Constable and myself, he going half with the King. Together they offered to bet that they would learn the name of the lady of my heart; I took them on. There's not a man detests the English more than I do. Why, have they not seized my Picardy estates? It was rather a dirty trick, don't you think, to try to use the arm of justice to outdo me? But, oho! my Lord Constable, a Court Chamberlain is your equal, and I am going to cheat you all.

'My dear Petit, I give you full licence to spend all night and all day rooting out all the corners of my house, provided you don't bring anyone else in here. Search this room for yourself, move the bed out, do whatever you please! Only do let me put a sheet of a kerchief over this fair lady of mine (for at the moment she is dressed like an archangel), so you cannot tell whose wife she really is.'

'Agreed!' cried the Provost. 'But I am an old fox, you know, don't you try to twist my tail! I must be sure it really is one of the Court ladies, not some Englishman. For those English have skins as white and soft as any wenches, and well do I know it, too, having strung up many a one.'

'Very well then,' said the nobleman, 'taking into consideration the crime of which I am maliciously suspected and of which I must clear myself, I shall beg my lady mistress to do without her modesty for a moment. She loves me too greatly to refuse that, if it will save me from a terrible slur. So what I will do is ask her just to turn over on her tummy and show you a physiognomy which will in no wise compromise her, yet will suffice for you to recognize a lady of noble blood—especially as she will be upside-down.'

'Agreed,' said the Provost.

Hearing all this with her three ears, the lady folded her clothes and tucked them under the pillow, also taking off her slip, in case her husband recognized the material of that. Then she wrapped her head in a sheet, and thus uncovered the rounded fleshiness which separated her pretty furrow from her pink spine.

'Come in, my dear fellow,' said the nobleman.

The Justiciary examined the hearth, he opened the cupboard and the linen chest, he felt the bed and he also felt under it, then he turned to examine what was on it.

'My Lord,' he said, with an envious eye on what were really his own legitimate appurtenances. 'I have seen young English lads with strapping shoulders like those. Forgive me for doing my duty, I must see differently from this.'

'What do you mean by see differently?' demanded the nobleman.

'I mean I must see the other physiognomy, or, if you prefer it, the physiognomy of the other.'

'Well, will it do if the lady covers her body and so places herself as to show only the minimum of what constitutes our good fortune,' asked the nobleman, not forgetting that the lady in question had certain moles easy to recognize. 'If so, turn your back a moment, so my dear lady may show what you require with all due modesty.'

The good lady gave her lover a broad grin, and a kiss for his quick-wittedness, and arranged herself so dexterously that when the husband, now provided with a full view of what his hussy had never let him see, was perfectly convinced that no English man could be so fashioned without being a delightful English woman.

'Yes, My Lord,' he whispered in his adjutant's ear, 'this is clearly a lady of the Court, since those of our burgesses are not so densely wooded, nor do they smell so good.'

Finally, the house searched and no Englishman found in it, the good Provost returned, as the Constable had instructed him, to the Royal residence.

'Killed him?' asked the Constable.

'Killed whom?'

'The man who was clapping the horns on you.'

'All I saw in the nobleman's bed, My Lord, was a woman with whom he was certainly having a great time.'

'You actually saw her with your own eyes, you damned old cuckold, and did not cut your rival down?'

'It was not merely a woman, My Lord! It was one of the ladies of Court.'

'You saw her?'

'Aye, and smelt her too, and both parts.'

'What on earth do you mean?' asked the King, bursting into laughter.

'I was saying, save Your Majesty's respect, that I checked her both fore and aft.'

'Do you mean to say you don't know what your wife's parts look like, you muttonheaded old tool? You deserve to be hanged!'

'In my wife, My Lord, I respect that of which you speak far too much to look at it! Besides, my dear wife is so pious about her goods that she would die rather than show a scrap of them.'

'True,' said the King, 'they were certainly not made to be shown.'

'You old cockdowel, but that woman was your own wife!' cried the Constable.

'My Lord Constable, my own dear spouse is fast asleep.'

'Then learn, learn the truth, man! To horse! Off we go, and if she is at home in bed, you'll get no more than a hundred strokes with ox-thongs.'

Followed by the Provost, the Constable went at once to the former's house, and in less time than it would take for a poor man to empty the poor-box. Hallo there, wake up! Whereupon, to the din of the rabble of soldiers threatening to break the walls down, the servant opened the door, yawning and stretching her arms. The Constable and the Justiciary then rushed into the bedroom, where with great difficulty they at last awakened the Provost's wife. She pretended to be very alarmed and to have been so sound asleep that she was quite bleary-eyed.

It was a great triumph for the Provost, and he told the Constable that he must have been tricked, that his wife was of most sober conduct. Indeed, the good lady did seem very astonished at all this, and the Constable quit.

The worthy Provost then made ready to get quickly into bed himself, for all this business had somehow reminded him of his wife. While he was stripping off his harness and his breeches his lady, still apparently astonished, said:

'But dearest, what is all this fuss about? What did the Constable and his men want of you? And why did they come to see if I was asleep? Is it now going to be one of the Constable's duties to check our . . .'

'I don't know,' said the Provost, interrupting her to tell her what had befallen him.

'And do you mean to say that without my permission you looked at *that* of one of the Court ladies?'

Boo-ho-hoo! And there she was in tears, sobbing away so miserably and shedding such copious moisture that the Provost was at a loss.

'Why, whatever is it, my pet? What do you want? What is wrong?'

'Oh,' cried she, 'you will not love me any more now you know what the Court ladies look like!'

'Silence, my pet,' he said, 'those are great ladies. It's for your ears only, but all their parts are also enormous.'

'True?' she asked, with a sly smile. 'Am I better?'

'Why,' said he, completely bamboozled, 'you are a good span less.'

'Then they must have so much more pleasure than I do,' she said, with a huge sigh, 'seeing that out of so little as I have I get so much.'

At this, the Provost sought better means of argument to convince his good wife, and convince her he did, seeing that she was at last persuaded what great pleasure God has implanted in small parts.

This proves to us that nothing here on earth can prevail against the confraternity of Cuckolds.

III

Concerning Brother Amador, Glorious Abbot of Turpenay

One drizzling day, just the weather when the ladies stay happy indoors, since they like moisture and then see the men-folk at their skirts, which they are far from disliking, the Queen was in her room at Amboise Castle, deep in the window curtains. Here ensconced in her high chair, she was working a rug, to while away the time, but she plied her needle very absently, her eyes more intent on the water pouring down into the Loire. She was silent and thoughtful, her ladies following suit. The good King was chatting with the members of the Court who had come back from Chapel with him, since there was a proposal to go back to the Dominican evensong. When he came to the end of all his tortuous arguments and reasoning, he glanced at the Queen and then noticed how moody she was, the ladies too, noted too that there was no one unacquainted with matters matrimonial.

'Why, surely I saw My Lord Abbot of Turpenay here just now?' he remarked.

Hearing this, he was approached by the very Monk who by his incessant demands for justice had so importuned King Louis XI that this monarch issued firm instructions to the Master of the Royal Household to get the man out of his sight. In the tale about this King in our first Decade the story has been told how, by the fault of Lord Tristan, the Monk escaped.

This Monk at the time was a man whose nature had most verdantly expanded in profundity, so much so indeed that his humours had suffused his countenance with a certain supercoloration. Hence he was most attractive to the ladies, who plied him heavily with wine and pasties and other tidbits of all the dinners, suppers and parties to which he was invited, for every hostess adores these worthy guests of the Almighty, with their flashing teeth and their ability to gush as many words as they guzzle gobbets of food.

This particular Abbot, moreover, was a rascal of a fellow who used to take advantage of his cassock to shower the ladies with endless merry tales at which however they were only aghast after they had heard them, seeing that one had to hear a thing before one can judge of it.

'Reverend Father,' said the King, 'this is one of those gloomy moments when feminine ears might well be treated to an engaging tale, especially as the ladies laugh without blushing or blush as they laugh, at their pleasure. Come tell us a good one, I mean a monastic one! I must confess I would like to hear it, I would like a little entertainment myself, and the ladies certainly would so too.'

'To this we submit solely to please Your Majesty,' said the Queen, 'because My Lord Abbot does go a bit far.'

'Very well,' replied the King, looking across at the monk, 'then read us a piece of Christian admonition, Father, to entertain Her Majesty.'

'Sire, my sight is feeble and it is a dim light.'

'Then tell us a tale which stops at the belt.'

'Ah, Sire,' said the Monk, with a grin, 'the one I have all ready does go no farther, but—starting from the feet.'

The gentlemen present then remonstrated, imploring the Queen and her ladies so gallantly that, good Breton girl as she was, she gave the Monk a forgiving smile.

'As you please, Father,' she said, 'you will answer to the Almighty for our sins.'

'Gladly, Madame. If you will graciously take over mine, you will be the winner.'

Everybody laughed, including the Queen. The King went over to his dear wife, whom as everybody knows, he loved greatly. The courtiers were then given permission to be seated, the elderly lords, of course, for with the ladies' permission the young ones stood in close by their chairs to laugh softly together with them. The Abbot of Turpenay was then kind enough to furnish them with the following Tale, slipping through the muddy parts in the flutiest of tones.

At least a century ago, great disputes broke out in Christendom, two Popes clashing at Rome, each claiming to be legally elected, which caused monasteries, abbeys and episcopal sees much harm, for in order to be the more recognized, each of these popes conferred rights to his adherents, which resulted in doubles all over the place. In such a situation, those monasteries or abbeys which were at litigation with neighbours could not recognize both popes, but found themselves much hampered by the other one favouring the enemies of the Chapter.

This shocking schism gave rise to countless evils and proved abundantly that in Christendom no disease is more harmful than adultery on the part of the Church. Hence it was that at this time when Old Nick was playing havoc with our miserable estates, the illustrious Abbey of Turpenay, of which I am at present the unworthy governor, had on its hands a serious lawsuit about certain rights with the redoubtable Count de Candé, an idolatrous villain, heretic and renegade, a very bad member of the nobility.

That demon, come to this world in seignorial shape, was indeed a good soldier, who stood well at Court, a friend of Lord Bureau de la Rivière, a follower of whom King Charles V of glorious memory was very fond. But under cover of the favour of this Lord Bureau, the Count de Candé had assumed the licence of doing whatever pleased him, without fear of punishment, all down the miserable Indre Valley, where he claimed universal submission from Mont-bazon to Ussé.

You must therefore realize that his neighbours were mortally afraid of him, and to keep their heads on their shoulders let him have his way, but they would rather have seen him pushing daisies than treading them and wished a thousand ills on his head, of all of which he cared absolutely nothing. Thus throughout the whole valley the only opposition to him was that of our noble Abbey since it has always been the doctrine of the Church for us to gather to our lap the feeble and the suffering and lend ourselves to the defence of the oppressed, particularly when their rights and privileges are threatened.

As a consequence, that uncouth military bully de Candé detested all monks, but above any those of Turpenay, for not letting him snatch their rights from them by force, trickery or any other means. You may imagine that he was therefore delighted with the schism in the Church, and was waiting to see which Pope our Abbey would plump for, to support the other and strip it bare, himself being ready to recognize whichever one the Abbot of Turpenay refused to obey.

Ever since he had come back to his castle, he had made a practice of tormenting and harassing any men of the Church whom he found on his lands, so badly indeed that a poor Monk who was caught by this nobleman on a road through his estate where it borders the river, could see no other way of saving himself but to jump into the water when, by a special miracle of the Lord, on whom the good man had passionately called, his cassock kept him afloat on the Indre waters and he floated nicely across to the other side, reaching this in full view of Count de Candé, who, totally unashamed, throughout made mock of the sufferings of a servant of the Almighty. Of such stuff was that accursed bird of prey made.

Assiduous in his devotions, the Abbot in whose hands our glorious Abbey then rested led a very saintly life, yet, so pious was he, had bought the tenfold salvation of his own soul, but still not discovered how to ensure the Abbey against that villain's claws. But although the ageing abbot was very worried and saw bad times ahead, he still trusted in God to save them, saying that He would never let the property of his Church be touched, He who had saved Princess Judith from the Jews and Queen Lucrece from the Romans would be bound to aid His most illustrious Abbey of Turpenay, and made other very sane remarks.

However, his monks (who, I must to our shame admit, were a rascally set), reproached him for his easy way of seeing things. On the contrary, they said if the Chariot of the Lord was going to get there in time, all the oxen in the whole province would have to be harnessed to it. Trumpets of Jericho, they said, were not made anywhere in the world today, and the Almighty had had such a lot of trouble with his Creation that He had given it all up as a bad job. In short, they said a multitude of things which showed certain scorn of, and doubts in, the Almighty.

At this distressing point a monk who went by the name of Amador suddenly got strangely excited. He had been called Amador in mockery, because in person he was the very spit of the false god Egipan. Like him, he was potbellied, like him he was bandy-legged, like him he had powerful arms as hairy as a buzzard's legs, like him he had shoulders strong enough to carry two sacks, one over each shoulder, he had too a drunkard's beefy face, gleaming eyes, tousled beard and a blank forehead, and was so rotund with bacon and good fare that you might have thought him in the family way. He even sang his matins halfway down the steps to the cellars and evensong among the vines of the Lord! Most of his time he spent sprawling like a beggar with sores. Otherwise his occupation was to rove up and down the valley, messing about, boozing, larking, poking and prying on girls piddling, and this despite the Lord Abbot's precise prohibitions. In short, he was a slacker, a scrounger, a bad soldier of the army of the Church, one whom nobody in the Abbey could manage, but out of sheer Christian charity let go idle, accounting him of unsound mind.

Now, getting wise that there was danger of ruin for this Abbey in which he could wallow like a hog in its straw, this Amador suddenly began to tear his hair and rush about, listening to all the news in the refectory, peeping into every cell, then all at once with quivering chaps announced that he had made up his mind he would save the Abbey. He took note of all the points at issue in the lawsuit; he got the Abbot to give him authority to settle out of court, and was even unanimously promised a sub-priorship by the Chapter, were he to succeed. Then, without giving a heed to the cruelties or ill-treatment he might suffer from the Count de Candé as he made his way across that man's land, he set out from the Abbey averring that he had a tool concealed under his cassock with which he could bring that braggart to heel.

Indeed, Amador made his way to Candé on foot with no other travel-money than that cassock of his, though here one should not forget that this was greasy enough to feed a dwarf. He further chose a day to call on this lord when rain was pouring down fit to fill all the housewives' butts. Hence he came within sight of Candé without seeing a soul. Looking like a drowned rat, he slipped boldly into the courtyard and took shelter under a penthouse roof to wait till Heaven's intemperance should end, then presented himself at the door of the hall where the Count must be. Seeing him there, and as it was now supper-time, a servant took pity on him and warned him to clear out, or the Count would lead off the conversation with a hundred lashes. What had made him so bold, the man asked, as to venture into the courtyard of a house in which monks were more loathed than the red leprosy?

'Oh,' said Amador, 'I'm on my way to Tours, on a mission for the Lord Abbot of Turpenay. If Count de Candé were less spiteful towards the Almighty's poor servants, I should not be in the courtyard in weather like this, but in the house. I only hope he may find mercy himself when his last hour comes.'

The servant reported these words to Count de Candé, and the Count's immediate reaction was to have the Monk, as a piece of filth himself, pitched straight into the castle moat, where all the sewage came out, but Lady de Candé had the whip hand of her spouse and was feared by him because he hoped to inherit quite a bit through her some day, for which she was inclined to nag him, and she now reproved him, saying that this particular Monk might well be a Christian, that in such weather a thief would shelter a constable and apart from that the man ought to be well treated, merely so as to find out what decision the monks of Turpenay had reached about the schism. It was indeed her advice to settle the disputes arisen between the Abbey and the Candé estates amicably. Never, she said, since the advent of Jesus Christ had there been any temporal lord as strong as the Church, and sooner or later the Abbey would bring the Castle down, not vice versa. In short, she produced endless sober arguments such as the fair sex do at life's climacterics, or when they are sick of storms.

Amador indeed did look so piteous and wretched and was such good bait for fun that it now struck the Count, who was depressed by the rain, that he might get some fun out of the man, teasing him, washing his chaps out with vinegar, so to speak, so he should have a bad memory of his reception at Candé. Therefore this Lord, who had a secret liaison with his wife's maid, a girl named Perrotte, charged her with the execution of his vicious intentions regarding poor Amador. When they had agreed all the details, this fine wench, who hated monks merely to please her master, went up to Amador still sheltering under the piggery penthouse, and just to trick him to the utmost put on her most pleasing appearance.

'Father,' she said, 'the Count indoors is ashamed to see a servant of God outside when there is room for him in the hall, with a good fire under the hood of the hearth and the table all ready for supper. So in his name and that of the Lady of the Castle, I invite you in.'

'I thank the Lady and the Count,' said Amador, 'not for their hospitality, for that is a Christian duty, but for sending as ambassadress to such a miserable sinner as myself an angel of such fine and delicate charms as yourself that I thought at first I beheld the Virgin on our Abbey altar.'

So saying, Amador raised his nose and poked the pretty maid with two shafts of flame which shot from his burning eyes, and she now found him neither so ugly nor so dirty, let alone brutish. But as he mounted the steps with Perrotte, Amador received the thong of a dog-whip across nose and cheeks and other parts of his face which made him see all the candles of the Magnificat, so well was it laid there by Count de Candé, who was just happening to be whipping in his hounds. Pretending not to have noticed Amador, the Count asked the Monk to pardon him the mishap and then went off with the dogs which had caused the visitor this misfortune. Forewarned, the laughing maid had of course nimbly got out of the way, but not so that Amador did not see through it all and at once guess the relationship of the Count to Perrotte and of Perrotte to the Count, though it is quite feasible that some hussies down the valley had already whispered a thing or two about this to their own washing-boards.

Now not a man of the company already in the hall made room for the man of God, who remained in the draughts between door and window, where he froze till the moment when Count de Candé, Lady de Candé and the Count's old maid sister (who looked after the young heir to the house, who was about sixteen), took their chairs at the top of the table, well away from ordinary folk, in the old-fashioned way which was very wrongly customary among lords at the time. Ignoring the Monk, de Candé allowed him to be set a place at the very bottom of the table, in a corner, where two rascals were appointed to treat him roughly; as indeed they did, trampling on his toes, jostling him with their elbows and shouldering him till it was a real torture. Instead of with water, they filled his tankard with white wine to befuddle him so they might have better sport of him, but they had poured seven big jugfuls down Amador without the hint of a gurk or a belch or a hiccup or a piss or a fart, which staggered them greatly, seeing that the Monk's eye also remained as clear as mirror glass. However, prompted by glances from their Lord and Master, they persisted in taking it out of Amador. Under excuse of waiting on him, they poured sauce into his whiskers, then scrubbed at them with a cloth, merely in order to pull out handfuls of hair by the roots. Next the scullion serving hot soup christened the monk with a ladleful, taking care to send the scalding stuff right down poor Amador's back.

The Monk, however, endured his trials with gentleness, for the spirit of God was within him. So, rest assured, was his assurance that by holding out inside the castle, he would terminate that lawsuit.

However, the malicious scoundrels so roared with laughter (the butler remarking that this was one way of trying to staunch the barrel), and shouted such scurrilities at this greasy baptism given by the monkey's son to the thirsty monk, that Lady de Candé could not but take notice of what was going on at the bottom of the table, and she saw Amador with an expression of perfect resignation wiping his face and then turning back to his efforts to get something edible out of a huge ox-bone which had been placed on his pewter plate. And here, planting a skilful thrust of his knife into that monster bone, the good Monk suddenly took this up in his two massive paws and, breaking it clean in two, sucked out the hot marrow and found it very tasty.

'Indeed,' said Lady de Candé to herself, 'God has certainly endowed this Monk with divine strength,' and, reflecting on this, she gravely told the pages, the servants and the others that they were to stop teasing the Monk, to whom as further mockery they were now serving a pile of mouldy apples and some wormy nuts. But, quick to twig how the old maid and her young ward, the mistress of the house and her maids had watched him cope with the bone, Amador now drew up one sleeve, to reveal the triple musculature of his arm, planted nuts on his wrist where the veins fork and crushed them one by one with such smart slaps of the palm of the other hand that they looked like ripe medlars, after which he proceeded to munch them, shell, nut and all, with teeth as white as those of a dog, turning it all into a sort of nut fool which he swallowed down as if it were hydromel, and when only the apples were left on his platter, he clipped them between two fingers, which he used like a pair of shears, to slice the fruit neatly in two in a jiffy.

As you may imagine, the womenfolk were all speechless with

319

admiration, while the menservants thought this monk must be possessed of the devil. Indeed, and had it not been for his wife and the fact it was now pitch dark outside, the Count de Candé would have had Amador tossed out, for he was mortally afraid of the man. As everybody was beginning to say, this Monk was capable any moment of tipping the whole castle into the moat.

Therefore, when all mouths were at last wiped clean, the Count took care to have this demon, whose strength was really a menacing sight, imprisoned, and Amador was taken to a wretched, stinking hole where Perrotte had arranged things so as to give him a very bad night.

By use of catmint, which puts them on heat, the Castle tomcats had been brought in to make him hear their confessions and the count of their sins, while a litter of pigs had also been introduced, with some fine platters of tripe for them under the bed, so as to prevent them becoming monks (which they wanted to do), by disgusting them with the *Libera* which the Monk would sing them. Further note that every time Amador fidgeted because of the chopped horsehair scattered about in his sheets, his movement would tip cold water down on to the bed and that there were countless others of the malicious little tricks which are the stock-in-trade of practical jokers in castles.

Now everybody was abed, in expectancy of this 'monk's sabbath', certain it would materialize, seeing that Amador had been lodged in the attic at the top of one of the turrets, the door at the bottom of which was carefully put under guard of some watchdogs howling for his blood. In order to have a front seat when Monk and cats and piglets all conversed together, the Count and his pet Perrotte got into bed in the very next room. But when Amador saw what was in store for him, the good fellow drew a penknife from his bag and with great skill forced open the lock.

His next step was to reconnoitre the lay-out of the castle thoroughly. Almost at once he discovered the Count in the next room, laughing and disporting himself with Lady de Candé's maid. Guessing what they were up to, Amador bided his time till the mistress of the house was also between the sheets, alone, and then went barefoot to her room, for he did not want his sandals to poke their noses into his secrets. Thus in the light of a lamp he suddenly appeared, in that state which monks do assume by night, that is to say, a glorious state which laymen cannot maintain for long at a time, for the monkish robes assist it, magnifying all things. Then, having thus allowed My Lady to see that he was undoubtedly a true Monk, he murmured sweetly to her as follows:

'Madame, God save you, now allow me to explain, I have been sent here by Jesus and the Virgin Mary themselves, to advise you to put an end to certain most unseemly excesses being committed to the detriment of your essential virtues, traitorously deprived as they are of your husband's best parts, with which indeed he gratifies your maid instead. Now, what is the good of being Lady of the Manor if the manorial fruits are thus stored in another barn? Is it not your maid who is thus the real Lady of the Manor and you but the maid? Are not all those pleasures which that girl acquires, yours by right? You may also find them stored in our Church, which is the solace of the afflicted. Behold in me a messenger, ready to pay those dues, if you do not renounce them.'

So saying, the good Monk slightly slackened his girdle, which, so worked up did he seem to be at sight of the good things which My Lord the Count disdained, was beginning to oppress him.

'If you speak the truth, Father,' she said, springing lightly from the bed, 'I shall consign myself to your guidance. You certainly must be a messenger of the Lord since in less than a day you have seen what I have not observed here for a long time.'

She then set out together with Amador to discover the truth, and when somehow or other she managed to brush a little against that very elevated cassock, she was so struck by the reality of it that she suddenly began to hope she would find her husband in the wrong. And so she did, for she heard him blatantly talking about the Monk, in bed together with her own maid. Faced with such felony, My Lady fell into a furious rage, and opened her lips wide, to express this in words, which is the particular way of women, and she would certainly have kicked up hell at once, before handing the girl over to justice, had not Amador told her that she would be wiser to avenge herself first and shout afterwards.

'Then avenge me quickly, Father,' she said, 'so I can let my tongue rip!'

At this the Monk avenged her most monastically with a fine big vengeance, in which she indulged as copiously as a drunkard with his lips on the tap of a barrel, for when a lady of noble birth is avenged, she has to get drunk with her vengeance or not taste it at all. Indeed, the mistress of Candé castle was finally so well avenged that she was utterly unable to move, she was archavenged, she was multiplavenged. But still, so she might retain the right to further vengeance, now here, now there, with this Monk, she would not pronounce forgiveness.

Seeing this love for his vengeance, Amador promised to help her to it just as long as her rage should last, and he now admitted to her that in his capacity of man of religion constrained to meditation on the nature of parts, he knew an infinite number of ways, methods and fashions of implementing vengeance, so now he taught her canonically how Christian it was to avenge oneself. For did not the Almighty, throughout Holy Writ, more than any other virtue claim that he was an avenging God, and, what was more in that resort known as Hell, further showed us how royally divine vengeance is, since there, vengeance is everlasting. Whence it followed, he argued, that both women and monks should avenge themselves liberally, lest they be not Christians and faithful minions of the laws of Heaven.

This dogma pleased Lady de Candé infinitely. She confessed that she had never before heard these commandments of the Church and she invited the beloved Monk to come and teach her to the very bottom. After this, her vital humours well excited by all this vengeance, which had in fact freshened them up, the Lady of the Manor went to the maid's room, to find that person with her hand on that on which she herself had often cast her eye, as merchants watch their valuable goods in order not to have them stolen from them.

Here indeed, as Judge Lizet said when he was in a good mood, was a couple caught in flagrant delight, a couple now thoroughly done, indeed, penally done. The sight was more displeasing to the Lady of the Manor than can be described. This was revealed by her speech, which became as fruity as the water in the main Castle moat when the sewage was drained into it. In fact, she delivered a three-point sermon, with high-pitched accompaniment of music, appoggiaturas on every note, not to speak of all the sharps in the key signature.

'Thank you for your virtue, My Lord,' she cried, 'I've had my fill. You show me that loyalty to married vows is an abuse. So now I see why I have no son! How many babies have you stuffed into that vulgar oven, that poor-box, that bottomless alms-bag, that lepers' porringer, the real graveyard of the House of Candé? Why should I care now whether I am barren by fault of my constitution or your fault? I'll leave the maids to you. For my part, I shall take on a few handsome knights, to give you an heir. You make bastards while I make some legitimate children.'

'Come, my pet,' said the Count, 'don't shout so.'

'Oh,' cried his spouse, 'but I intend to shout, and I shall shout too, shout so I am well heard, heard by the Archbishop, heard by the Papal Legate, heard by the King, heard by my brothers, all of whom will avenge this infamy.'

'You surely won't dishonour your own husband?'

'You think that this would be a dishonour? Perhaps you are right. But, my Lord, it's not going to come from you, but this skivvy, whom I am going to have sewn in a sack and thrown into the Indre, so your dishonour gets a good washing. Hallo there!' she cried.

'Please do be quiet,' urged her husband, as ashamed as a blind man's dog, for this great man of war, so ready to do others to death, was *vis-à-vis* his wife like a mere child, a common phenomenon in soldiers, for in them resides strength and a concentration of the dense fleshinesses of matter, whereas in woman there is a subtle spirit with a little spike of sweet-smelling flame which, to the great perplexity of the male sex, illuminates Paradise. This is why wives tend to manage their husbands, for spirit rules all matter.

(At this, the ladies burst out laughing, and so did the King.)

'I won't be quiet,' declared Lady de Candé (the Abbot resumed his story), 'I am far too outraged. So this is your return, is it, for the great fortune I brought you and my discreet conduct? Have I ever refused to obey you, even in Lent or on fasting days? Am I so cold that I chill the sun? Do you imagine I do things by force, duty or pure complaisance? Is my part consecrated? Is it a holy relic? Do you need a Papal chit to enter it? God's virtue, have you had so much of it that you are tired of it? Have I not done everything you have wanted? Do serving-maids know more than ladies about it all? Ha, that no doubt is true enough, since she has shown you how to plough her field without sowing it. Teach me how you do that, won't you? Then I can practice it with those I shall take to serve me, for that's settled, I am a free woman now! That is fine! Your company irked you too much. Besides, you sold me a bad truss of fun at too high a price! Thank heavens, I'm quit of you and your fancies. I shall retire into a monastery! . . .'

She of course meant to say *nunnery*, but that avenging Monk had nonplussed her tongue too well to get it straight.

'. . . I shall be better off there,' she continued, 'with my daughter than in your den of low vice. You can inherit now from my maid. Oho! A fine Lady de Candé she will make!'

'What has been happening here?' demanded Amador, suddenly putting in an appearance.

'What has happened, Father,' she replied, 'is that somebody is talking about vengeance. To start, I am going to have this drab thrown into the river sewn in a sack, for misappropriation of the crops of the House of Candé. That will save the executioner a job. For the rest, I intend . . .'

'Please forget your wrath, my daughter,' said the Monk. 'In the

Our Father the Church bids us forgive those that trespass against us, if we wish to go to Heaven, for God pardons those who in turn have pardoned others. God only takes everlasting vengeance on the evil. Those he has pardoned he keeps with him in Paradise. Thence comes Jubilation, which is the Great Day of Delight, when all debts and offences are remitted.

'Hence it is great fortune to forgive. Forgive, forgive, for pardoning is a sanctified deed. Pardon Lord de Candé, and he will bless you for your gracious mercy and will love you greatly from now on. Such forgiveness will restore the flowers of youth to you. Further believe me, my dear lovely young lady, forgiveness is sometimes a way of taking vengeance. Forgive your maid, and she will pray to God for you. Thus beseeched by all, God will look after you and will grant you a fine quiverful of sons in return for so much forgiveness.'

Having said this, the Monk took the Count's hand, placed it in that of the Countess and said: 'Now go and discuss your pardon,' while in the ear of the Count he whispered these wise words: 'My Lord, draw out your big argument and by confronting her with that you will silence her, for the mouth of a woman only spews words when the gap is disengaged. So argue away, and you will always have the better of your wife.'

'God's body!' thought the Count, withdrawing, 'there is good in this Monk.'

Once Amador was alone with Perrotte, he addressed her as follows:

'You are at fault, my pet, for having ever had the notion of maltreating a poor servant of the Lord. That is why you have fallen under the thunderbolt of a Celestial wrath which will come down on you. Wherever you choose to hide, it will inevitably attain you and strike at all your joints, even when you are dead, and will bake you like a pasty in the oven of hell, where you will boil for ever, every day receiving seven hundred thousand lashes of the whip for that which by your instigation I suffered.'

'Oh, Father,' cried the maid, throwing herself at the Monk's feet, 'you alone can save me, for if I could but draw your glorious cassock on, I should be protected from the wrath of the Lord.'

So saying, she raised his skirts, as if to see how to find room for herself, then cried out:

'I' faith, monks are handsomer than counts.'

'By Old Nick's roast! Have you never either seen or felt a monk?'

'No,' said the maid.

'You really don't know the service in which monks sing soundlessly?'

'No,' said Perrotte, and thereupon the Monk gave her a sound demonstration, as on double-bar feasts, with all the bob majors customary in monasteries, psalms well sung in F major, candles ablaze, choirboys illuminating her on the *Introit* and also the *Ite missa est*, so that he withdrew at last, leaving her so sanctified that you could not have found a trace of the wrath of the Lord in any part of that girl which had not been most amply monasticated.

At his command, Perrotte now took him to the room of the Count's sister, and to her he presented himself with the inquiry whether it would not perhaps be her good pleasure to confess to him, for monks rarely called at the Castle. The old maid proved to be as glad as any good Christian woman would have been at this chance of furbishing her conscience. Amador indeed asked her to show it him and when at last the poor old maid did let him have a look at what he had explained to her was a virgin's conscience, he found it very black indeed, and told her that all women's sins were made there and that to be sinless in future she had better bung it up with a monk's indulgence. So dazzled now was her sight by that treasure from which in every way she had hitherto been cut off, that her brain was quite befuddled and with such heartfelt passion did she wish to believe in the monk's relic, that she most piously indulged now in indulgences, quite as vigorously, indeed, as Lady de Candé had indulged in that vengeance.

Her confession at last awakened the little de Candé daughter, and she went in to have a peep. Bear in mind that this was an event for which the Monk had been hoping, for much water had been discharged into his mouth at sight of that pretty fruit, which he now devoured, since the good old maid could not prevent his giving the little girl, when she wanted it, a left-over indulgence.

Bear in mind, however, that all this was well due to the Monk for his trouble. Morning come, the piglets had devoured their platter-fuls, the cats were all disenamoured, by force of much spraying of the places rubbed with the catmint, and Amador went at last to take a little rest in his bed, which Perrotte had now freed from hindering devices. Everybody then slept, thanks to the Monk, and so long that there was nobody about in Candé Castle before noon which was the hour of dinner.

All the servants were now quite convinced that the Monk was a demon, that he had spirited the tomcats away, together with the piglets and also their masters. But despite these fears everybody assembled in the hall for the midday meal.

'Come, Father,' cried the Lady of the Manor, offering the Monk her arm and seating him in the Baron's own chair, to the great

astonishment of all the servants, since the master of Candé did not
breathe one word against this.

'Page, serve Father Amador with this,' said the Lady of the
Manor.

'Father Amador requires some of that,' said the Baron's old maid
sister.

'Fill Father Amador's goblet,' said the Baron.

'Father Amador wants some bread,' said the little daughter.

'What is your pleasure, Father Amador?' asked Perrotte.

All through, it was Amador here, Amador there, and good Amador was fêted like a pretty little virgin on her bridal night.

'Do help yourself, Father,' said the Lady of the Manor, 'You
made such a poor supper last night.'

'Do take a glass, Father,' said the Baron, 'God's blood, you are
the grandest Monk I ever met.'

'Father Amador is a fine Monk,' said Perrotte.

'An indulgent Monk,' said the old maid.

'A beneficent Monk,' said the little Candé daughter.

'A great Monk,' said the Lady of the Manor.

'A Monk whose name is correct in every detail,' said the Manor
Chaplain.

Amador gorged and gorged again, simply rolling in good food.
He guzzled sweetbreads, he licked his chops, he belched, he harked,
he strutted and paraded about like a bull in clover. All the rest of the
company looked on in great trepidation, sure he was a necromancer.

Dinner over, Lady de Candé, her sister-in-law and her daughter
engaged de Candé with endless delightful topics to round things off.
The Lady of the Manor had quite a lot to say, arguing to her husband
about how useful it was to have a Monk permanently in a castle, the
Baron's old maid sister talked about the need for daily furbishing of
her conscience, the daughter tugged at her father's beard and asked
if this good Monk could not stay at Candé for ever. If ever a dispute
were to be settled, the Monk was the man for it. The Monk was a
man of great understanding, a very gentle man, and wise as any
saint. It was a misfortune to be at loggerheads with a monastery in
which there were such monks. If all monks were like this one, the
Abbey would win over the Castle every time and in the end would
ruin it, because this Monk was a most powerful man. In short, these
ladies brought forth a thousand reasons which constituted a flood of
words dispersed in such a constant downpour that de Candé gave
way altogether, seeing that he would never have peace there till the
matter was settled as the womenfolk wanted.

He then sent for the clerk who secretaried for him and also for

Brother Amador. Now it was that Amador gave him a great shock by producing from his bag ready-written charters and letters of credence which prevented the Baron and his man delaying a settlement any longer. And when the Baroness de Candé saw them winding up the lawsuit, she went straight to the linen cupboard to select a length of fine linen to make dear Amador a new gown. Everybody in the castle had seen how worn-out his own was, and it would have been a poor way of doing things to leave such a fine tool of vengeance in such a wretched sheath.

Now it was a question as to who was to make it. The Baron's lady cut out, the maid-servant made the cowl, the Baron's old maid sister insisted on the sewing, and the young daughter undertook the sleeves. Thus they all set to work to fashion it with such great longing to dress up the Monk that the gown was ready by supper-time, as also was the charter of agreement, drawn up and signed by the Baron de Candé.

'Oh, Father,' cried Lady de Candé, 'if you have any affection for us, you will rest after such hard work by steeping yourself in a bath which I have had Perrotte prepare.'

Amador was then bathed in scented water. When he emerged, he found his new cloak of fine woollen stuff and fine sandals, which made him the finest Monk in the world in the eyes of them all.

Meanwhile, in great fear for Amador, the fraternity of Turpenay had charged two of their numbers to reconnoitre round Candé Castle, and these scouts came out by the moat at the precise moment when Perrotte was throwing Amador's dirty greasy old robes in, stuffed with a lot of bricks, seeing which they got the idea that this was the end of the poor madman. They then went back and said that it was certain that Amador had suffered a cruel martyrdom for the Abbey's sake. Learning this, the Abbot ordained a special service in chapel to solicit God's aid for his devoted servant in torment.

Meanwhile, having supped, Amador now tucked the charter in his belt and decided to return to Turpenay. At the bottom of the steps leading from Candé Castle he found the Baroness's hack, bridled and saddled, held by an ostler. The Baron then ordered his men-at-arms to escort the good Monk, lest any misadventure befall him. Seeing this, Amador forgave the misdeeds of the previous day and pronounced a benediction on them all before he withdrew his sandals from that converted place. You may be sure that he was followed by the eyes of the Baroness, who remarked what a magnificent rider he was. Perrotte said that when mounted, he bore himself more erect than any of the men-at-arms. The old maid just sighed. The daughter still longed for him to confess her.

'He has sanctified the castle,' they all said, when they re-entered the hall.

When the cavalcade of Amador reached the entrance to Turpenay Abbey, the scene was really lamentable, for the guard thought that the Bardon de Candé's appetite for monks had been excited by the death of poor Amador, and that villain now intended to sack the whole Abbey. But in his great and grand, lusty voice Amador shouted out, to be recognized and admitted to the courtyard. And when he dismounted from the Baroness's hack there was an uproar loud enough to make the monks as mad as red moons. They also uttered a tremendous cheer later, in the refectory, when all came to congratulate Amador, who brandished the charter.

Candé's men-at-arms were regaled with the best wine in the cellars, which was a present made to the Turpenay monks by those of Marmoustiers, who own the Vouvray vineyards. When the good Abbot had had the Baron de Candé's charter read out to him, he took his leave of this world, saying:

'These many junctures indicate the finger of the Lord, to whom we must give thanks.'

However, as the good Abbot, thanking Amador, would thus keep harping on the part played by this said forefinger of the Almighty, Amador was piqued to hear his dodrantal thus made light of, and he cried to the Abbot:

'Let's call it my arm, Father, and drop the matter!'

The termination of this suit between the Baron de Candé and the Abbey of Turpenay was followed by fortune which made Candé a most devoted son of the Church, for he had a son at the end of the ninth month from this date.

Two years later, Amador was elected Abbot by the monks, for they assumed that under the madman they were in for a jolly time. But when Amador became Abbot he also became sober and very austere, for by his labours he had mastered his evil desires, and recast his nature in that female forge, in which there is a fire which clarifies all things, seeing that it is the most lasting, the most persevering, the most persistent, the most perfectissimal, the most perennial, the most perprising, the most perscrotant and the most perineal fire that there is in all this world. Thus is it a fire which can ruin everything, and it so well ruined the evil in Amador that it left in him only that which it could not chew up, namely, his native wit, which remained clear as a diamond, which as everybody knows is a residuum of the great fire in which at an earlier epoch our globe was carbonized.

Thus was Amador the instrument elected by Providence to reform our illustrious Abbey, since in it he put everything to rights, watching night and day over his monks, making them rise at the hours appointed for the offices, counting them in chapel as a shepherd counts his sheep, keeping them on a tight lead and punishing short-comings so seriously that he made them into very sober monks indeed.

This teaches us to give ourselves to women rather as a means of self-chastisement than to acquire delight. Further this story is abundant teaching that we should never fight ecclesiastical gentry.

IV

Magdalene Bertha

I. How Bertha Remained a Virgin in the Married State

About the time of the first absconding of His Royal Highness the Crown Prince of France, by which our good Sovereign Charles the Victorious was much aggrieved, misfortune befell a noble family of Touraine. Later this family died out completely, so that their most lamentable story can now be given to the light of day. In this task may the Holy Confessors, Martyrs and other Heavenly Lords be the Author's succour, for by the commands of Almighty God they strove for good in the matter.

By a character failing, Baron Imbert de Bastarnay, one of the greatest landowning lords of our land of Touraine, was utterly devoid of trust in the mentality of the female of the species. He considered them too fluctuating owing to their circumbilivaginations. Perhaps he was right. By this unfavourable conception of things, anyway, he reached a great age *sans* life partner, which was not at all advantageous to him. Always alone, he lost all notion how to be pleasant to others. His whole life had been one long series of military campaigns and carousals with bachelors with whom he never knew restraint.

Thus it was that he, Baron de Bastarnay, went foul-breeched seamy with sweat, grimy-handed and monkey-visaged. In short, while in his person he looked the most villainous man of all Christendom, as far as heart and head and other hidden parts went, he was the possessor of properties which made him very estimable. A messenger of the Lord (take this from me) would have gone far to find a soldier more reliant at his post or a lord with so spotless an honour, of word more definite, or loyalty so perfect.

Some who had heard his discourse maintain that he talked wisely and was a counsellor of value. Was it indeed not purposive on God's part, for he does make mock of us, to have planted so many perfections in so ill-kempt a man?

Having made himself look like a sexagenarian while still only fifty, this nobleman resolved at last to take to himself a wife, in order to have an heir. Inquiring then as to where he might find a mould suited to him, he heard praise of the great merits and perfections of a girl of the illustrious family of Rohan (which at that time held fiefs in the province), the Christian name of the girl being Bertha. Going to

Montbazon Castle to inspect her, Imbert was so struck by the prettiness and also the very innocent virtue of the said Bertha de Rohan that he was at once seized with so powerful a desire to enjoy her that he made up his mind there and then to take her for spouse, for he reckoned that a girl of such lofty lineage would never fail in her duty.

The marriage took place very shortly after, for Baron de Rohan had seven daughters and did not know how, in a period in which everybody was recovering from the wars and reconstructing their ruined businesses, he was ever going to provide for them all. Good Bastarnay's first great stroke of fortune, however, was the discovery that Bertha really was a maid, which was witness of her excellent upbringing and perfect maternal instruction. Hence, the very first night in which he was able to tackle her, he loaded her up with a baby with such brusqueness that he had ample proof when the first month of his marriage was over, which was very delightful for him.

To round off this first point in the case, let us at once record that in due course, from this lawful seed, was born young Lord de Bastarnay, the one who by the grace of King Louis XI became Duke and Royal Chamberlain, also his Ambassador to various European countries, much beloved and honoured by his sovereign, whom he never once failed, which loyalty he inherited from his father, who from a very early date had taken a fancy to the Crown Prince, all of whose vicissitudes he followed, even the rebellions, being so staunchly fond of him that he would have put Christ back on the cross, had the Prince asked it of him, a flowering of friendship such as is most rare in the entourage of princes and the great.

At first, in this marriage, the gracious Lady de Bastarnay bore herself so loyally that her company dispersed that dense fog and those black clouds which in the good Baron's mind had veiled the brilliance of female glory. Now, like any other converted man, he switched with such violence from mistrust to trust that he handed over the management of the house to this Bertha, making her the mistress of his acts and his deeds, sovereign of it all, Queen of his honour, guardian of his white poll, and without hearing a single word of justification would have struck down any man who in his presence uttered any slur on that mirror of virtue, in whom, for all their flaccid chilliness, there had been no other breath but that issuing from his own conjugal marital lips.

In all fairness, it should be added that in this she was greatly aided by her little son, with whom the pretty mother occupied herself night and day uninterruptedly for six years, from the first attention of suckling him with her own milk, turning him into a lover's adjutant, letting him have his way with her lovely titties, which he nibbled as hard as he wished, ever the constant lover. But this good mother knew no other love delicacies than those of his little hands, as they ran over her like happy little mouse paws, nor did she read any other book than those dainty bright eyes of his, reflecting the azure heavens, or listen to any music but that of his cries, which to her were angelic speech. So you may be sure she was always fondling him, from early morning hungry to kiss him, at eventide too still kissing him and, so 'tis said, even getting out of bed in the night hours to devour him with lovely caresses, making herself little beside him in his littleness, bringing him up in the perfect faith of maternity. In short, she behaved like the best and happiest mother there ever was, which is said without detriment to Our Lady the Virgin. After all, she cannot have had much trouble to bring our Saviour up well, since he was God.

This upbringing and the fact that Bertha had little taste for the business of married life, delighted good old Bastarnay, who would in any case have been unable to offer her much in bed. Indeed, on that score he was diligently saving up, in order to get together enough stuff to make a second child. But when the boy's first six years were completed, the mother was obliged to abandon him to the hands of the grooms and other men to whom his father confided the business of toughening him up, so that, together with the family estates and title, the boy, his heir—might inherit the virtues, the qualities, the nobility and the courage of the de Bastarnays.

When this weaning took place and Bertha was bereft of her good fortune, she wept copiously. Indeed, to her great motherly heart having her beloved son only for a few fleeting hours after others was like having no son at all. As a result, she fell into a deep melancholy. Hearing her weeping, that worthy man, her husband, then bent himself to the task of making another, but now without success, which greatly vexed the poor lady, since, as she said, this making of a baby distressed her greatly and cost her dearly.

That indeed was true enough, or nothing ever was and if you do not credit that unaffected statement, the gospels should be burned as false. However, as for many a woman (the menfolk I do not mention, they know a thing or two) this will look like pure fiction, the Author has taken care to elucidate the unspoken reasons for this eccentricity of Bertha's, that is to say how she could thus dislike what as a rule the ladies like above all else, without that lack of delight agonizing her heart or ageing her countenance.

Now, could a scribe be found more accommodating or who was more of a worshipper of the ladies than I am? No, I do not think he could. Indeed, I have worshipped them a lot, though still not as much as I should have liked, since I spend more time wielding my goose-quill than tickling their lips with those beards that make them part in smiles and innocent fun, I mean myself with them. Anyway here is how it all happened.

Good old Bastarnay was no youngster, lewd of heart and well informed about niceties of behaviour. For instance, he never bothered much about how he struck down an enemy soldier, provided the man was dead after the blow, he was ready to deal it out back, front or sideways without turning a hair—in a scrimmage, of course—and this utter indifference in the matter of death was completely matched by his carelessness about the matters of life, such as procreation and how to bake a baby in that delightful oven you know all about. Our worthy baron was utterly ignorant of the endless preparations and processings, the interlocutions, the dilatations, in a word, the niceties of it, how you prime or warm up the oven with light brushwood, all those little twigs which flare like resin and are to be gathered one by one in the forests of love, those handlings and dandlings, those cuddlings and huddlings, all that minor exchange, all those sweeties you both nibble at together, all those pussy-wise sips of the goblet, all the little licences and intimate traffic of love confected by lovers, known to rascals, and adored more than is good for them by the womenfolk of the nobility, who are cattier than they are human, which stands out a mile in their feminine morals. If as a species they interest you at all, just watch them a bit while they are eating. Not one—speaking here of course of the nobility and the well-brought-up—not one that will cut herself a good hunk of anything and eat it straightaway, in the brutish fashion of the men. No, she will fiddle her food about, picking it over and over to find the tidbits that suit her, she will lick away at the sauces and leave the lumps, playing with spoon and knife as if only eating because some law commanded it, so much does she hate going straight at a thing, always finessing, always resorting to endless roundabout devices, all manner of fiddling tricks. Which is the creature's real nature, and why the sons of Adam go crazy about them, just because they do things so differently from what they do, and do well to do so differently.

Agreed? Good, we're friends. Well, Baron Imbert de Bastarnay, an old soldier ignorant of such petirogeries used to make his entry into the Garden of Venus as if taking a city by storm, regardless of the wailing of the poor weeping inhabitants, and when he tried to implant a babe he might have been using a cross-bow and shooting blind with it. You may well imagine that dainty Bertha, a mere child when he took her, was utterly unused to be treated like that—she was only in her sixteenth year—but the result was that in her virginal credulity she concluded that the benediction of motherhood demanded that frightful, terrifying, loathsome, bullying act. Hence, though she always suffered it, she would inwardly implore the Almighty to aid her, and murmur *Aves* to the Virgin, thinking to herself how lightly that maid had come off with only a pigeon's weight to put up with.

Thus, having had nought but unpleasantness from conjugal life, she never took the initiative or called on her husband to do anything about his vows, and now, seeing that the good man was hardly up to it any longer (as we have already remarked), she lived in complete isolation, like a nun. Male company she hated, never suspecting for a moment that the architect of the world had imbued with such delight that which had given her but infinite unpleasantness. At the same time, through this she merely loved the more that child which had cost her so much before he was conceived. Consequently, you must not be at all surprised that she should shun that pretty jousting in which the good mare has the better of the rider, leading him on and wearing him out and abusing him if he stumbles.

That, so old men and women aver, is the true story of some wretched marriages, and the undoubted cause of the madness of some women who late in life, I know not how, suddenly realize that they have been cheated of something, when they go all out to cram the twenty-four hours with more than they can hold, just to get their share of life. Very philosophical, too, my friends. Therefore pay attention to this page so you may see wisely to the management of your wives and mistresses and all females whatsoever in general who by any chance may be given into your care, from which God preserve you.

Thus, essentially a virgin, although a mother, Bertha de Bastarnay in her twenty-first year was indeed a noble blossom, an honour to the province, and the glory of her good man, who found considerable pleasure merely in seeing her like a child herself, going about her tasks, whippy as a sallow, frisky as a fish, naïve as her little boy, for though he was a child of great common sense and perfect intelligence, he never undertook anything without first asking his mother, for when the mind of these angels has not had its limpidities disturbed, it rings true, whenever it be that you test it.

When these events took place, this noble wife was living in her lord's castle near the town of Losches, where she never gave a thought to anything in the world outside her domestic affairs, quite in the style of the circumspect wives of an earlier age, a way of living from which the wives of France were led astray when Queen Catherine and her Italians came, they being great folk for festivities, to which King François I and his successors lent a hand, their rascally behaviour doing France quite as much harm as did the evil living of the men of the church, which is not solely my view.

About this time, Baron de Bastarnay and his lady were invited by the King to go to his town of Losches where His Majesty was making a stay together with the Court, in which the beauty of the Lady de Bastarnay had suddenly been noised about. So Bertha came to Losches, to be the recipient of much flattering attention from the King himself and the centre of homage paid by all the younger lords, whose eyes feasted on that love apple, as well as the elder ones, who found new warmth basking in that sunlight. You may indeed be sure that all of them, young or old, would have suffered a thousand deaths to be able to make use of such lovely instruments of joy, dazzling to the sight, confounding to the brain. There was as much talk of Bertha the Loschian as there was of God or the Gospels, to the fury of countless ladies who did not happen to be so well furnished with pleasing parts and would have been prepared to let the ugliest men at court sleep with them for a fortnight, could they thereby have dispatched that lovely harvester of smiles to her castle, and so obvious was it to one younger lady that a certain friend of hers was mad about Bertha that the jealous excess of her feelings originated all the subsequent misfortunes of Lady de Bastarnay, though it must be added that they were also the source of Bertha's good fortune and her discovery of all-soft-embracing realms of love of which she had hitherto been so ignorant.

It was like this. The jealous lady happened to have a relative who the moment he saw Bertha confided to his cousin that he would so much like to have his pleasure of her (that is, of Bertha) that for a month with her he would gladly give his life. Let it be added that this said cousin was as good to look at as any girl is beautiful. Beardless of chin, he would further have obtained mercy of an enemy merely by crying the word once, so melodious was his young voice. He was barely twenty.

'My dear cousin,' said the jealous one to him, 'leave this assembly and go to your lodging at once, and I will contrive to give you your delight. But take care not to be seen, either by Bertha de Bastarnay or that baboon grafted by error of Nature on a Christian stock, to whom that fairy of loveliness belongs.'

The handsome cousin lying low, there was this jealous hussy rubbing her treacherous muzzle up against Bertha's, calling her *dear friend*, *treasure* and *beauteous star* and striving in endless ways to please her, so as to be the more certain of her vengeance over the poor darling who, without in the least suspecting it, had made the jealous one's lover jilt her (which for any woman with love aspirations is the worst of infidelities), and after considerable conversation this criminal woman herself realized that poor Bertha was a virgin in love matters, for her eyes swam abundantly with limpid moisture and there was not a hint of crow's foot at her temples, no little black spot on the lovely tip of her snow-white nose, where as a rule love's disturbances show, not a wrinkle on her brow, in short, there was no hint in her countenance of being accustomed to making love, it was as clean as that of an ignorant virgin. And, putting a number of precise feminine questions to Bertha, this traitress from the replies obtained absolute confirmation that for all that she had had maternal profit of dealings with a man she had undoubtedly missed all the pleasures of love-making.

This discovery made the jealous one, kindly woman that she was, very confident on her cousin's account and she now told Bertha that there was a girl who belonged to the de Rohan family at that moment living in Losches who needed the assistance of a lady of standing to get the head of the family to take her up, and that if this girl equalled in kindness of heart what she possessed in physical beauty, Bertha might well take the girl into her own household, when she could see for herself as to the sanctity of her way of living and obtain some arrangement with Baron de Rohan, who was otherwise loath to have his relative at his home.

To all this Bertha agreed without any hesitation. She had in fact already heard about the misfortunes of the de Rohan girl in question (Sylvia her name was), though she had not actually met her, indeed, had had the impression that the girl was somewhere abroad.

Here it should be made clear why His Majesty had been fêting Baron de Bastarnay. The King had got wind of the Dauphin's first abscondence to the States of Burgundy, and he was anxious to win away from him so good a supporter as Bastarnay. But, true to My Lord Louis, the old fellow had already on the quiet made his plans in the matter, so his immediate reaction was to take Bertha back to their castle. He now learned from her that she had acquired a companion, whom she introduced to him, this companion being the young nobleman disguised as a girl with the aid of that cousin of his who was jealous of Bertha and out to make a whore of her, so furious was she at Bertha's chaste mode of life. When Bertha intimated that she had acquired this companion, Imbert looked black for a moment, especially when he understood this companion to be Sylvia de Rohan, but, a moment later, touched to the quick by Bertha's kindness, he actually thanked her for undertaking thus to bring a lost lambkin back to its fold.

So it was that, toasting his worthy wife heartily, Bastarnay left some men-at-arms at the castle that very night and himself set out for Burgundy with the Dauphin, thus without the slightest suspicion leaving behind a cruel enemy in his lap. The countenance of this delightful fellow was quite strange to him, for the young man was a page who had but recently entered the royal household, where he was maintained by Cardinal Dunois, whom he served as novice-in-arms. Believing him to be a girl the old Baron had indeed found him —or her—a very pious and timid damsel indeed, for, apprehensive of what his eyes might betray, the young miscreant kept them downcast, and when he felt Bertha's kiss on his lips shook all over, from fear lest his skirts should give the game away. He also kept away from the windows, so afraid was he of being recognized as a man by Bastarnay and cut down before he had had enjoyment of his dear one. Thus when, the drawbridge lowered, the old Baron rode away through the fields, the pseudo-damsel was as happy as any other lover would have been in his place. He had indeed been in such terror that he now at once vowed he would erect a column at his own cost in Tours Cathedral for having come through the first perils of his undertaking, and he did indeed fork up fifty marks of silver to reimburse the Almighty for his happiness, only to have to pay up a second time to the Devil, as will be shown in the following details if the story pleases you enough to incline you to follow out a narration which shall be made succinct, as indeed all good speech should be.

II. Bertha's Misconduct When She Learned the Facts of Love

The novice-at-arms in question was young Lord Jehan de Sacché, a cousin of the Duke de Montmorency, to whom on the death of this Jehan the fiefs of Sacché and other places returned in pursuance of the tenure. He was twenty years old, glowing like a brazier, so you may be sure his first day was hard enough to bear. However, when old Imbert rode off into the landscape, the two girls perched on the drawbridge windlass to see him as long as possible, with endless waves of kerchiefs to bid him farewell. Then, once the cloud of dust raised by the horses no longer smoked on the horizon, they came down and retired into the hall.

'Now what shall we do, fair cousin?' said Bertha to the pseudo-Sylvia. 'Are you fond of music? Let's make music together. Let's sing some old minstrel's song, us two, shall we? Wouldn't you like that? Come to my organ, do! Do play it, if you love me! Let's sing!'

She then took Jehan by the hand and led him to the organ

keyboard, and this boon companion seated himself at this daintily enough, in the feminine manner.

'Oh, fair cousin!' cried Bertha, when, the first notes sounding, the novice-at-arms turned towards her, so they might sing their duet, 'oh, fair cousin, you have got a terrible light in your eyes, you quite disturb my heart, I know not why.'

'Ah, cousin,' replied the false Sylvia, 'that's just what has been my undoing. A delightful milord of that oversea land also told me that I had lovely eyes and he then kissed them so well that I was quite undone, I found so much pleasure in letting them be kissed.'

'Is love then to be caught through the eyes, cousin?'

'That indeed is where Cupid's arrows are forged, my dear Bertha,' said the lover, darting forth fire and flame.

'Let us sing, cousin.'

And sing they did, Jehan's whimsical choice being a *tenzone* by Christina of Pisa, in which there was powerful talk of love.

'Oh, cousin, what depths of voice, what volume you have! It draws the life out of me.'

'No, surely not! . . .' said this accursed Sylvia.

'But it does, just here!' replied Bertha, indicating her dainty diaphragm, where indeed the accords of love are better heard than with the ears, since this said diaphragm lies closer to the heart and you know what, which is doubtless the primeval brain, second heart and the third ear of the ladies. This I say with the best and most honourable intent, solely as physical explanation.

'Let us quit this singing,' now said Bertha, 'it disturbs me all through. Come to the window embrasure, and let us sew a fine seam till eventide.'

'Ah, dear soul, cousin, I simply do not know how to hold a needle, for to my perdition I have been used to employ my fingers for other things.'

'Really? What then did you use to do to while away your time?'

'Oh, I just let myself drift on love's stream, for that turns days to instants, months to days and years to months and, were it to last, would devour eternity like a mere strawberry, since all in it is fresh and sweet perfume, gentleness and infinite delight.'

Here the boon companion lowered his lovely eyelashes and remained as melancholy as any poor love-forlorn lady lamenting her lover, wishing she could have kept him, and pardoning him any treachery, would he but have the heart to find the sweet track back to the fold he used to love.

'Cousin, does love blossom in the married state?'

'Oh no!' said Sylvia, 'for in the married state everything is duty.

But in love it is all freedom of the heart. This distinction impregnates the caresses which are the flowers of love with incredibly soothing balm.'

'Cousin, let us drop this conversation, it is more disturbing even than music was.'

Swiftly she called a servant and told him to bring her son, who entered, when, seeing him, what did Sylvia cry out but:

'Oh, he's lovely as love itself!' then planted a smacking kiss on the boy's forehead.

'Come, my dear child,' said the mother, into whose lap the little one leapt. 'Come, your mother's delight, her unadulterated fortune, her constant pleasure, her crown, her jewel, her pure pearl, her white soul, her treasure, her evening light and morning light, sole flame of her heart! Give me your hands, so I may devour them, give me your ears, so I may nibble them, give me your head, so I may kiss your hair! Be happy, my little flower, if you wish me to be happy!'

'Why, cousin,' said Sylvia, 'you talk the language of love to him.'

'Is love then a childhood?'

'Indeed, cousin, the pagan world always thus depicted it.'

With countless other turns of conversation proliferating love, the two pretty cousins played with the child till supper.

'Don't you want another?' suddenly asked Jehan, taking advantage of an opportune moment to whisper this into his cousin's left ear, and at the same time accidentally to brush it lightly with his hot lips.

'Oh, Sylvia darling, yes, I would, would Almighty God but give me that delight, I would endure a hundred years in Hell-fire. But despite all the efforts, hard work and labour of my Lord my husband, all most distressing for me, my girth is still the same.

'Alas, to have an only child is to have nothing at all. If I hear a cry anywhere in this castle, it so upsets me it destroys my heart. I mistrust every animal and every other human where this innocent child is concerned, I fear every *volte*, every *passado*, when he fences. I fear any handling of weapons at all, in short, I fear everything. I have no life of my own because I live too much in him. And, alas, I even love those tribulations because so long as I fear, it means that my progeny is safe and sound. All my prayers to the saints and the apostles are for him. And, to cut short a matter of which I could go on talking till morning light, I sometimes feel as if my own breath were not in me at all, only in him.'

So saying, she crushed the child to her breasts as mothers will with an inspired vigour which makes mincemeat of nothing but their own hearts. If you doubt this, just observe a cat carrying her little ones in her jaws. Not one utters a sound. The boon companion, who had been afraid lest it were wrong to water this lovely barren plot with love's delights, was greatly comforted by this talk, till he conceived it would be following God's will to win this soul for love, and conceived well. When evening came Bertha, following the custom which has prevailed among noble ladies from ancient times to this day, asked her companion to sleep with her in the big baronial bed, to which, of course merely to maintain her role of young lady of noble birth the alleged Sylvia replied that she would be delighted so to do.

Thus, when curfew was rung, there were the cousins withdrawn to an apartment which was deep in rugs, royal tapestries and other fancy upholsterings, and Bertha, aided by her maids, proceeded to undress. You may be sure that in his modesty the novice-at-arms was loath to be touched, pretended to blush with shame, telling her cousin that ever since she had no longer had her beloved to aid her, she had taken to undressing all by herself. He had undressed her with such delicacy as to give her a distaste for feminine hands to do it. Further, she said, alas, such preparations for bed recalled to her the lovely things he used to tell his love, and all the little rogueries he practised as he unrobed her, all of which, to her great confusion, used to make the water come to her mouth.

All this talk perplexed Lady Bertha greatly, but she allowed her cousin to say her prayers and make her other preparations concealed behind the curtains of the four-poster in which, all afire with the utmost desire, the said young nobleman was soon hidden, though not without the fortune of a passing glimpse of the wonderful, totally undamaged charms of the Lady of the Manor. Bertha, for her part, being confident she was with a girl who knew the facts of life, left out none of her little habits, washed her feet, for instance, without bothering about whether she lifted her legs little or much, revealed her delightful shoulders, and did the other things that ladies do do when going to bed. At last, however, she too mounted the four poster, to stretch out luxuriously and then give her 'cousin' a good kiss on the lips, which she found surprisingly hot.

'Are you not ill, Sylvia dear?' she demanded, 'you seem so burning.'

'I always burn like that when I go to bed,' said the young nobleman, 'because in that moment my memory fills with the delightful little things my dear love used to think of to give me pleasure, and they used to make me burn still more.'

'Oh, cousin dear, do tell me what he did! Tell me the good things of love, for I live under the shadow of a hoary head, the snows of which protect me from such fierce heats. Tell me, you who have been cured. It will be such a good lesson to me, and thereby your misfortunes will have proved to be salutary advice for two poor female natures.'

'I do not know if I should heed your request, fair cousin,' said the boon companion.

'And why not, pray?'

'Oh, because those are things that it is better to do than to say,' she said, and heaved a sigh as hollow as the organ's deepest C. 'Then, I am afraid lest my dear lord has so filled me with delight that I pass a touch of it on to you, which would be enough to give you at least a baby girl, as that which makes babies would be weakened in me.'

'Indeed,' said Bertha. 'Now, between you and me, would that be a sin?'

'On the contrary, there would certainly be rejoicing both here and in Heaven, the angels would make their music, and spread their perfumes in your person.'

'Then tell me quickly, cousin,' cried Bertha.

'Well, then, this is how my dear love turned me into nothing but delight.'

So saying, Jehan took Bertha in his arms and strained Bertha to him with unparalleled desire, for in the lamplight and clad as she was in white linen in this infernal bed, she was like the lovely nuptial parts of the lily deep in its virginal calyx.

And Jehan murmured: 'When he had me in his arms as I now have you, in a little voice softer than mine is now he said: "Oh, Sylvia, you are my everlasting love, my endless treasure, throughout the twenty-four hours you are my delight, brilliant far more than day is day and sweeter than all else on earth, I love you more than God Almighty and would gladly suffer a thousand deaths in return for that boon which I seek from you." Then he kissed me, not as spouses do, which is brutishly, but like a dove.'

Now without restraint, to make quite clear how much better the lovers' way was, Jehan sucked all the honey from Bertha's lips and taught her how she could use that lovely tongue, dainty and pink as that of a little cat, to say much to the heart without utterance of a single word, then, glowing the fiercer from all this play, he extended the fire of his kisses from her mouth to her throat and then from her throat to the more gracious fruits which she herself had once encouraged her own little son to hold between his gums to draw their milk. And no man in his place would be thought wicked to imitate him.

'Ah!' cried Bertha, caught in the lime of love without knowing it, 'this is certainly better, I simply must tell Imbert about it.'

'Are you in your senses, cousin? Not a word to your husband, for that would never make his hands as gentle and pleasing as mine when they are clumsy as washerwomen's bats, why, his tough old venerable beard would be sure to chafe this centre of delights, these rosy petals which are all our soul, our goods, our substance, our love, our happiness. Did you not know that this is a living flower which requires to be fondled so, not merely plucked as if it were a soldier's catapult? Look, here is the lovely way my English lover did it!'

With these words, Bertha's 'girl' companion behaved so boldly that certain exudations were engendered, upon which poor ignorant Bertha suddenly cried out:

'Oh, cousin, I see angels, their music is so lovely that I am deaf to all else and their fire darts forth so dazzlingly that my eyes are sealed to light.'

She did indeed swoon back under the burden of the pleasures of love which blazed out in her like the topmost scales of the organ, gleaming bright like the most wondrous daybreaks, coursing through her veins like the finest musk, and she lost all hold on life as she was given a child of love, the which, as it takes up its position, makes a perturbation of the whole body such that it is more upsetting than anything else ever known. In the end Bertha thought she really must be in the heavenly realms of paradise, she felt so good. From that lovely dream she awakened in Jehan's arms, murmuring:

'Oh why was I not married in England?'

'My lovely mistress,' whispered Jehan, who had never experienced such delight, 'you are married now to me in France, where things are still better arranged, seeing that I am a man who would give a thousand lives for you—if I had them.'

Poor Bertha now uttered so loud a cry that it pierced the walls. She leapt from the bed as one of the locusts of the plague of Egypt might have done. Then, falling to her knees at her praying desk, she clasped her hands and wept more pearls than Mary Magdalene ever wore.

'Oh, this is the end of me,' she moaned, 'I have been tricked by a devil which assumed the countenance of an angel, I am lost, I am sure I am a mother now, of a fine babe, without being any more guilty than you were, oh Blessed Lady! Intercede with God for me, for I lack human mercy on earth, or bring me death, so I blush not when I face my Lord and Master.'

Noticing that she did not breathe a single word of condemnation of him, Jehan rose, utterly aghast to see Bertha take their lovely two-step like that. But quicker than she heard her Gabriel move she had leapt to her feet. Tear-faced she confronted him, her eyes ablaze with a saintly rage which made them most lovely to look at.

'Advance one step towards me,' she cried, 'and I shall take one into death!'

She took a lady's dagger in her hand, upon which, so distressing was the tragic sight of her anguish, Jehan replied:

''Tis not meet for you to die, but me, my lovely darling, better loved than ever woman was on this earth.'

'Had really you loved me well,' she said, 'you would never have undone me as you have, for I would rather die than be open to my husband's reproach.'

'Die?' he cried.

'Of course,' she said.

'Very well, if with many blows I am stabbed to death, you may be sure of your husband's pardon, for you can say that though your innocence was taken by surprise you avenged his honour by killing the man who deceived you, while for me it will be the greatest fortune I could know, to die for your sake, once you renounce living for mine.'

Hearing these gentle words, which he uttered with eyes brimful of tears, Bertha let her weapon fall, whereupon at once Jehan rushed to it and then stabbed himself, crying: 'Such good fortune must be paid by death,' and fell lifeless.

Bertha was so frightened that she called her maid. The maid came, and she too was most alarmed to see a man in sorry state lying on the floor in her lady's chamber, with my lady supporting him in her arms and murmuring: 'Dear one, what have you done now?'

For, believing Jehan dead, recalling her superabundant pleasure, and also realizing how handsome he must be for everyone, even Imbert, to have taken him for a girl, she lost all restraint. In her grief she told her maid everything, weeping and declaring that it was quite enough to have a baby on her conscience, without also having the death of a man. But this the lover heard, and made great efforts to open his eyes, though all he succeeded in doing was to show a flicker of the whites.

'Oh, My Lady,' said the maid, 'let us not cry out, and lose our heads, let us save this handsome knight. Not to let any physician or surgeon into the secret I will go and seek out Fallotte. She is a witch who, to please My Lady, will perform a miracle and seal up this wound without its ever showing.'

'Run!' cried Bertha. 'I shall love you and know how to reward you for this aid.'

Before all else, however, the Baroness and her maid agreed never to say a word about what had happened, and to conceal Jehan from all eyes. As it was already dark, the maid went at once to fetch Fallotte, her mistress going with her as far as the side door, for the guard was not allowed to lower the draw-bridge without express orders from Bertha.

Returning, Bertha found her handsome love now unconscious from his wound, for blood was streaming continuously from the gash. At this sight, and thinking Jehan had shed it for her, she sipped a little of the blood. Deeply moved by this great lover and the perilous situation, she smothered the cheeks of this handsome rascal with kisses and tended his wound by washing it with her tears, whispering to him that he must not die, and that to make him live she would love him greatly.

You may well imagine that the lady of the manor of Bastarnay was by now very smitten, observing what diversity there was between a young nobleman like Jehan, fair-skinned, all bloom and flue of fair down, and an old one like Imbert, hoary and coarse of hair, tanned and furrowed. The difference was a reminder too of the diversity she had found in the delights of love.

Realized to a high degree by the remembrance, she now gave kisses so honeyed that suddenly Jehan came round. His colour improved, and he was able to distinguish Bertha, of whom in a feeble voice he begged forgiveness. Bertha however forbade him to talk at all till the woman leech had seen him, so the pair of them occupied the time exclusively with making love with their eyes, for in those of Bertha was naught but compassion, and in these matters compassion is closely related to love.

Fallotte was a certain female hunchback greatly suspected of dealings in necromancy, sabbath assemblies and broom-stick riding, witch-fashion. Some had even seen her harnessing her broom in the witches' stables which, as everybody knows, are to be found in the drains. To tell the truth, this woman did possess secrets of healing and had afforded the ladies, and indeed the menfolk too, such good services in certain matters that she could now live out her days in perfect peace, without having to give up the ghost on a hundred faggots, but on a featherbed. Fallotte had also amassed skepfuls of crowns, for all the doctors' prosecuting her and alleging that she sold poisons, which was true, as this tale will show. The servant and Fallotte came to the castle mounted on the same donkey, but making such speed that day had still not broken when they got there. As she entered the chamber, the old hunchback cried:

'Well, my dears, whatever have we been up to, eh?'

This was her style, full of familiarity with the great ones, who in her eyes were very small.

She now put on her spectacles and examined the wound with great skill.

'Now that's good blood, that is, my dear,' she said, 'and I can see you've had your taste of it. It's all right, the bleeding is outward.'

So saying, under the noses of Lady de Bastarnay and her maid, breathless both of them, she washed the wound with a fine sponge. To cut a long story short, she then declared with surgical solemnity that the young nobleman was not going to die of this blow, although, she added, after looking at his palm, this night of love would in the end bring him to a violent end, a chiromantic declaration which greatly alarmed both Bertha and her girl. Fallotte then prescribed urgent medicaments and promised to come again the following night.

And so she did. Indeed, she tended the wound for a whole fortnight, coming in secret every single night. The castle servants were told that Sylvia de Rohan had an enlargement of the belly, by which she was in mortal danger, but that for the sake of the Lady de Bastarnay's honour, Bertha being the girl's cousin, this must not be allowed to leak out. Everybody swallowed this lie, which they found meaty enough to pass on to others.

The good folk thus thought it was Jehan's illness which constituted the danger, but oh no, not at all, it was the convalescence, for the stronger Jehan became, the weaker was Bertha herself, so weak in fact, that she just slipped down and down into that paradise which Jehan enabled her to attain. Nevertheless, even at the peak of her delights, which she achieved in spite of the fears engendered by Fallotte's ominous prophecy, and also being racked by her own great piety, what she was really afraid of was Baron Imbert, to whom she felt compelled to write that before his departure he had given her a baby, which would be his delight on his return, which was a falsehood far greater than the babe.

The whole day on which she wrote that deceitful letter she avoided her Jehan, weeping so that she could not keep a handkerchief dry. Finding himself thus avoided (for now they no more left one another than fire leaves the forest in which it has got a hold), Jehan conceived the notion that she now hated him, so he too wept. That same evening, upset by his tears, revealed by his red eyes and also by his frequent wiping of them, Bertha confided to him why she was so miserable, at the same time admitting her fears as to the future. She told him straight that they were both to blame, and such lovely, such Christian, sermons did she now read him, so rich with divine tears and contrite implorings, that Jehan was stirred to the very profundities of his heart by his dear one's faith. This love so naïvely combined with repentance, this nobility amid guilt, this compound of feebleness and strength, are alleged by writers of antiquity to have been so

M   345

powerful that they would have changed the very nature of tigers and made them gentle animals. So you must not be at all astonished that Jehan now gave Bertha his word as novice-in-arms for knighthood that for her salvation he would obey her any behest in this world or the next.

Hearing this assurance of trust in her and seeing this absence of malice in him, Bertha threw herself on the ground and kissed Jehan's feet.

'Oh dearest one,' she said, 'you whom I am forced to love, though it is mortal sin, you who are so kind, so pitying towards your poor Bertha, if you want her always to think of you with tenderness, if you wish to staunch the torrents of her tears, of which you are the cause so delightful and so delectable'—and here, to prove her words, she let him steal a kiss—'Jehan,' she resumed, after the act, 'if you wish the memory of our heavenly delights, the angelic music we have made together and the sweet scent of our loving not to weigh heavily on me, but rather be my solace in evil days, do what the Virgin had told me in a dream to command you. For in a dream I implored her to show me light in our present situation, and when I thus asked her to come to me, she came. I then displayed to her the frightful burning pains in which I should be, trembling for the babe already stirring here in my womb and also for that babe's true father, who would be at the mercy of the other, and might expiate his paternity in a violent end, for Fallotte may have seen clearly what the future holds in store for us. Then, smiling, the beauteous Virgin told me that the Church offers us forgiveness for our sins if we follow her commandments, but that I must be my own fires of Hell by mending my ways in good time, before Heaven is moved to wrath. With her finger, she showed me a Jehan exactly like you, though attired not as you are, but as she said you should be, and as you shall be, if you love Bertha with a lasting love.'

Raising her from her knees, seating her on his own, and kissing her well, Jehan then assured her of his perfect compliance. Poor Bertha then said that the garment in question in which she saw him robed in the dream was the cowled frock of a monk, and, trembling greatly, lest he refuse, she now requested him to take the tonsure and retire to the Monastery of Marmoustier, on the far side of Tours, swearing on her faith that she would give him one more night of love, after which she would never more be his or any other's in this world. But she also promised that every year, in recompense for this, she would let him come to her for a day, to see his child.

Bound by the oath he had given, Jehan promised to become a monk as his love required of him, telling her that in this way at least he would be faithful to her, and would have no other enjoyment of love than that which he had known in her divine union with him, and would live on the precious memory of that.

Hearing these tender words, Bertha told him that, however great his sin, and whatever God might have in store for him, the passage of time would enable him to bear anything, for she did not believe she had been with a man, but an angel.

They then lay down in the nest where their love had first blossomed, though now to bid a supreme farewell to all its lovely flowers. It must be supposed that Lord Cupid himself intervened in this festival, since never in any place in the world did any woman acknowledge such delight, nor ever man took so much, for the essential of true love-making is a high degree of harmony which ensures that the more the one gives, the more the other gets, and vice versa, as in certain mathematical relationships where things are multiplied by themselves to infinity.

This equation is not to be explained to those of little knowledge otherwise than by what they may see in Venetian mirrors, when they behold thousands of profiles deriving from one alone. In this wise, in the hearts of two lovers the roses of pleasure are multiplied in a caressing profundity which makes the lovers themselves marvel that there should be so much essential delight therein, without anything giving way.

Bertha and Jehan would have liked that night to be their last, and by the swooning languor which flowed into their veins did indeed for a time think that love had decided to carry them right away on the wings of one immortal kiss, but despite the said infinite multiplication, they emerged from it all sound enough.

The following day, as the return of My Lord Imbert de Bastarnay was at hand, the alleged maid, 'Sylvia de Rohan', had to take her leave. The poor girl said farewell to her cousin, watering her alike with tears and kisses, each ever the last, and the last lasting till nightfall. Then they simply had to desist and he left her, although the blood of his heart congealed thereby like wax fallen from an Easter candle.

In pursuance of his oath, Jehan made his way to Marmoustier, where he entered a little before eleven o'clock that night and from novice-at-arms became a novice-at-monkhood. Baron de Bastarnay was informed that Sylvia had returned to her milord, which is the English for *seigneur*, and as Jehan had now consecrated himself to God, Bertha did not thereby lie.

The delight of her husband, when he beheld Bertha ungirdled, since she could no longer bear a belt, so big with child she was, began this poor woman's martyrdom. She was not good at deceit and for every lying word she spoke had to have recourse to her prayer-stool, weeping tears of water and of blood, dissolving in prayer, confiding herself to the Holy Saints in Paradise.

It happened at last that one day she cried out so loudly to God that the Baron heard her, for he heard everything, he heard even the pebbles rolling on the river bed, he heard the poor groaning, he heard even the flies as they fly through the air. This it is right for you to know, otherwise you would never credit what now happened: the Lord God ordered the Archangel Michael to see that this repentant woman went through Purgatory on earth, so that she might enter Paradise without examination. Therefore Saint Michael came down from Heaven to the vestibule of all hells and delivered this triple soul to Satan, telling him that by reason of Bertha, Jehan and the child it was permissible for him to torment it for the rest of its days. And Satan, by the graciousness of the Almighty Lord of all evil, assured the Archangel that he would execute this commission.

While Heaven was issuing these directives, life was pursuing its normal course here on earth. The gentle lady of Bastarnay furnished Baron Imbert with the loveliest child in the world, a boy all lilies and roses, as intelligent as a little Jesus, as laughing and roguish as a heathen Cupid, handsomer with every day that passed, while the elder son gradually grew into a baboon like his father, whom he resembled to a horrifying degree. The younger son gleamed bright as a star in the firmament, the image of his true father and of the mother, whose bodily and spiritual perfections had in him produced a compound of illustrious graces and wondrous understanding.

Seeing this eternal miracle of flesh and soul so essentially combined, Bastarnay declared that for his eternal salvation he would like to be able to make the younger son the elder and by Royal Grace would see what could be done about it.

Bertha was now beside herself with anxiety. She adored Jehan's child and could only love the other feebly, yet despite this partiality she strove to protect him against good old Bastarnay's ill intentions of making him take second place. Yet so satisfied was Bertha at heart with this new turn of events that she cloaked her conscience with lies. Indeed, she thought everything was now at rest, seeing that twelve years had gone by unclouded by more than the anxieties which constantly poisoned her happiness. Every year, in pursuance of the promise given, the Marmoustier monk, unknown to everybody save the maid, came to pass twenty-four hours at the castle to see his child, though many a time had Bertha begged her 'friend'

Brother Jehan to renounce his right. But Jehan would then point to their son and say:

'You see him every day of the year, I only one.'

Then the poor mother could find no word to say against him.

Some months before the final rebellion of His Highness Louis against his father, the boy was on the verge of his twelfth birthday and seemed to have the makings of a great scholar, so learned was he in every branch of knowledge. Never had old Bastarnay felt happier at being a father, and he now decided to take his boy with him to the Court of Burgundy, where since he was no detester of intelligent men, Duke Charles promised to establish this much-beloved son in a position which princes would envy.

Seeing matters thus arranged, Satan decided that the time for evil doing had come at last. He took his tail and thrust it as fiercely as ever he could plump into the heart of this good fortune, so as to stir things up as suited him.

III. The Terrible Punishment of Bertha and the Atonement by which She Died Forgiven

Lady de Bastarnay's maid, when in her thirty-fifth year, fell madly in love with one of the Baron's men-at-arms, and was ninny enough to let the fellow bake a batch of those long French loaves in her oven. This resulted in a natural swelling which charming folk in these parts sometimes call the nine-months dropsy. The poor woman implored her kind mistress to speak to the Baron on her behalf and get him to compel the rascal to complete at the altar what he had begun in bed. Lady de Bastarnay had no difficulty in getting her Lord to promise this favour, and the maid was very satisfied.

However, the veteran warrior, still devilish blunt of speech, had the man-at-arms on the carpet and dressed him down before he ordered him on pain of death to marry the girl, which the soldier did prefer, prizing his neck more than his peace. But old Bastarnay then had the woman up, thinking it his duty, for the honour of his house, to give her a curtain-lecture too and call her a few names. However, he made such a terrifying hullabaloo about it all that the woman was afraid that as punishment she was not going to be married after all, but at least cast into a dungeon. This made her suspect her mistress of wanting to get rid of her, in order once for all to bury the secrets of the birth of her pet son. So, when the old baboon began saying shocking things to her, such as that only a loony would keep a trollop about his house, she felt sure her suspicions were right, and retorted that he certainly was a double-loony, if ever there was one, his own wife had been trolloped long since, what was more, by a monk, the worst possible thing for a soldier to hear.

Imagine the worst storm you have ever seen in your life, and you will have a feeble notion of the tempest which raged in the old man when thus touched in that part of his heart where dwelt a triple life. He seized the maid by the throat and was on the point of slaughtering her without another word, when, to bear out her story, she gave the why and the wherefore of it all and said that if he did not believe her, perhaps he would believe his own ears when Dom Jehan de Sacché, Prior of Marmoustier Monastery next came to spend a day at the Castle, for he would hear the talk of the boy's father when he solaced himself for his year's fasting and in one day gave his son a whole year's due of kisses.

Imbert now told the woman to clear out of the Castle, for if her charge proved true he would murder her just as surely as if it were all invention on her part. He quickly handed her a hundred crowns (apart from the gift of her man), and told them both not to put head to pillow in Touraine that night. Indeed, to make quite sure, they were taken straight across into Burgundy by one of the Baron's officers. He then told his wife they had gone, adding that anyway that maid was a wormy fruit, and he thought it better to throw it out, giving her a hundred crowns and finding a job for the man at the Burgundy Court.

Bertha was astounded to learn that her maid had left the Castle without even bidding her good-bye, but she did not murmur a word. Soon after that, indeed, she had other things to worry about, suddenly becoming all apprehension for her husband's manner had completely changed and he had begun to find likenesses between his eldest son and himself, but nothing of his nose or his forehead or this or that in the younger one, whom he had loved so much.

'But he's just like me,' replied Bertha, one day when he was expressing these misgivings. 'Surely you know that in good families the sons are made by the husbands and the wives in turn, or often enough together, because the mother merges her humours with the vital humours of the father? Or that some doctors say they have seen many children produced without any resemblance to either, declaring these mysteries to be by the whim of the Almighty?'

'You have become learned, my dear,' replied Bastarnay. 'But, ignoramus that I am, I reckon that a child like a monk . . .'

'Would have been made by a monk?' said Bertha, looking him fearlessly straight in the eyes, for all that there was ice instead of blood in her veins.

350

The good fellow was now inclined to think that he was wrong and cursed the maid. This, however, only made him the more intent on checking the truth. As the day set apart for Dom Jehan's visit was drawing near, Bertha, put on her guard at all this talk, wrote to him that she would rather he did not come at all this year, she would tell him why later, then she went to ask Fallotte at Losches to pass the letter to Dom Jehan, and thought that so far she was safe. She was indeed the gladder that she had written to her love, the Prior, since Baron Imbert, who had as a rule travelled through the province of Maine, where he owned large estates, about the time set apart for the poor monk's annual holiday, this year decided not to travel, his reason being the preparations for the rebellion proposed by Prince Louis against his father, who was so grieved by that resort to arms that, as everybody knows, he died of it. Hence her husband's reason was such a good one that poor Bertha felt quite snug and was not really worried.

On the appointed day, however, the Prior did not fail to turn up. When she saw him, Bertha lost colour and asked if he had not received her message.

'What message?' asked Jehan.

'Then we are lost, the boy, you and me,' she replied.

'Why?' asked the Prior.

'I cannot tell you now,' she said, 'but, I assure you, our last day has come.'

When she inquired of her beloved boy where Bastarnay was, the young man said his father had been summoned to Losche by an urgent messenger and would not be back till nightfall. Hearing this, Jehan, despite what his love said, insisted on staying with her and his dear child, assuring her that no mishap could arise now that twelve years had elapsed since the boy's birth.

These annual days of celebration of that night so full of doings of which you already know, poor Bertha used to spend the whole day with the poor Monk in her room, till supper. On this occasion, however, pressed by Bertha's apprehensions, shared by Dom Jehan as soon as his love had told him about it, the two lovers dined early, although the Prior of Marmoustier fortified Bertha's heart by arguments about the privileges of the Church and how, already in disfavour at court, Bastarnay would never dare lay hands on a dignitary of Marmoustier.

When they sat down to table the boy was playing about, and in spite of the repeated requests of his mother, refused to leave his sport. He was galloping round and round the courtyard on a fine Spanish jennet which Prince Charles of Burgundy had given his father, and as young lads like to be grown-up, serving-boys pretending they are novices-at-arms, and novices-at-arms that they are knights, this youngster's pleasure was to demonstrate to his friend the Monk how grown up he was, and he made the jennet jump like a flea in a bed, keeping his seat as if he had been many years in the saddle.

'Let the boy have his fun, my darling,' said the Monk to Bertha, 'disobedient lads often turn into great personalities.'

Bertha, however, scarcely touched her food, her heart swollen like a sponge full of water, while the Monk, who was a great student, at the first mouthful or two felt a queasiness in his stomach and an acrid sting on his palate which made him suspect that the Baron had poisoned the ham. Before he was sure of this, Bertha too had eaten some.

All at once the Prior tipped over the table and threw everything into the fire, telling Bertha his suspicion. Bertha thanked the Virgin that the boy had been so insistent on his riding. Without losing his head, Dom Jehan recalled his early training as a page, ran down into the courtyard, whipped his son off the jennet, leapt on it himself and galloped off at such speed that you would have thought him a meteor, had you seen him digging his heels into the jennet's flanks, fiercely enough to gut the animal.

Dom Jehan reached Fallotte at Losche in a time so short only the devil could have equalled it. He put the situation to her in a couple of words, for the poison was already gnawing at his bowels, and demanded an antidote.

'Alas!' said the witch, 'had I but known that it was for you that I was supplying my poison, I would have let the dagger which threatened me plunge into my throat and would have quit my wretched life to save that of a man of God and the nicest lady who ever blossomed on this earth, for, my dear friend, the contents of this little bottle are all the antidote I have left.'

'Is there enough for her?'

'Yes, if you're quick,' said the old woman.

The Monk returned still more swiftly than he came, so swiftly, indeed, that the jennet expired under him in the courtyard. Reaching the chamber where, thinking her last hour come, Bertha was kissing her child, while she writhed like a lizard on hot coals, uttering no cry for herself, but only for the boy, abandoned to the rage of Bastarnay, so that her vision of the cruel fate that awaited them all three made her forget her own sufferings.

'Take this,' cried the Monk, 'my life is saved.'

This Dom Jehan had the grand courage to say with unfaltering expression, although he already felt the claws of death seizing at his

heart. No sooner had Bertha drunk the antidote than the Prior fell
dead, though not without kissing his son and, as he expired, keeping
his eyes on his love, with an expression which did not change even
after his last gasp.

The sight of Jehan's death froze Bertha de Bastarnay like marble
and left her so aghast that she lay at his feet on the floor as if dead
herself, clutching the hand of her child, who was weeping, though
she on the contrary was as dry of eye as the Red Sea was when the
Jews passed over it led by Baron Moses, for she felt as if sharp grains
of sand were caught under her lids. Pray for her, charitable souls, for
never was any woman so harrowed as she was, when she realized
that her loved one had saved her life at cost of his own.

Assisted by the boy, with her own hands she laid the Monk out on
the bed and took her stand beside him, praying together with her
son, whom she now told that this Prior was his real father.

Like this she awaited her evil hour, and the evil hour indeed arrived, for Bastarnay came at about eleven o'clock, to be told at the
drawbridge that the Monk was dead but not Lady de Bastarnay or the
boy, and to see his jennet dead. Then, stirred with furious desire to
kill Bertha and the Monk's son, he bounded up the steps. But at sight
of the corpse for whom, deaf to his loud complaints, blind to his
gestures and threats, his wife and son were murmuring endless
prayers, he had not the courage to commit that sombre deed.

His first fire spent, Baron Imbert de Bastarnay did not know what
to do. Like a coward and criminal he paced the hall terribly moved by
the prayers still being recited over the Monk, and the night wore
away in sobs and moaning and prayer. Meanwhile, by Lady de Bastarnay's order a maid had been to Losches to purchase the outfit worn
of custom by a *feme-sole* of noble birth, and, for the boy, a small horse
and the outfit of a squire, seeing which, the Baron, aghast, sent for
his wife and the Monk's son. But neither heeded him. They merely
donned those garments purchased by the maid.

On Bertha's orders, this maid now drew up an inventory of all
Bertha's effects and laid out her married wardrobe, her pearls, her
jewellery, her diamonds, as is done when a widow renounces her
rights. To make the ceremony perfect, Bertha even gave instructions
to add her own purse to these things.

Rumour of all these preparations ran swiftly through the house.
Everybody now saw that the Lady of the Manor was going to leave
it, which wounded every heart, even that of a little scullion engaged
only a week before this. He too wept, for Lady Bertha had not omit-
ted to speak kindly to him.

Horrified by these preparations, old Bastarnay went up to his wife's chamber, to find her there at Jehan's body, weeping, for now at last the tears had broken, though when she saw her Lord and husband there, at once she stayed them, and her eyes were dry. To his repeated questions, she replied curtly, freely admitting her guilt. She told him now how she had been tricked, how upset the poor young man had been. She showed Bastarnay the scar of that dagger wound on the corpse, told him how slow the recovery had been, then added how, in obedience to her and as penitence to the men of God, Jehan de Sacché had abandoned his fine career as knight and, wiping out his name, retired to a monastery, which was worse than death; how, avenging her honour, she had thought that even God would not grudge one day a year to the Monk to see the son to whom he had sacrificed his all; how, refusing to live with an assassin, she was abandoning all her goods and leaving his house, and finally, that if the honour of the Bastarnays was sullied, it was he, not she, who was the cause, for in the misfortune which had struck them, she had settled things as best could be. She added that it was her desire now to cross mountains and valleys, with her son, to be wanderers on the face of the earth till all was atoned, for she could atone for it all.

Having, pale of countenance and noble in bearing, made this declaration of great beauty, she took her child by the hand and departed, in full mourning, more magnificently lovely than the maid Hagar when she left the house of Abraham the Patriarch, and so dignified that all the men of the household knelt at her passage, and laying their hands together in prayer uttered their pleas to her as if she were Our Lady de la Riche. It was pitiful, too, to see Baron de Bastarnay himself now weeping, convinced she had done right. He followed her, admitting his fault, as desperate as a man being led to the scaffold for execution.

Bertha would not hear a word. The sorrow was so great that she found the drawbridge ready lowered and quickened her pace to get out of the Castle, fearing lest the bridge be suddenly raised. But no man had the mind or heart to do this. She now sat down on the edge of the moat, in view of the whole Castle, which weeping still implored her to stay, while the poor Baron stood, his hand on the drawbridge chain, silent as any of the saints carved in stone above the gatehouse lintel. He now watched Bertha as she instructed her son to shake the dust of his shoes on to the approach to the bridge, so as to take away not a thing of the Bastarnay's and did the same herself. Then, pointing out the Baron to her son, with grave gesture, she addressed the boy as follows:

'Child, there stands your father's assassin for, as you now know, your father was that poor Prior. But you have taken this man's name, so now see to it that you give it back to him, just as you have shaken off the dust which your shoes took from his Castle. As for the food you have eaten in his house, that account too we shall in time settle, with God's aid.'

Hearing this cry, old Bastarnay would have allowed a whole monastery full of monks to have his wife, only not to be deserted by her and by this young squire capable of being the glory of his line, and his head fell back against the chains.

'You Devil!' cried Bertha, 'blind to the part you played in this, are you satisfied? Then may God and the saints and the archangels, to whom I have prayed so ardently, be our succour in this ruin!'

Her heart was at once full of holy solace, for the banner of the great monastery came round a corner of the road through the fields, accompanied by the hymns of the church, breaking over them like voices of Heaven. Informed of the murder of their beloved Prior, the monks were come in solemn procession, supported by ecclesiastical justices, to claim his body. Seeing this, Baron de Bastarnay scarcely had time with his men to slip away through the postern gate. He went now to join Prince Louis, abandoning all he had.

Poor Bertha, riding pillion behind her son, went now to Montbazon to bid her father farewell, telling him that she would die of this blow, and she was comforted by her family, who made every effort to restore her heart, though without success. Old Baron de Rohan made his grandson a present of a fine suit of armour, telling him he must win such honour and glory by great deeds that he would transform his mother's mistake into eternal glory. Lady de Bastarnay, however, had planted in her son's mind no other thought but that of making good the damage, so as to save her and Jehan from eternal damnation. So mother and son now went together to the parts where rebellion had been raised, desiring to render such service to the said Baron de Bastarnay that he should get back more than life from their hands.

Now, this sedition had flared up, as everybody knows, in the neighbourhood of Angoulême and Bordeaux, in Guyenne, and also in other places in the kingdom where there were to be great battles and clashes between the rebels and the Royal forces. The principal one, which terminated the war, was fought between Ruffec and Angoulême, where the prisoners taken were hanged and executed.

This battle, led by veteran Bastarnay, took place about November, seven months after the murder of Dom Jehan, and when Bastarnay's forces were routed the good man found himself hard pressed between six men-at-arms determined to capture him. He then realized that they wanted to take him alive so as to be able to take proceedings against his house, ruin his name and confiscate all his properties. The poor nobleman preferred to die, thereby to save his line and keep the lands for his son, and he began to defend himself like the true lion that he was.

Despite their number, the soldiers, seeing three of their number cut down, were compelled at last to attack Bastarnay, even at risk of killing him, and they threw themselves on him together after striking down his two squires and a page.

In this extreme peril, a squire with the de Rohan arms suddenly came down like a thunderbolt on the assailants, at once killing two of them, and crying: 'God save the Bastarnays!' The third man-at-arms, who already had a hold on old Bastarnay, was so terrified by this young squire that he was compelled to let the Baron go and turn against the new assailant, dealing him a dagger thrust through a fent in his gorget.

Bastarnay was too good a companion now to take flight without lending a hand to the young man who had freed his house, whom when he looked about him he saw lying wounded. With one blow of his mace he brought down the last man-at-arms, then took the squire across his horse and got away to open country, led by a guide who brought him to la Rochefoucauld Castle, which he entered by night, in the great hall to find Bertha de Rohan, there afforded retreat. And when he took off the armour of his rescuer, he recognized the son of Jehan, who, by a last effort kissing his mother and saying loudly to her: 'Mother dear, we are quit regarding him now!' now expired on the table where they had laid him.

Hearing these words, the mother embraced the body of her son of love and joined with it for ever, passing away herself from grief, without giving a thought or heeding the forgiveness and repentance of Bastarnay.

This extraordinary misfortune so advanced the last days of the poor nobleman that after all his efforts he never saw the accession of good King Louis XI. However, he endowed a daily mass in the la Rochefoucauld Church, where in the same tomb he interred son and mother, with a large tombstone inscribed in Latin rendering great honour to their lives.

The moral which every man may imbibe from this tale is very profitable in life's conduct, for the story shows that noblemen should be courteous even to their wives' lovers. It is also abundant instruction that all children are treasures sent by God himself and that their fathers, real or false, should have no right of murder over them, as they once did in Rome, under an abominable pagan law which does not at all fit Christendom, in which we are all sons of God.

V

How the Portillon Beauty Scored
over the Magistrate

As everybody knows, the Belle of Portillon, before she married Taschereau—'Jobber' the dyer—and became Mme Tascherette (or 'Jobbette') was a washerwoman at Portillon, whence her name. In case any do not know Tours, better add that Portillon is on the Loire, downstream from Tours, on the St Cyr side, as far from the bridge across to the Cathedral as the said bridge is from Marmoustier, that is to say, the bridge comes midway along the dyke between the said place, Portillon and Marmoustier. Clear? Yes? Right you are, then!

Well, this girl did fine laundering at Portillon. In a jiffy she could be down at the river to beat her linen, or to have a ferryman row her across to St Martin, which was on the opposite bank, where she had most of her business, at Château Neuf and other places.

It was the seventh St John's Day before she married old Taschereau, that the Belle of Portillon was ripe to be loved, but, being a harum-scarum lass, she let all the lads who were after her pay her court without choosing one of them. Although she had Rabelais's son serenading her (he with seven boats plying on the Loire, too), and the eldest Jahan, Marchanieau the tailor and Peccard who did all the church gilding, she led them all up the garden path times without number, because she wanted to go properly to the altar before she burdened herself with a man, which is proof she was a decent girl till her maidenhood was broached. She was one of those fillies who take great care not to get into a mess, but if they do get caught, go the whole hog, thinking absolution is the same whether it's for one blot or umpteen. Such souls deserve their absolution.

Now, one day one of the young lords at Court saw her go down to the river. It was on the stroke of midday, in dazzling sunshine, which brought out all her ample glories, and on the spot he asked who she might be. An old fellow working the foreshore land said that was the Portillon beauty, a laundry-girl famous for her tart tongue and her level head.

As well as a suit of ruffles to starch, this young lord also had a quantity of very valuable embroideries and furnishings, so he thought he might as well give all this to the Belle of Portillon to do, and at once tackled her about it. She thanked him, warmly too, seeing he was none other than the Royal Chamberlain Lord du Fou. This

357

lucky meeting made our beauty most happy, she could talk of nothing else now but du Fou. She chattered away to the St Martin folk and when she got back to her washing-board spilled a bibful about it, till Lord du Fou cropped up more often in Portillon than Lord God in the pulpit, which was too much.

'If that's the way her clapper goes cold, what'll it be hot?' asked an old relic of a washerwoman. 'She's asking for it, she is. He'll warm it up for her, du Fou will.'

The first time, all blab about du Fou, the silly girl had to deliver him his linen, the Chamberlain wanted to see her and sang lauds and compline to her about her lively tongue, finally remarking that being very pretty had certainly not blunted her wit, but he could give her as good as she gave him. And followed the word by the deed, for, the moment his servants left the room, he started caressing her, whereupon, thinking he was fumbling in his codpiece at a pile of coins and, like any decent girl bashful about being paid, shy to stare at the said purse, she murmured:

'Being as you are a new customer . . .'

'Being as I'm a quick customer,' was his quick reply.

Some say he had a hard job taking her and in fact scarcely dipped at all, others say she got it strong, being that she left that room like any girl with a full charge, and at once broke out a-moaning and a-groaning and went straight to the beak.

As luck would have it, that gentleman was out on his land, so our Portillon beauty waited for him in tears, in the hall, telling the maid she had been robbed, as all that Lord du Fou had given her was his wickedness, a Canon of the Chapter was always offering her very big money for what Lord du Fou had pinched, if she loved a man, she would reckon it decent to give him his pleasure for what she got out of it herself, but the Lord Chamberlain had hustled her and bustled her, he had not treated her nice at all like she counted to be, so he owed her those thousand crowns which the Canon offered.

Coming home and finding the Belle waiting for him, the magistrate would have got fresh with her, but she faced up to him and told him she was there to lodge a plaint. The magistrate then said that if it depended on him she could have a man strung up, he would turn the town upside down to please such a pretty girl. The good lass said she did not want her man to pay with his life but with his pocket, a thousand crowns sterling, because, against her will, she had been raped.

'Oho!' cried the beak, 'that's a flower the plucking of which costs a bit more.'

'A thousand crowns'll do me,' said she, 'then I could give up laundering for my living.'

'Is the fellow who took his pleasure well lined?' asks the beak.

'Very well lined,' said she.

'Then let him fork out. Who is it?'

'Lord du Fou.'

'Ah, that alters your suit,' says the beak.

'What about my rights?' says she.

'I said alters your suit not your rights,' replied the beak. 'But I must know exactly how Lord du Fou did it.'

Without more ado the girl related how she was putting the ruffles away in the young noble's linen cupboard when he started fiddling with her skirts, whereupon she turned round and said, 'Stop it, My Lord!'

'Enough said,' cried the beak. 'When you uttered those words he thought you were telling him to be quick with his plug. Ho! Ho! Ho!'

The Portillon beauty then told the magistrate that she had struggled, she had cried and she had shouted, and that all turned it into rape.

'Maidenly flibbertygibbeting,' says the magistrate, 'to egg the man on.'

Finally, said the Belle of Portillon, in spite of all her efforts, she felt herself 'took from about the middle' and 'backed on to the bed'. She jumped and she shouted, she said, like anything, but, seeing no help came, in the end she lost heart.

'Tophole,' says the magistrate. 'And did you enjoy it?'

'No,' says she. 'I didn't. And only one thousand crowns sterling will make good my damage.'

'My pet,' says the beak, 'I reject your plaint, because I don't believe a girl is ever violated but willingly.'

'Ha-ha!' she jibed, through her tears. 'You just ask your own maid and hear what she has to say.'

The magistrate's maid then declared that there were rapes pleasant and rapes very unpleasant, and if this poor girl got neither cash nor enjoyment out of hers, either enjoyment or cash was owing to her.

This sober counsel greatly perplexed the good magistrate.

'Jacqueline,' said he, at last, 'before I eat that chop I must settle this. Bring me that bodkin I use for stitching my papers together, and a length of red thread, will you?'

Jacqueline returned, bearing in her hand a bodkin which certainly had a very pretty eye, with a length of that red thread which legal gentry use. She now stayed, to see the case judged. Like the Portillon beauty, she was rather agog at these mystifying preparations.

'Now, my pet,' said the magistrate, 'I will hold up this bodkin, the

359

eye of which, as you see, is amply big enough to have this red thread poked into it, isn't it? Well, if you can get it in, I'll see to your suit and the good Lord du Fou can compound with you and cough up.'

'What's that?' cried the girl, 'I'm not letting him compound with me any more!'

'I don't mean what you mean,' said the magistrate. 'Compound is only a legal word, when a respondent admits the truth of your plight.'

'What I suppose you mean,' she said, 'is: when justice plights its troth.'

'My pet,' said the beak, 'I see the act which let his sharpness in also let yours out. Get me?'

'I do,' said she.

Now the roguish beak had a great game with his plaintiff, offering her the hole in the bodkin fair and square, but whenever she was about to poke in the thread (which she had twisted to make straight), shifting a little, so she was bound to fail to get it in. She now guessed his line, so, moistening her thread well she held it up stiff and started again. The man of law shifted and fidgeted and wriggled as well as any timid virgin ever did. Hence that damned thread never did get in, and the harder the Portillon beauty tried, the more our fine magistrate shallied, so the union never was consummated, the eye of the bodkin stayed virginal, till, laughing her head off, the magistrate's maid cried out to the laundress that she was certainly a better rapee than a raper. Thereupon the good magistrate laughed too, but the Portillon beauty still bemoaned her crowns.

'If you won't stay still,' said she to him, losing patience, 'I never shall shoot these rapids.'

'Therefore, my girl,' he said, 'had you done likewise, the good Chamberlain would never have shot yours. And think too what an easy opening this is and how tight is that of a virgin!'

The good lass who declared herself raped now became pensive, wondering however she was to convince the magistrate and show him how it was she who had been forced to yield, which was particularly important since it concerned the honour of every poor girl prone to suffer the same fortune.

'Sir,' she said, 'to make the trial fair, I ought to do what the Lord Chamberlain did. If fidgeting alone had been enough, I should still be fidgeting now, but, you see, he got up to other tricks.'

'What tricks?' demanded the magistrate.

Now the Belle of Portillon dressed her thread thoroughly, rubbing candle-wax into it so it would stay stiff and straight. Having thus dressed her thread, she poked away at the eye-hole which the magis-

trate held out to her, wriggling it all the time to right and to left.
But this time the lass simply showered him with ribaldries, such as:
'Oh, the pretty little hole! What a dainty bull's eye 'tis! Never did I
see such a pretty little pussy! Oh, what a lovely bit of drawn-thread
work! Just let me insert this plausible little thread! Oh deary me,
you'll hurt my poor little thread, my dainty little thread, do please be
still! Come now, Your Honour! Darling Magistrate, come, my love!
I declare, my little thread is afraid of this iron gate of yours. It must
use up a lot of thread, since mine always come out limp.' And the
laundress roared with laughter, seeing she was able to keep up this
game longer than the magistrate. But he also laughed, she was so
droll, with such dainty monkey-tricks, poking out that thread and
drawing it back again. She kept the good magistrate till the clock
struck seven holding the eyelet to her, wriggling it and jiggling it up
and down like a monkey off its chain, but seeing this lively hussy so
set on getting her end in he had no other course but to keep on holding her the hole till, catching a whiff of his supper burning, and getting really tired, he rested his hand for an instant on the table, whereupon the damsel thrust her waxy piece home.

'There,' she said, 'that's how it happened.'

'But my bit of meat was burning,' he protested.

'So was mine,' said she.

Thus scored over, the magistrate told the girl that, having seen
that the young gentleman had indeed taken her by force, he would go
and see Lord du Fou and dun him, but for certain valid reasons he
would postpone the visit till the following day.

In the morning, the magistrate did indeed go to Court and see
Lord du Fou. The young nobleman having admitted there was truth
in the story, the King inquired if he had found the girl difficult of
access. Since Lord du Fou's unaffected reply was that he had not so
found, the King pronounced the tapping to be worth only one hundred crowns, which, not to be dubbed tight-fisted, the Chamberlain
paid the magistrate forthwith, though not without the observation
that at that rate starching was going to bring in the Belle of Portillon
a nice little penny.

The magistrate returned to Portillon, and, with a smile, told his
plaintiff that he had raised one hundred crowns sterling for her, but
if she wanted the balance of her thousand, there were at that very
instant a number of lords in the Royal Chamber who, having heard
all about her suit, were willing to pay their share. The beauty was
nothing loth, and declared that she would gladly have her suit laun-
dered a bit more, in order afterwards not to have to do any more
laundering, and, lavishly rewarding the magistrate's efforts regarding

the said suit, had in a month earned her thousand crowns sterling. Hence arose the slanders and lies at her cost, jealous hussies turning the ten into a hundred, whereas, in distinction from them, once she had her thousand the Portillon girl put the shutters up on her little boutique. Even a duke who would not have made a fuss over five hundred crowns would have found her deaf to his entreaties, which goes to show she kept a tight hand on her goods.

True, the King did send for her to his little love-nest in Quin-quangrogne Street just off Chardonneret Mall, and finding her both comely and very rampageous, had fine sport with her, after which he forbade his officers to worry her in any way, whereupon, seeing her so beautiful, the King's own poppet, Nicole Beaupertuis, gave the Belle a further hundred crowns to take herself to Orleans to see if the Loire was the same colour there as at Portillon.

The ex-laundress was all the more ready to comply since she did not fancy herself as the King's mistress. But when that worthy ecclesiastic who confessed the King *in extremis* and was thereafter canonized called to see her, to him she did unveil her conscience, doing penance and endowing a bed in the Leper Hospital of St Lazar of Tours.

There is many a lady of quality of your own acquaintance who has willingly been 'raped' by more than a dozen lords without bothering about any other bed than her own. This is a fact which should be put on record to cleanse the good name of this honest maid who once washed other folks' filth but later was so famed for her decency and her wit. She finally gave proof of her qualities in marrying old Taschereau, whom, as related above in *The Last Word*, she certainly cuckolded very thoroughly, though to their mutual satisfaction.

All of which well proves that by dint of vigour and patience justice itself can be compounded.

VI

Proof that Luck is Invariably of Feminine Gender

In the age when knights courteously lent each other aid and support in the search for fortune, it happened that in Sicily (which, if you happen not to know it, is an island situated in a corner of the Mediterranean Sea which was once famous), in a forest one knight came upon another who looked like a Frenchman. To all appearances this Frenchman had by some mischance been stripped bare, for he was on foot, he had no squire or any other followers, and he was so badly attired that had it not been for his princely manner he might have been taken for a common rascal. It is feasible that the horse had died of hunger or exhaustion after disembarkation from the overseas land whence by reason of stories of the great careers which French-men were making in this Isle of Sicily, which were in no sense true at all, his master had come.

The Sicilian knight, whose name was Pezara, was a Venetian who had long since emigrated from the Republic of Venice and, having got a foothold at the court of the King of Sicily, never thought to return home. The fact is, having not a clue how to trade, he had been given up by his family as a bad job; so was left penniless at home, for all that the family was a very distinguished one. He had stayed on with the Sicilian Court, at which he greatly pleased the King. He was making his way not on foot, but on a fine Spanish jennet, yet he was telling himself how lonely he was here too, in this alien court. He had not one trusted friend. How cruel, he was just thinking, in such circumstances fortune could be to a man with no backing and how treacherous, when he beheld this poor Frenchman, who looked an even barer knight than he was himself, for he at least had got fine weapons, a fine horse, some servants and quarters at an inn, where his men were at this moment preparing an ample supper.

'You must have come far to have so much dust on your feet,' remarked the Venetian.

'Farther than I've the dust of,' said the Frenchman.

'If you have travelled so far,' retorted the Venetian, 'you ought to be a man of learning.'

'Yes,' said the Frenchman, 'I have learned to take no heed of those who take no heed of me. I have learned that however high a man puts his head, his feet are still on the same level as my own. What is

363

more, I have also learned not to trust a warm spell in mid-winter, the slumber of enemies or the humbug of friends.'

'Then you are richer than I am,' said the very astonished Venetian, 'seeing that you expound maxims I never even thought of.'

'Every man to his own thoughts,' said the Frenchman. 'In return for your questions I ask your kindness to put me on the right road for Palermo, or a wayside inn, for, look, night is upon us.'

'Do you mean that you know neither Frenchman nor Sicilian of noble blood at Palermo?'

'Not one.'

'So you are not even sure of being accommodated?'

'I am ready to forgive any who turn me away. Good Knight, the road, if you please.'

'I am as lost as you are,' said the Venetian. 'Let us seek it together.'

'That means travelling together. But you are on horseback, I am on foot.'

The Venetian thereupon took the Frenchman up behind him on his horse.

'Do you guess with whom you are?' he now asked.

'Apparently, a man.'

'You think you are safe?'

'If you are a brigand, it's you who ought to be afeared,' said the Frenchman, jabbing the hilt of his poniard in the region of the Venetian's heart.

'I must say, French Knight, you seem to me a man of great wit as well as elevated knowledge. Know then that I am a nobleman established at the Sicilian Court, but alone, and, in fact, in search of a companion. You seem to be in the same position. Nor, to all appearances, are you really satisfied with your lot. Indeed, you seem to have need of everybody.'

'Do I stand any chance of being any happier, were the whole world to meddle with me?'

'Damn it, man, you cap my every word! By Saint Mark, unknown sir, are you a man to be trusted?'

'More than yourself, I think, for you would initiate our federation by tricking me. You guide your horse like a man who knows his road, but you said you were lost.'

'And did you not trick me too,' cried the Venetian, 'by making a wiseacre as young as yourself foot-slog it and giving a noble knight the appearance of a brigand? But here is our inn, my men will have pottage ready for us.'

Consenting to partake of his supper, the Frenchman dismounted and entered the inn with the Venetian knight. The two therefore at once sat down to table. The Frenchman now fenced so well with his jaws and with such celerity rent flesh from bone that he revealed himself quite knowledgeable too regarding suppers. He further showed his knowledge in the great dexterity with which he could empty his cups without losing any clarity of eye or becoming at all fuddled of thought. You may therefore be sure that the Venetian thought he had certainly met a proud son of Adam, one sprung from the right side, not the wrong.

As they quaffed their wine together, the Venetian knight made great efforts to find some crack through which to sound the secret stores of thought that his new friend possessed. When he came to recognize that it would be easier to make the Frenchman part with his shirt than his caution, he thought it might be wiser to earn the man's confidence by unbuttoning to him a little himself. So he outlined the situation which then held in Sicily, where King Leufroid and his charming wife were on the throne. He told of the great gaiety of their court and the gentle manners which flourished there, adding that there were many personalities from Spain, France, Italy and other countries, nobles of most elevated lineage, possessed of great apanages, and many princesses as rich as they were noble and as lovely as they were rich.

He further said that this King of Sicily had set his cap very loftily indeed, to such heights as the conquest of the Morea, of Constantinople, of Jerusalem, of the lands of the Sultan and of other African parts. There were, he said, men of great intelligence in charge of affairs and they were busy rallying round them the whole flower of Christian chivalry, maintaining this splendour with the intention of making this island (which had been so opulent in antiquity) the ruler of the whole Mediterranean, to the ruin of Venice, which had not a handsbreadth of land.

These designs had all been put into the King's mind, he said, by himself, Pezara, but for all that he stood high in the monarch's favour, he felt himself in a weak position, having no backing among the other courtiers. This was why he wished to find a friend, and, reduced to this critical state, had indeed ridden out of Palermo expressly to think things over and evolve some plan. This was the reason why, having with such thoughts in mind come upon a man of such intelligence as the French knight had proved to be, he now proposed they should join hands as brothers. He would open his purse to the Frenchman and give him the run of his own mansion for lodging. They would advance together equally through honours and through pleasures, without any *arrière-pensée*. In the Crusade they would aid one another, whatever came, as brothers-in-arms, and,

seeing that the Frenchman was seeking his fortune and himself
needed help, the Venetian thought this suggestion for mutual support was not one to be turned down.

'As a matter of fact,' said the Frenchman, 'I really have no need of
any assistance at all, I rely on a thrusting weapon which will get me
all I need. Nevertheless, dear Knight Pezara, I would like to give
recognition to your courtesy, and you shall soon see yourself obliged
to Sir Gauttier de Montsoreau, of the gentle land of Touraine.'

'Have you then some magic charm, in which your fortune resides?'
asked the Venetian.

'I have,' replied the Frenchman. 'A talisman, gift of my dear
mother, tool with which castles and cities alike are both built and
demolished, a die with which to strike coins, a cure-all, a traveller's
staff which one can pledge, and is worth much when loaned, a master
tool guaranteed to do wonderful engraving in any forge without
making a sound.'

'Why, by St Mark, you have got a mystery in your hauberk!'

'No, Sir Knight,' said the Frenchman, 'not in my hauberk. My
talisman is a very natural, ordinary thing. Here it is!'

And without hesitation, as he rose from the table to go to bed,
Gauttier showed the Venetian the loveliest tool for making love's
delight that the Venetian had ever seen.

'This little bauble,' said the Frenchman, when after the fashion of
the age, both were in bed together, 'this little bauble levels out all
obstacles and renders you master of feminine hearts. And since the
ladies are the queens of this Court, your friend Gauttier will soon be
reigning there.'

The Venetian could not get over his tremendous astonishment at
sight of the hidden charms of the said Gauttier, who by reason of
having been remarkably well set up by his mother (his father perhaps
also, playing some part), was thereby bound to triumph over everything, since to this perfection of body were adjunct the spirits of a
young page and the knowingness of a veteran rascal.

These two therefore swore perfect companionship, accounting
female hearts to be trifles and swearing to be of one and the same
thought, as if their heads were capped with the same mortar-board
and, delighted with their brotherhood, they slept on the same pillow.
This is how things were done in those days.

The following day, the Venetian presented his friend Gauttier with
a handsome jennet and a purse full of gold bezants, fine linen hose,
a doublet of gold-embroidered velvet and an embroidered cloak, garments which enhanced his fine appearance and so set off his charms
that in the Venetian's opinion he was bound to turn all the ladies'

heads. Pezara's servants were instructed to obey Gauttier as himself, to the point that the retinue said their master must have been fishing deep to have caught this French pox.

The two friends then made their entry into Palermo just when the Prince and Princess were promenading on the *Corso*. Pezara presented his friend the Frenchman in great style, chanting his praises, and at once secured for him such a charming welcome that the Monarch kept him back to supper.

The French knight now conned the Sicilian Court with prudent eye, to discover very many strange things about it. The King was a handsome, valiant monarch and his Consort was a temperamental Spanish woman, the loveliest and most estimable person in the Court. Yet she was clearly in a melancholic state. From this observation the Tourainian judged that she was sparsely served by His Majesty, for it is a recognized law of Touraine that a cheerful countenance comes from good cheer of something else.

Indeed, in no time Pezara had indicated to Gauttier a number of ladies to whom the King was forthcoming, every one of them envious and ready to snap at who ever engaged him, in a constant contest of love interest, with remarkable feminine inventions. From all of this Gauttier drew the further conclusion that despite having the loveliest woman in the world, the Monarch did a lot of wenching about his Court, constantly engaged assessing the customs dues of all the ladies of Sicily, anything to be able to put his nag in their stables for a change of fodder and find out how the different countries mounted.

Seeing the life that King Leufroid was leading, and convinced that there was not a man at Court who had dared to enlighten the Queen, Sir Gauttier de Montsoreau made up his mind that his first step must be the master stroke of planting his flagstaff straight in that lovely Spanish lady's own paddock. Now, at supper, to show the strange knight courtesy, the King took care to seat him next the Queen, and as first step Gauttier gave her his arm to take her in to the hall, leading her swiftly with brisk step, to get ahead of those behind them so that without delay he could whisper a word on that subject which always delights the ladies, whatever condition they are in. But just think what he chose to say to her, and how straight a path he forged through the cabbage-patch into the ardent bushes of love:

'Madame,' he whispered, 'I know why you have grown so pale.'

'Why?' she asked.

'You are so lovely to mount that His Majesty is up night and day, so that you really abuse your advantages. He will perish of love.'

'What then should I do to keep him alive?' asked the Queen.

'Forbid him to worship at your altar beyond three prayers a day.'

'You are trying to be funny, sir,' she said, 'and in true French style, for the King has told me that the maximum of his prayers, under pain of death, is a short *Our Father* once a week.'

'You have been tricked,' said Gauttier as they sat down. 'I can prove to you that love should say daily mass, vespers and compline, with an occasional *ave* thrown in and that goes for Queens as it does for ordinary women, and those daily services should be fervent, just like those of the monks in their monasteries, though in your particular case the lovely service should never end.'

The Queen flashed at the handsome French knight a glance utterly devoid of irritation. Then she nodded, and retorted:

'In this menfolk are great liars.'

'Well, I myself have a large veracity,' replied the knight, 'and I will show it to you if you like. I guarantee to give you Queenly fare and put you in veritable clover of delight, so that you will make up for lost time, the more so since the King ruins himself on other ladies, whereas I shall reserve all my resources for your service.'

'If the King were to know we had agreed that he would put your head on a level with your feet.'

'Even were I so unfortunate after the very first night, I should count that I had lived a hundred years for the delights I should have taken, for though I have seen all the Courts, I have never seen Queen or Princess your equal in loveliness. But to be businesslike in this matter, if I do not die by the sword, then it shall be by your act, since I am determined to spend my life in our love, supposing life to be spent in the same place through which it is given.'

The Queen of Sicily had never in her life heard such speech as this, and it delighted her heart more than the best church service. This showed clearly in her face, which became scarlet, for Sir Gauttier's words made her blood boil in her veins to such extent that the strings of her lute were agitated and set into vibration by it, resonating in her ears with a pinnacle of overtones, for with their sounds their lutes do fill ladies' bodies with a most delightful confection of that instrument's vibratory nature.

How maddening too to be young, lovely, a Queen, a Spanish woman moreover, and yet ill served! The Queen now conceived great and righteous scorn for the men of the Court who from fear of the King had kept their mouths sealed about this, and she decided that she would avenge herself and with the help of this handsome Frenchman who was so indifferent about life that in the very first words he addressed to her in carefree wise he delighted her by making a suggestion which had she done her duty meant death. Far from doing that, she now squeezed his foot with hers in unmistakable meaning, while out loud she said:

'Sir Knight, let us change the subject, it is bad of you so to attack a poor Queen in her weak spot. Tell me what the ladies of the Court of France are busy with just now.'

Thus the French knight received the delightful intimation that the cat was in the bag. He now began an account of wild and delightful things which throughout supper kept the Court, the King, the Queen and all the courtiers cheerful, so that at last when he, Leufroid declared that he had never laughed so much. They then went out into the gardens, which were the loveliest in the world and the Queen made the knight's stories the excuse to stroll down a grove of flowering orange trees which scented the air most sweetly.

'Lovely, noble Queen,' said good Gauttier at once, 'in all countries I have observed that the cause of the death of love resides in putting the emphasis on so many formal rules of polite behaviour. If you trust me, let us as persons of intelligence agree to love mutually without forcing such wretched formalities on each other. Thereby we need give rise to no suspicion, we can be happy without risk, and a long time too. That is how Queens need to behave, if they are to escape impeachment.'

'Well spoken,' said the Queen. 'But, as I am a novice in this craft, I cannot think however we are to arrange things.'

'Among your women have you not one in whom you can have great confidence?'

'Yes,' she said, 'I have. This is a woman who came with me from Spain. She would jump into the fire for me, as St Laurent did for God, but she is always ailing.'

'Excellent!' cried this charming fellow, 'because of course, you visit her.'

'I do,' said the Queen, 'and sometimes in the night, too.'

'Oho!' said Gauttier, 'I swear to St Rosalie, patron saint of Sicily, I will endow an altar of gold in commemoration of good luck like this!'

'Sweet Jesus!' cried the Queen. 'My happiness is double to know that so charming a lover should also be so fond of the church.'

'Why, dear lady,' said Sir Gauttier, 'today I have two Churches, with a Queen to love in Heaven and another down here on Earth, two loves, moreover, which fortunately do not clash.'

This gentle observation moved the Queen beyond measure. It wanted but little for her there and then to have eloped with this so quick-witted Frenchman.

'In Heaven,' said the Queen, 'the Virgin Mary is very powerful, do make love so that I be like her.'

'Just listen!' cried the King, suddenly, 'talking about the Virgin Mary!'—for he had covertly come to eavesdrop on them, being prompted by a glancing shaft of jealousy directed at his heart by a Sicilian courtier who was furious to see how rapidly this accursed Frenchman was getting into the Royal favour.

The Queen and the Knight, however, had made their arrangements, and everything was already neatly set to trim the Royal bonnet with invisible ornaments. The Frenchman rejoined the company, delighting everybody, then returned home to Pezara to assure his friend that their fortunes were made, for the next night, he would sleep with the Queen. So rapid an ascent dazzled the Venetian, but like the good friend he was he at once concerned himself with the fine scents, the Brabant linen and the other costly articles of apparel to which Queens are used, and with which he armed his dear Gauttier, so that the wrappings might match the magic word within them.

'Oh my friend,' he said, 'are you sure you won't stumble, are you sure you can go it hard enough, serve the Queen well and give her such a good time in her Roguey Castle that she clings to that master wand of yours like a shipwrecked man to his plank?'

'Get away with you, don't you fear, dear Pezara,' cried Gauttier, 'I have some travelling arrears to make up, I shall eat into her like any skivvy as if I were a pack of starving hounds, I'll show her all the tricks of our wenches of Touraine, who are better at love than any others, since they make love and remake it and unmake it to make it again and even when remade still keep on making and have nothing else to do but this job which always needs doing. But let us now agree. Here's how you and I are going to run this island. I shall keep a hold on the Queen, you the King. Before all the courtiers we shall now pretend to be great enemies, so we may split them into two factions under our rule, though in secret we remain friends. Like that, we shall know what they are hatching and shall outdo them, you eavesdropping on my enemies, I on yours. So, in a few days' time let's pretend to have a quarrel and set us one against the other. The cause of our quarrel will be the favour whereby, through the Queen's part, I force you into the King's heart, which will give you supreme power to my detriment.'

The very next day, after having pretended in front of the courtiers to have known her well in Spain, good Gauttier suddenly moved to the Spanish woman's house, and he spent a whole week there. As may be imagined, the good Tourainian now served the Queen as a loved woman is served and showed her so many unknown districts of love, so many French byways, nooks, niceties and comforts, that she nearly went out of her mind and declared that it was certainly only Frenchmen who knew how to make love. And that is how the King was punished for having filled her lovely love barn with chaff.

This supernatural junketing so excited the Queen that she vowed love everlasting to good Montsoreau for awakening her and revealing to her all the sweets of love's delight, and it was agreed that the Spanish woman would take care to remain an ailing woman. The only man the lovers trusted was the Court Master Physician, who was very fond of the Queen. Now, it so happened that this doctor had glottal cords in every detail like Gauttier's, so that by a mere trick of nature these two had the same voice, which greatly amazed the Queen. This Master Physician swore on his life that he would serve the handsome couple well, for he had greatly deplored the King's sad neglect of that lovely woman, and was pleased to know that, rare happening, she was now being served as a Queen should be.

The month up, everything went as the two friends wished. They so contrived to pull the strings which the Queen held as to bring the Government of Sicily into the hands of Pezara as against Montsoreau, whom the King prized for this great knowledge, whereas openly the Queen refused to have anything to do with him, saying she hated the man, he was uncouth. Leufroid now dismissed the Duke of Cataneo, his principal gentleman-in-waiting, and put Pezara in his place. The Venetian meanwhile ignored his friend the Frenchman. Then Gauttier seethed with indignation, complained of treachery and of sacred friendship being scorned—and at once had Cataneo and his faction his devoted servants and pacted with them to overthrow Pezara.

As soon as he was in command, the Venetian, who was a crafty fellow, most skilled in state administration (which is the great *forte* of the Venetians), did wonders in Sicily. He repaired the ports, he attracted traders by alleviations of his own devising and other facilities, he provided many poor folk with work, he attracted skilled men of all the trades, so that there were ample holidays and also idlers and rich men from on all sides, even the East.

In this way the warehouses were crowded out with produce, home and foreign, with galleys and other bottoms coming in regularly from the Orient, all of which made the King the most envied and happy monarch in the whole of Christendom, for in this way his Court became the most famous in Europe, and the excellent policy behind it was due to the perfect agreement of these two men, who got on greatly together, one of them looking after the pleasures of the State, himself directly responsible for those of the Queen. And now she invariably showed a cheerful countenance, for she was well served in the Tourainian fashion and hence enlivened everything with the glow of her good fortune. Gauttier, however, also looked to it to keep the King happy too, finding him ever fresh mistresses and devising countless distractions. Thus, the King to his amazement found the Queen invariably good-tempered, though ever since de Montsoreau set feet on the island he had not touched her any more than a Jew does pork.

Thus busily occupied, their majesties each left the care of their kingdom to the other friend, who conducted the business of administration, directed government institutions, shared out finance, kept a firm hand on the army and all very efficiently too, for he was a pastmaster at nosing out where there was cash and also at getting it into the treasury and preparing the great undertakings mentioned above.

This excellent concord lasted three years, some say four, but the monks of St Benoist failed to establish the exact time, which remains as obscure as the cause of the quarrel between the two friends. Probably it was that the Venetian got the too lofty ambition of reigning without any kind of check or discussion, and totally forgot the services which the Frenchman had rendered him. That is how men do behave in high places for (according to something Aristotle has said in his writings), what ages most rapidly in this world is a good deed (although on the other hand one must remark that dead love is also sometimes very high-smelling).

Hence, trusting in the perfection of friendship of King Leufroid, who now called him his 'partner' and would have taken the shirt off his back to give him, had he asked for it, the Venetian got the idea into his head that he would now rid himself of his confederate by revealing to the King the secret of his cuckoldom and showing him how to undo the Queen's contentment, for he had not the slightest doubt but that, when he knew, the first thing Leufroid would do would be to lop off de Montsoreau's head, following the practice of Sicily in such matters. Thereby good Pezara would acquire all the funds which in secret Gauttier and he had been busily transferring for their joint account to a Genoa bank. This fund had grown greatly, on the one hand by reason of presents from the Queen, who was most generous to de Montsoreau, for she had her own large estates in Spain and had inherited some lands in Italy, and on the other hand by the presentations made by the King to *his* good minister, to whom he gave certain rights over the merchants and other little takings.

Determined now to be crooked, this traitor of a friend took care to ensure that he had got a secure grip on Gauttier's heart, for he knew the Tourainian to be capable of outwitting the most crafty opponent, and then, one night when Pezara knew that the Queen was sleeping with de Montsoreau, who, so skilled was she now in love matters, loved her as if every night were a bridal night, the traitor promised the King he would show him proof of the matter through a hole which had been made in the wardrobe of the Spanish woman, who was still pretending to be on the point of death. To have as good a view as possible Pezara waited till daybreak.

The Spanish woman, however, quick of foot and eye and with a mouth sensitive to the bit, caught the sound of footsteps, stuck out her muzzle, and, through a crack of the closet in which she slept those nights that the Queen had her lover between the sheets, which is the best way of having one's loved one, saw the King, followed by the Venetian. She sped at once to warn the lovers they were betrayed, but the King already had his eye at that accursed hole.

And what did Leufroid see? He saw that lovely, divine lantern which consumes so much oil and lights the world, that lantern which is decked with the most magnificent frills and is most ardent, and which he now found lovelier than all others, because he had so badly lost sight of it that it seemed quite new to him. But the smallness of his spy-hole prevented his seeing anything more, except a man's hand. That hand with sudden modesty all at once hooded the lantern, and then he heard Montsoreau's voice asking: 'And how is this little pet this morning?'—a nicely foolish turn of speech, of usage when lovers play together. For in all countries that lantern is indubitably love's, for which reason men give it countless dainty names, comparing it to the loveliest of things, such as: 'my grenadine, my rose, my shell, my ickle hedgehog, my gulf of love, my treasure, my master, my iddle-one.' Some even go so far as most heretically to call it their 'god'. Ask one acquaintance after another, if you do not believe this!

At this point, by a sign, the woman indicated that the King was there.

'Is he listening?' asked the Queen.

'Yes.'

'Can he see?'

'Yes.'

'Who brought him here?'

'Pezara.'

'Get the doctor up,' said the Queen, 'and get Gauttier away to his room,' and before you could wink she had swaddled her lantern in linen and tinted rags, so you might have thought she had a horrible wound and some frightful inflammation.

When, enraged by what he had heard, the King broke open the door, it was to find the Queen stretched out on the bed exactly as he had seen her through the hole. But with her was the Master Physician, his hand on that swathed-up lantern, and he was saying: 'And how is the little pet this morning?' precisely as the King had heard before. A delightful, humorous way of speaking, for physicians and surgeons do use pet words with the ladies and particularly when they treat that luminous flower their speech simply proliferates such blossoms.

The sight that he thus found left the King as foxed as Reynard in a trap. The Queen started up scarlet with shame, demanding who the man was who dared enter her room at that moment. Then, seeing it was the King, she cried:

'Oh, my Lord, now you have discovered what I was taking such pains to hide from you, namely, that through being so sparsely served by you I have fallen sick of some sort of inflammation of which for dignity's sake I could not complain, but which calls for secret poulticing to extinguish the savage effects of the vital humours. To save my honour and yours, I felt forced to retire here, to my dear Doña Miraflor, who is a great solace in my tribulations.'

After this, the doctor furnished Leufroid with a statement full of Latin quotations gathered like precious grain from Hippocrates, Galen, the Salernian school and others, all to show him how serious for a woman it was to have the field of Venus unattended, and that there was even danger of death for Queens of Spanish make-up, for their blood was very amorous. This argumentation he produced with all gravity, keeping his beard straight and his tongue lengthy, all to give Montsoreau time to get home and into bed. Next the Queen took up the story, to make the King cubit-long speeches, then insisted on taking his arm, with the excuse that to avoid tongues wagging, he ought to relieve the poor sick Spanish woman, who usually took her home.

As they passed the house where Montsoreau lodged, the Queen suddenly jokingly said:

'I say, you really must play a trick on our Frenchie. I bet he's not at home, but out with some lady of the Court. All my ladies are just mad silly about him, and that will give him something to contend with. If you only took my advice, that man would be turned out of Sicily.'

Leufroid at once forced his way into Gauttier's room, to find him sound asleep, snoring like a monk in a choir. The Queen then went home with the King, keeping him at her side, but passed a word to the watch to bring in the nobleman whose place Pezara had taken.

374

Then, cosseting the King as she breakfasted with him, she took the displaced nobleman aside the moment he appeared.

'Set up a gibbet on the tower,' she said, 'then go and seize Pezara and see to it without fail that he is hanged without the chance of writing a word or saying anything to anybody. That is our good pleasure and supreme command.'

Cataneo did not object. While Pezara was busy thinking that his friend Gauttier had already lost his head, Duke Cataneo suddenly appeared, seized him and led him to the tower, whence, at the Queen's window, he saw Montsoreau and the King together with the Queen and some courtiers, so he realized that the man who had served the Queen had come off better than him who had the King in his hands.

'My love,' said the Queen now to her husband, leading him to the window, 'there you behold a traitor who was plotting to take from you that which is dearest in all the world. If you like I will give you the proofs, when you have the time to study them.'

Seeing the preparations for the ultimate ceremony, Montsoreau now threw himself at the King's feet to beg mercy for the man who had been his mortal enemy. By this the King was greatly moved.

'De Montsoreau,' cried the Queen, turning angrily to him, 'do you make so bold as to oppose our good pleasure?'

But the King insisted.

'You are a noble knight,' he said, and he raised de Montsoreau to his feet, 'but you have no idea how bitter an enemy you had in that Venetian.'

Pezara was then very gently constrained 'twixt head and shoulders, the Queen proving his treachery to the King by the statements of a banker of the town as to the immense sums that Pezara had dispatched to the Genoese bank—all of which, of course, was now inherited by Montsoreau.

This lovely, noble Queen died as described in the history of Sicily, namely, in consequence of a laborious childbirth, in which she gave birth to a son who was as great as he was unfortunate in his enterprises. On the assurances of the Queen's physician, the King believed that the damage caused by bleeding in his consort's confinement resulted from the excessively chaste life that she had led, whereupon, reproaching himself with guilt for the death of so virtuous a woman, he did penance and founded the church of the Madonna, one of the loveliest edifices of the city of Palermo. Witnessing the King's sorrow, Montsoreau told His Majesty that when a King brought a Spanish Queen to the throne, he ought to have known that she wanted to be better served than any other woman, Spanish women being so vital that they counted for ten, whereas if he merely wanted a wife for show, he should have drawn one from the north of Germany, where women are cold.

The good French knight now returned to Touraine as a very wealthy man, and there lived a long life, though most silent as to his Sicilian days. He made one trip back to Sicily. This was to aid the son of the monarch in his main enterprise against Naples. But he left Italy again when as recorded in the Chronicles, that handsome prince was wounded.

Apart from the lofty moral contained in the title to this tale, in which it is stated that Fortune is of female sex, and always takes the distaff side, consequently men would do well to serve the ladies well, it shows us that a still tongue is nine-tenths of wisdom. Nevertheless, the monkish author of this story was inclined to draw therefrom another moral, as follows, one which is no less clever; that self-interest, which makes so many friendships, also undoes them. You, however, must choose between these three precepts that which best suits your outlook and your momentary requirements.

VII

About a Beggar known as Old Parchemins

The old chronicler who provided the hemp to weave the present yarn states that he was alive when this happened in Rouen City, which lodged the matter in its archives. In the neighbourhood of that lovely town, where Duke Richard then lived, there was a worthy beggar, Tryballot by name, but to whom folk had added the nickname of *Old Parchemins*—not *parchment* because he was dry and yellow as vellum, though he was, but *par-chemins*—'about the roads'—because he was always everywhere, up hill and down dale, sleeping out with the sky for roof, dressed in rags. In spite of his way of life he was a great favourite in the dukedom. Everybody was accustomed to him, so that if a month went by without him there, holding out his bowl, people would ask: 'Where be the Old Man?' To which the response was always: *Par-chemins!*

This man had had a Tryballot for father who in his time was a real business man, so steady and such a saver that he left a nice little sum to his son. But this the young fellow soon dissipated in gay living, for he was the exact opposite of the old man, who on his way home from the fields always gathered a stick here, another there, piles of scraps of firewood abandoned left and right, and insisted in all seriousness that one should never come home empty-handed.

In this way, he warmed himself in winter at the cost of the heedless, and did well. Everybody recognized what a fine example that was for folk, and indeed, a year before he died nobody any longer left wood about the roads; he had induced the most spendthrift to be frugal and steady. But his son just poured it all away and nohow followed his sound example. The old man indeed had prophesied that this would happen. When from an early age old Tryballot set the lad to scare the birds which came to eat the peas, beans and other crops and to keep off feathered pilferers, particularly the jays, which made a mess of everything, the boy just watched them and enjoyed seeing with what grace they came and went, flying away out of the garden laden, soon to come back again, with merlin eye scouting out the snares and nets, and he laughed loudly when he saw their skill in avoiding these.

Tryballot *père* got enraged, finding two- and often three-sevenths less yield, but though he pulled the lad's ears when he caught him

sitting like a ninny under the hazels, the queer boy was always
astonished by this and returned to his watching of the industry of the
blackbirds, sparrows and other learned peckers, till one day his
father told him he had better model himself completely on them,
because if he went on like that, in his old age he would be obliged
to pilfer as they did and like them would be harried by those who
watched over the fruits of industry.

This was true, seeing that, as already stated, in a very few days he
had dissipated all the crowns which his frugal father had accumulated
during a lifetime. He behaved the same with men as with sparrows,
letting each and all poke their fingers into his purse, while he marvelled at the delightful charming ways in which they said by your
leave.

Thus, he soon ran through it all. When only Old Nick was left,
Tryballot was not in the least troubled, saying that he refused to ruin
himself over mere worldly goods, he had studied philosophy in a
bird school.

After he had had a thoroughly good time, all that remained of his
possessions was a mug bought at Landict fair and three dice, equipment enough anyway for drinking and gambling, especially as he
was not encumbered by furniture, since the great are unable to travel
without coaches, rugs, dripping pans and countless servants. He
would of course have liked to go on seeing his old companions, but
there was not one now recognized him. That left him free to recognize nobody. Seeing how it was, and with hunger sharpening his
teeth, he resolved to assume a station in which he would have
nothing to do and a lot to earn. Asking himself what that might be,
worthy Tryballot recalled the charming ways of the blackbirds and
the sparrows, whereupon he elected that calling in which one takes
a mite from every house.

At once compassionate folk began to give him cash, and Tryballot
was happy. He found begging a good trade. There was no fuss about
laying money out, let alone getting it in. On the contrary, all was convenience, and he plied this trade so cheerfully that he was liked everywhere and afforded many a solace denied the rich. The worthy fellow
watched country folk planting, sowing, harvesting, vintaging, telling
himself that they were partly doing all this for him, for he who had a
pig in his larder owed him a portion, nor was the pork-owner ever
in any doubts about it, and whoever was baking a loaf in her oven
baked one for Tryballot and never questioned it. He took nothing
by force. He did not need to. Everybody had a kind word as they
gave him things.

'I say, Par-chemins, old chap,' they would declare, 'here's something for you, enjoy yourself! Suit you? Right, and take this, true, the cat's been at it, but you finish it off.'

Par-chemins went to weddings, christenings and also funerals, because he was everywhere involving enjoyment or festivity, open or concealed. He kept religiously to the statutes and regulations of his calling, namely: never do a stroke of work, for, had he done so, however little, nobody would have given him anything. And when his belly was full this wise man would stretch out in a ditch or up against a church porch, dreaming of the common weal, that is, philosophizing, like those kindly masters of his, the blackbirds, the jays and the sparrows. And as he begged, he thought much. For if his accoutrements were poor, was that any reason for his mind not to be rich?

His philosophy entertained his clients greatly, for it was his custom, as a form of thanks, to give them the finest aphorisms that he knew. According to him, slippers gave the rich gout, he himself claiming to be fleet-footed because his shoemaker gave him shoes that sprouted in alder groves; diadems rested on headaches, which never afflicted him, his head not being constricted by either cares or other cappings; while jewelled rings hindered the circulation of the blood, whereas, although in pursuance of the laws of beggardom he was sores all over, you may be sure he was really healthier than a babe at christening.

Old Par-chemins had a grand time with other beggars, gambling with his three dice, which he stuck to, as a reminder to spend whatever pence he had, so as always to be poor. For, like the Mendicant Orders, despite his oath he was so well off that one Easter Day when another beggar wanted to pay up a gambling debt incurred that same day, Par-chemins rejected the two crowns offered him, and at evening spent fourteen others on fêting his benefactors, since the statutes of beggary enjoined him to show gratitude to donors.

While he took such trouble to get rid of all that caused others such cares (who, over-encumbered with chattels, brought themselves misfortune), he was happier with nothing in the world than he had been when he still had his father's crowns. As for the conditions of nobility, he was always fit for a title, seeing that he never did aught but what pleased him, and lived nobly without working. Once abed, he would not have risen if you had offered him thirty crowns. He always reached the morrow like anyone else despite this lovely way of life, which, according to Master Plato (whose authority has already been invoked in these pages), certain sages of antiquity also lived in those distant ages.

At last Old Par-chemins reached the age of eighty-two without having known a day when he did not get some coin, and still he had the loveliest complexion you could imagine. Thus he did believe that, had he persisted on the road of worldly wealth, he would have been a ruined man and long since laid to earth. And he may have been right.

In his early youth Old Par-chemins' outstanding quality was his tremendous love of womenflesh, and he alleged that his plentiful love-making was a fruit of his academic work under the tutelage of sparrows of house and hedge. Thereby he was ever ready to lend a woman his aid to count her rafters, a generosity which also had its physical reason in that, doing nothing, he was always ready to do them. The laundrywomen (otherwise known, in those parts, as washerwomen), always said that they never needed starch for the ladies of the gentry while Par-chemins could manage so well. It was his hidden qualities, it was said, that gave rise to the favour he enjoyed throughout the province. Some averred that Lady de Caumont had summoned him to her Castle at first hand to learn the truth about those qualities, and then kept him concealed there for a week to prevent him begging, but the dear fellow escaped into the hedgerows, from fear of being rich.

As he got older, however, this great distiller of vitality found himself neglected, despite the fact that his outstanding ability in loving had suffered no diminution. That unfair fickleness of the female species gave rise to Old Par-chemins' first trouble and the notorious Assay of Rouen to which it is time we came.

In this eighty-third year of his, Old Par-chemins had been compelled to be continent for about seven months, during which he did not meet one single woman of good will, and he told the judge that this was the greatest surprise in his long and honourable life. In this most lamentable state, one day out in the open country, in the lovely month of May, he saw a girl who happened to be a virgin and was tending a herd of cows. The heat was so fierce that this cow-girl had stretched out on the greensward in the shade of a beech, face downwards, as field workers are wont, to take a nap while her cattle ruminated. She was suddenly awakened by the act of the old man, who had by then robbed her of what a poor lass cannot provide more than but once.

Finding herself deprived of maidenhood without having received either pre-notification or pleasure, she shouted out so loudly that the folk working in the fields came and were taken by the lass as witnesses while that damage which is made in brides on their wedding night was still to be seen. She wept and wailed, saying that the intemperate old baboon could have gone and raped her mother and her mother

would not have complained at all. The old man's reply to the field-workers, however, when they raised their mattocks to slaughter him, was that he had been taken short, in a manner of speaking. These folk then quite rightly objected that a man could still take his pleasure without raping maids, which was an indictable offence leading straight to the gallows, and Old Par-chemins was with much commotion taken to Rouen Gaol.

Interrogated by the Provost, the girl deposed that for want of better to do she was taking a nap, and she dreamt of her lover, with whom she had quarrelled because of his wish before marrying her to see if he was up to the job, and in this dream, for fun, she was letting him see if the parts matched up so neither of them should be at a loss when, despite her prohibition, the boy went farther than she had given him permission to go, whereupon, finding more hurt than pleasure, she had awakened to find herself forced by Old Par-chemins, tackling her like a monk with a ham at the end of Lent.

This case excited so much comment in Rouen that the Provost was sent for by the Duke, who was seized with a great desire to know if all he heard was really true. On the Provost's confirmation of it, he ordered them to bring Old Par-chemins to his palace, so he might hear what defence the man could offer.

The poor old fellow then appeared before the Duke and with simple directness described to him what a bad case he had been in through sheer force of circumstance and will of nature, alleging that he had been like any stripling compelled by very imperious desires, that prior to this year he had regularly had his women, but had been fasting for eight months, that he was too poor to resort to prostitutes, that the decent women who formerly had been wont to grant him such solace had become disgusted with his hair, which had had the indecency to whiten, despite the green freshness of his love-making, and so he had been compelled to take his love wherever he found it, namely, through seeing this accursed virgin, who, stretched out full length under the beech revealing the lovely lining of her frock and two hemispheres which, snow-white, had clouded his reason and the fault was therefore the girl's, not his, because virgins should never be allowed to tickle the palate of passers-by through showing them that which earned Venus the appellation Callipygous.

Finally, he said, the Duke ought to know how hard a job a man has at midday to keep his hound on the lead, because it was at that hour that David was smitten with the wife of his master Uriah, and that where a Jewish monarch beloved of God had slipped up, a pauper deprived of satisfaction and reduced to pinching his wherewithal could not well have been at fault and that for that matter he would readily agree to sing psalms for the rest of his life on a lute as a sort of penance, in imitation of the said monarch, who had committed the serious crime of murdering a husband where he had only slightly damaged a country lass.

The Duke appreciated Old Par-chemins' arguments and made the pronouncement that he was a man of good outfit. Then he made the unforgettable decision that if, as this beggar assured him, Old Par-chemins had such great need for love play at his age, he granted him licence to prove it at the foot of the gibbet he was to mount to be hanged, to which the Provost had condemned him unconditionally. Namely, if, 'twixt priest and executioner, with the rope round his neck, he was taken with like fancy, he would be pardoned.

When this decision was made known there was a tremendous crowd to see the old fellow taken to the gibbet. People lined the road thick as at a Ducal procession, and there more women's head-dresses than men's were to be seen. And Old Par-chemins was now saved by a noble lady who also wanted to see how this invaluable raper ended his life. Telling the Duke that religion ordered her to give the fellow a fair chance, she dressed as if for a festive dance, deliberately bringing out two spheres of vital flesh so white that they made the finest linen of a ruff look dingy. Indeed, those lovely love fruits thrust firm and rounded above her bodice like two large apples and made water come to one's mouth, so dainty they were.

This noble lady, one of those who make any man feel he is one when he sees them, curved her lips into a smile for the worthy fellow. Clad in a tunic of coarse canvas, more sure of being in a raping posture after than before his suspension, Old Par-chemins came along, surrounded by guards, very downcast, glancing this way and that, but unable to see anything but coifs. He would, so he then said, have given a hundred crowns for a girl with her petticoats up as that cowgirl had hers, whose fine plump white columns of Venus, which had ruined him and might still save him, he could not forget, yet, being old, could just not remember vividly enough. Then, at the very foot of the gibbet catching sight of the lady's twin cuddles and the lovely V formed by their intermelting curves, his Master John Thomas came into such a state of heat that his canvas smock indicated it quite blatantly by a major rise.

'Come on then, quick, check the event,' cried Old Par-chemins to his guards, 'I have earned my pardon, but I don't answer all that long for the tricky rogue.'

The lady was delighted with this homage, which she said was greater than any rape. The officers charged to lift up the canvas and see the situation thought the old man must be the devil himself, for never in their documents did any man see a capital I as straight as that worthy's stand.

So Old Par-chemins was now paraded in triumph through the town to the Ducal palace and the officers and others swore to the event. In that ignorant age such judicial instrumentation was viewed with such honour that the City of Rouen now provided funds for the erection of a memorial column at the site where this good man had earned his pardon. On this, Old Par-chemins was depicted in stone exactly as he was at sight of that virtuous, pure-hearted lady. The statue was still to be seen when the city of Rouen was taken by the English, and authors of the period recorded the story of it as one of the notable events of the reign.

As for the subsequent offer of the town to provide the good man with wenches to look after his living, clothing and board, the good Duke introduced some order into this by giving the deflowered maid a thousand crowns and marrying her to Old Par-chemins, who now lost that name altogether and was by the Duke made 'Lord of the Manor of Good Parts'.

At the end of nine months his wife gave birth to a boy of perfect form and vitality, born with two teeth, and from this marriage arose the family of the Bonne-C——s or Good-Parts, which later, for reasons of modesty (though very mistakenly), beseeched our beloved King Louis XI to issue them *Letters Patent* to soften the name down into Bonne-Chouse, which might equally be Good-Thing *or* Good-Parts. Good King Louis did indeed argue with Bonne-Chouse that in the State of Venice there was an illustrious family known as the *Coglioni*, whose coat of arms portrayed three bare outfits, but the Bonne-Chouse family argued back to His Majesty that their wives were greatly embarrassed by being thus called before full drawing-rooms of people. The King's reply was that they were losing a lot, for with the name went the part in question.

Nevertheless, he did issue the *Letters Patent*, and since then the family has been known by its new name, and has spread into several provinces.

The first Lord of the Manor of Bonne-Chouse lived another twenty-seven years and had another son and two daughters. He was only rather aggrieved thus to die rich and no longer to seek his living about the roads.

From this you can draw one of the finest of pieces of edification and most solid of moral precepts of all the stories you will ever read (save, of course, others among these hundred glorious Droll Stories), namely, that such a chance happening could never have fallen to the lot of the flabby, shabby rascals at Court or any rich men or others who all dig their graves with their teeth by their excessive guzzling and tippling of wine, which is to the detriment of the joy-making tools, which these much-corporationed men swaddle in expensive cambrics and bury in soft feather-beds while Lord de Bonne-Chouse slept hard. Why, if with their constitutions they had eaten his kale they would have died of the squits. Perhaps this will prompt many of those who read this tale to change their way of life so as to be able to emulate Old Par-chemins in their old age.

VIII

The Unwise Chatter of Three Pilgrims

When the Pope left his good seat at Avignon to dwell in Rome, there were many pilgrims undone who had set out for the County, but now had to cross the high Alps to reach the city of Rome to achieve their aim of pleading for a *remittimus* of their outrageous sins.

At that epoch, on the roads and in the inns were to be seen many men who wore the collar of the Confraternity of Cain. In other words, the cream of penitents, rascals all, leprous of soul, thirsty for a dip in the Papal piscina, laden with gold and other valuables with which to redeem their evil deeds, pay for an indulgence and reward the saints. Bear in mind that those who drank water going, insisted on holy cellar water if any innkeeper again suggested that beverage when they were returning.

At this juncture, among others there were three pilgrims who entered Avignon to their distress, since that city was already mourning the Pope. While they then made their way down the Rhône to reach the Mediterranean coast, of these three pilgrims one, who had his boy of ten years or so with him on a lead, left the company, but when quite close to Milan, showed up again, but now without the boy. So that evening they turned supper into a feast, to celebrate the reunion with this fellow-pilgrim, who, they assumed, had been disgusted with penitence by the absence of the Pope at Avignon.

Of these three romipetal fellows, one originated from the City of Paris, another came from Germany, while this third man, who without doubt had originally intended the trip to further his son's education, had come down from the Duchy of Burgundy, in which as a younger son of the house of Villers-la-Faye, or *Villa in Fago* (his family name being de la Vaugrenand), he held certain fiefs.

Thus foregathering at the landlord's board, the three pilgrims let their tongues wag freely and agreed to finish the journey to Rome in company, so they might resist thieves, night-birds and other cut-throats who made it their business to relieve pilgrims of whatever weighed down their bodies before the Pope freed them of whatever burdened their souls, and after some rounds of drink the three were chatting freely, for the tankard is the master key of discourse. They now each confessed in turn that the reason why they left home was

385

a woman, and the girl who was serving them and watching them drink interjected then that ninety-nine per cent of the pilgrims who put up at that inn were on the road for the same reason.

This made these three wise men reflect how harmful woman is to man. The Baron exhibited the heavy gold chain which he was carrying for safety in his hauberk to reward Saint Peter, and said that his own crime was such that he doubted if ten such chains would redeem it; the Parisian slipped off his gauntlet, to reveal a ring with a white diamond, adding that he was taking a hundred times that value to the Pope, while the Burgundian undid his cap and showed some wonderful pearls, intended to be fine ear-drops for Our Lady of Lorette, though, he confessed, he would far rather have left them round his wife's neck, whereupon the maid remarked their sins must have been as big as those of the Visconti, to which the pilgrims replied that they indeed were so great that in their heart of hearts they had vowed never more in their lives to diverge from the straight and narrow path of virtue—and this apart from any penance the Pope imposed—or however lovely the womenfolk might be.

The young servant then expressed astonishment that they should all three have made the same vow, and the Burgundian added as proof of his seriousness that his vow was in fact the direct cause of his being delayed so at Avignon, for he had been extremely afraid lest despite his tender years his son took the same false road. He had sworn he would let neither beast nor any of his household nor any on his lands misbehave in future. And when the Baron inquired what exactly had happened, this nobleman told them the following:

'You know, I expect that some time ago the good Countess Jeanne d'Avignon issued an Ordinance concerning whores, compelling them to live in a special district, in brothels, with closed shutters, painted red. Well, as with you gentlemen I passed through that accursed district, my lad spotted those houses with closed red painted shutters, and his curiosity was at once whetted. As you know, these imps of ten have an eye for everything, and he plucked at my sleeve and would not stop pestering me till I told him what those houses were.

'To end the matter I said that they were places in which young boys had no business. They should not go into them under pain of death, I said, because they were the workshops where they made men and women, and if anybody not in the secret did go in, his face would be attacked by flying cankers and other wild beasts. The terrified lad stuck close to me all the way to the inn in a great state and did not dare even glance at those brothels.

'But while I was out at the stables later, seeing the horses bedded

down, the young rascal slipped off like a thief and the maid just could not tell me where he had gone. But for all my apprehensions about whores, I was still inclined to trust the regulations which prohibit the entry of boys under age. At supper-time the rascal turned up, as self-assured as ever our divine Saviour was among the learned men in the Temple.

'"Where've you been?" I asked.

'"I've been to those houses with the red shutters," he said.

'"You little rapscallion," I said, "you shall have a good tanning for that."

'He then made such a fuss that I told him that if he confessed all that had happened to him I would spare him.

'"Why," he said, "I took good care not to go inside, because of those flying cankers and other savage things, I just held on to the window grill, to see how they do make men."

'"And what did you see?" I asked.

'"Oh," he said, "I saw a lovely woman just being finished off, all she lacked was a dowel-pin and there was a young joiner ramming that in furiously. As soon as he had finished she looked up, whispered something and gave her manufacturer a kiss."

'"Hurry up and finish your supper," I said, and that same night, I set off back to Burgundy, where I left him with his mother, I was so afraid lest in the next town we reached he rammed his own dowel-pin into a girl.'

'As you say, children often say things like that,' said the Parisian. 'My neighbour's boy once disclosed his father's cuckoldom by something he blurted out. It was like this. One evening, to find out if they taught him religion sufficiently well at school, "What is Hope," I said. "Oh," said he, "he's that Royal Crossbowman, who comes to see us whenever my daddy's out." Bad luck had that the Sergeant of the local Company of the Royal Archers was named Hope. My neighbour was absolutely done when he heard that, though his mind was easier when he took a peep in the mirror, and could not see any horns.'

Here the Baron observed that this boy's remark was really rather apt, since it was quite true that Hope was a hussy who only sleeps with a man when he really lacks something.

'Now tell me this,' said the Burgundian. 'Is a cuckold made in the image of the Almighty?'

'No,' said the Parisian, 'because God was wise, and never married, hence he is eternally happy.'

'All the same,' said the maid, 'before they get their horns cuckolds are fashioned in the God's image, aren't they?'

Whereupon the three pilgrims cursed womankind, averring that they caused all the ills of this world.

'With their backsides gaping like a helmet,' said the Burgundian.

'With their hearts as straight as billhooks,' said the Parisian.

'And why does one see so many men pilgrims and so few women?' asked the German baron.

'Because their damned backsides don't sin,' replied the Parisian. 'Backsides know no father or mother, neither the commandments of God nor those of the Church, neither heavenly nor human laws. Backsides know no doctrine, they are blind to heresy, there's no reproaching backsides, they are innocent of everything, always a-grinning, there's no understanding at all in backsides, that is why I have such a horror of them and profoundly detest them.'

'So do I,' said the Burgundian, 'and I am beginning to grasp the different version of certain lines in the Bible, those about Creation, which a certain scholar has made. In that commentary of his, which in our country we call a *Noël*, you can see the reason for the imperfection of the human female's backside—the thirst of which, in distinction from that of the backsides of the females of other species, no man can slake, such devilish combustion is there in it. For that *Noël* says that while he was making Eve, an ass brayed for the first time in his Paradise, and God turned round to look, and Satan took advantage of it to stick his finger into the creature, because it was too perfect, and like that he made a wound so inflamed that the Lord was at pains to seal it up with a stitch or two, whence our females' initial maidenhood. Because of those stitches, women were to have stayed sealed up for ever, and children be made the same way Lord God made the angels, and that is by means of delight as much superior to our physical delight as Heaven is to earth.

'But, the moment he spotted that sealing up, Satan was furious, and, not to be outdone, what did he do but plucked hold of our Lord Adam by his skin, for, you see, Adam was asleep, and tugged it so hard that he stretched it out just like his own diabolical tail, but as the father of all men was lying on his back, Satan pulled the appendage out forwards, and then by that law governing likes which God instituted to govern his worlds those two diabolical parts conceived a lust for combining together. Thence came man and woman's initial sin and all the sorrows of humankind, because, seeing what Satan had done, Lord God himself was a bit curious to see what would come of it.'

At this the waitress then remarked that there was a lot of sense in what they were saying, because women were indeed vicious, she knew some she would rather have pushing daisies than cropping them, when the three pilgrims suddenly noticed that this girl was quite a beauty, which made them alarmed lest they backslided from their vows, and they took themselves off to bed. But the girl then went to tell her mistress what rascally fellows she had taken in, and all they had said apropos of women.

'Peugh!' said the landlady, 'a lot I care what my customers think, so long as their purses are well lined.'

But when the girl went on to mention the wealth the pilgrims carried, the landlady became very excited.

'Now that is something that concerns all women,' she said, 'let's go and have a word with them, I will take on the two nobles, you can have the burgher.'

The landlady, who was the biggest trollop of a burgess there ever was in the whole Duchy of Milan, went up to the room where Lord de la Vaugrenand and the German Baron were quartered, and congratulated them on their vows. She added that these of course did not cause womenfolk much loss, but that if they were going to fulfil them, they would have to know if they could resist a little temptation. She then made them an offer. She would sleep in bed with them, so curious was she to see if they could fail to mount her, as that had never happened to her any time she had slept in the same bed as a man.

The following day at breakfast, the maid had that ring on her finger, while the landlady had the golden chain round her neck and the pearls in her ears. The three pilgrims stayed in the town about a month, and there spent all the money they had in their purses, agreeing that if they had uttered such slanders on womenfolk, that was only because they had not tasted those of Milan.

When at last he did get back to Germany, the Baron remarked that he was guilty of only one single sin, that was coming home. The Parisian returned all blisters, to find his wife full of Hope. The Burgundian found his mistress so desolate that for all that he had said, he almost killed himself with the consolation he gave her.

This goes to show that in public inns we should keep our tongues between our cheeks.

IX

Innocence

By the double red crest of my cock and the pink lining of my love's black slipper, by the horns of all dear cuckolds and the virtue of their sacrosanct wives, the loveliest accomplishment of man is neither poetry nor painting, music nor castle, neither is it statuary, however well sculped, nor any galley whether under sail or sweep—it is children. Hereby is meant children up to the age of ten, for after that they become men or women and, acquiring reason, are never worth their cost, and the worst are the best.

Indeed, just think now of children, at their play, so unaffected, playing with everything—with shoes, particularly old ones with holes in them, or with kitchen pots and pans! They just drop whatever displeases, they cry for whatever pleases, they gobble up all the nice things and sweetmeats of the house, they nibble away at all stores—once they have cut their teeth—and they are always a-laughing. You will agree that they are utterly delicious, as well as being at once flower and fruit, flowers of love, fruits of life.

Likewise, so long as their minds are not misdirected by life's turmoils, there is in all the world nothing more sacred or more delightful than the things they say, which maintain a very high level of innocence. This is as true as that cattle chew the cud. Hence you will never hear of a man's being as unaffected as a child, for in the unaffectedness of an adult there is always to be found some element of reason, whereas that of a child is utterly candid and pure. All a young mother's delicacy is there. And that comes out in the following tale.

Queen Catherine was at the time only the wife of the Crown Prince, and to be in the good books of her father-in-law, then King, and in a poor state of health, from time to time she used to make him presents of Italian pictures, knowing that he was very fond of them, and being herself a friend of Master Raphael d'Urbino and Masters Primatice and Leonardo da Vinci, to whom she used to send large sums of money, thereby obtaining the cream of their works for her family, for the Duke de Medici then ruled Tuscany, a most estimable region much painted by a Venetian named Titian, who was painter to the Emperor Charles and, when he portrayed Adam and Eve at the moment when God left them to discourse in the earthly paradise, greatly valued, for he did them life-size in the costume of that period, on which it was difficult to go very wrong, seeing that it consisted solely of Adam and Eve's innocence. They were caparizoned solely by the Heavenly grace which enveloped them, a difficult thing to paint because of the colour, but precisely that in which this said master, Titian to wit, excelled.

This particular picture was hung in the poor King's own chamber. He was at the time suffering greatly from the complaint of which he eventually died. This canvas enjoyed a great success at the Court of France. It became the rule for everyone to go to see it, though nobody was really allowed to do so before the King died, but at his wish this picture was after his death left in that room in which he had lived his last days.

Now, one day Princess Catherine took her son François to see the King, with little Margot, and the two children began to chatter without rhyme or reason, as children all do. Now, from time to time these little ones had heard talk of this picture of Adam and Eve, and they had plagued their mother to take them to see it, and as the children sometimes cheered the old King up, one day the Princess did take them.

'You wanted to see Adam and Eve, our first parents,' she said, 'here they are,' and left them staring in utter amazement at Master Titian's picture, while she herself sat down at the Royal bedside, for the King liked watching the little ones.

'Which is Adam?' asked François, nudging his sister Marguerite.

'Silly duffer,' replied the girl, 'you can't tell, they aren't dressed.'

This reply, which delighted the King and their mother, was forthwith sent to Florence in a dispatch from Princess, later Queen Catherine, and as no other writer has ever brought it to light, it shall be a flower blossoming in a corner of this collection of tales, even though it has nothing at all of their particular drollness in it and there is no other moral to be extracted therefrom than that, if one wishes to hear these lovely things, one has first to make children.

X

The Married Life of Fair Imperia

How Milady was Caught in the Nets She used Herself to Spread for Her Love-birds

That great beauty, the Lady Imperia, who since she was the glory of her age forms a glorious introduction to these Tales, was compelled to go to the city of Rome after the holding of the Council of Constance, for the Cardinal of Ragusa had become enamoured of her to the point of losing his biretta and insisted on keeping her at his side. That rapscallion had such panache that he gave her that magnificent palace of hers in Rome. It was approximately at this time that she had the misfortune of being made pregnant by the Cardinal. As everybody knows, this terminated in the birth of a lovely daughter, of whom the Pope humorously remarked that she would have to be christened Theodora, meaning Gift of God. And this is how she was in fact baptized, a girl of marvellous beauty.

The Cardinal made a will in favour of this daughter, whom fair Imperia established in that Roman palace, herself fleeing the city as a treacherous place where babies were made and she had risked ruining her amorous figure's illustrious perfections, namely, its beauteous lines, the curves of her back, all those lovely surfaces and undulating delicacies which put her above all other women of Christendom as much as the Holy Father was above other men.

Nevertheless, all her lovers knew that with the assistance of eleven doctors of Padua, seven master physicians of Pavia and five surgeons from all over the place, who all attended her in childbed, she was saved from any damage. Some even said that childbearing had augmented that delicacy and whiteness of her complexion on which a distinguished member of the Salernian school based a book to show how advantageous a confinement was for the freshness, health, preservation and beauty of the fair sex. In that very learned book it was made clear to the readers that the part which was loveliest to see in Madame Imperia was that which only her lovers were allowed to look upon, and even that was rare, since she did not undress at all for the minor princes of Germany, whom she called Margraves, Burgraves, Electors and Dukes, like a Captain talking of his men.

Everybody knows, too, that when she reached the age of eighteen, fair Theodora, to redeem her mother's loose life, decided to become a nun and bequeath all her worldly goods to the Convent of St Claire. With this in mind she had recourse to a Cardinal, who prepared her for her dedication. However, that bad shepherd found his ewe-lamb so marvellously beautiful that he tried to possess her, when, rather than be contaminated by the said ecclesiastic, Theodora stabbed herself to death, an event recorded in contemporary histories which greatly alarmed the City of Rome and caused universal mourning, such a favourite was the daughter of Madame Imperia.

When this took place, that noble courtesan returned to Rome in great grief, to mourn her poor daughter, reaching the city in her thirty-ninth year, which year, according to the authorities on the subject, was the most flourishing period of her remarkable beauty, everything in her then being at perfection, as in a ripe fruit. Grief made her very dignified, also very spiteful to any who suggested love to her in order to dry her tears. The Pope himself called at her house to admonish her for this, but she maintained her mourning, declaring her intention to give herself to God, since so far no man had ever really satisfied her, though she had known many, for in the end they had all tricked her, even a certain little priest whom she had worshipped like a shrine, but that Almighty God would never do.

This decision of Imperia's made everybody so uneasy, for she was the delight of an untold number of noblemen, that at last when people met in the street the first thing they asked each other was: 'What's the latest about Madame Imperia? Is she going to deprive the world of love?'

Ambassadors wrote home about it. The Emperor of the Romans himself was greatly upset, for at one time, for eleven weeks on end, he had quite lost his head with Lady Imperia, and even then only tore himself away to go to the wars, and still loved her as much as the most precious part of his body which, to him, he said, despite the different opinion of his courtiers, was his sight, since that embraced the whole of his darling Imperia at once.

In this extremity the Pope sent for a Spanish doctor and took him round to call on fair Imperia, and with arguments based on and tricked out with quotations from both Greek and Latin authors this physician with great adroitness proved to her that so much weeping and vexation diminishes beauty and it is through the opening of grief that wrinkles slip in.

Backed by the doctors of rhetoric of the Holy College, this argument resulted in the palace being opened up that very evening. The younger Cardinals, the Foreign Envoys, the very rich and all the leaders of Rome society came, crowding the drawing-rooms and conducting themselves most festively. The lesser townsfolk meanwhile lit bonfires and thus the whole world fêted the return of the Queen of Pleasure to her labours—for at this time Imperia was the sovereign of love.

Artists of all kinds were very fond of her, because she spent considerable sums of money on a church in the city, where the tomb of Theodora was to be seen. This was eventually destroyed in the sack of Rome, in which that traitor Constable Bourbon fell, for the holy maid had been laid in a coffin of heavy silver-gilt, which the accursed soldiery were set on acquiring. This church, it was said, cost more than the pyramid built in an earlier age by Lady Rhodepa, an Egyptian courtesan, one thousand eight hundred years before the advent of our Divine Saviour, which is evidence of the antiquity of that delightful calling. How lavishly the wise Egyptians paid for their delights, and how everything does tend to dwindle, seeing that for a teston of silver a chemise-ful of white flesh is yours today in Petit-Heuleu Street in Paris. Abominable, isn't it?

Never had Lady Imperia seemed so beautiful as the night of that first party after her mourning. All the Princes, Cardinals and others present said she was worthy of the homage of the whole world, which was that night in her palace represented by a nobleman for every known country, thereby amply demonstrating that in all places it is love that is the queen of all things.

The Ambassador of the King of France, a younger son of the de l'Isle-Adam family, arrived late, although, never having set eyes on Lady Imperia, he was most curious to have sight of her. This de l'Isle-Adam was a handsome young knight who had risen rapidly in the favour of the French monarch, at whose court he had a mistress whom he loved with infinite affection, she being a daughter of the Montmorency family, whose estates adjoined those of the l'Isle-Adams. Without a penny to his name, this younger son had been charged with a number of missions in the Duchy of Milan, which he had accomplished with such circumspection that as reward he had now been sent to Rome, where he was to further those negotiations of major importance of which historians have written amply.

Thus, though penniless, poor little de l'Isle-Adam was confident that he had made a good start. Though not very tall, he was well fashioned, straight as a column, dark, his brown eyes shot with sunlight and the beard of an old legate to whom nobody is going to sell a pup. This sharpness of intelligence of his was, however, cloaked under the air of being but an innocent boy, which made him as charming and gentle as a laughing slip of a girl.

However, the moment this young blue-blood strode into her mansion and she set eyes on him, Lady Imperia felt an overmastering fancy begin to bite and pluck at her lute, producing a resonant note that she had not heard for a very long time. Indeed, so intoxicated with real love was she at once at the sight of that freshness of youth that had it not been for her imperious dignity she would there and then have kissed those bonny cheeks which gleamed like ripe apples.

Make no mistake about it, the women we pronounce modest, and ladies with armoured petticoats too, are ignorant all round about what love really is, since, like the Queen of France, who believed all men's breath must stink, like the King's did, they stick to one only, whereas a great courtesan like Imperia knew men thoroughly, having handled a great number of them. Once in her retreat a man had no more shame than a puppy tumbling with its mother, telling himself that he would not see her long, he concealed nothing from her. Imperia had often lamented that lack of restraint, and sometimes said that whereas some folk suffered because others discharged their sorrows on them, she suffered rather from discharging of pleasures.

Herein was the reverse of her medal. And bear in mind here that often enough a suitor needed a whole mule-load of crowns to buy a night in her bed. Some overweening ones were even driven to slitting their throats by her refusal to countenance them. Thus it was a real carnival for her to feel again a youthful fancy, just like that she had felt for that little priest, the story of whom heads this collection, but since she was now older than in those fine days, love bit the more deeply into her and flourished so that it was like a conflagration which lost no time making itself felt. Indeed, her skin felt like that of a scorched cat, so much so that she felt an urge to leap at this newcomer and bear him off to her nest as a kite does its prey, but, though with great difficulty, she restrained herself beneath her petticoats, and when de l'Isle-Adam approached to pay his respects, drew herself very erect and bore herself with her most queenly grandeur, as a woman will when she feels the quick of love within her heart.

Indeed, her *hauteur* towards this young Ambassador was so marked that some guessed at once that she had something she wanted him to do, which was double-talk, of course, after the fashion of the time. He, however, knowing how well his own mistress loved him, was little concerned whether the great courtesan was cold or hot, and he comported himself as airily as a goat off the hobble.

This vexed Imperia greatly and she changed her tune at once, switching from moroseness to being gracious and graceful. Joining him again in conversation, she fluted her voice and sharpened her glance, her head a little to one side, her sleeve brushing him close. She called him her dear Mr Ambassador, she knotted him all about with snaky speech, her fingers played in the palm of his hand and then at last, close-up, she smiled, but, never dreaming that such small fry as himself could suit her, since he was penniless and had not a clue that to her his good looks were worth all the world's wealth, he was just not caught in the net she spread and merely continued, hand on hip, to exchange light banter with her.

This failure to grasp her fancy was such irritation to the lady's heart that the initial conflagration spread to her whole being. If you doubt this, that is because you have no notion of Lady Imperia's calling, for by the mere plying of her profession she might be compared to a hearth on which so many jolly fires had blazed that its chimney was well sooted-up, and in such a state that though a hundred bundles of damp firewood might have smoked away without anything untoward happening, one really good flare could set it all ablaze. So there she was, all aglow inside from top to bottom, in a frightful state, in fact, and nothing capable of putting it out but the waters of love.

Young de l'Isle-Adam left the Imperia mansion without having even noticed the heat. Desperate when he left, My Lady lost her head completely, to such an extent indeed that amid all the whirl of the party she sent a messenger post-haste to find him and invite him to sleep with her. You may be quite sure she had never committed such a craven act before, neither for King nor Pope nor for Emperor, for the high price of her body resulted from the serfdom in which she kept all men, so that the lower she sank the higher she rose.

So the disdainful young fellow was now informed by Imperia's first maid, who was a clever ambassadress herself, that he would have a glorious reception in bed, for without doubt the Lady Imperia would entertain him with her daintiest turns of love. Therefore, very pleased at so unforeseeable a piece of luck, de l'Isle-Adam returned to the rout.

When the French envoy reappeared, just as everyone had seen her lose colour when he left, now an oecumenical delight swept through the whole party, everybody being relieved to see she really was resuming her lovely life of loving. An English Cardinal who had sipped from more than one dainty-bellied flagon and would have liked to sample lovely Imperia too, went across to de l'Isle-Adam and whispered:

'Ply her hard with the staff, so she never escapes you.'

When he rose next morning, the Pope was given an account of this night, and his immediate reaction was: '*Laetamini, gentes, quoniam surrexit Dominus*', a quotation which the elder Cardinals found an abominable profanation of Holy Scripture, seeing which, the Pope gave them a severe dressing-down, and took advantage of the occasion to point out that though they might be good Christians, they were bad politicians. The fact was, he counted on lovely Imperia to tame the Emperor and with that in view was prepared to water her with flattering remarks.

The lights of the Imperia mansion extinguished, golden flagons strewn empty about and drunken types sleeping it off on the carpets, Imperia entered the room in which she slept, leading her dear lover-elect by the hand and very pleased with herself, later admitting that her fancy was so stiff that she nearly lay down where she was on the floor like any beast of burden and told him to tread her as hard as he could. De l'Isle-Adam now undressed, and climbed into bed as if at home, seeing which, the great lady bounded over the tail-board, trampling in her half-loosened skirts, coming to her man with a violence which astounded her maids, who knew her as a woman usually as circumspect in bed as ever any was.

Their astonishment was to spread to the whole country, for the two lovers remained in that bed for nine days on end, eating and drinking there and playing crocquet-cricket in masterly and superb style. Imperia confided to her woman that she had lit on a veritable phoenix of love, rising fresh to every blow. All Rome, all Italy, talked of nothing else but this defeat of Imperia's, who had always vowed she would never let any man have the better of her and scorned them all, even the Dukes, for when it came down to Burgraves and Margraves, all she gave them was her train to hold, saying that if she had not trampled on them, they would on her. To her maids she confessed that, in distinction from the other men she had supported, the nicer she was to this child of love the more she came to like being so and could never more do without him, neither his lovely eyes, which blinded her, nor his coral branch, for which she always had an appetite and a dry tongue.

She also said that, had he wanted it, she would have let him suck her blood and nibble her bubbies, which were the loveliest in the world, even cut her locks, of which she had only given away one, to her good Emperor of the Romans, who wore it at his throat like a precious relic. Finally, she asserted that it was only from that night that her real life began, this man really did excite her to it, he changed her blood three times before a fly could fart.

When these pronouncements became known, everybody was very vexed. The very first time she came out, she told the Roman ladies she would die a bad death were she abandoned by de l'Isle-Adam. Like Queen Cleopatra, she would sting herself with a scorpion or an asp. Finally, she said very frankly that she was saying farewell for ever to all her wild fancies and would show the whole world what virtue was by relinquishing her fine realm for that of this Villiers de l'Isle-Adam, whose servant she would rather be than any Queen of Christendom.

The English Cardinal protested to the Pope that this grant to one single man of true love in the heart of a woman who was the joy of all men was a shocking deprivation, and by an *in partibus* decree the Holy Father ought with fourfold nullity confound this marriage, which was world robbery. But the love of this poor girl, who thereby avowed the misery of the life she had hitherto led, was so beautiful a thing and so moved the bowels of the most vicious of men that she silenced all talk and everybody forgave her her good fortune.

One day of Lent, good Imperia made her household fast and ordered them to confess and return to God, then went to the Pope, to fling herself at his feet and, thus prostrate, so repented her love-life that he gave her remission of all her sins, in confidence that this absolution of the Pope would restore to her soul the virginity that she could not count on offering her dear one. One is however forced to believe that the papal font did have some virtue, since the poor young man was caught in the toils and so well limed that he now thought himself in the seventh heaven and abandoned his representation to the King of France and his love for the Montmorency girl too, to marry Imperia. Such was the effect of the clever devices of that great light-o'-love, once her experience was turned to the profit of a sound affection.

The Lady Imperia then gave a regal wedding breakfast, to bid her pets and her petters all farewell. The wedding itself was magnificent, attended by all the princes of Italy. It is said that she possessed a million gold crowns. This was such a vast sum that everybody, far from blackening l'Isle-Adam's name, showered him with praises, for it had been made abundantly clear that neither Imperia nor her young husband cared a thing about this fortune which lay between them, so preoccupied were they with another one in like position.

Their marriage was blessed by the Pope, who said it was grand to see a loose virgin come to such an end, returning to Almighty God through the gateway of matrimony. Nevertheless, during that final night on which it was still permitted to all to look upon that queen of loveliness, about to become a simple lady of the manor in the French lands, there were a considerable number of men who lamented those nights of rich laughter, those *medianoches*, those masked balls, those delightful routs and those gentle hours when any man could unburden his heart to her. Finally, they lamented the many advantages which that superb creature presented, for now she

seemed more enticing than ever she had been in the springtide of her life, for her exceeding conflagration of heart made her glow like a sun.

Many were sorrowed by her having had the saddening fancy to end her days living decently. To these, however, Lady de l'Isle-Adam replied humorously that after twenty-four years of busy life in the public service she merited a rest. Some remonstrated that though the sun was a long way off, everybody could warm themselves in its light, whereas they would now see nothing at all of her. To these she replied that she would still have a smile for any lords who came to see how she played the party of a lady of society. To this the English ambassador remarked that she was capable of anything, even of pushing virtue to the supreme point.

She left a present for every one of her friends and considerable sums for the poor and suffering of Rome, then to the convent in which her daughter was to have been a nun and to the church she was building she relinquished the money Theodora left and that which she herself had received from the above-mentioned Cardinal of Ragusa.

When the married couple set out, they were accompanied a considerable part of the way by knights in deep mourning and even by common folk, who all wished her a thousand good wishes, for Lady Imperia had never restricted herself to the great and had been universally kind to the poor. Thus was this lovely queen of love-making fêted on her passage through all the towns of Italy, where rumour of her conversion had spread, and everyone was curious to see a husband and wife who were such lovers, a rare sight. Many princes received the handsome pair at their courts, saying they had to show this Queen honours who had been brave enough to renounce her authority over everybody to become a simple married woman.

There was however one bad rascal, and this was the Duke of Ferrara, who told young de l'Isle-Adam that he had acquired his great fortune cheap. At this first insult, Imperia showed her dignity of heart, for she gave away every penny she had had from her love-birds and spent it on decorations to the dome of St Maria del Fiore in Florence, which made a laughing-stock of d'Este, for he too, despite his small resources, had said he would build a church, so you may imagine that his brother the Cardinal told him off roundly for such empty boasting.

All Imperia retained were her personal belongings and what since her departure the Emperor had given her out of pure friendship, which anyway was a considerable amount. Young de l'Isle-Adam also fought a duel with the Duke d'Este, in which he wounded him. Thus neither Lady de l'Isle-Adam nor her husband could be reproached in any way. That chivalrous gesture of de l'Isle-Adam's was received with great acclaim wherever he passed on his way home, and especially in Piedmont, where the festivities were most boisterous. The poetry—sonnets, epithalamia and odes—which the poets then composed have been included in more than one collection, but any poetry was bound to be poor compared with her who, according to a statement of Master Boccacio, was poetry itself.

In this round of festivities and gallantry the palm must however go to the good Emperor of the Romans who, aware of the folly of the Duke of Ferrara, sent an emissary to his love bearing letters in Latin in which he said he loved her greatly for herself and was very glad to hear she was happy. He said that he was only sad because all her fortune was not of himself, but he had near lost the right to make her presents, but if the King of France was frigid towards her, he would hold it an honour to acquire one like her husband in his Holy Empire and would grant him whatever dukeries he cared to choose in his domains.

Lovely Imperia's reply was that she knew the Emperor was very great, but that even if she had to endure a thousand insults in France, she intended to end her days there.

II. How this Marriage Ended

Not knowing whether she would be received or not, Lady Villiers would not go to the French Court, but lived in the country, where her husband set her up in good style by the purchase of the manor of Beaumont-le-Vicomte, which gave rise to that naughty quip of Rabelais's in his very fine book. This younger son of the de l'Isle-Adams further acquired the manor of Nointel, Carenelle Forest, St Martin and other places adjoining Isle-Adam, where lived his brother, also a Villiers. These acquisitions made him the most powerful lord in Isle-de-France and the County of Paris.

He now bent himself to the erection of a marvellous castle, Les Beaumont, subsequently destroyed by the English. This he adorned with fine furniture, hangings, exotic rugs, chests, paintings, statues and *objets d'art* of his wife's, she being a great connoisseur, whereby this mansion came to be the equal of the most magnificent castles known.

The couple led a life which everybody envied so much that at Paris and Court it was the sole topic to talk of their marriage, the lavishness of Beaumont Castle and above all the perfect, loyal, gracious, pious way of life of his wife, whom by sheer habit some still called *Lady Imperia*, but who was no longer haughty or cutting as steel, but had the calm virtues and qualities of a married woman and could have given points to any Queen. She was much beloved of the Church for her great piety, seeing that she had never forgotten God, for as she used humorously to say, she had had a lot of commerce with all sorts of churchmen, abbots, bishops, cardinals, priests, who had all sprinkled a deal of holy water in her little vessel and behind the bed-curtains had laboured her eternal salvation.

The praise spoken of this lady had such an effect that the King travelled to Beauvoisis to have a chance to see the wonder, and then honoured Sir Villiers by sleeping at Beaumont Castle. Indeed, he stayed three whole days and a royal hunt was arranged, with the Queen and all the Court. Rest assured that His Majesty was astounded, as were also the Queen and her ladies-in-waiting, by their lovely hostess's fine manners. Indeed, Imperia was declared a lady of courtesy and beauty and first the King, then the Queen, then everybody else complimented de l'Isle-Adam on having chosen such a wife. The essential modesty of the lady of the house did more than any haughtiness would have done, since she was now invited to Court and everywhere else, so noble was her greatness of heart, so absolute her violent love for her husband. Yet you may be sure that though her charms were concealed by the wrappings of virtue, they were none the less lovely for that.

The King now gave the vacant post of Lieutenant Royal of Isle-de-France and the Provostship of Paris to his former ambassador, with the title of Count Viscount Beaumont, which established him up as Governor of the whole province and set him well up at Court.

That visit, however, also caused a wound at Lady de Beaumont's heart, for a wretched man who was envious of this undivided fortune asked her jokingly if Beaumont had ever told her of his earlier dalliance with the Montmorency girl, who was then twenty-two, having been but sixteen at the time of that Rome marriage, but was still unmarried, rejecting any suggestion at all of marriage, saying she would die in her petticoats of mortification, because she was unable ever to forget the lover stolen from her, and intended to enter Chelles Convent some day.

In all the six years of her good fortune, Madame Imperia had never once heard that name, which she took as a sign that she was truly loved. Bear in mind here that all these years had slipped by as if they were but a day, that both husband and wife felt it was but yesterday that they had married, that every night was a bridal night, and that if official business ever took the Viscount temporarily away from his wife, he was most depressed, unable to lose her from mind, nor she him.

The King, who was very fond of the Viscount, also said something which was like a thorn embedded in the heart, remarking one day: 'Have you no children?' To which Beaumont replied like any man touched on the raw: 'Sire, my brother has, so our line is assured.' It was just after this that it happened that both his brother's sons were suddenly taken from this world, one by falling from his horse in a tournament, the other by illness, while the brother was so cut up that he too died, so fond of the boys had he been. Hence now the Viscounty of Beaumont, the Carenelle, Martin and Nointel acquisitions and all the estates about them were joined to the de l'Isle-Adam estates and the adjoining forests and the younger son suddenly became head of the house.

Imperia was now forty-five and still capable of child-bearing, so fine was her body, but she did not conceive. Then, seeing the de l'Isle-Adam line thus extinguished, she craved for children. But as for seven years she had not had the slightest hint of pregnancy, she now, on the advice of a clever physician whom she brought from Paris, got the idea that this failure to conceive came from the fact that both of them, she and her husband likewise, still more lovers than husband and wife, took too much pleasure in the act and that thereby pregnancy was prevented.

Hence for some time, good lady, she strove to remain as unmoved as a hen under the cockbird, for this doctor had pointed out that in the natural state the creatures never failed to produce, which was, he said, because their females made no use of any artifice, love-play, tendernesses or any of the countless ways in which women dress the Poissy olives. That, said Imperia, was why they were called *brutes*, but she nevertheless took an oath never more to play with her beloved coral branch and to consign to oblivion all the love delights she had invented.

Alas, even while she lay stretched out as sober as that German woman whose modest bearing resulted in her husband mounting her when she was dead, when, poor baron, he went to ask the Pope for absolution and the Pope issued that famous Encyclical in which he implored the ladies of Franconia to move just a little when in the act so there might never be repetition of that sin, Lady de l'Isle-Adam did not conceive, and she then fell into a profound melancholy.

Next she began to notice how thoughtful her husband sometimes was, which she observed when he thought he was not seen, for then he would shed tears for having no fruit of his love. Soon the two of them mingled their tears together, for all in this marriage was in common and as they were always together, the thought of one was the thought of the other.

If in those days Imperia happened to see a poor man's child she died of grief and was inconsolable for a whole day after. Seeing this great sorrow, de l'Isle-Adam gave orders that all children were to be kept out of the way of his wife, while to her he addressed the sweetest of words, such as suggesting that children often turned out badly, to which she replied that had they who loved each other so ever made a child, it would have been the loveliest in the world. He argued that their sons would have stood just as much chance of losing their lives as those of his poor brother. To this she replied that she would never let them away from her skirts more than a hen its chicks, which are always under its eye.

In short, she had an answer to every false argument.

Imperia now called in a woman suspected of necromancy and said to have made study of these mysteries, and this female told her that she had often seen women who did not conceive, despite their study of how to give love satisfaction, do so at last in animal fashion, which is the most simple. So then Imperia made a point of doing it like the brute animals, but from this too came no increase in girth, her belly remaining white and firm as marble.

She returned then to the physical science of master physicians of Paris, and also sent for a famous Arab doctor, then come to France to furnish new knowledge. This doctor, trained in the school of a certain Master Averroës, made her this cruel pronouncement: that she had received too many men in her boat and, as was her wont, in pursuing the lovely craft of love had too greatly yielded up to their whims, so that thereby she had for all time ruined certain vines upon which Mother Nature had affixed a number of ova which, fecundated by the males, were hiddenly incubated, to hatch out in the confinement of any female with breasts, which was shown by the caul some babies brought with them into the world.

This argument, however, seemed so mammalianly stupid, brutish, idiotic and counter too to the Holy Scriptures, in which it is laid down that the majesty of man is made in the image of God, in short, it seemed quite contrary to the systems then followed, to common sense and to good sound doctrine, that the doctors of Paris made much mock of it. The Arab physician then left the school, where his master, Averroës, was never more considered.

The doctors then told Imperia, who had come secretly to Paris, that she should go on in her own way, as during her life of love she had had fair Theodora by the Cardinal of Ragusa, that the right to make babies was woman's so long as she had periods and took care to multiply the chances of conception. This advice seemed to her so wise that she now multiplied her victories again, but this was only to multiply her defeats, for all she got was flowers without fruit.

The poor thing in her affliction then wrote to the Pope, who was very fond of her and had sent her his condolences, and he replied in a gracious homily writ in his own hand that where human science and earthly things failed one must turn to Heaven and beg the mercy of God. She then decided to go barefoot, with her husband, to Notre-Dame de Liesse, famous for her intervention in a like case, and made a vow to build a magnificent cathedral there in gratitude for a child. But though she tortured and ruined her pretty feet, she conceived no more than the most violent mortification, so great that some of her lovely locks fell out and others turned white.

At last the faculty to make babies was withdrawn altogether from her, whence certain dense humours issued from her hypochondria, and sallowed her complexion. She was then forty-nine years old, living at her castle of l'Isle-Adam, where she grew thin as a leper in a lazar-house. The poor dear thing became so much the more desperate since de l'Isle-Adam was still loving and kind to her who had so failed in her duty through having formerly been too much known by men, and was now no more, she said scornfully, than a pot to cook chitterlings in.

'Ah!' she said one evening when her thoughts rent her heart, 'whatever Church, King and all may say, Lady de l'Isle-Adam is still the evil Imperia.'

Indeed, she fell into fits of terrible despair when at the sight of that nobleman in his prime, with everything a man could desire, great properties, Royal favour, unparalleled love, a wife without pair, pleasure in love such as no woman could equal, yet a failure in the dearest point of all to the head of a family, namely, the acquisition of an heir.

Thinking this, Imperia longed to die, having in mind how noble and great he had been towards her and how greatly she had failed in her duty by never giving him a child and now being incapable of so doing. She concealed her sorrow in the depths of her heart and conceived a devotion worthy of her great love. To implement that heroic intention she became still more loving, took extreme pains about her looks and employed learned precepts for preserving the beauty of her body, which radiated incredible light.

Towards this time, the Duke de Montmorency overcame his daughter's revulsion from marriage and there was much talk of an alliance with a Baron de Châtillon. One day Imperia, being about ten miles from Montmorency, sent her husband out hunting and rode over to the castle where the Montmorencys were living at the time. Reaching the grounds, she strolled through them, instructing a man to inform the young lady of the house that a certain unknown lady had something very urgent to tell her, would she grant an interview and come out to see her. Very troubled by what she was told of the loveliness, the courtesy and the suite of the unknown woman, the girl rushed out into the park, and there met her rival, though without knowing who it was.

'My dear,' said the poor lady, tears springing to her eyes to see the girl as lovely as she herself had been, 'I know you are being pressed to marry de Châtillon, though you still love de l'Isle-Adam. Have confidence in the prophecy I am now going to make you, that the man you have loved all this time, who let you down merely because of an ambush which would have trapped an angel, will be freed from his ageing wife before the fall of the leaves. Thus your steadfast love will have its crown of flowers. So do have the steadfastness to refuse this union that is now mooted, and you will enjoy your loved one. Give me your word to love de l'Isle-Adam well, for he is the most gracious of men. Never do him any hurt, but tell him to show you all the secrets of love which Lady Imperia invented, for, since you are still young, if you practice them it will be easy for you to erase memory of her from his mind.'

Lady de Montmorency was so astonished that she did not know what to reply and let that queen of loveliness depart, then assumed she must be a fairy, till a workman told her that the fairy was Lady de l'Isle-Adam. Though the whole incident seemed inexplicable, the girl did tell her father that she would not give her reply on the proposed marriage till the autumn was over, so natural is it for Love to marry Hope, despite the ridiculous false jewels that that false if gracious companion gives it to swallow as honey-cakes.

During the month of vintage, Imperia would not let her husband leave her side and employed her most fiery delights, so one might have thought that she wanted to ruin him, since for his part de l'Isle-Adam thought it was a new wife he had to do with every night. And when they wakened, his dear spouse would beg him never to forget that love which they now accomplished to absolute perfection. Then, to learn the truth what her dear one really thought, she said:

'My poor dear, we were not wise to marry, a young fellow as you were, in your twenty-third year, and an old woman getting on for forty.'

He replied that he had been so fortunate that he had made a thousand men envious, that even at her age there was not her equal among the younger women, and that if ever she did grow old, he would love her wrinkles, and was sure that in the grave she would be beautiful and her bones lovable.

To such replies, which brought moisture to her eyes, she responded maliciously one morning with the statement that the Montmorency girl, too, was very beautiful and very true. This made de l'Isle-Adam say that she put him at great disadvantage, thus reminding him of the one bad thing he had done in his life, by letting down his first sweetheart, love for whom was extinct in his heart.

These frank words prompted her to take him in her arms and hold him very tight, for she was deeply moved by his answering so firmly where another would have faltered.

'Dear love,' she said, 'for some days past I have been feeling heart stabs which since my youth have threatened to be my end, an opinion which that Arab doctor confirmed. If I die, I want you to make me the most binding oath of a knight, to take the Montmorency girl for wife. And, indeed, so sure am I that I am soon going to die that I leave all I have to your family on condition you marry her.'

Hearing this, the colour left de l'Isle-Adam's cheeks and he felt weak at the mere thought of being for ever separated from his dear wife.

'Yes, my treasure of love,' she said, 'God has punished me where I sinned, for the great delight I always experience has dilated my heart and, according to the Arab doctor, enfeebled its vessels which must one day rupture in a moment of supreme transport. But then, I always have begged God to take my life in my present age, so I might never see my beauty ruined by time.'

That great, noble woman then saw how much she was loved. That was how she had obtained the greatest sacrifice of love ever made on this earth. She alone knew what attraction there was in the fondlings and follies and delicacies of the marriage bed, such that poor de l'Isle-Adam would have rather died than consent to be robbed of the love delights which she confected there. To this admission of hers that in a frenzy of love her heart would burst, the chivalrous man flung himself on his knees at her feet and told her that to preserve her he would never seek love-making any more, that he would live happy merely to see her and feel her beside him, satisfied with kisses planted on her head-coif or by brushing his lips on the hem of her skirts. At this she dissolved into tears and said she would rather die earlier than lose a single one of her wild rosebuds, that she would perish as she had lived, since it was her fortune that she knew, without need to utter a word to him, how to contrive that a man rode her when it was her whim.

Here it must at once be indicated that the above-mentioned Cardinal of Ragusa had given her a precious gift which that old rascal succinctly named *in articulo mortis*. You will forgive those three words of Latin, they originate from the Cardinal. It was a phial of fragile glass made in Venice in the size of a bean, containing so subtle a poison that if one broke it with one's teeth death came suddenly and painlessly. The Cardinal had obtained the phial from Signora Tophana, that excellent poison maker of Rome. The phial was concealed in a hollowed-out ring in which a number of gold plates protected it from everything.

Poor Imperia put that glass between her lips more than once without bringing herself to bite, so greatly did she revel in the coming which she counted as her last, and she indulged now in going through all the ways of making love before biting the glass, telling herself meanwhile that when she knew which was the most perfect of all those delights, she would crush the phial.

The poor thing departed this life in the night of the first day of October. A great clamour was then heard in the woods and in the clouds of heaven, as if all the Cupids had cried out: *The Great Cnut is dead!* in imitation of Pagan gods, which at the advent of the Saviour of Mankind fled into the skies, with the cry: *Great Pan has passed away!*, a cry overheard by certain mariners sailing the Euboean Sea and preserved by a Father of the Church.

Imperia died unspoiled, so careful had the Lord been to fashion in her an irreproachable model of a woman. It is said that by reason of the proximity of the burning wings of Pleasure, which wept and groaned over her, she had a wonderful complexion in death.

Her husband went into profoundest mourning, never suspecting that she had died to free him from a barren wife, for the doctor who embalmed her breathed not a word on the cause of her death. Her lovely act, however, was disclosed six years after the marriage of de l'Isle-Adam to Lady de Montmorency, for that nitwit one day told him all about Madame Imperia's visit to her, after which the poor wretched nobleman declined into a melancholy and died, incapable of banishing memory of the delights of love which such a nincompoop was incapable of restoring. Thereby he gave proof of a truth asserted at the time, that Imperia was a woman who never did die in any heart in which she had reigned.

The moral of this is that virtue is only known to those who have practised vice, because there are very few among decent women who would thus have left the world, in whatever lofty regions of religion you seek them.

Epilogue

Oh, you naughty girl—yes, you, told to entertain the house!—in spite of all you have been told, so many times, you have gone and wallowed in that midden of melancholy, fishing out Bertha from it, to come back with your hair all loose, like a girl who has seduced a platoon of soldiers! Where are those lovely gold pins with little bells, where are those Arabian fancies in filigree flowers? Where have you left your scarlet cap with its precious bells, which cost a wealth of pearls? Why spoil your black eyes with pernicious tears, they are so nice when a salty yarn makes them twinkle so the popes would all forgive the spiciness, provided it is cloaked in laughter, they feel the ivory of your teeth steal their souls and the delicate pink of your darting tongue-tip pluck their hearts. Yes, they would swap their very slipper for a hundred of those grins which enrich your lips with good scarlet blood. You laughing hussy, if you would stay forever fresh and young—no tears! Dream of riding flies unbridled, but bridle your own chameleon fancies, with lovely clouds dream you transform quick reality into multicoloured shapes that ride crimson dreams with winged sleeves of partridge blue. By Body and Blood, by Censer and Seal, by Book and Sword, by Rag and Gold, Sound and Colour, if I see you back in that elegiac hovel where eunuchs recruit ugly-mugs for loony sultans, I'll curse you, I'll lambaste you —and as for the sweets of love, it's Lent for you, I'll . . .

Ouf! And here she is, riding a sunbeam together with a Decade of tales that spatter in aeroform meteors, in the prisms of which she dances, with step so frank, so bold, so unwary, so contrary, so wilful altogether that you've got to know her very well indeed to follow the way that silver-sequined siren's tail of hers whisks about the whims of her latest jokes.

Heaven's alive, look, the moment evening service is over she rushes out like a hundred schoolboys at a raspberry thicket! Confound the schoolmaster, this Decade is now complete! To hell with work! Come on, my lads!